itty bitty

HELLBOY™

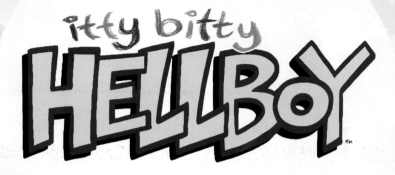

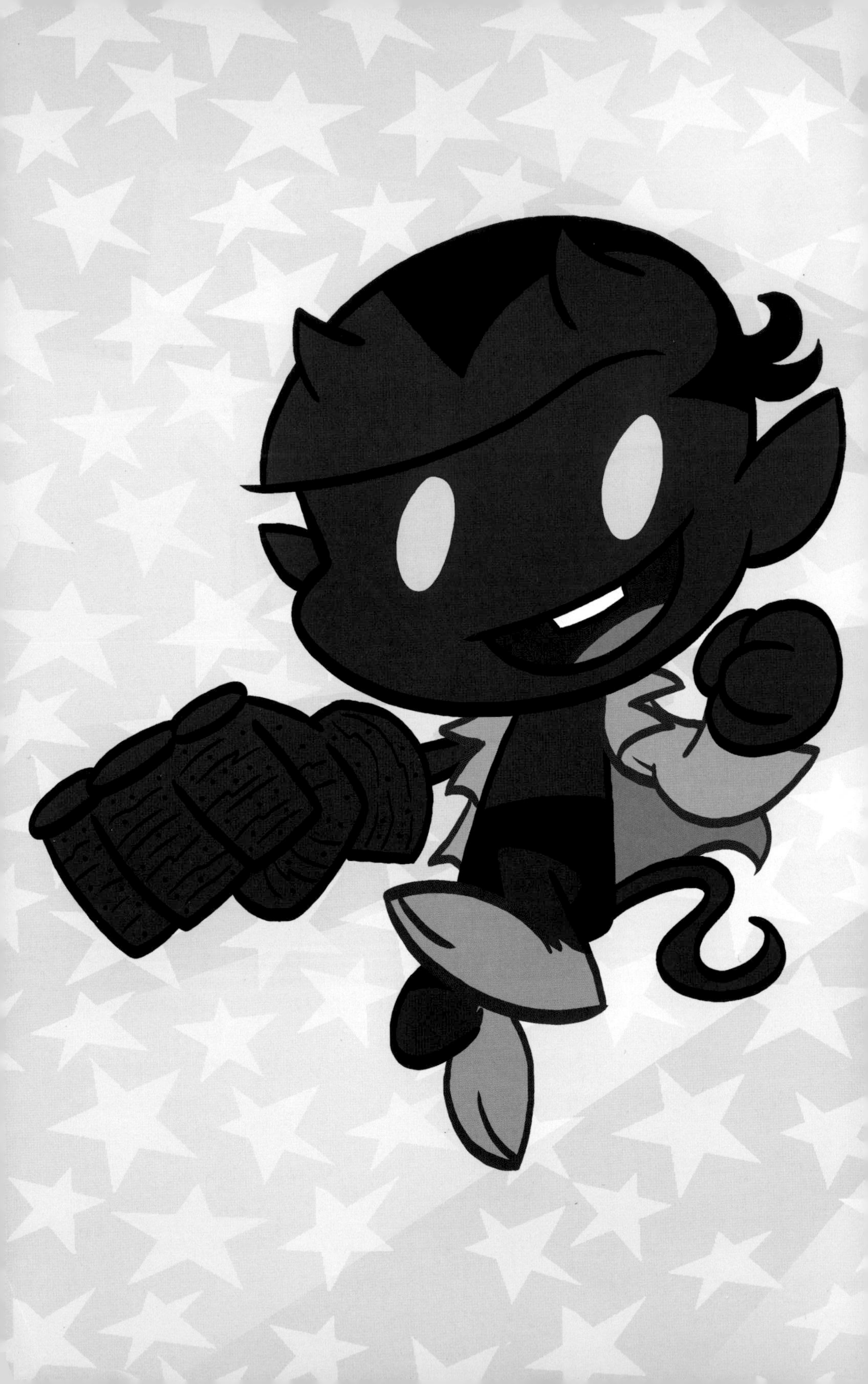

itty bitty HELLBOY™

ART BALTAZAR & FRANCO

WRITER & ARTIST   WRITER

HELLBOY CREATED BY MIKE MIGNOLA

Designers CARY GRAZZINI &
KRYSTAL RANDOLPH

Associate Editor DANIEL CHABON

Editor SCOTT ALLIE

Publisher MIKE RICHARDSON

Dark Horse Books®

MIKE RICHARDSON President and Publisher • NEIL HANKERSON Executive Vice President • TOM WEDDLE Chief Financial Officer • RANDY STRADLEY Vice President of Publishing • MICHAEL MARTENS Vice President of Book Trade Sales • ANITA NELSON Vice President of Business Affairs • SCOTT ALLIE Editor in Chief • MATT PARKINSON Vice President of Marketing • DAVID SCROGGY Vice President of Product Development • DALE LAFOUNTAIN Vice President of Information Technology • DARLENE VOGEL Senior Director of Print, Design, and Production • KEN LIZZI General Counsel • DAVEY ESTRADA Editorial Director • CHRIS WARNER Senior Books Editor • DIANA SCHUTZ Executive Editor • CARY GRAZZINI Director of Print and Development • LIA RIBACCHI Art Director • CARA NIECE Director of Scheduling • TIM WIESCH Director of International Licensing • MARK BERNARDI Director of Digital Publishing

Published by
Dark Horse Books
A division of Dark Horse Comics, Inc.
10956 SE Main Street, Milwaukie, OR 97222

First edition: April 2014 • ISBN 978-1-61655-414-9
Convention exclusive edition • ISBN 978-1-61655-544-3

Special thanks to Elisabeth Allie.

ITTY BITTY HELLBOY

This volume collects Itty Bitty Hellboy #1–#5, originally published by Dark Horse Comics.

1 3 5 7 9 10 8 6 4 2
Printed in China

CHAPTER ONE

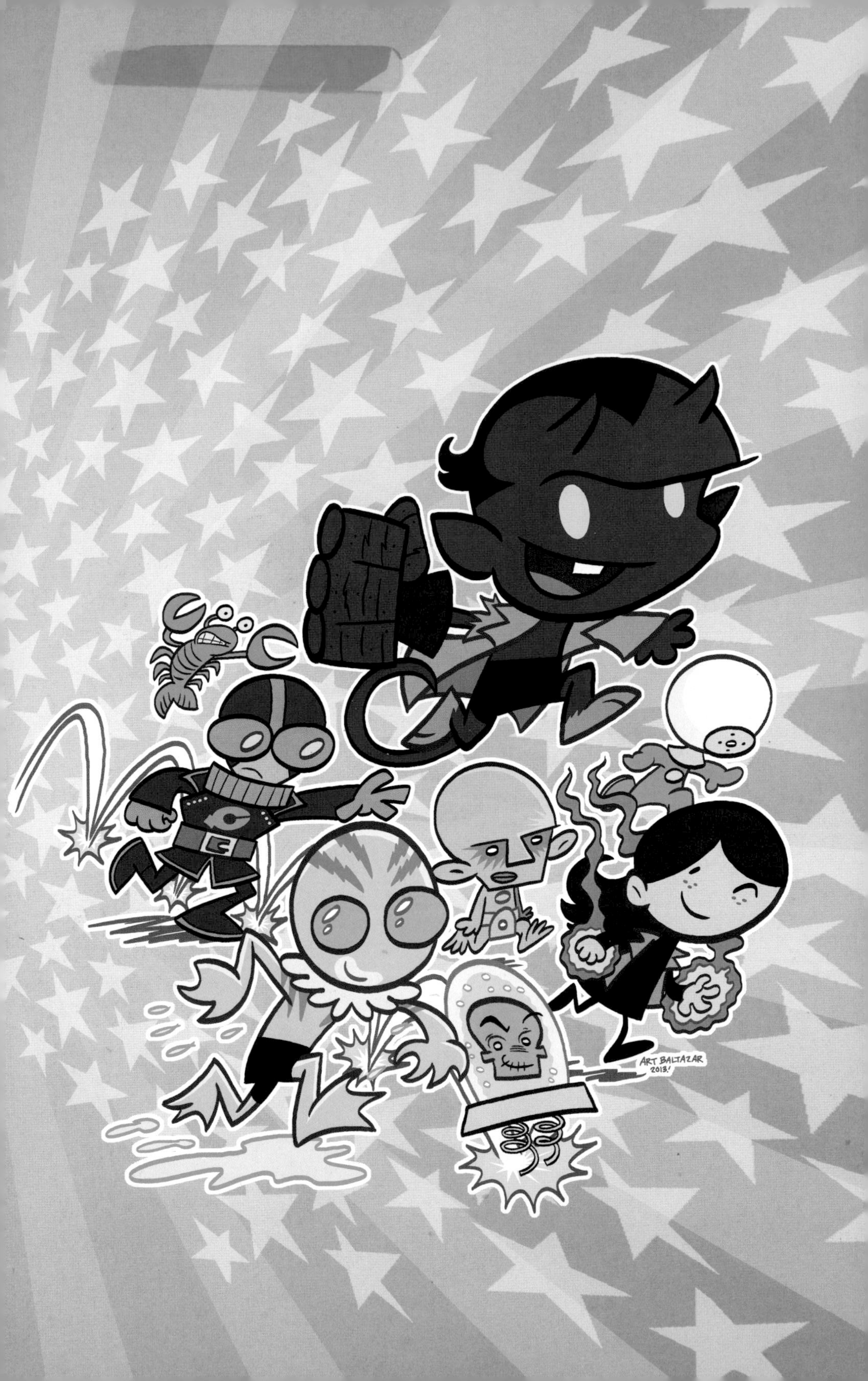
ART BALTAZAR
2013!

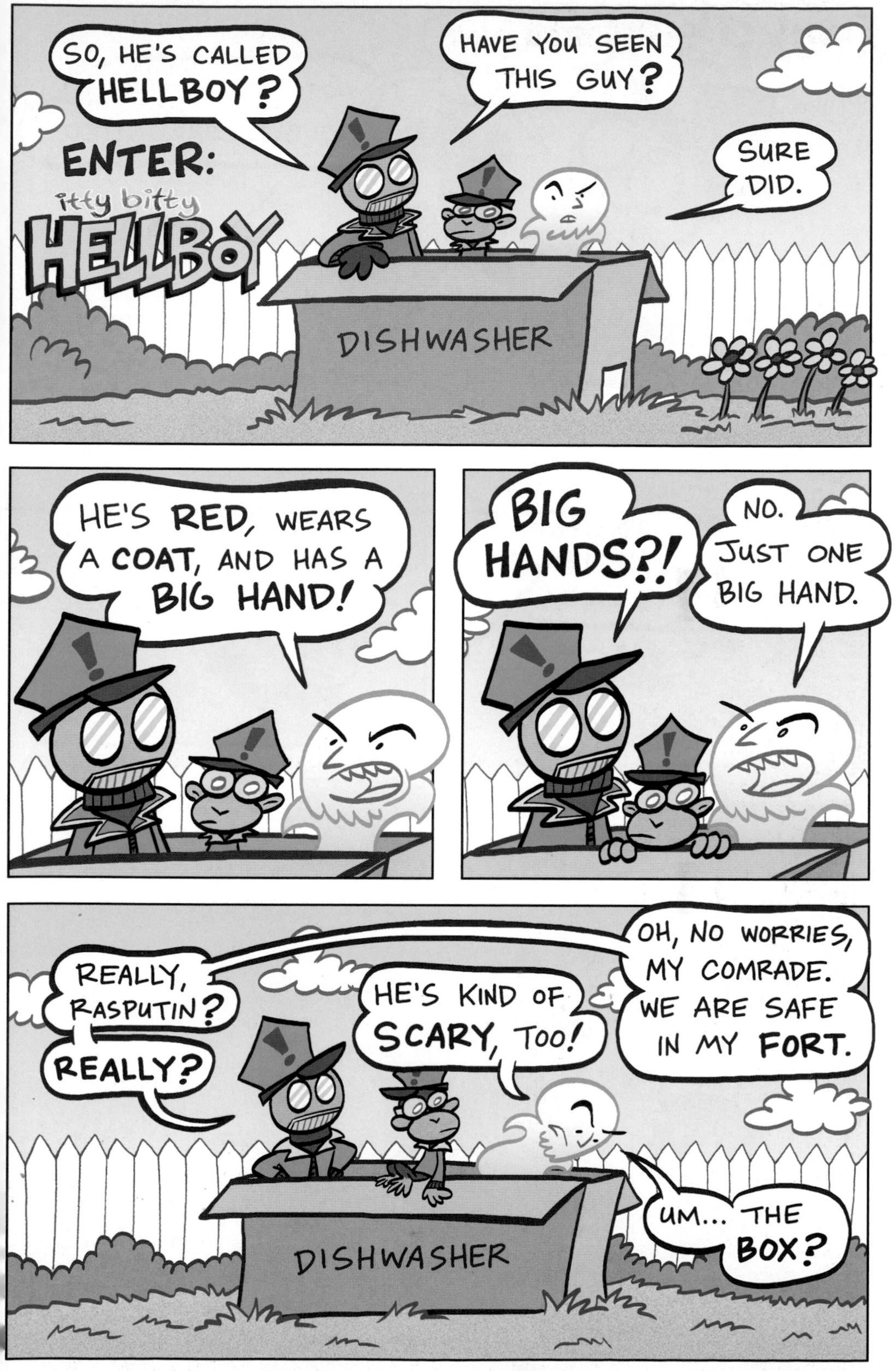
SO, HE'S CALLED HELLBOY?
HAVE YOU SEEN THIS GUY?
SURE DID.
ENTER: itty bitty HELLBOY
DISHWASHER
HE'S RED, WEARS A COAT, AND HAS A BIG HAND!
BIG HANDS?!
NO. JUST ONE BIG HAND.
REALLY, RASPUTIN?
REALLY?
HE'S KIND OF SCARY, TOO!
OH, NO WORRIES, MY COMRADE. WE ARE SAFE IN MY FORT.
UM... THE BOX?
DISHWASHER

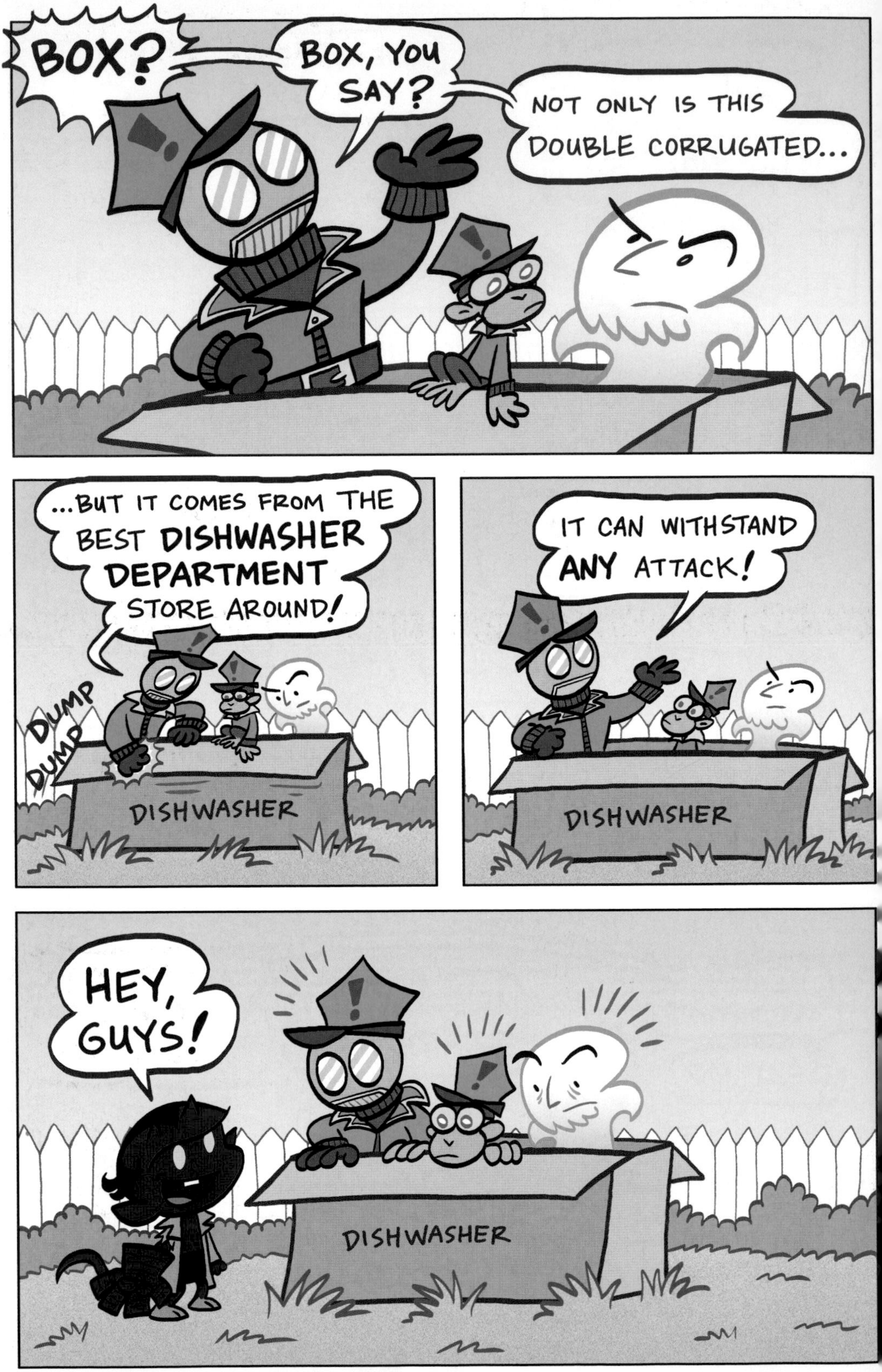
BOX?
BOX, YOU SAY?
NOT ONLY IS THIS DOUBLE CORRUGATED...
...BUT IT COMES FROM THE BEST DISHWASHER DEPARTMENT STORE AROUND!
DUMP DUMP
DISHWASHER
IT CAN WITHSTAND ANY ATTACK!
DISHWASHER
HEY, GUYS!
DISHWASHER

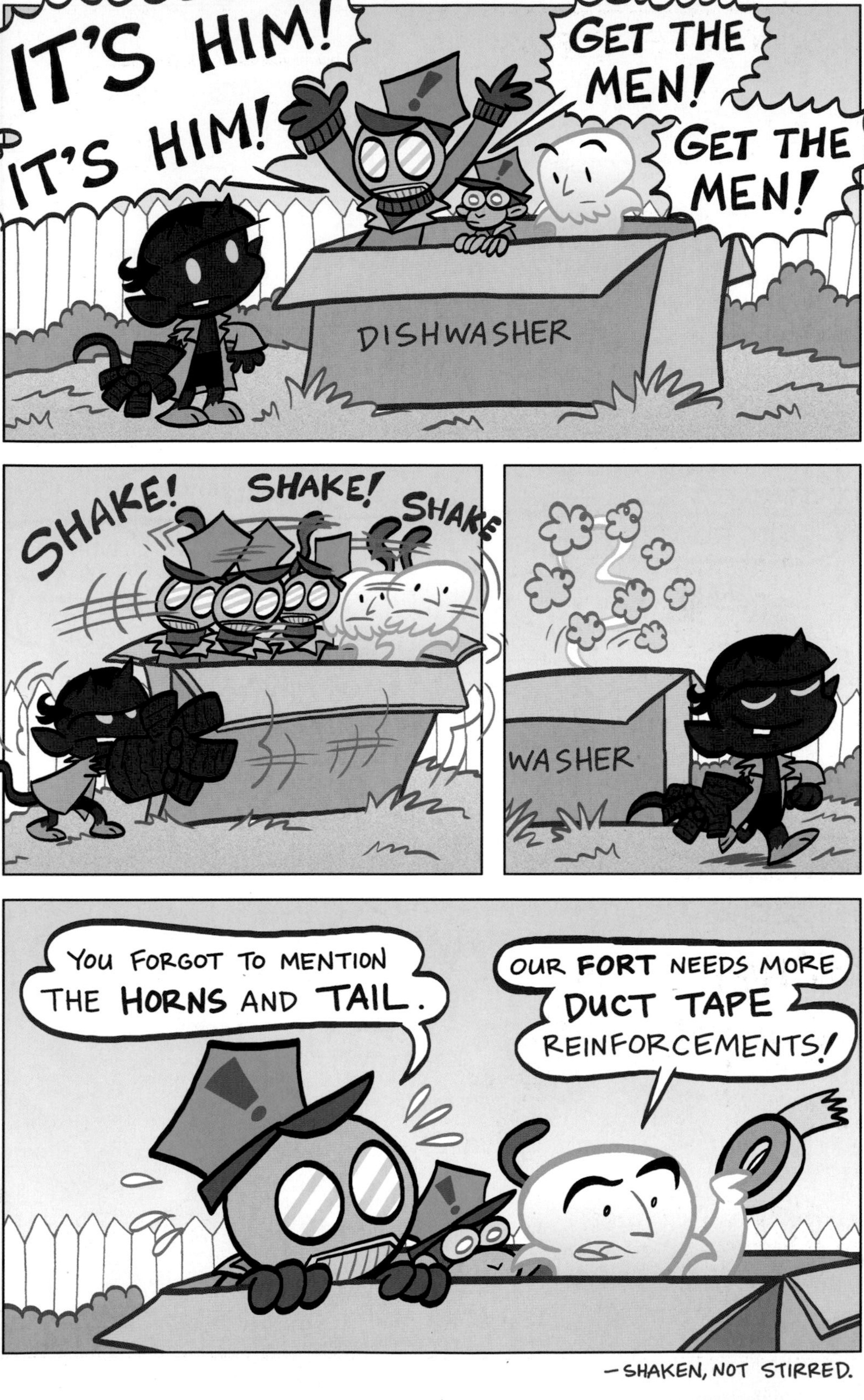
IT'S HIM! IT'S HIM!
GET THE MEN!
GET THE MEN!
DISHWASHER
SHAKE! SHAKE! SHAKE
WASHER
YOU FORGOT TO MENTION THE HORNS AND TAIL.
OUR FORT NEEDS MORE DUCT TAPE REINFORCEMENTS!

—SHAKEN, NOT STIRRED.

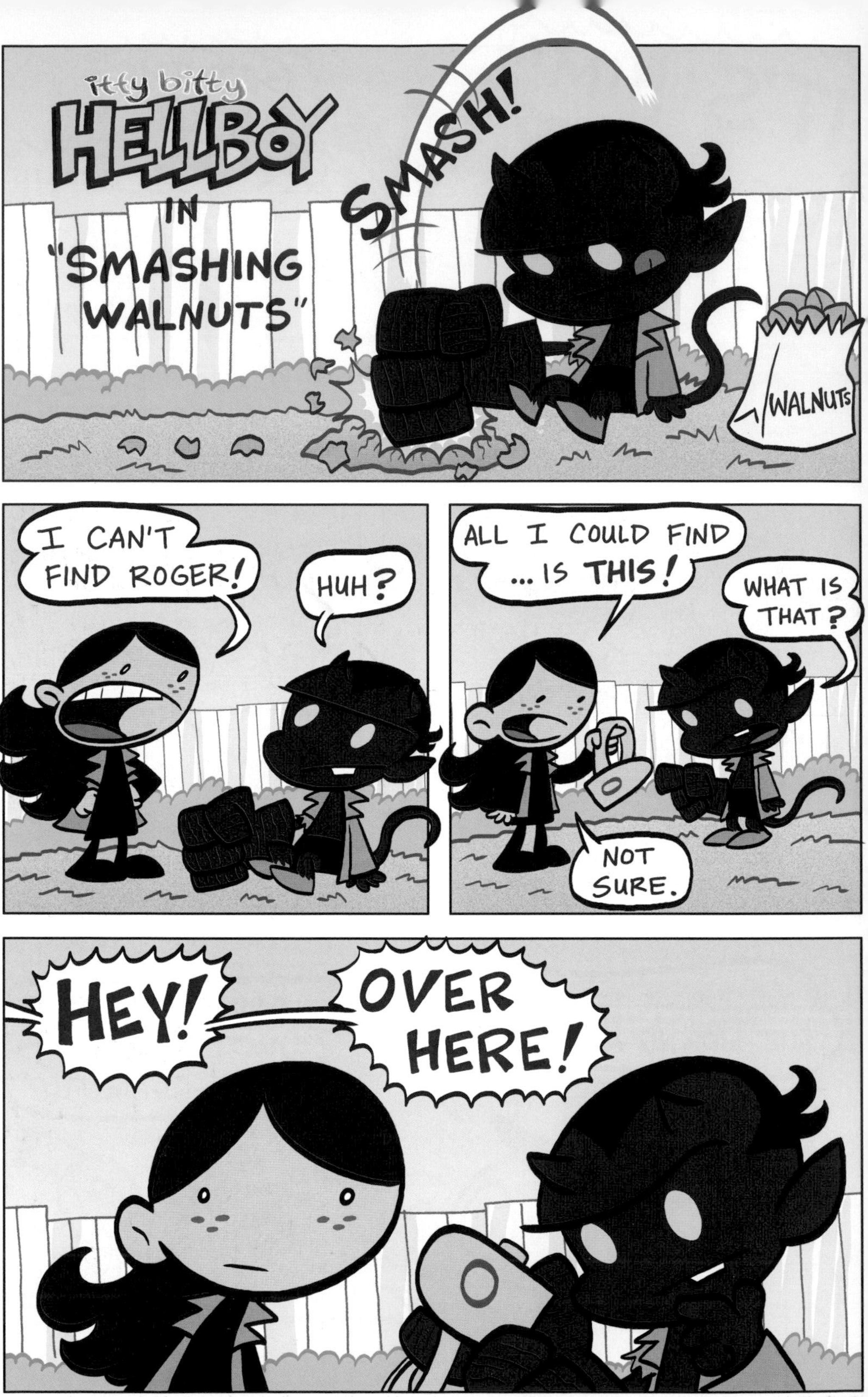
itty bitty
HELLBOY
IN
"SMASHING WALNUTS"
SMASH!
WALNUTS
I CAN'T FIND ROGER!
HUH?
ALL I COULD FIND ... IS THIS!
WHAT IS THAT?
NOT SURE.
HEY!
OVER HERE!

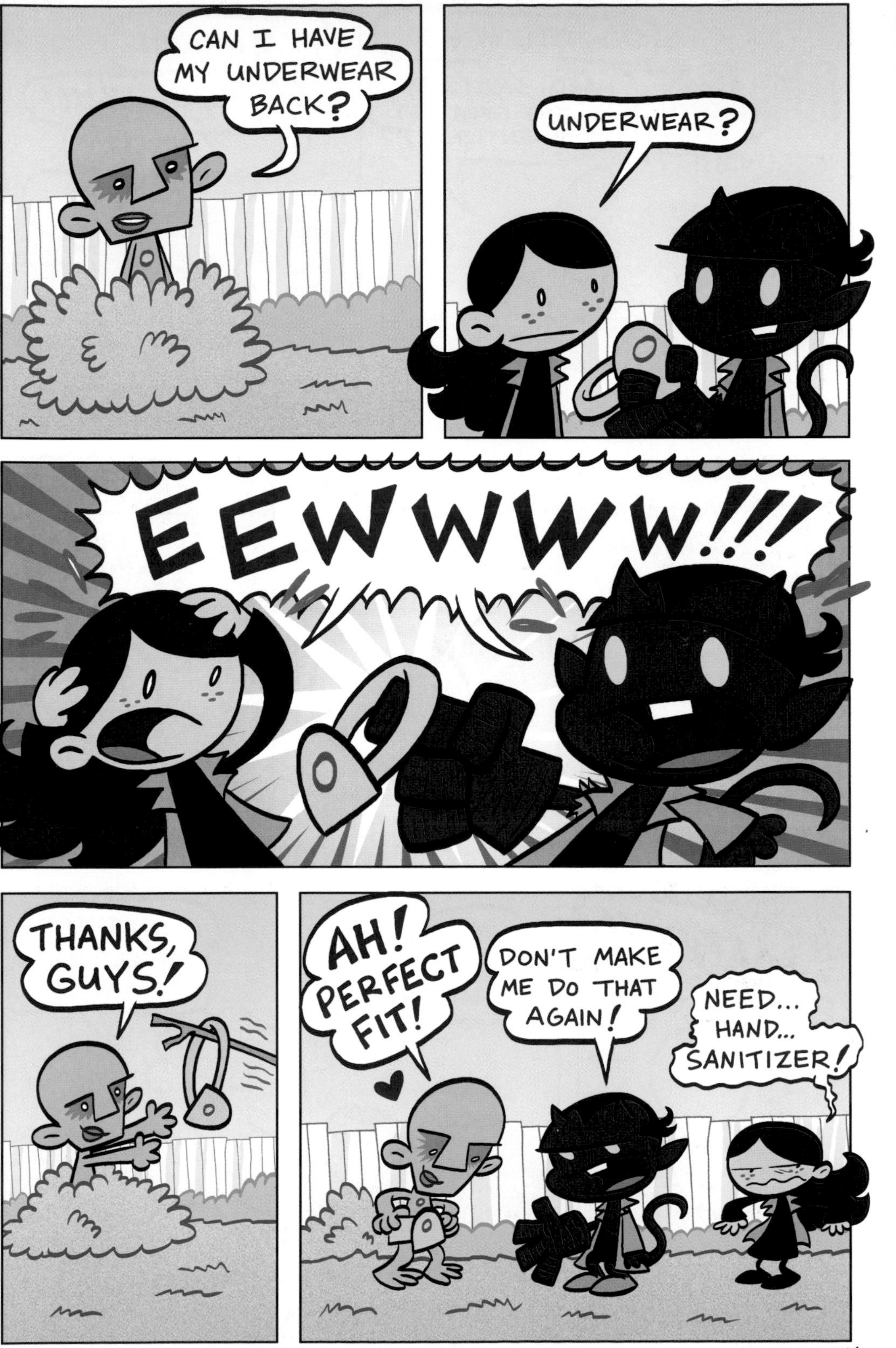
CAN I HAVE MY UNDERWEAR BACK?
UNDERWEAR?
EEWWWW!!!
THANKS, GUYS!
AH! PERFECT FIT!
DON'T MAKE ME DO THAT AGAIN!
NEED... HAND... SANITIZER!

–MMM, COMFY!

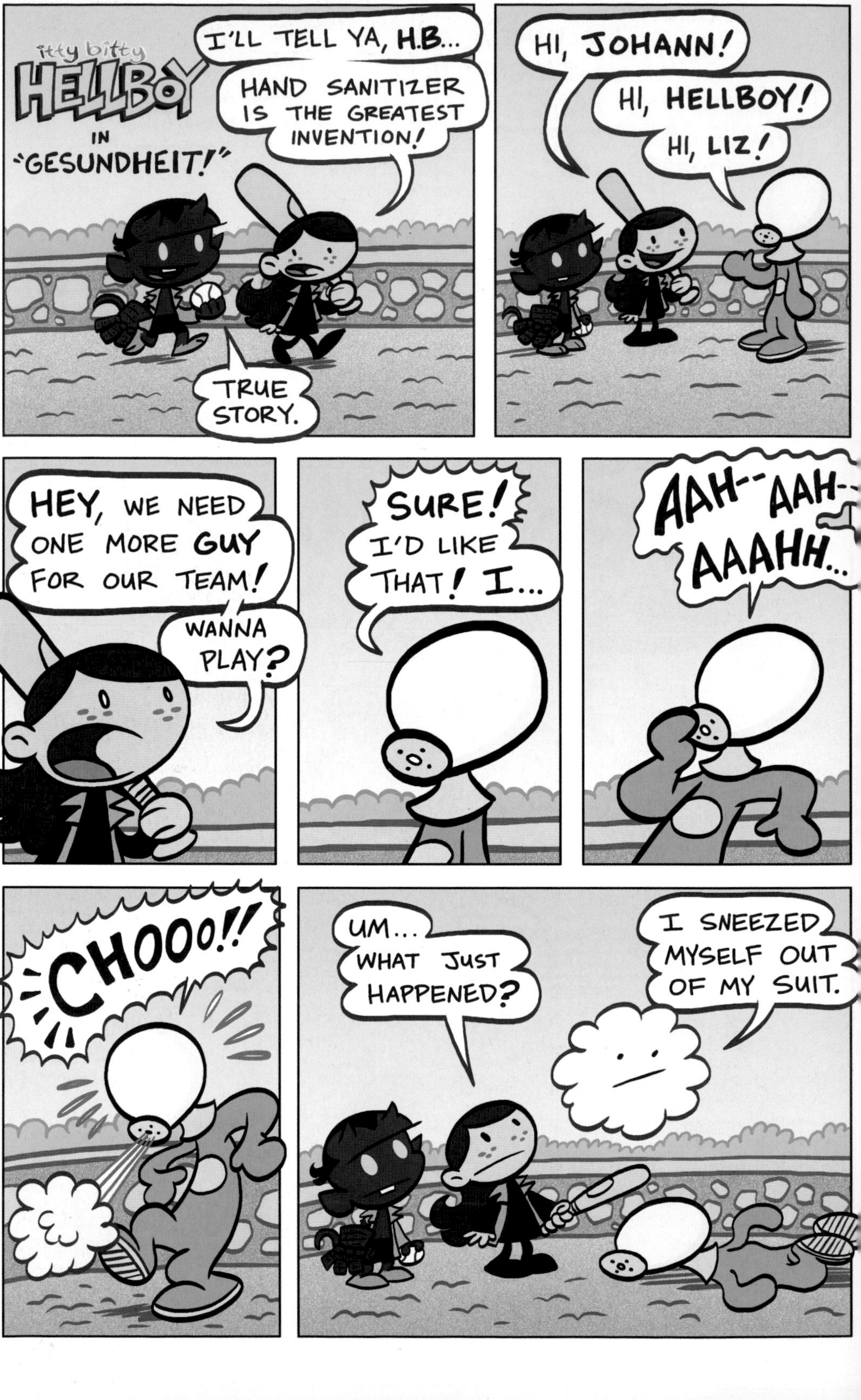
itty bitty HELLBOY
IN "GESUNDHEIT!"
I'LL TELL YA, H.B...
HAND SANITIZER IS THE GREATEST INVENTION!
TRUE STORY.
HI, JOHANN!
HI, HELLBOY!
HI, LIZ!
HEY, WE NEED ONE MORE GUY FOR OUR TEAM!
WANNA PLAY?
SURE! I'D LIKE THAT! I...
AAH--AAH--AAAHH...
CHOOO!!
UM... WHAT JUST HAPPENED?
I SNEEZED MYSELF OUT OF MY SUIT.

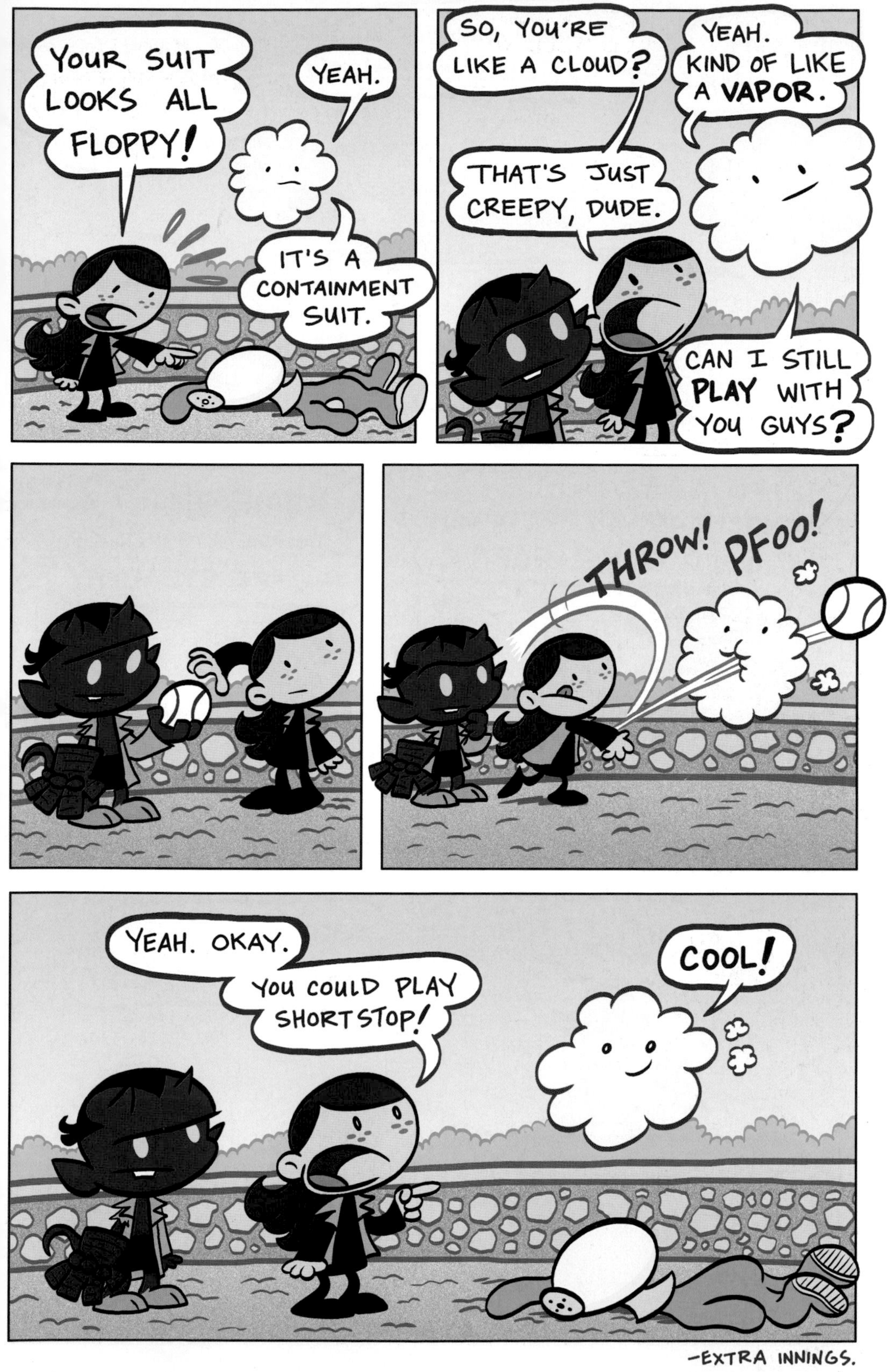
YOUR SUIT LOOKS ALL FLOPPY!
YEAH.
IT'S A CONTAINMENT SUIT.
SO, YOU'RE LIKE A CLOUD?
YEAH. KIND OF LIKE A VAPOR.
THAT'S JUST CREEPY, DUDE.
CAN I STILL PLAY WITH YOU GUYS?
THROW!
PFOO!
YEAH. OKAY.
YOU COULD PLAY SHORTSTOP!
COOL!

-EXTRA INNINGS.

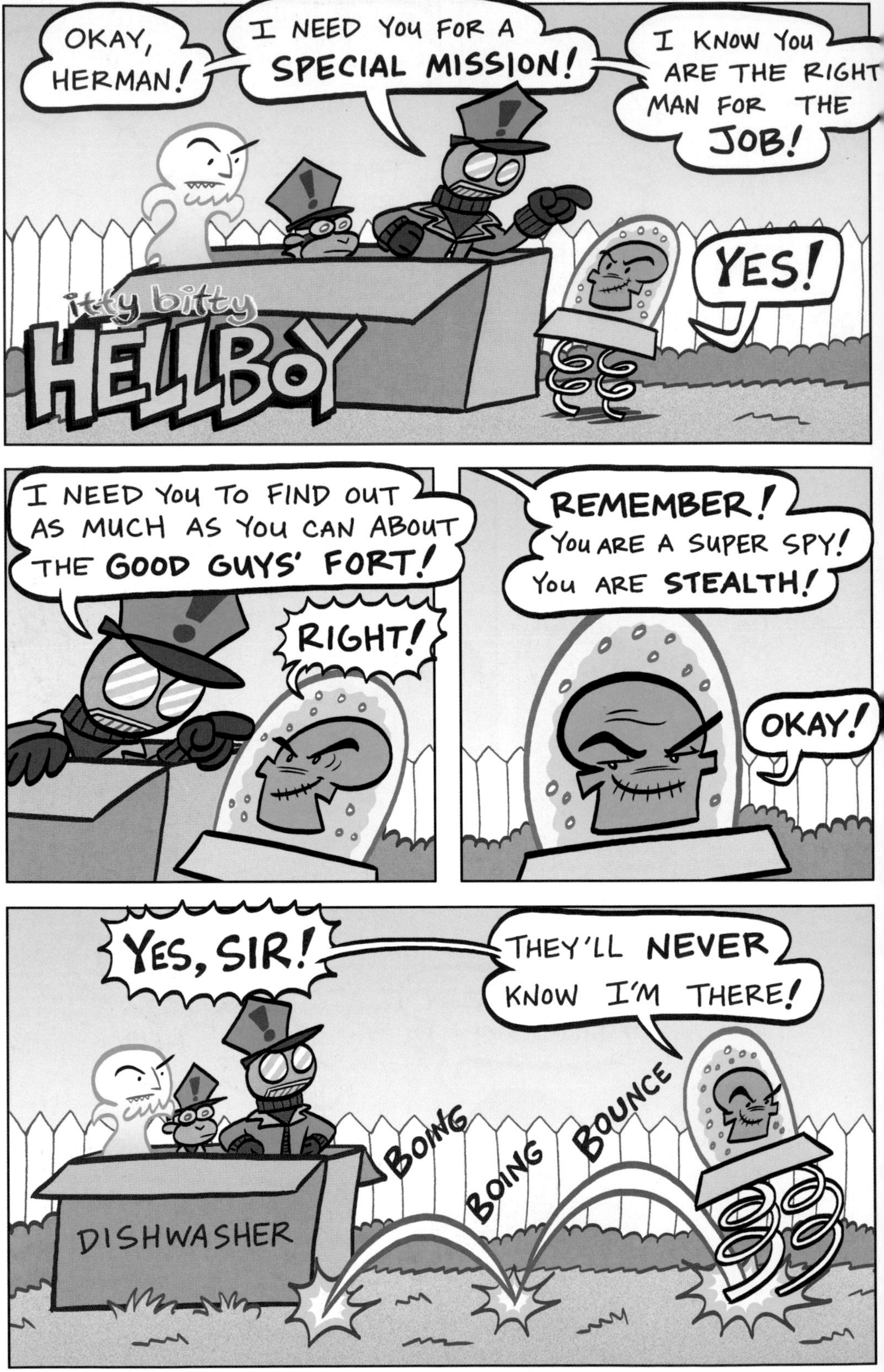
OKAY, HERMAN!
I NEED YOU FOR A SPECIAL MISSION!
I KNOW YOU ARE THE RIGHT MAN FOR THE JOB!
itty bitty HELLBOY
YES!
I NEED YOU TO FIND OUT AS MUCH AS YOU CAN ABOUT THE GOOD GUYS' FORT!
RIGHT!
REMEMBER! YOU ARE A SUPER SPY! YOU ARE STEALTH!
OKAY!
YES, SIR!
THEY'LL NEVER KNOW I'M THERE!
DISHWASHER
BOING
BOING
BOUNCE

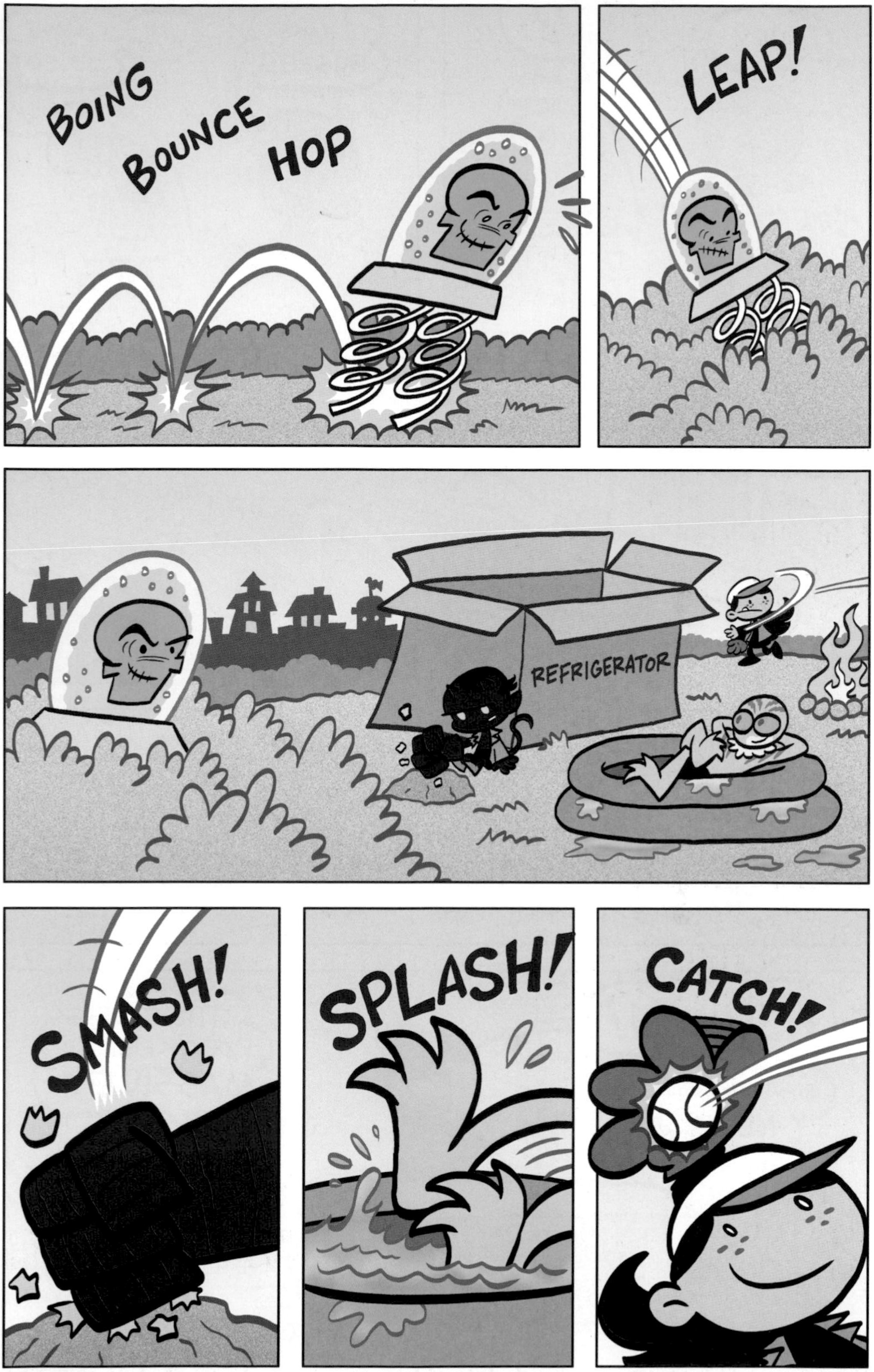
BOING
BOUNCE
HOP
LEAP!
REFRIGERATOR
SMASH!
SPLASH!
CATCH!

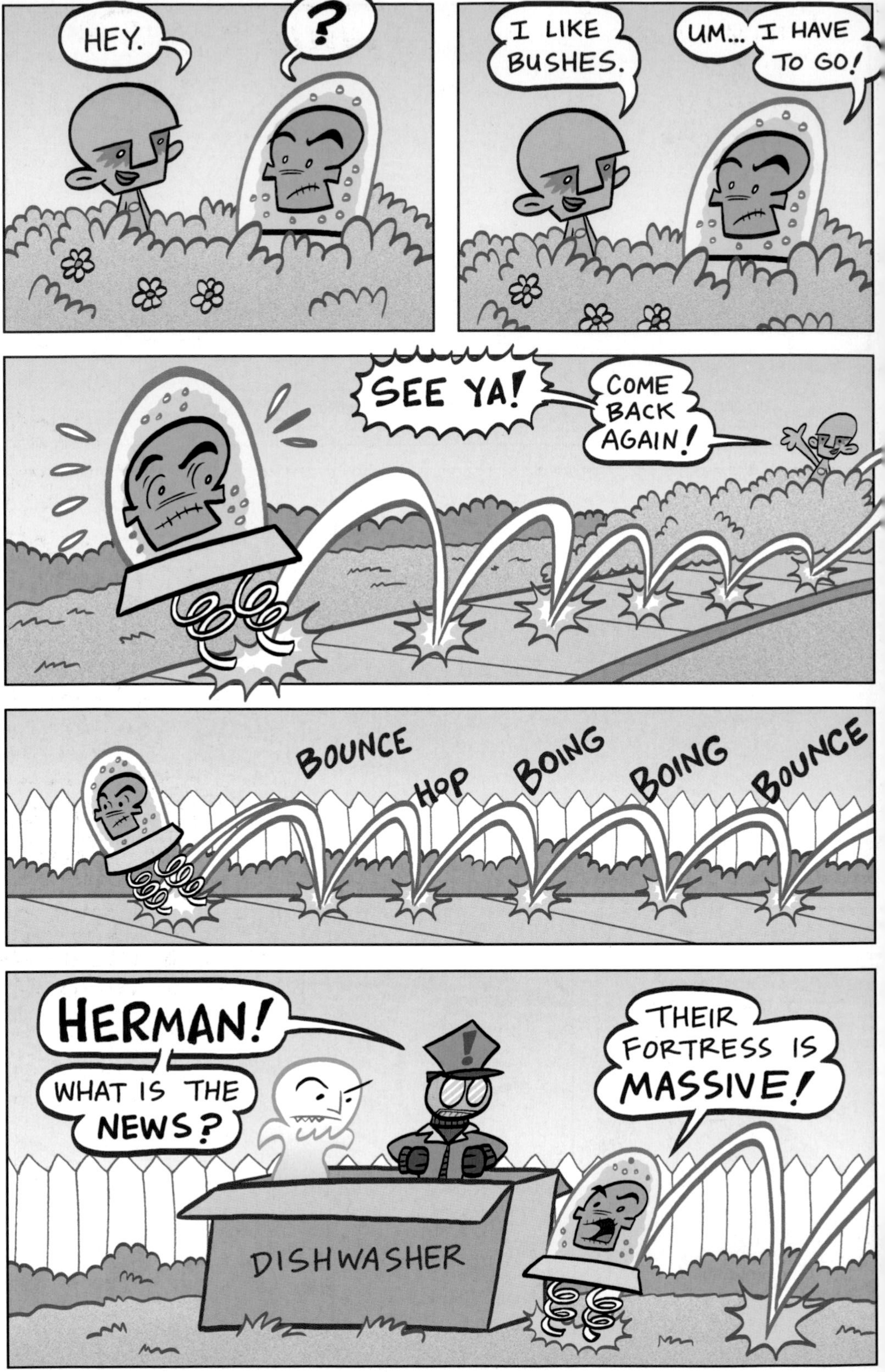
HEY.
?
I LIKE BUSHES.
UM... I HAVE TO GO!
SEE YA!
COME BACK AGAIN!
BOUNCE
HOP
BOING
BOING
BOUNCE
HERMAN!
WHAT IS THE NEWS?
THEIR FORTRESS IS MASSIVE!
DISHWASHER

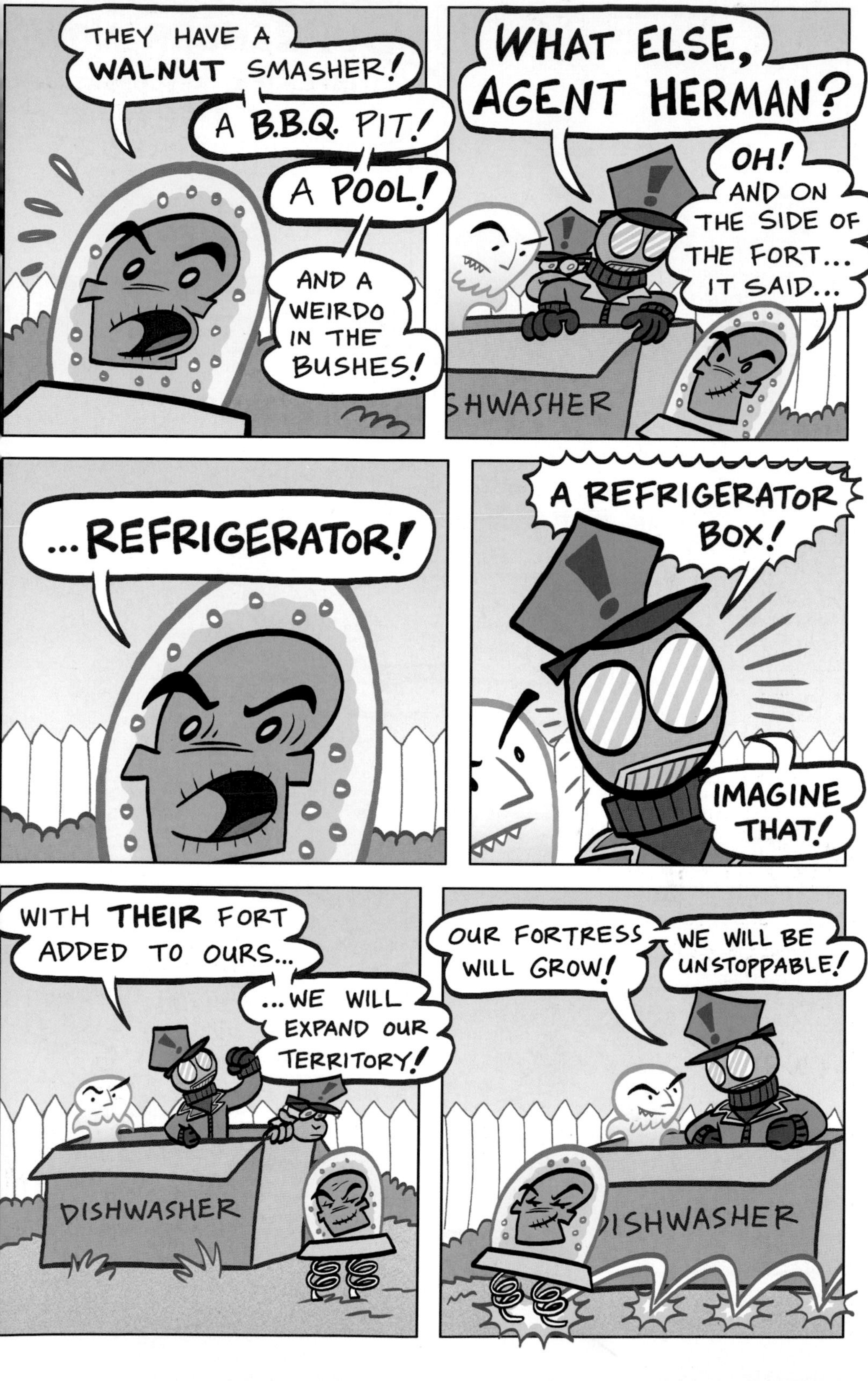
THEY HAVE A WALNUT SMASHER!
A B.B.Q. PIT!
A POOL!
AND A WEIRDO IN THE BUSHES!
WHAT ELSE, AGENT HERMAN?
OH! AND ON THE SIDE OF THE FORT... IT SAID...
SHWASHER
...REFRIGERATOR!
A REFRIGERATOR BOX!
IMAGINE THAT!
WITH THEIR FORT ADDED TO OURS...
...WE WILL EXPAND OUR TERRITORY!
DISHWASHER
OUR FORTRESS WILL GROW!
WE WILL BE UNSTOPPABLE!
DISHWASHER

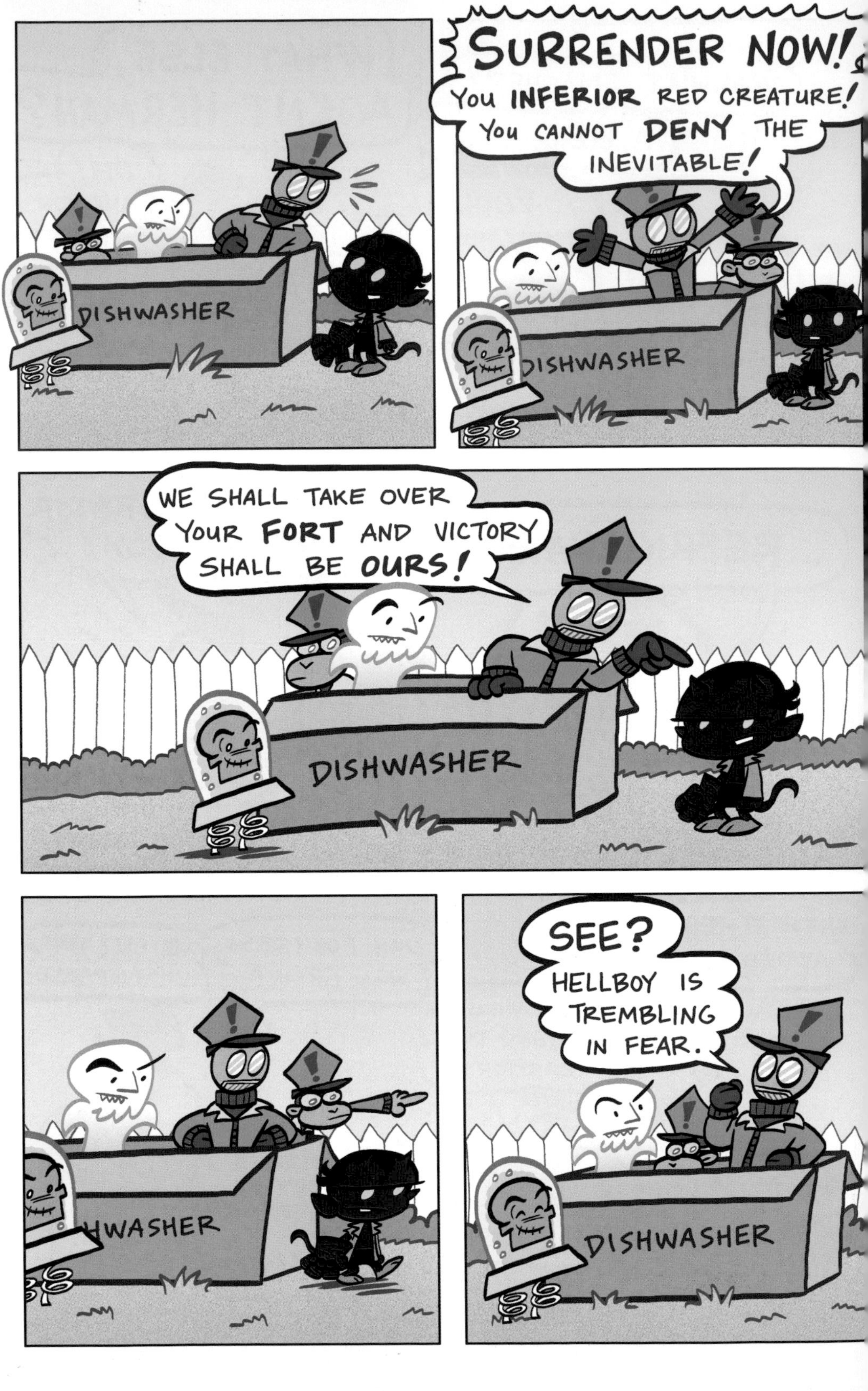
SURRENDER NOW!
You INFERIOR RED CREATURE! You CANNOT DENY THE INEVITABLE!
WE SHALL TAKE OVER YOUR FORT AND VICTORY SHALL BE OURS!
DISHWASHER
SEE?
HELLBOY IS TREMBLING IN FEAR.

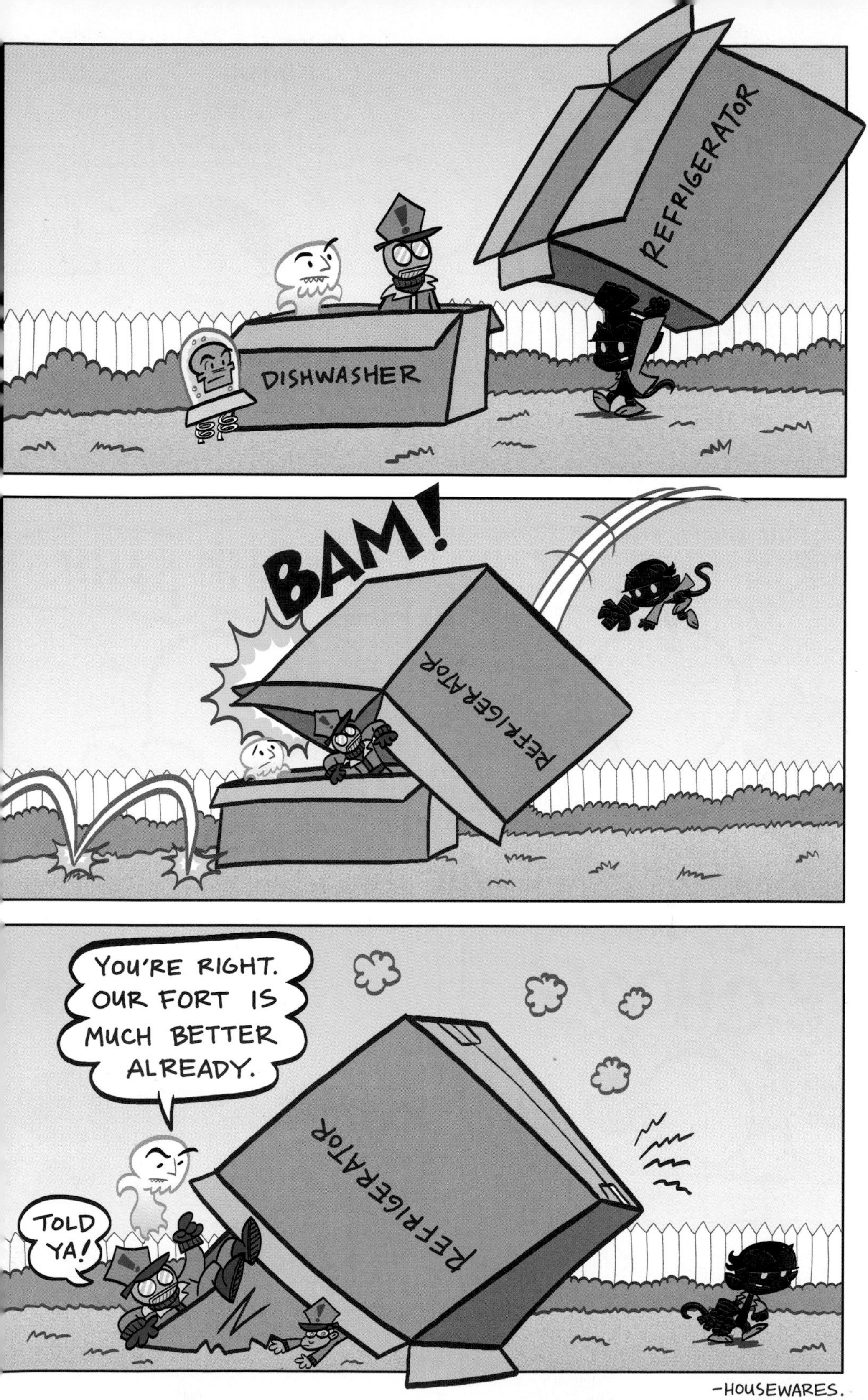
REFRIGERATOR
DISHWASHER
BAM!
REFRIGERATOR
YOU'RE RIGHT. OUR FORT IS MUCH BETTER ALREADY.
TOLD YA!
REFRIGERATOR

-HOUSEWARES.

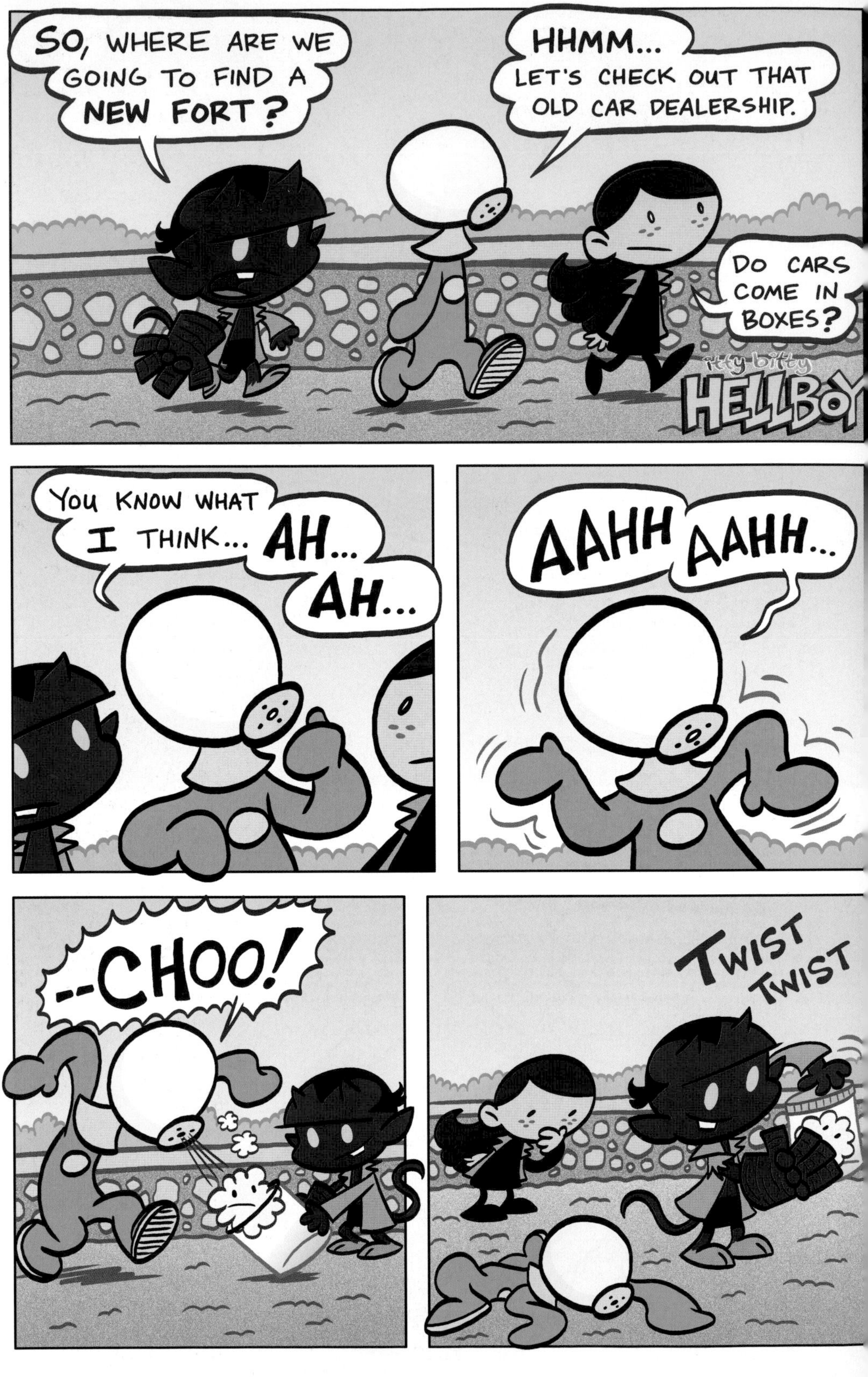
SO, WHERE ARE WE GOING TO FIND A NEW FORT?
HHMM... LET'S CHECK OUT THAT OLD CAR DEALERSHIP.
DO CARS COME IN BOXES?
itty bitty HELLBOY
YOU KNOW WHAT I THINK... AH... AH...
AAHH AAHH...
--CHOO!
TWIST TWIST

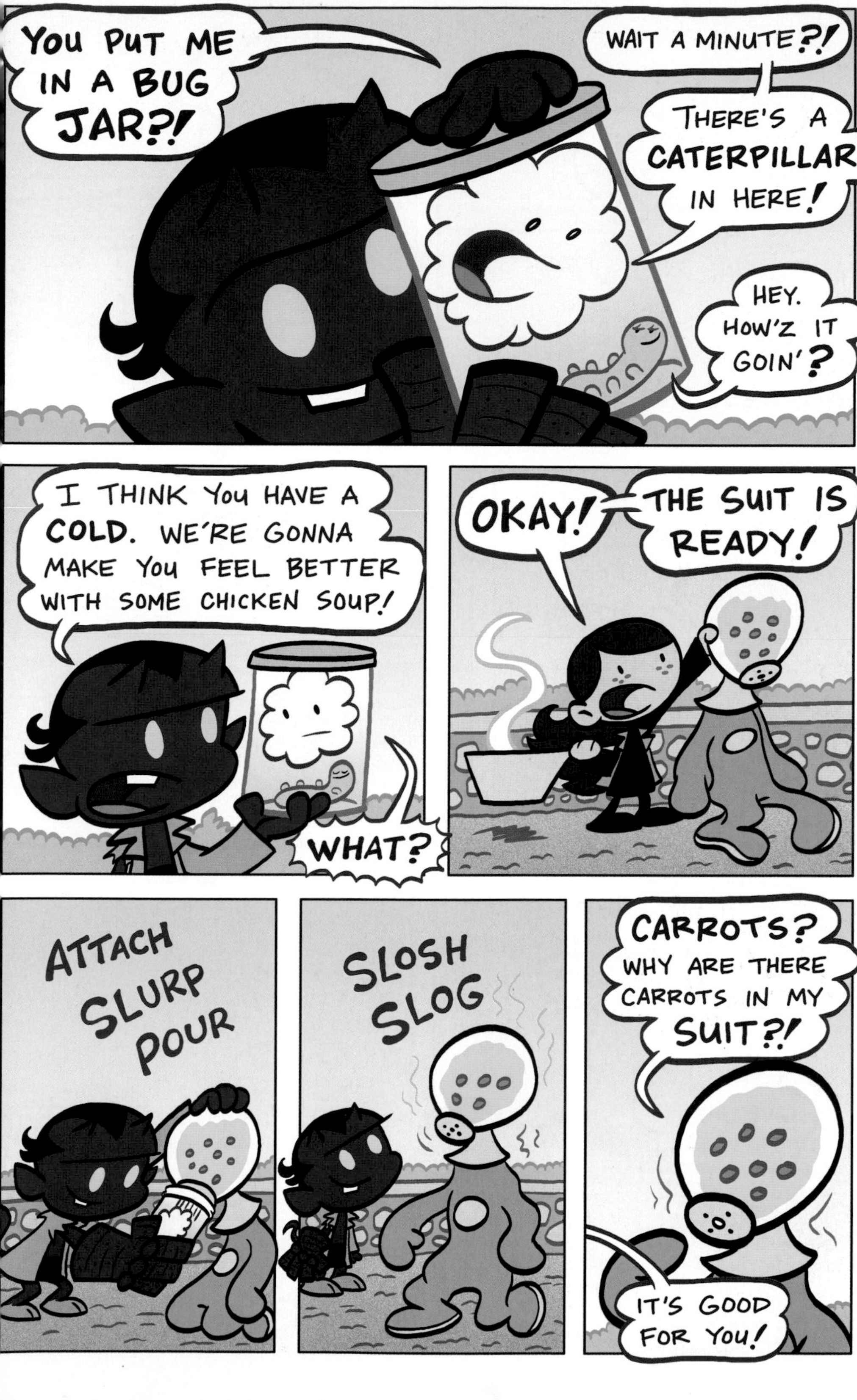
YOU PUT ME IN A BUG JAR?!
WAIT A MINUTE?!
THERE'S A CATERPILLAR IN HERE!
HEY. HOW'Z IT GOIN'?
I THINK YOU HAVE A COLD. WE'RE GONNA MAKE YOU FEEL BETTER WITH SOME CHICKEN SOUP!
WHAT?
OKAY!
THE SUIT IS READY!
ATTACH
SLURP
POUR
SLOSH
SLOG
CARROTS? WHY ARE THERE CARROTS IN MY SUIT?!
IT'S GOOD FOR YOU!

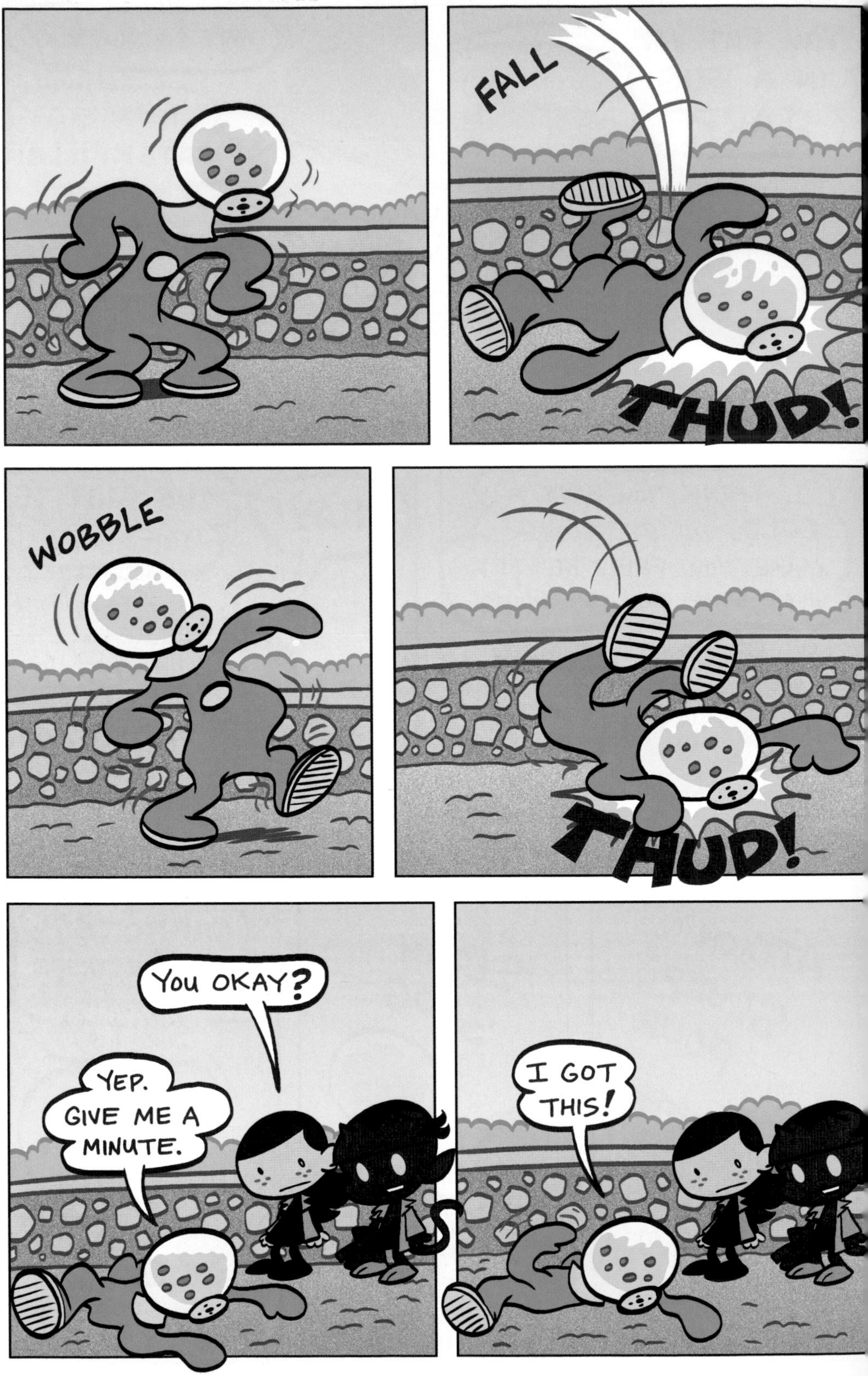
FALL
THUD!
WOBBLE
THUD!
YOU OKAY?
YEP. GIVE ME A MINUTE.
I GOT THIS!

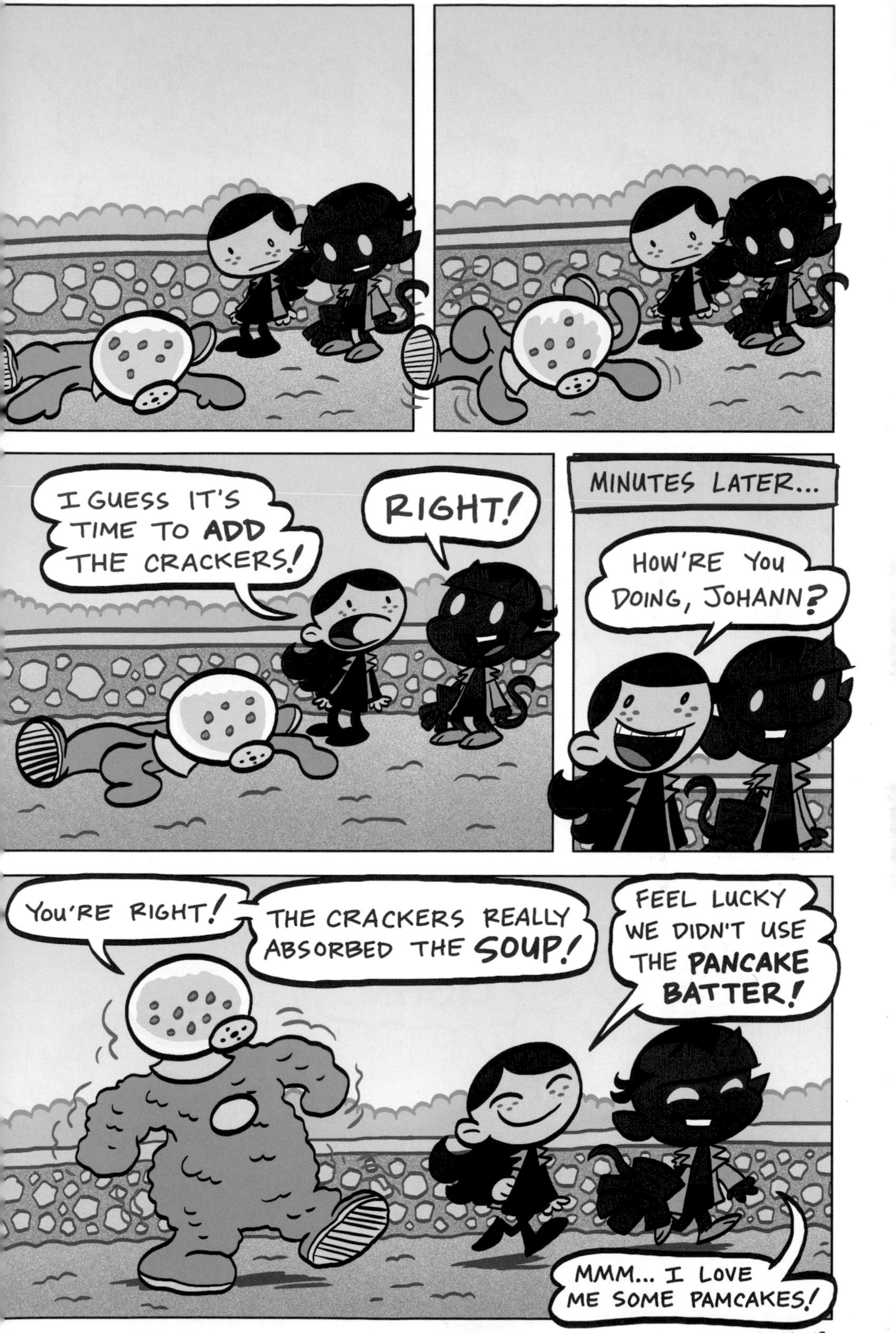
I GUESS IT'S TIME TO ADD THE CRACKERS!
RIGHT!
MINUTES LATER...
HOW'RE YOU DOING, JOHANN?
YOU'RE RIGHT!
THE CRACKERS REALLY ABSORBED THE SOUP!
FEEL LUCKY WE DIDN'T USE THE PANCAKE BATTER!
MMM... I LOVE ME SOME PAMCAKES!
-WHERE'S THE BACON?

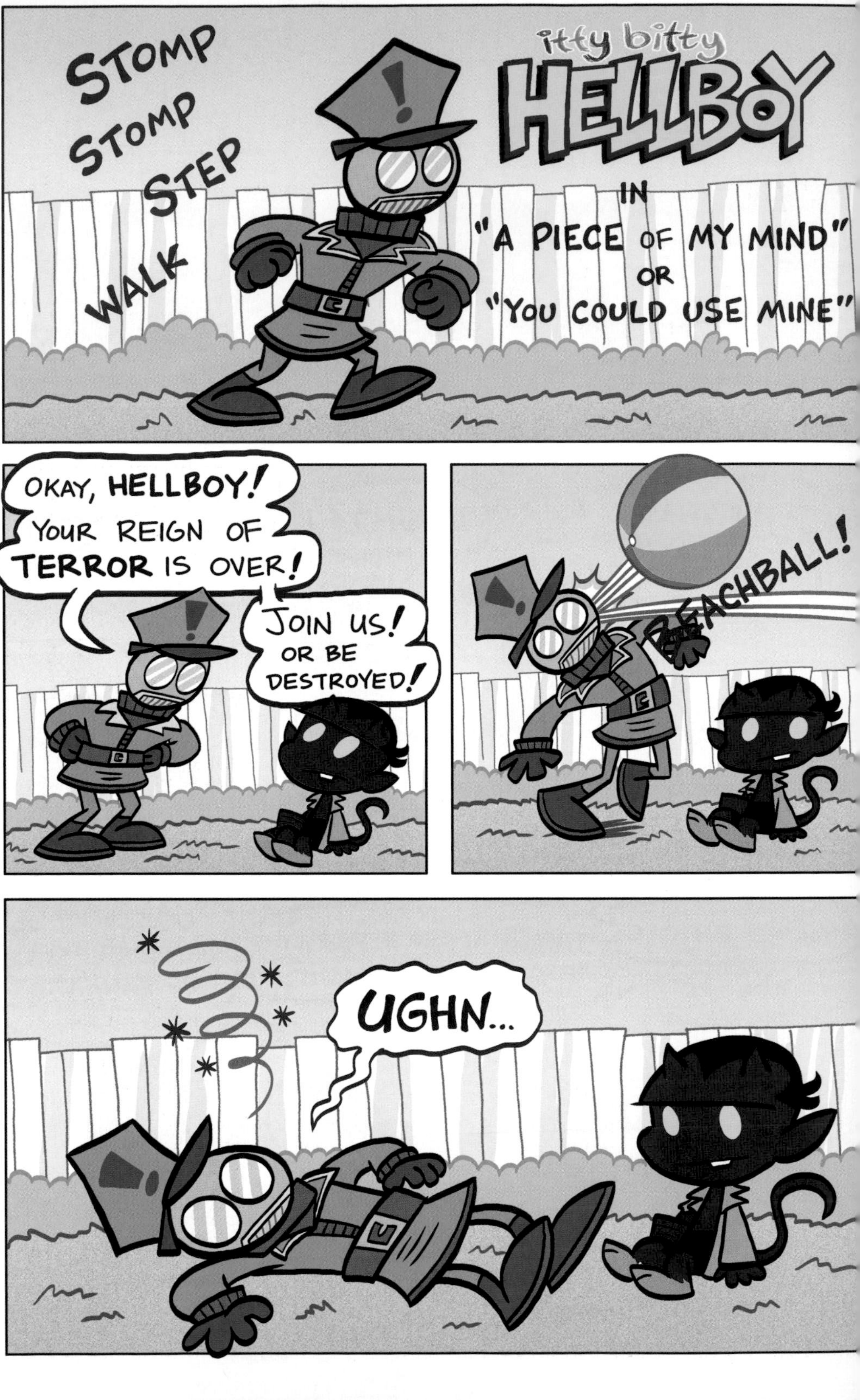
STOMP
STOMP
STEP
WALK
itty bitty HELLBOY
IN
"A PIECE OF MY MIND"
OR
"YOU COULD USE MINE"
OKAY, HELLBOY! YOUR REIGN OF TERROR IS OVER!
JOIN US! OR BE DESTROYED!
BEACHBALL!
UGHN...

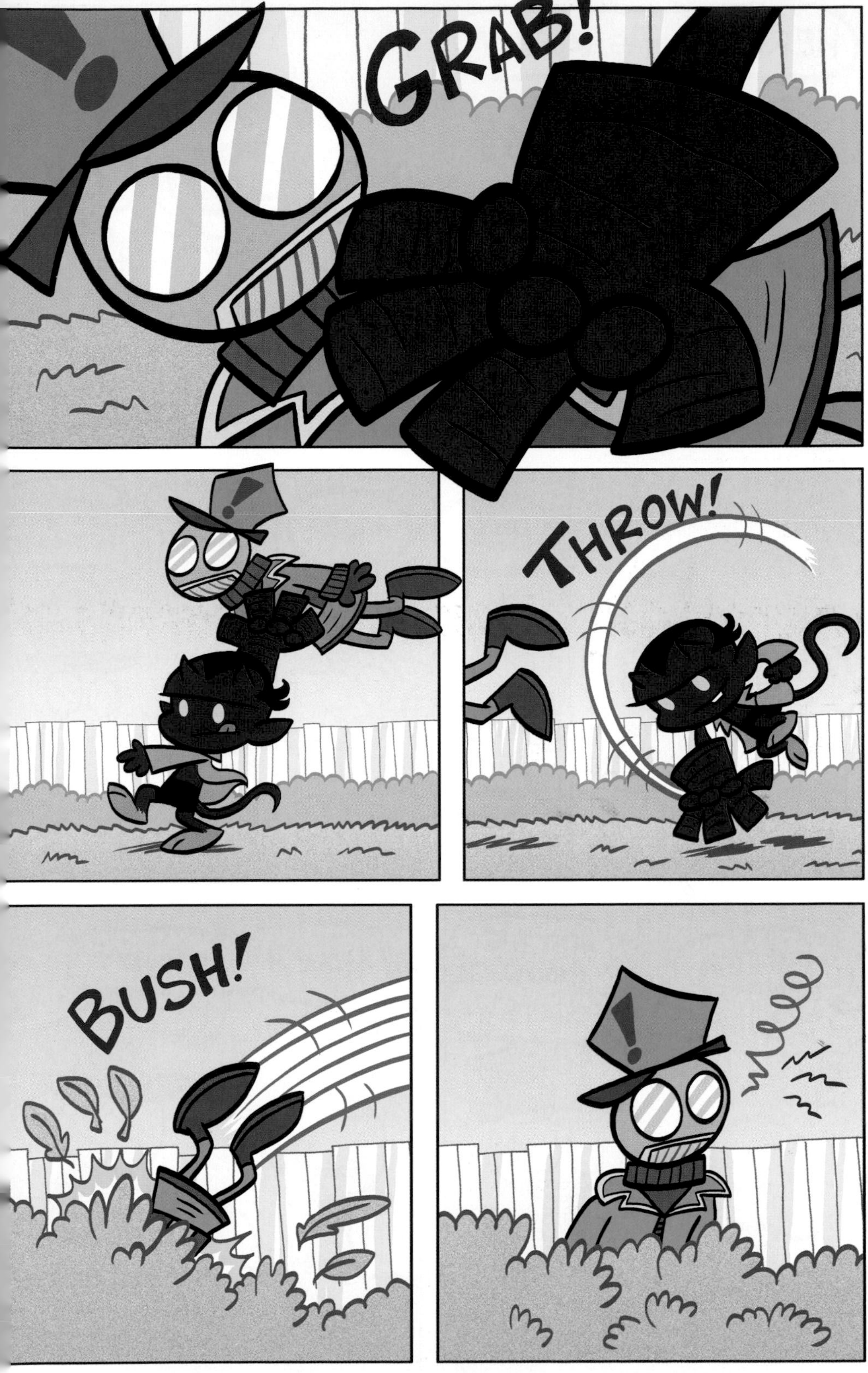
GRAB!
THROW!
BUSH!

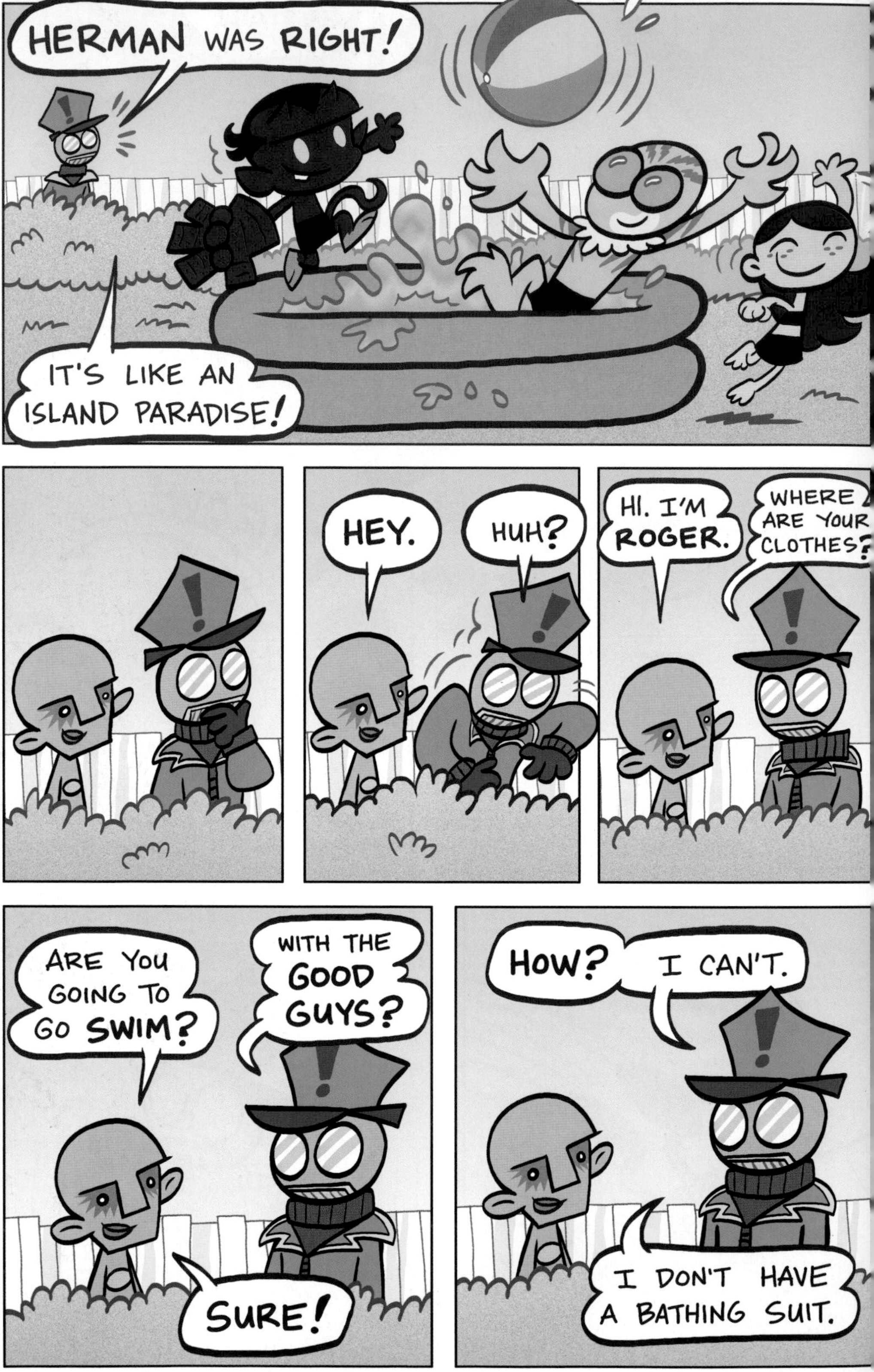
HERMAN WAS RIGHT!
IT'S LIKE AN ISLAND PARADISE!
HEY.
HUH?
HI. I'M ROGER.
WHERE ARE YOUR CLOTHES?
ARE YOU GOING TO GO SWIM?
WITH THE GOOD GUYS?
SURE!
HOW?
I CAN'T.
I DON'T HAVE A BATHING SUIT.

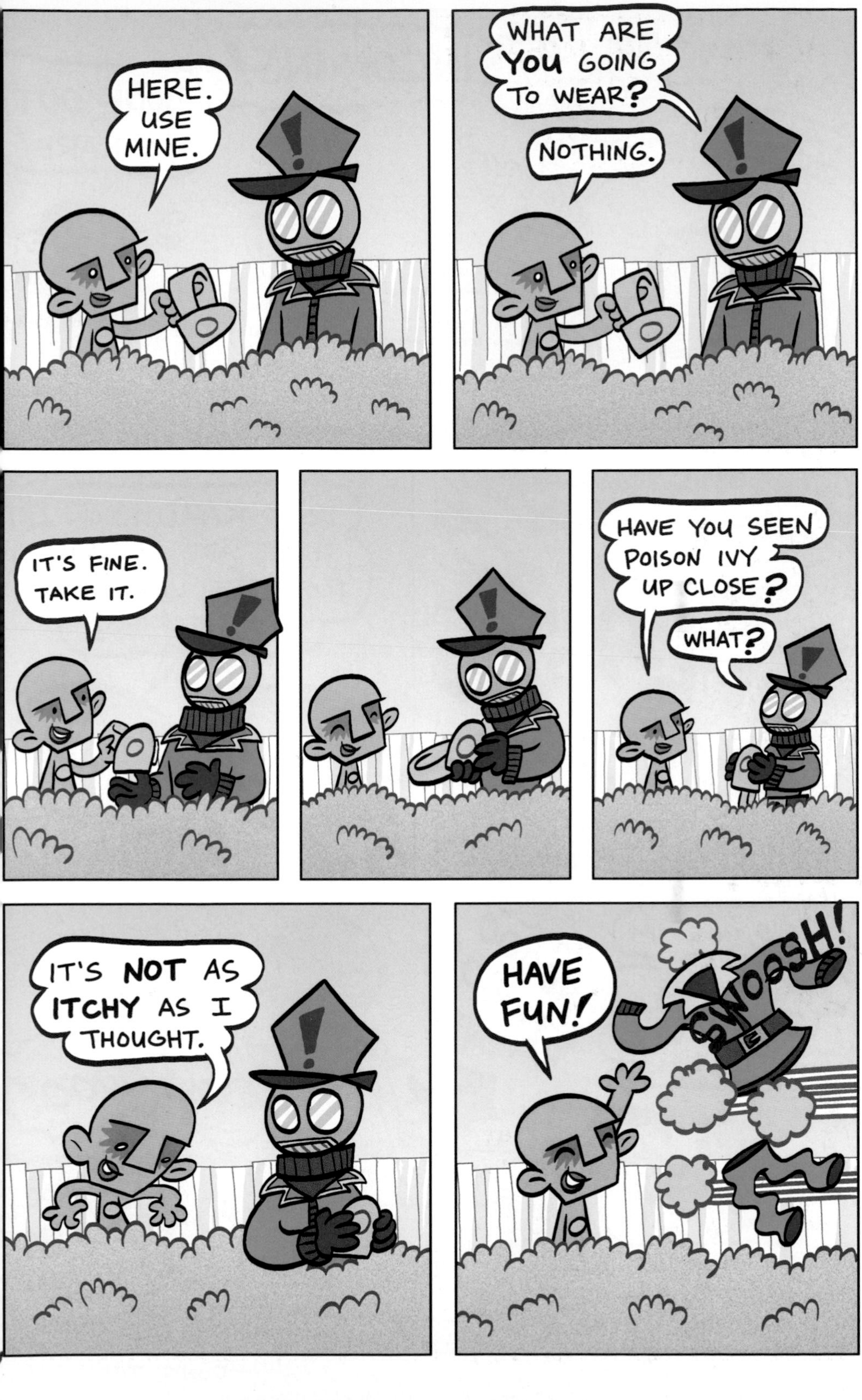
HERE. USE MINE.
WHAT ARE YOU GOING TO WEAR?
NOTHING.
IT'S FINE. TAKE IT.
HAVE YOU SEEN POISON IVY UP CLOSE?
WHAT?
IT'S NOT AS ITCHY AS I THOUGHT.
HAVE FUN!
SWOOSH!

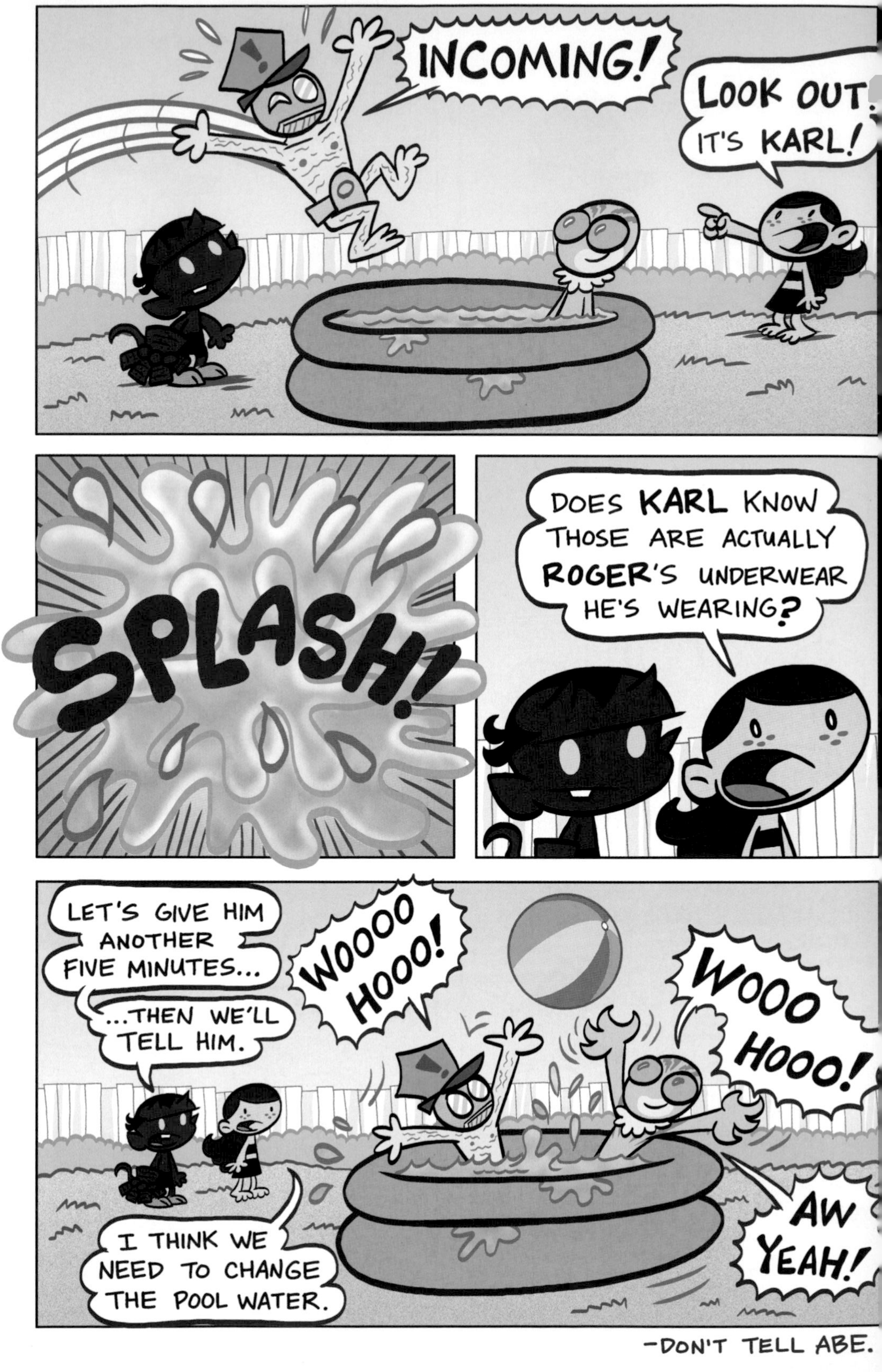
INCOMING!
LOOK OUT! IT'S KARL!
SPLASH!
DOES KARL KNOW THOSE ARE ACTUALLY ROGER'S UNDERWEAR HE'S WEARING?
LET'S GIVE HIM ANOTHER FIVE MINUTES...
...THEN WE'LL TELL HIM.
WOOOO HOOO!
WOOO HOOO!
AW YEAH!
I THINK WE NEED TO CHANGE THE POOL WATER.

-DON'T TELL ABE.

CHAPTER TWO

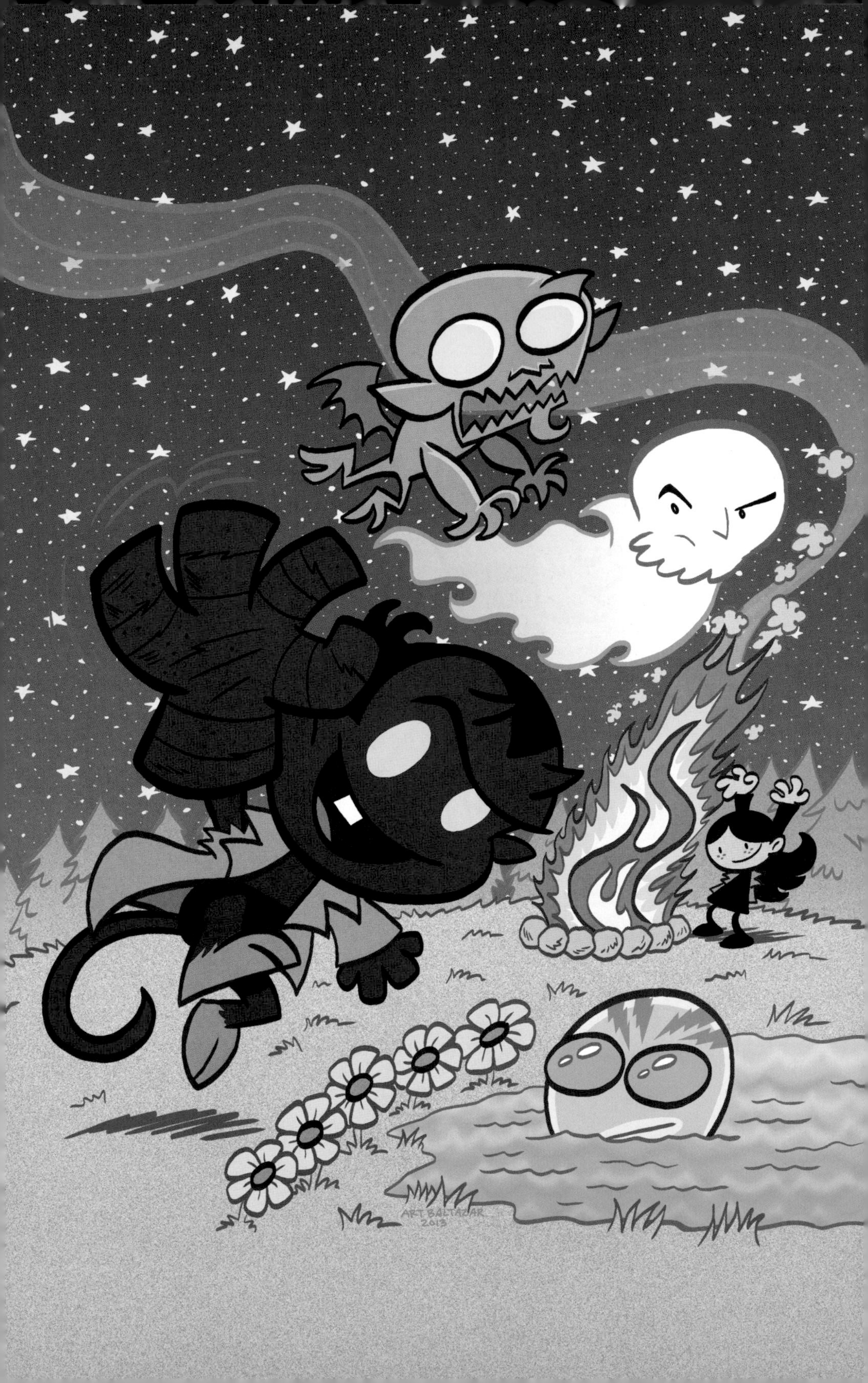
ART BALTAZAR
2013

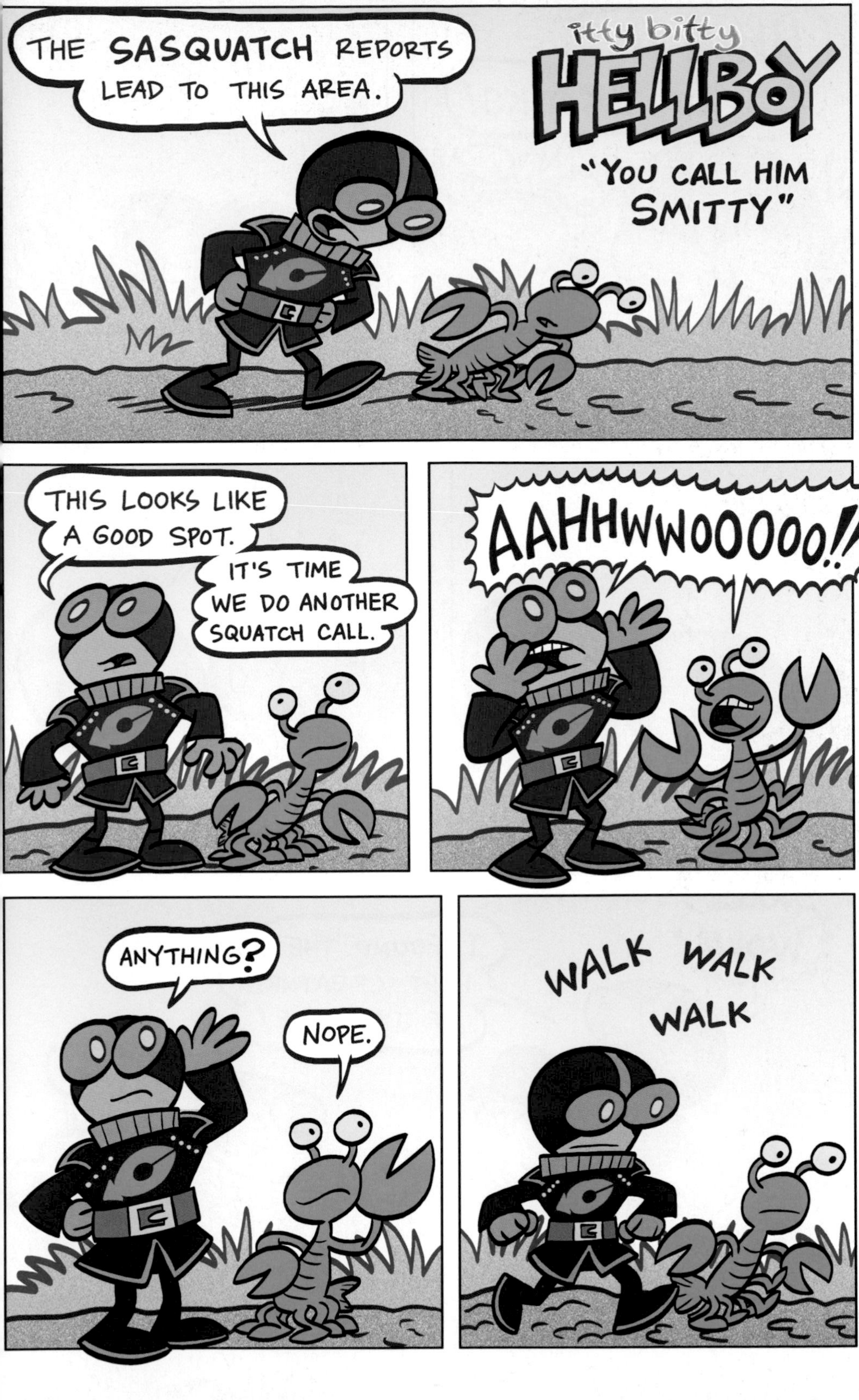

THE SASQUATCH REPORTS LEAD TO THIS AREA.
itty bitty HELLBOY
"YOU CALL HIM SMITTY"
THIS LOOKS LIKE A GOOD SPOT.
IT'S TIME WE DO ANOTHER SQUATCH CALL.
AAHHWWOOOOO!!
ANYTHING?
NOPE.
WALK WALK
WALK

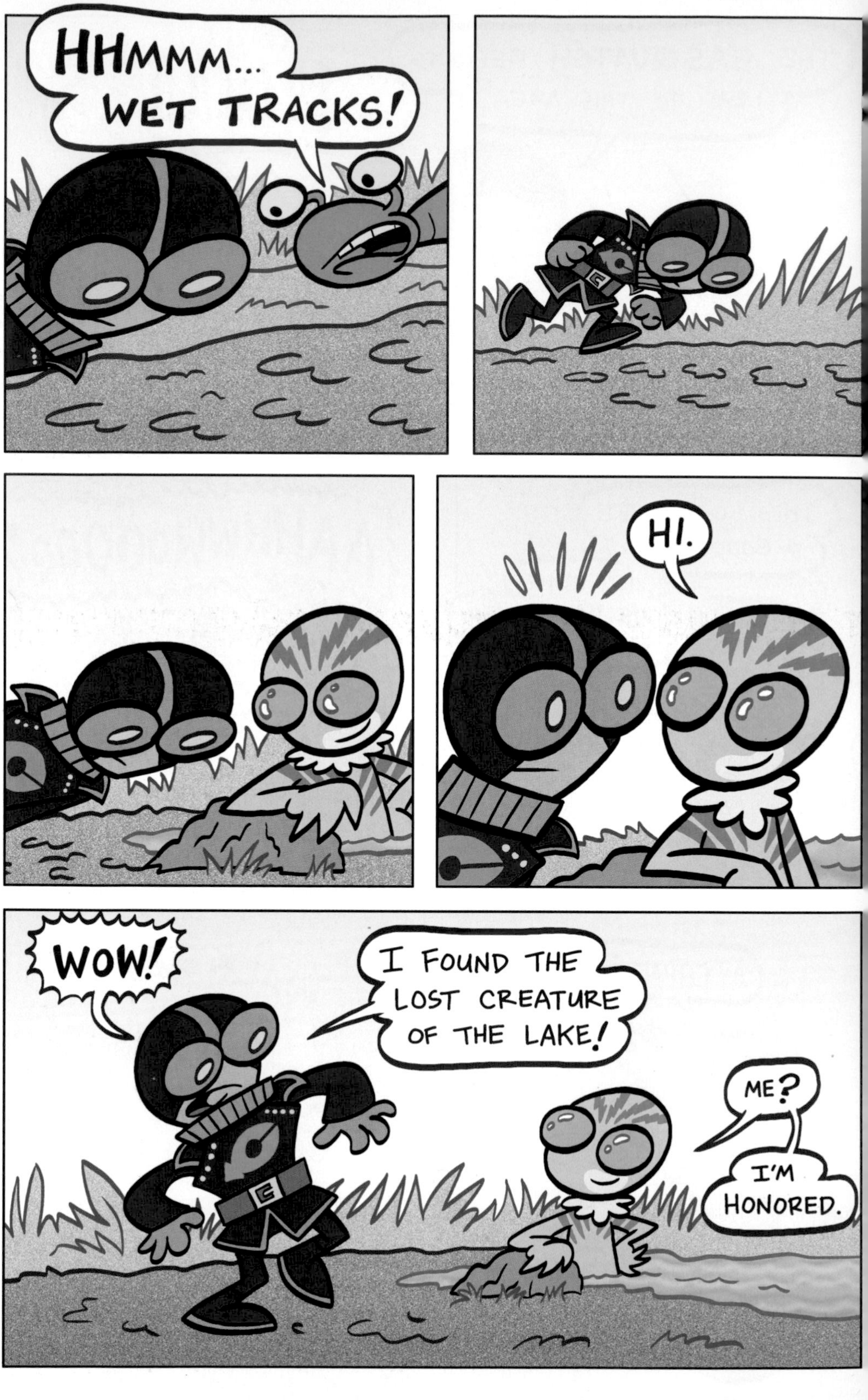
HHMMM... WET TRACKS!
HI.
WOW!
I FOUND THE LOST CREATURE OF THE LAKE!
ME?
I'M HONORED.

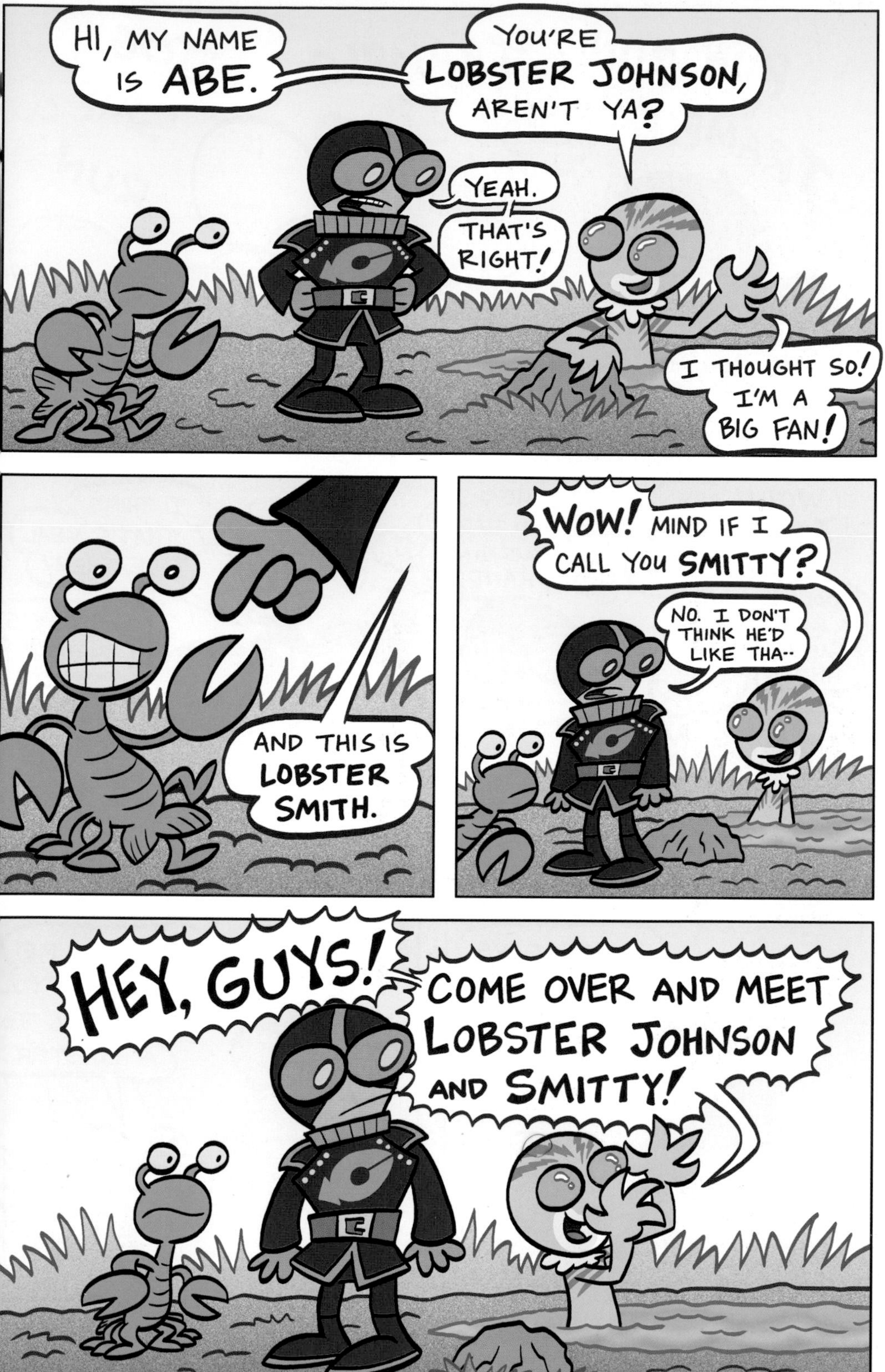
HI, MY NAME IS ABE.
YOU'RE LOBSTER JOHNSON, AREN'T YA?
YEAH. THAT'S RIGHT!
I THOUGHT SO! I'M A BIG FAN!
AND THIS IS LOBSTER SMITH.
WOW! MIND IF I CALL YOU SMITTY?
NO. I DON'T THINK HE'D LIKE THA--
HEY, GUYS!
COME OVER AND MEET LOBSTER JOHNSON AND SMITTY!

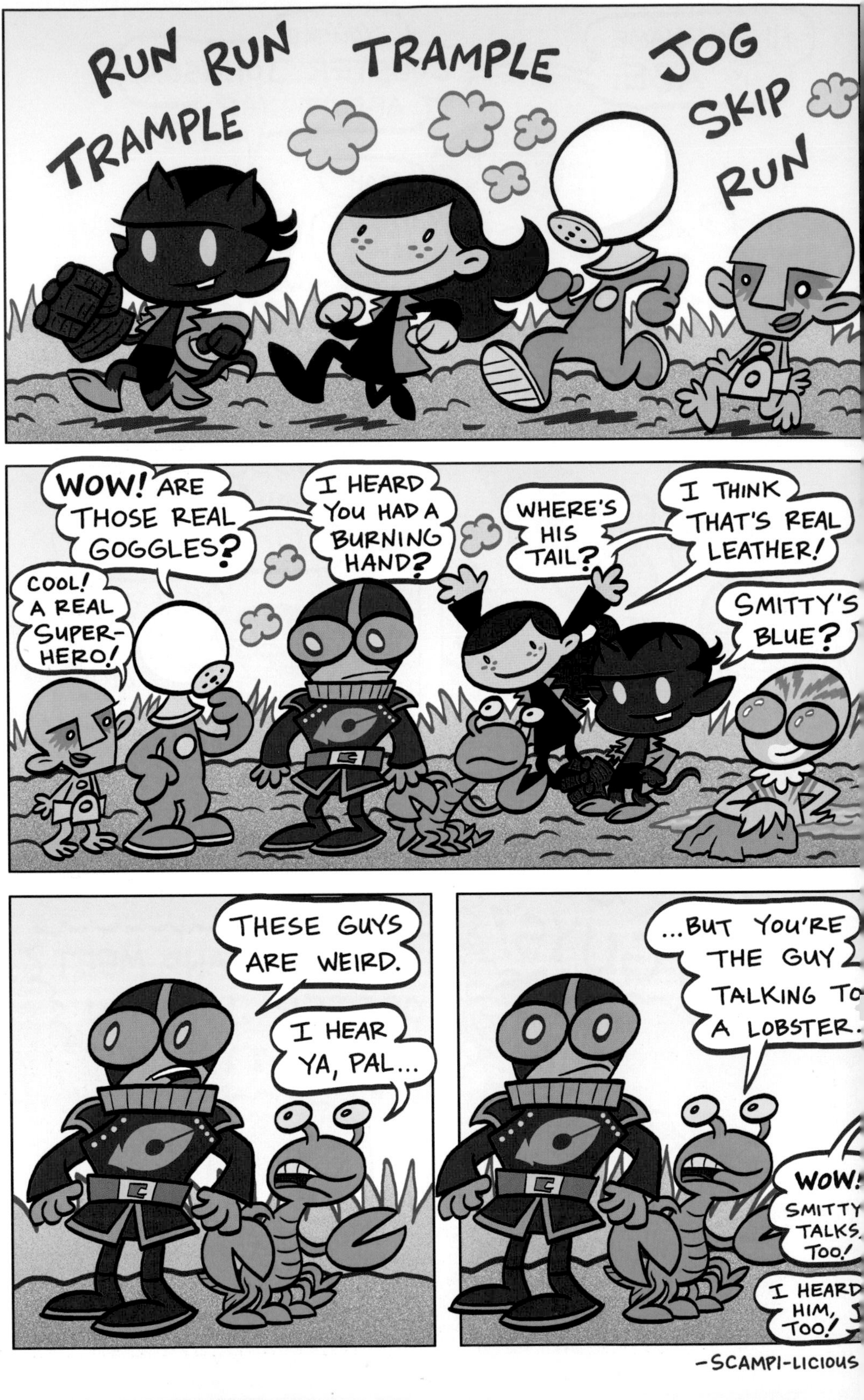
RUN RUN
TRAMPLE
TRAMPLE
JOG
SKIP
RUN
WOW! ARE THOSE REAL GOGGLES?
I HEARD YOU HAD A BURNING HAND?
WHERE'S HIS TAIL?
I THINK THAT'S REAL LEATHER!
COOL! A REAL SUPER-HERO!
SMITTY'S BLUE?
THESE GUYS ARE WEIRD.
I HEAR YA, PAL...
...BUT YOU'RE THE GUY TALKING TO A LOBSTER.
WOW! SMITTY TALKS, TOO!
I HEARD HIM, TOO!
-SCAMPI-LICIOUS

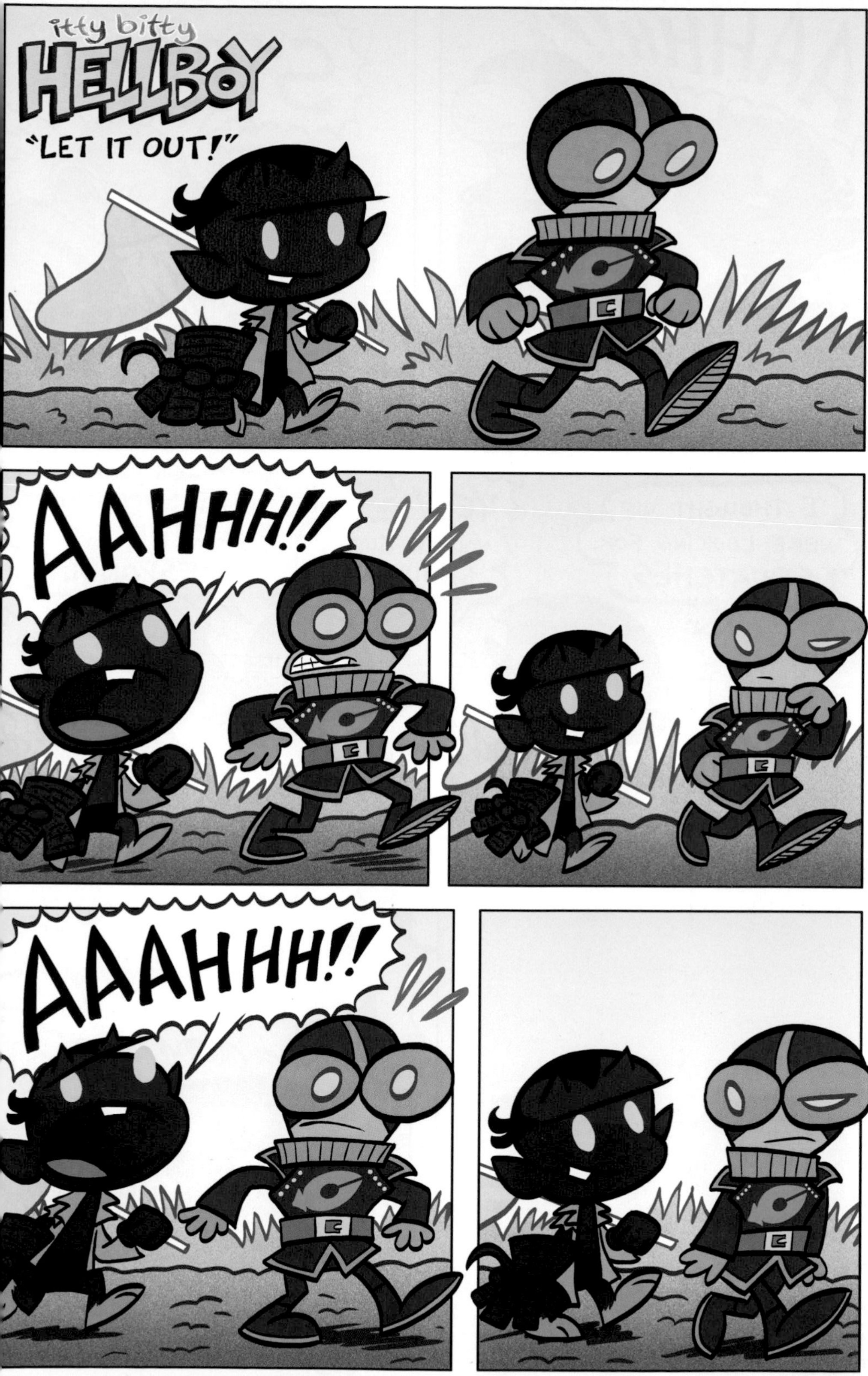
itty bitty
HELLBOY
"LET IT OUT!"
AAHHH!!
AAAHHH!!

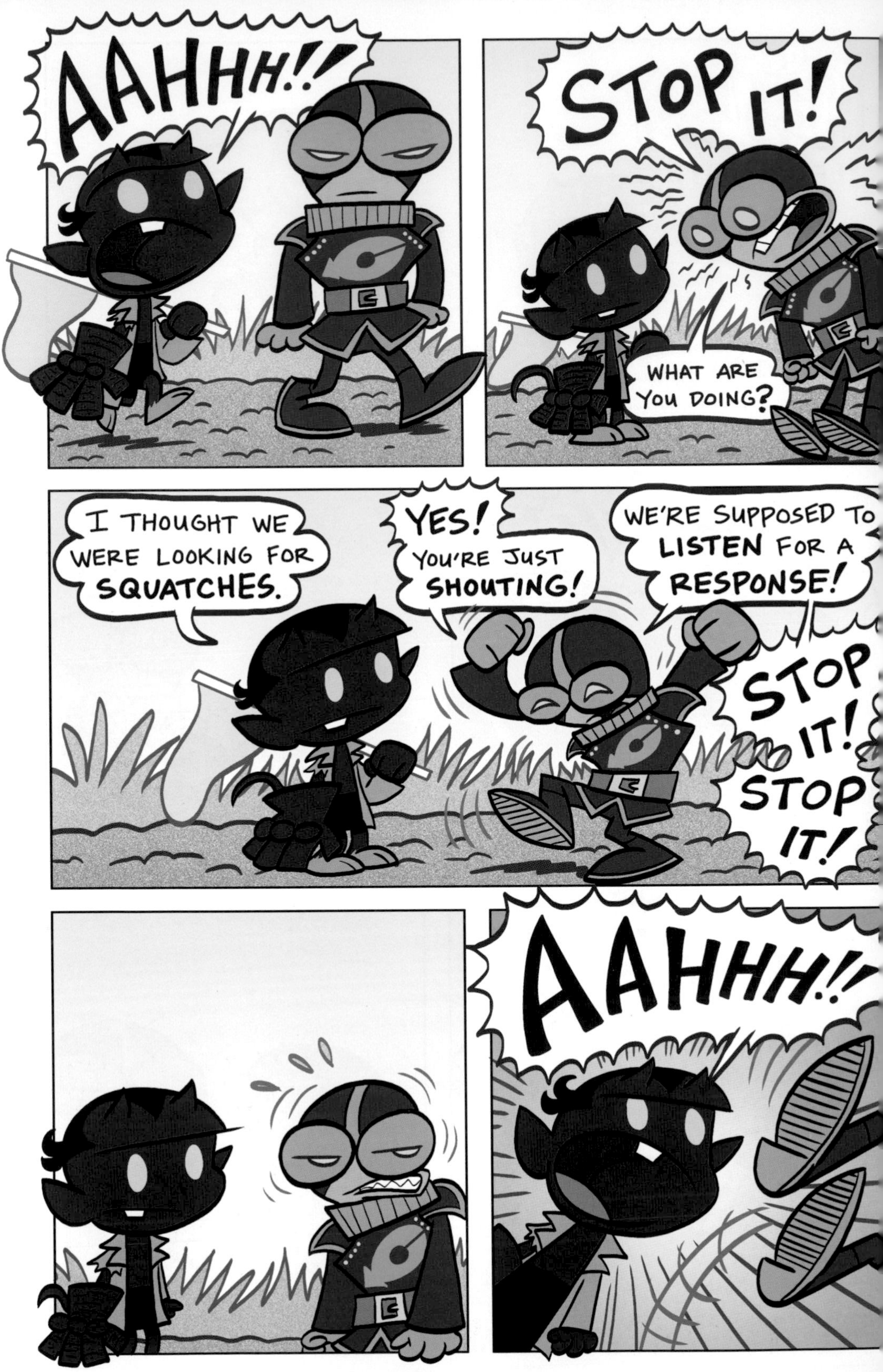
AAHHH!!
STOP IT!
WHAT ARE YOU DOING?
I THOUGHT WE WERE LOOKING FOR SQUATCHES.
YES! YOU'RE JUST SHOUTING!
WE'RE SUPPOSED TO LISTEN FOR A RESPONSE!
STOP IT! STOP IT!
AAHHH!!

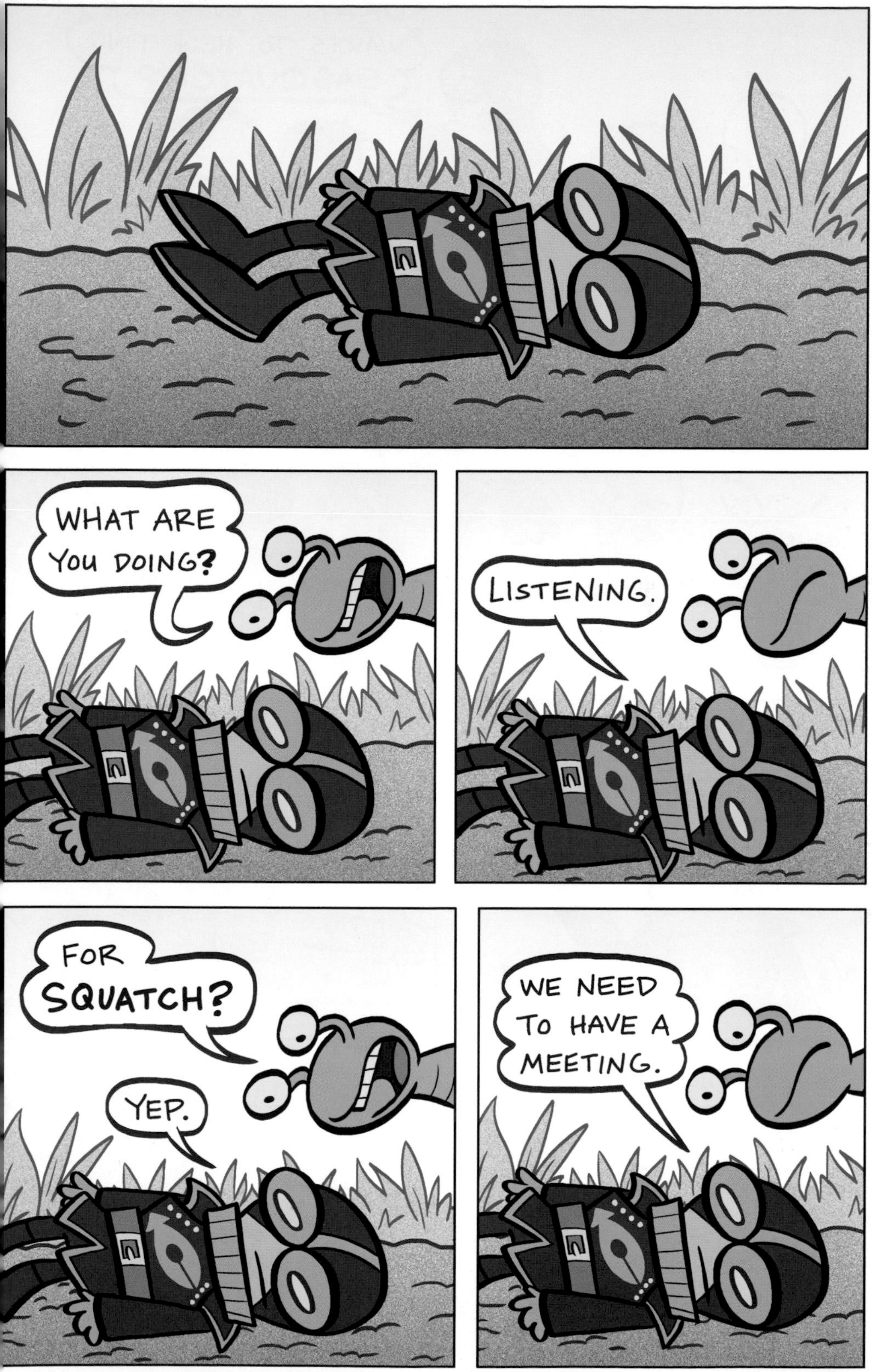
WHAT ARE YOU DOING?
LISTENING.
FOR SQUATCH?
YEP.
WE NEED TO HAVE A MEETING.

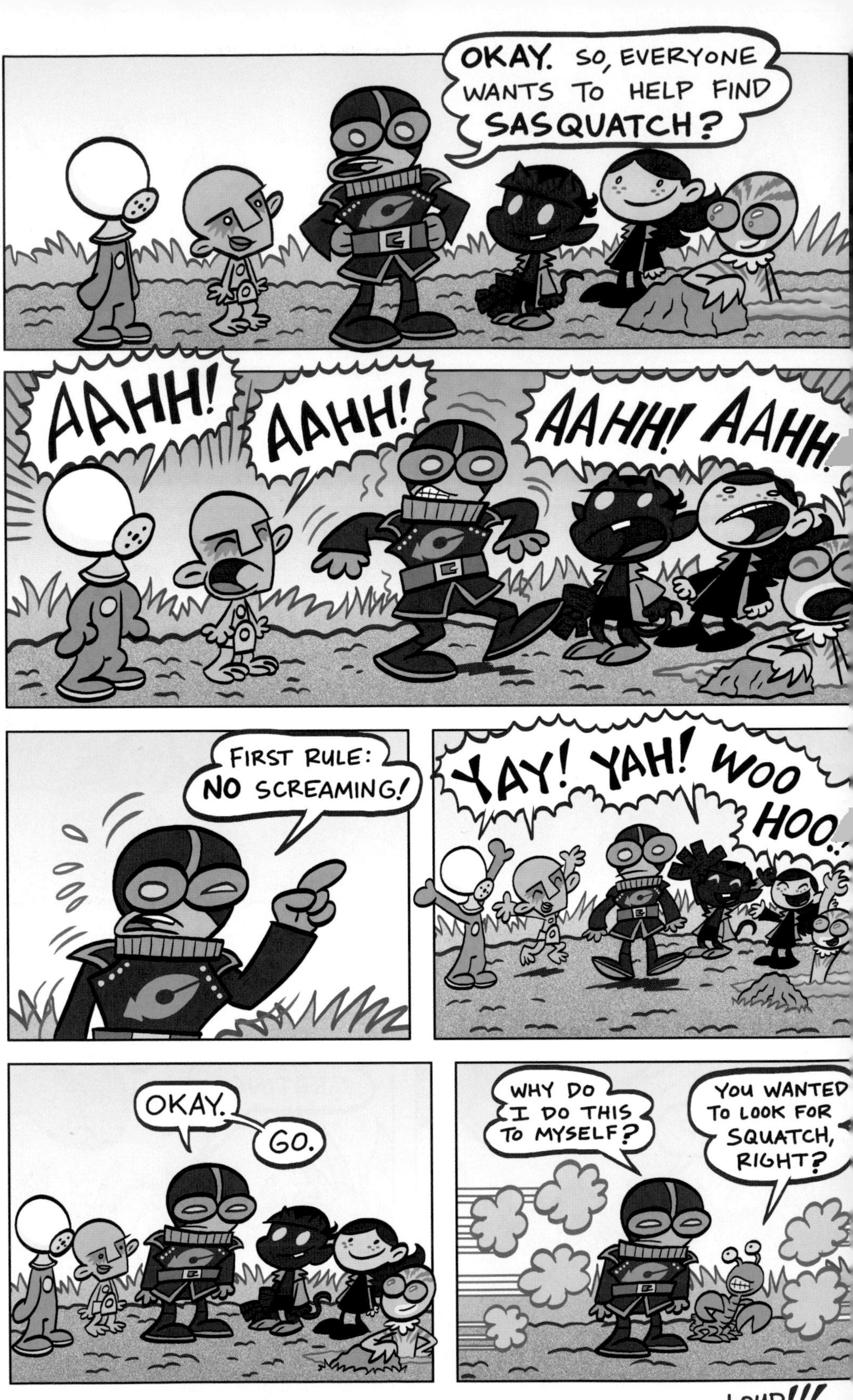
OKAY. SO, EVERYONE WANTS TO HELP FIND SASQUATCH?
AAHH!
AAHH!
AAHH! AAHH
FIRST RULE: NO SCREAMING!
YAY! YAH! WOO HOO...
OKAY.
GO.
WHY DO I DO THIS TO MYSELF?
YOU WANTED TO LOOK FOR SQUATCH, RIGHT?
LOUD!!!

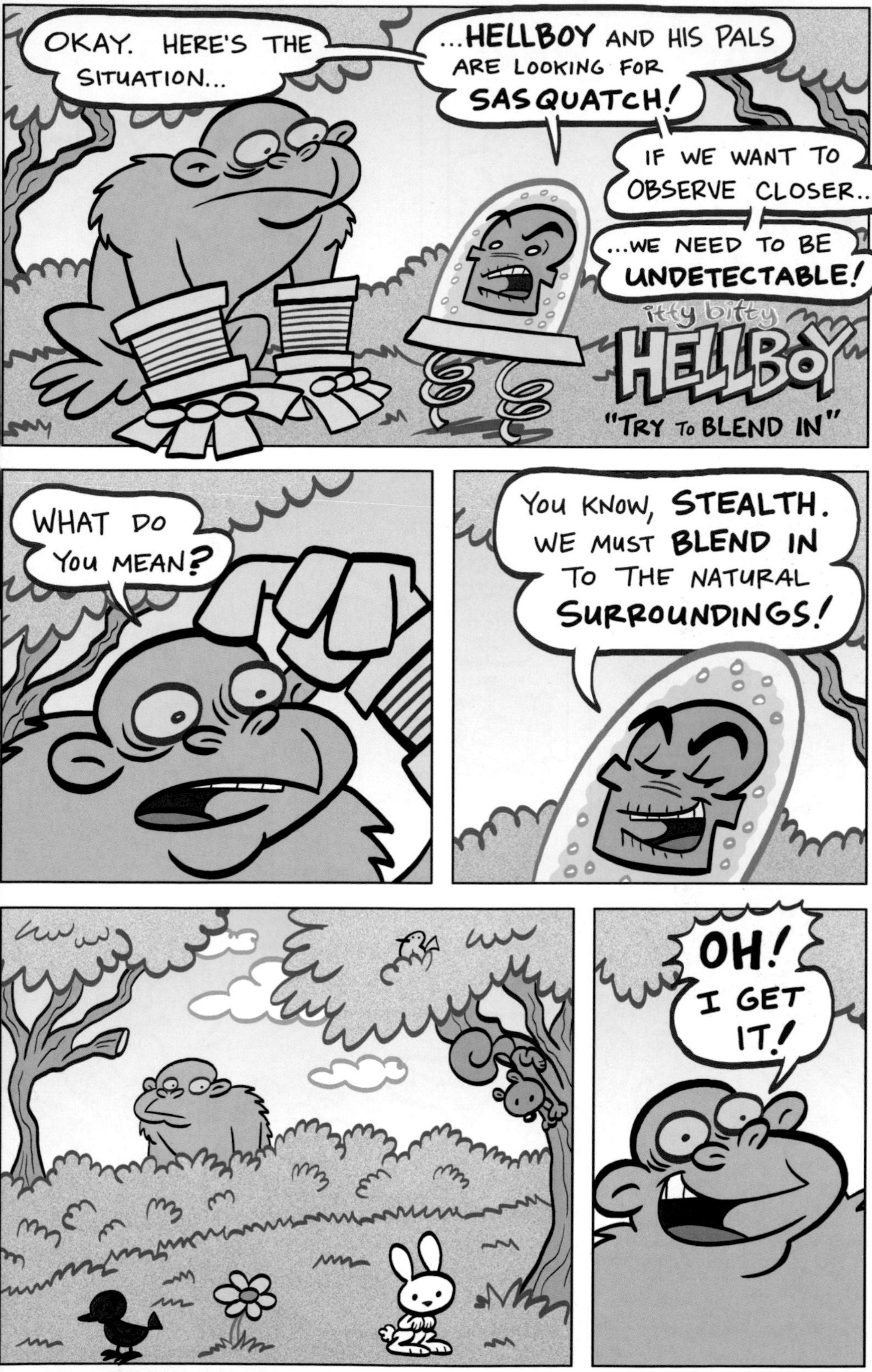
OKAY. HERE'S THE SITUATION...
...HELLBOY AND HIS PALS ARE LOOKING FOR SASQUATCH!
IF WE WANT TO OBSERVE CLOSER..
...WE NEED TO BE UNDETECTABLE!
itty bitty HELLBOY
"TRY TO BLEND IN"
WHAT DO YOU MEAN?
YOU KNOW, STEALTH. WE MUST BLEND IN TO THE NATURAL SURROUNDINGS!
OH! I GET IT!

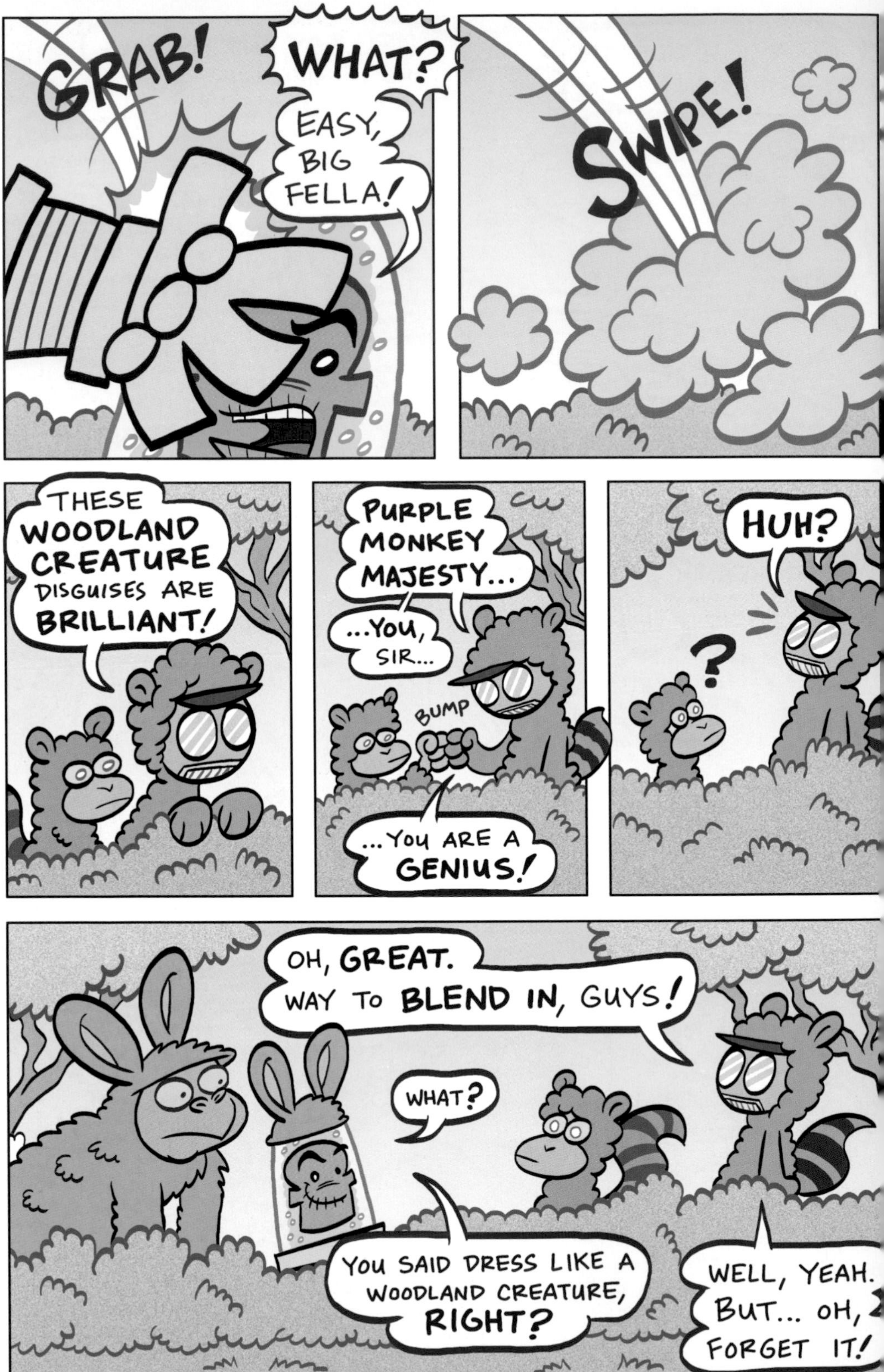
GRAB!
WHAT?
EASY, BIG FELLA!
SWIPE!
THESE WOODLAND CREATURE DISGUISES ARE BRILLIANT!
PURPLE MONKEY MAJESTY...
...YOU, SIR...
BUMP
...YOU ARE A GENIUS!
HUH?
?
OH, GREAT. WAY TO BLEND IN, GUYS!
WHAT?
YOU SAID DRESS LIKE A WOODLAND CREATURE, RIGHT?
WELL, YEAH. BUT... OH, FORGET IT!
-MIX-IT-UP.

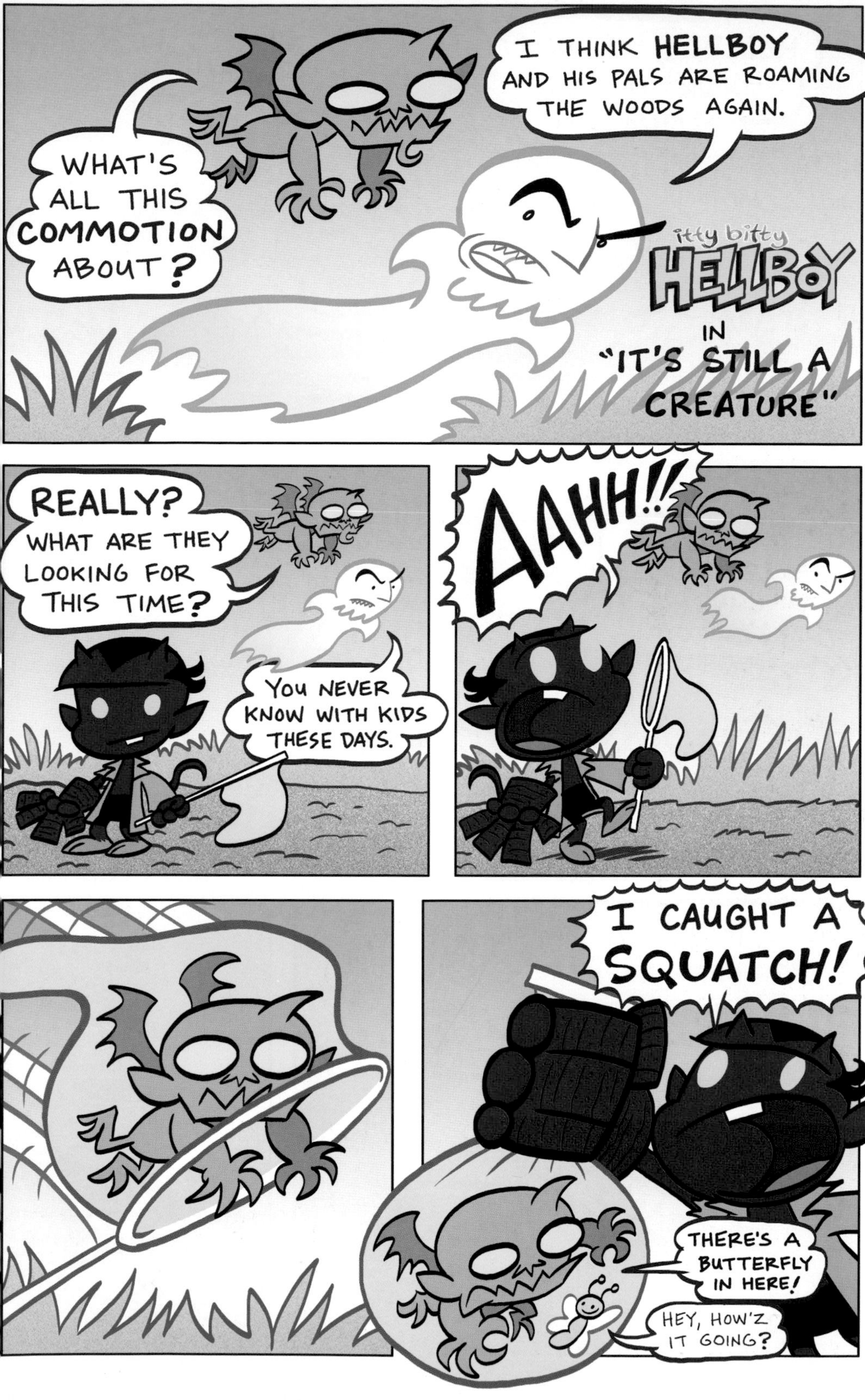
WHAT'S ALL THIS COMMOTION ABOUT?
I THINK HELLBOY AND HIS PALS ARE ROAMING THE WOODS AGAIN.
itty bitty HELLBOY
IN "IT'S STILL A CREATURE"
REALLY? WHAT ARE THEY LOOKING FOR THIS TIME?
YOU NEVER KNOW WITH KIDS THESE DAYS.
AAHH!!
I CAUGHT A SQUATCH!
THERE'S A BUTTERFLY IN HERE!
HEY, HOW'Z IT GOING?

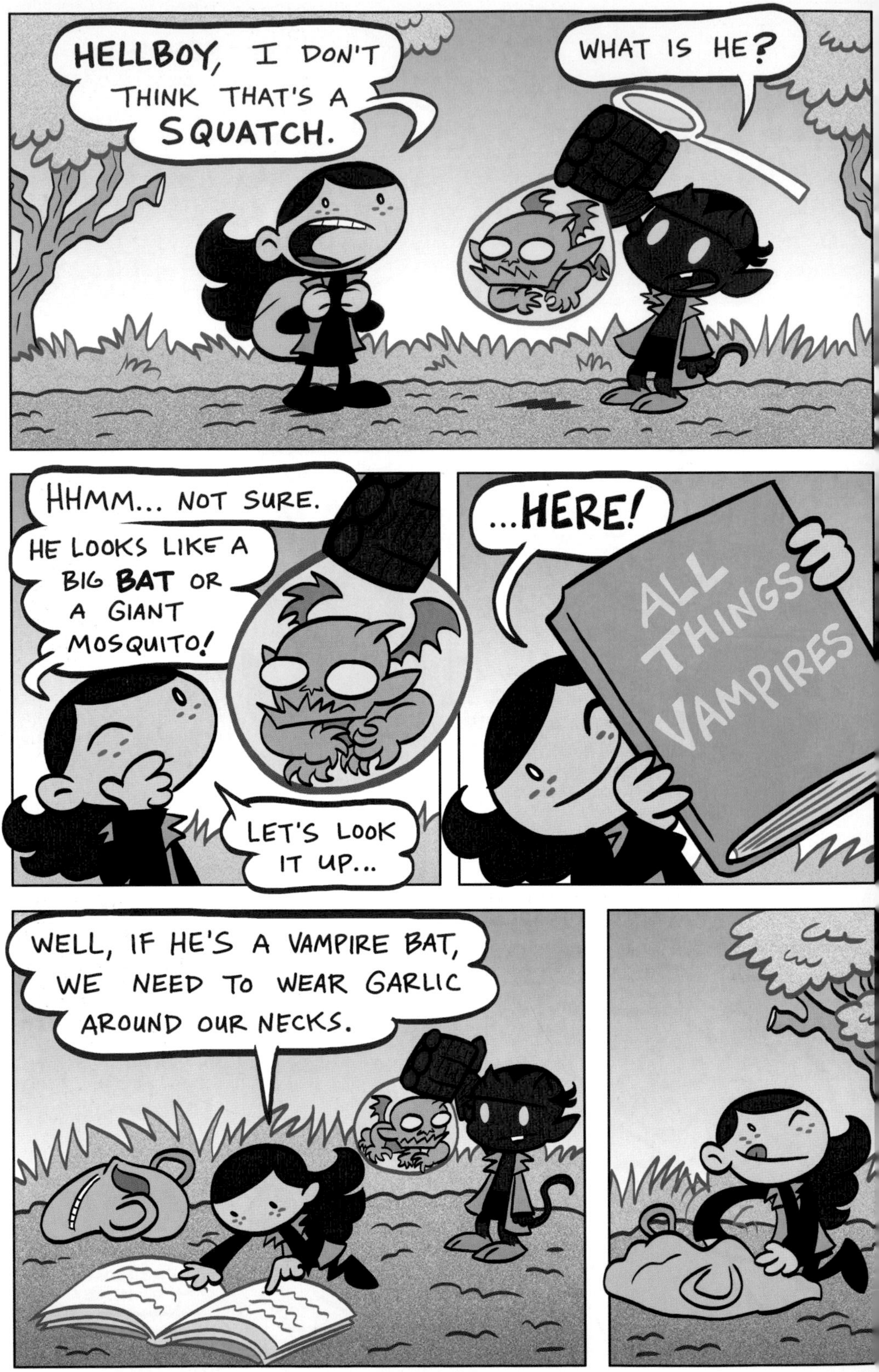
HELLBOY, I DON'T THINK THAT'S A SQUATCH.
WHAT IS HE?
HHMM... NOT SURE.
HE LOOKS LIKE A BIG BAT OR A GIANT MOSQUITO!
LET'S LOOK IT UP...
...HERE!
ALL THINGS VAMPIRES
WELL, IF HE'S A VAMPIRE BAT, WE NEED TO WEAR GARLIC AROUND OUR NECKS.

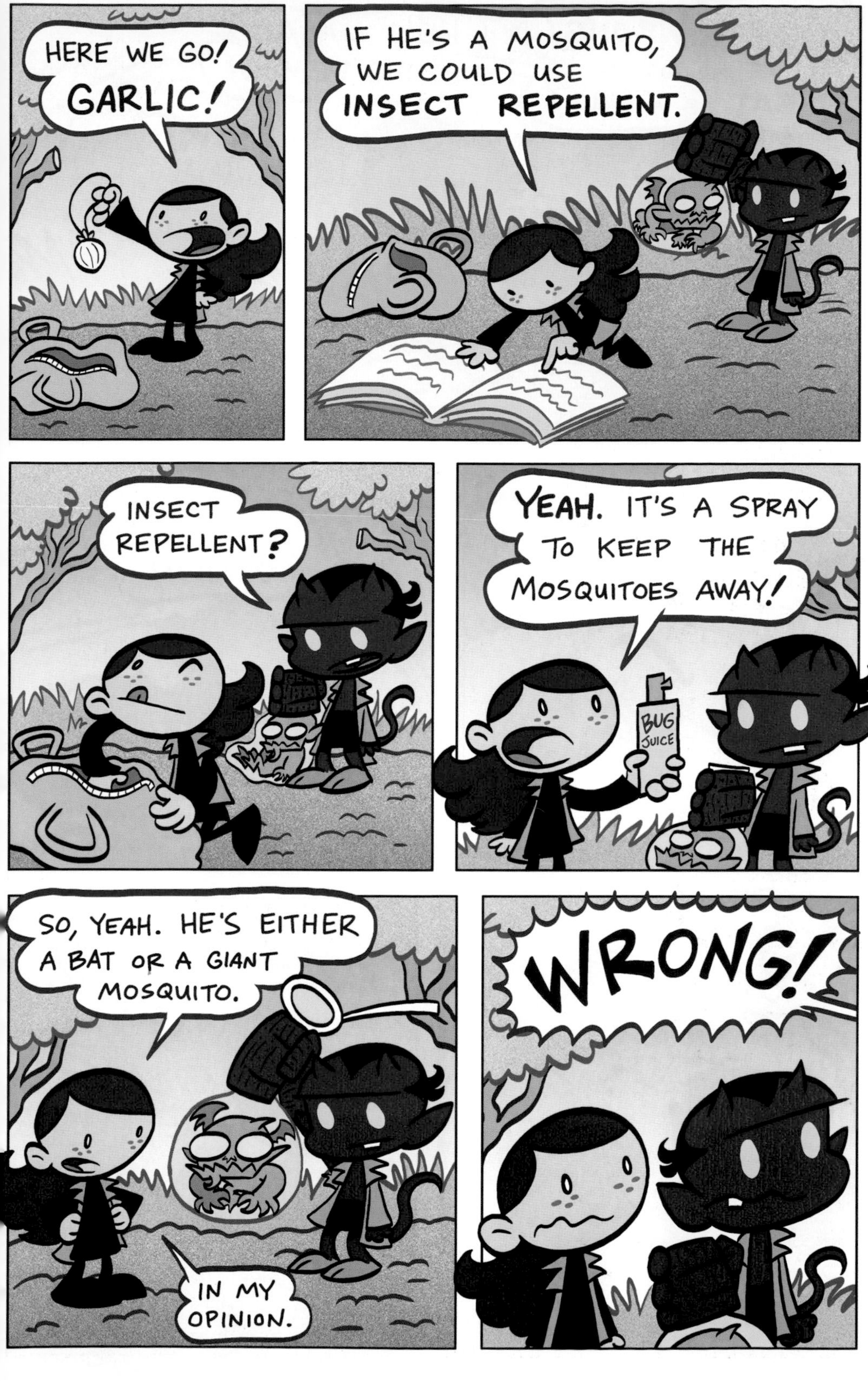
HERE WE GO! GARLIC!
IF HE'S A MOSQUITO, WE COULD USE INSECT REPELLENT.
INSECT REPELLENT?
YEAH. IT'S A SPRAY TO KEEP THE MOSQUITOES AWAY!
BUG JUICE
SO, YEAH. HE'S EITHER A BAT OR A GIANT MOSQUITO.
IN MY OPINION.
WRONG!

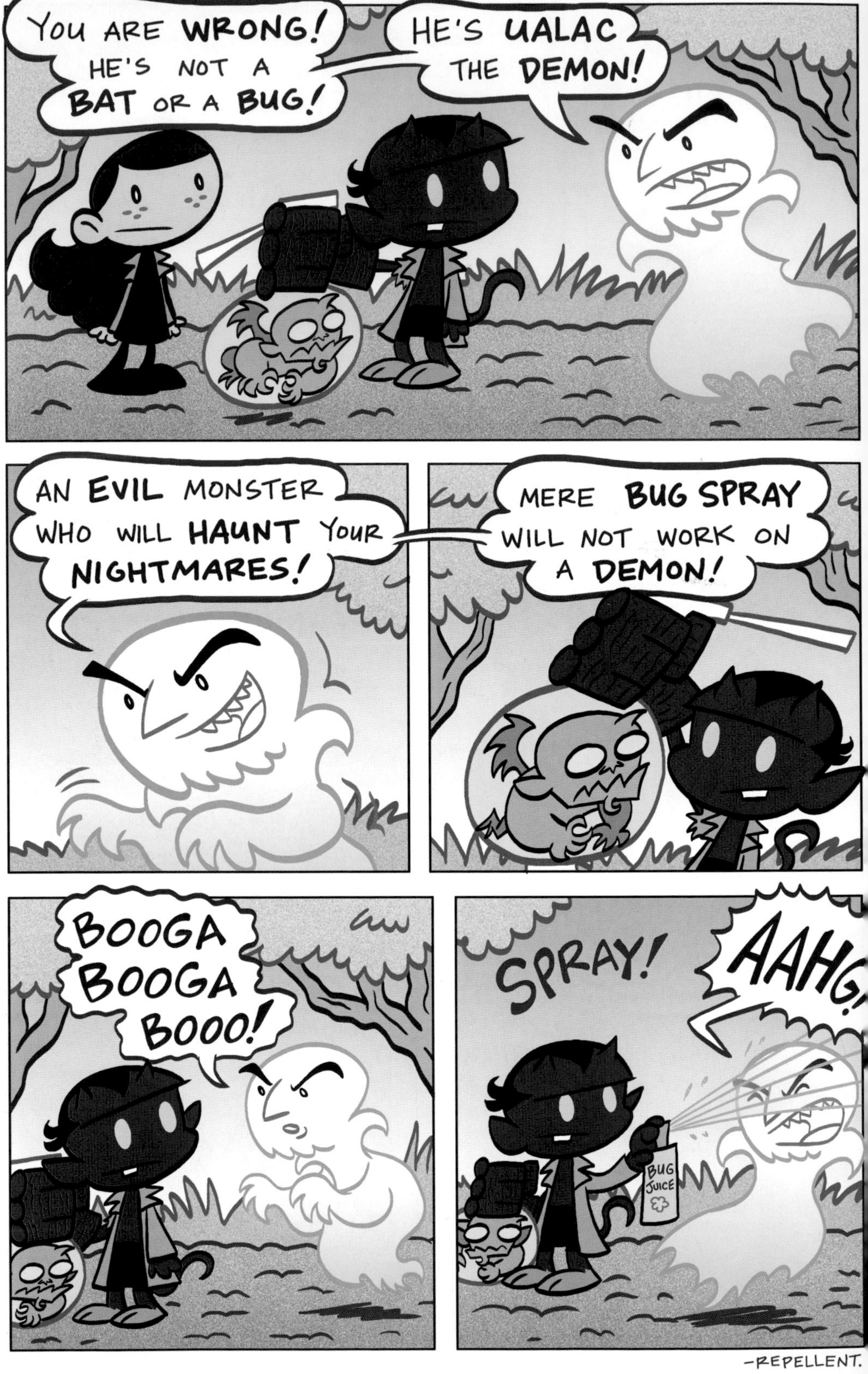
YOU ARE WRONG! HE'S NOT A BAT OR A BUG!
HE'S UALAC THE DEMON!
AN EVIL MONSTER WHO WILL HAUNT YOUR NIGHTMARES!
MERE BUG SPRAY WILL NOT WORK ON A DEMON!
BOOGA BOOGA BOOO!
SPRAY!
AAHG!
BUG JUICE

–REPELLENT.

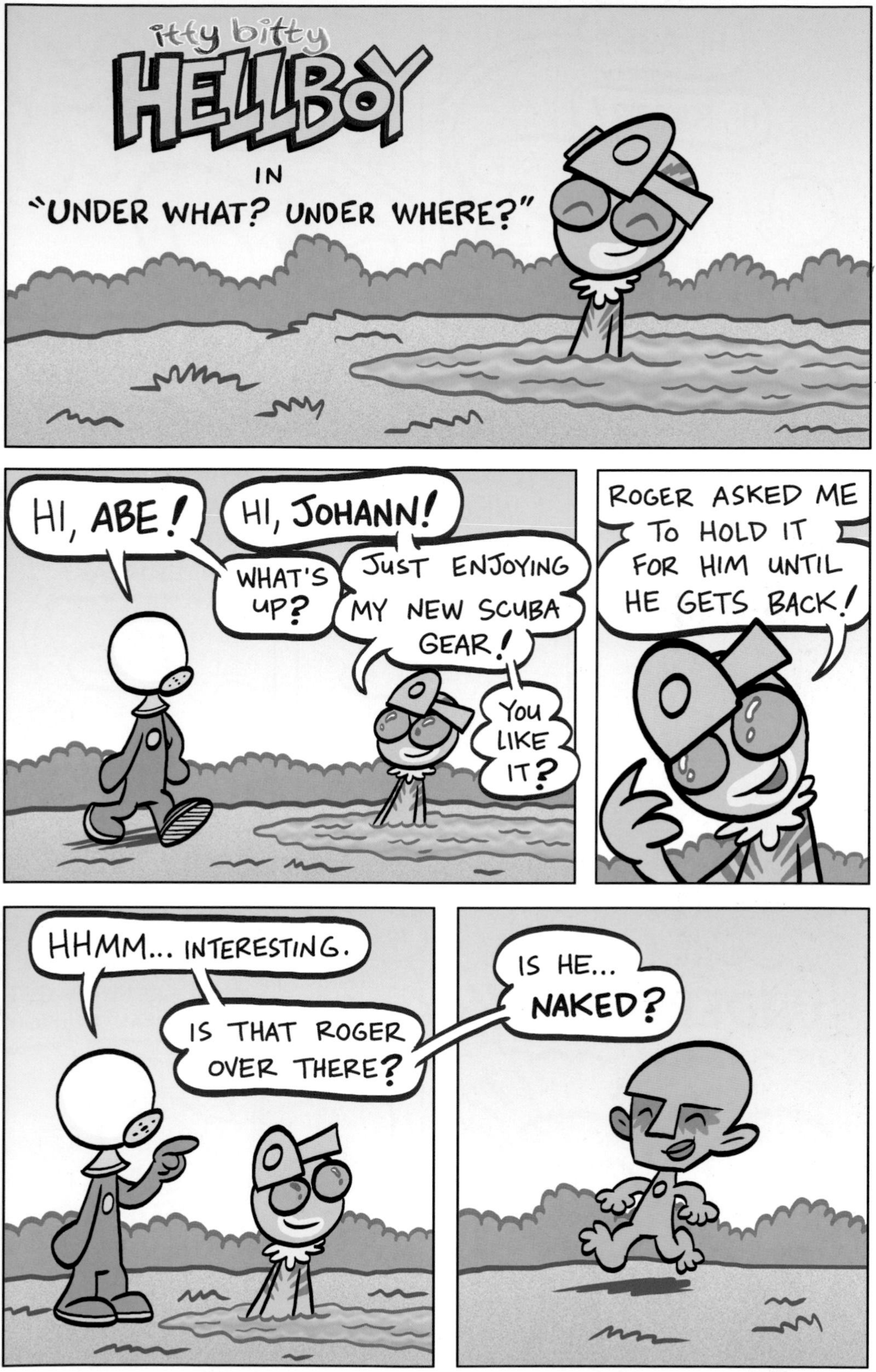
itty bitty
HELLBOY
IN
"UNDER WHAT? UNDER WHERE?"
HI, ABE!
HI, JOHANN!
WHAT'S UP?
JUST ENJOYING MY NEW SCUBA GEAR!
YOU LIKE IT?
ROGER ASKED ME TO HOLD IT FOR HIM UNTIL HE GETS BACK!
HHMM... INTERESTING.
IS THAT ROGER OVER THERE?
IS HE... NAKED?

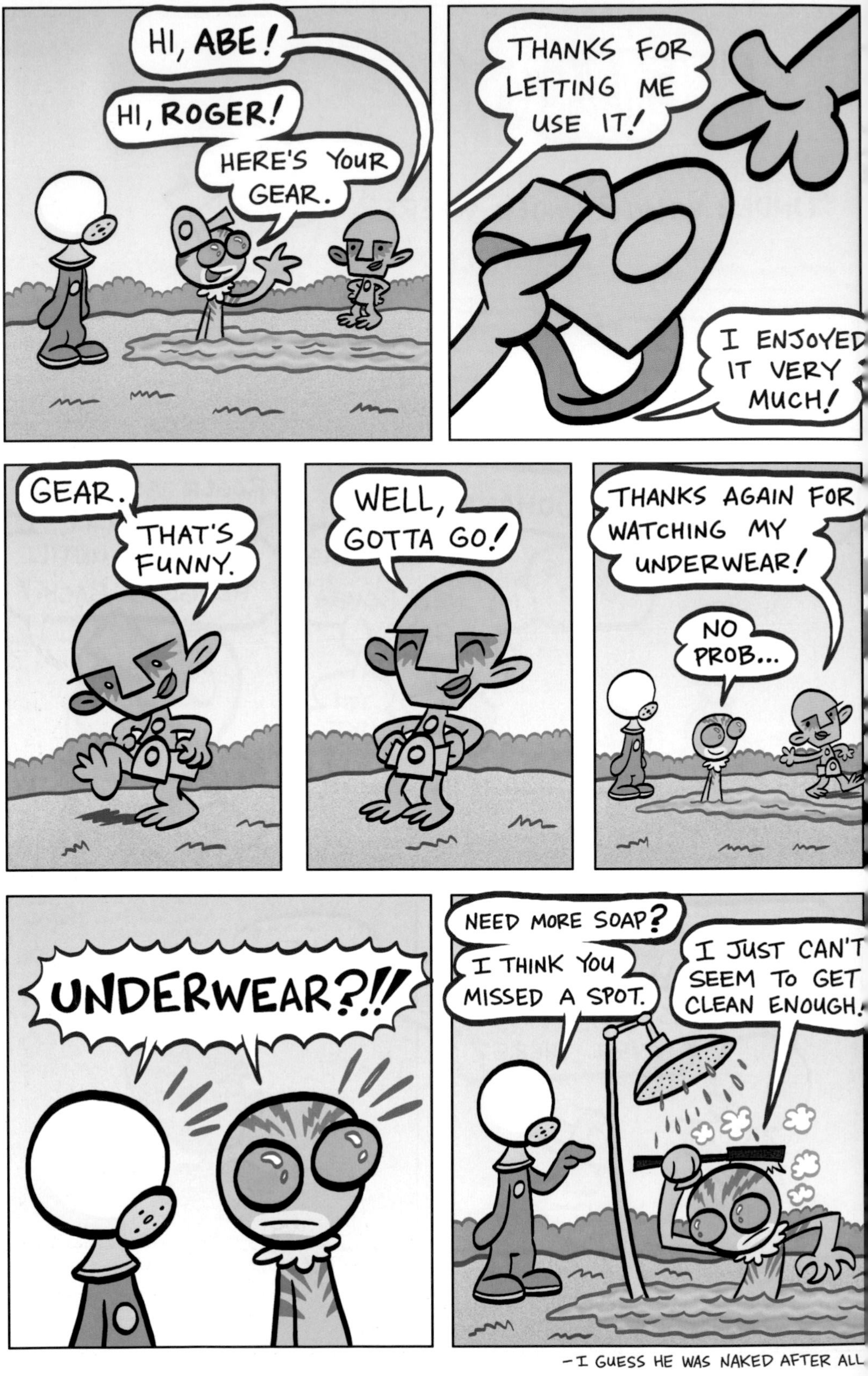
HI, ABE!
HI, ROGER!
HERE'S YOUR GEAR.
THANKS FOR LETTING ME USE IT!
I ENJOYED IT VERY MUCH!
GEAR.
THAT'S FUNNY.
WELL, GOTTA GO!
THANKS AGAIN FOR WATCHING MY UNDERWEAR!
NO PROB...
UNDERWEAR?!!
NEED MORE SOAP?
I THINK YOU MISSED A SPOT.
I JUST CAN'T SEEM TO GET CLEAN ENOUGH.

—I GUESS HE WAS NAKED AFTER ALL

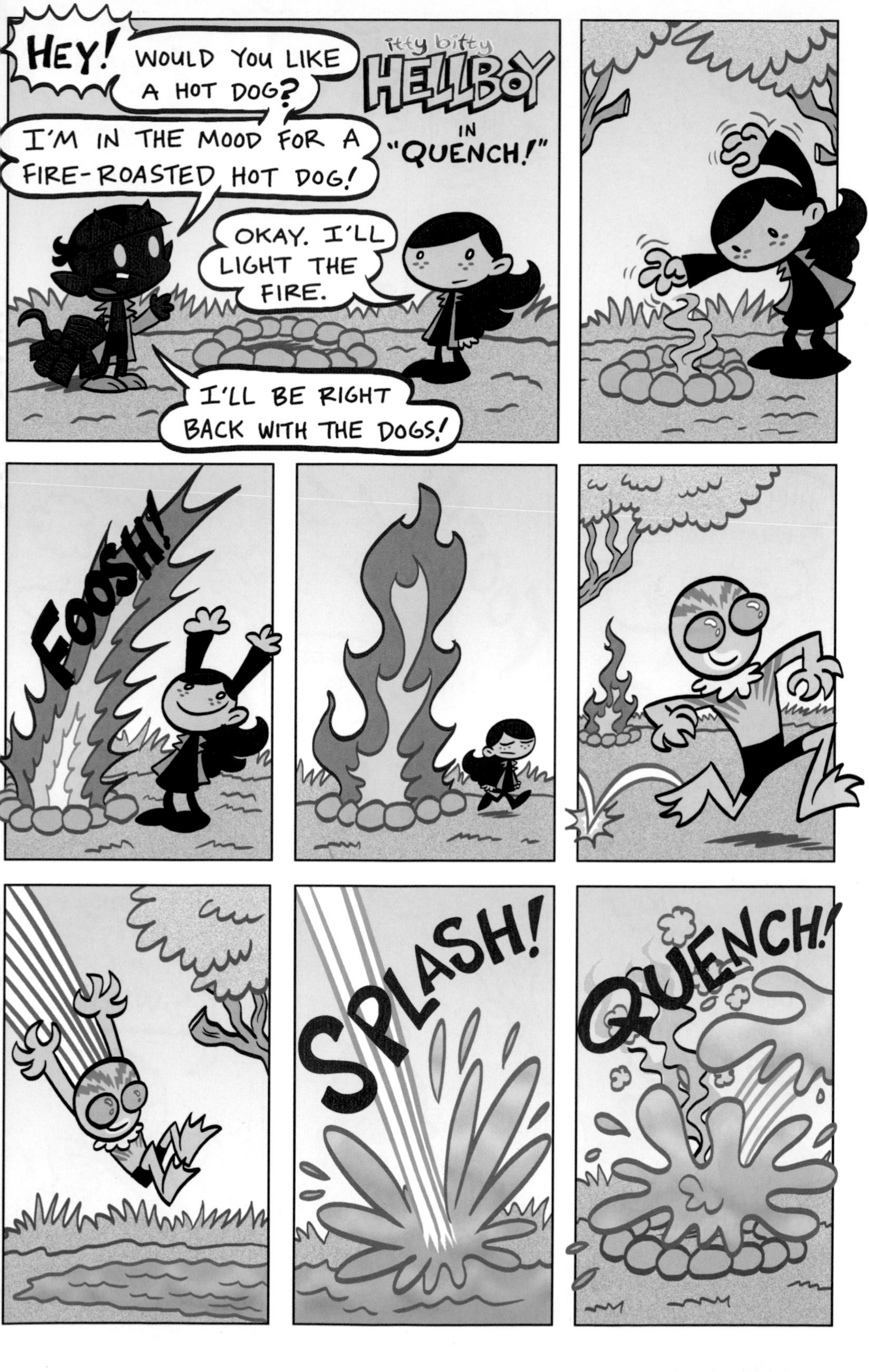
HEY! WOULD YOU LIKE A HOT DOG?
I'M IN THE MOOD FOR A FIRE-ROASTED HOT DOG!
itty bitty HELLBOY IN "QUENCH!"
OKAY. I'LL LIGHT THE FIRE.
I'LL BE RIGHT BACK WITH THE DOGS!
FOOSH!
SPLASH!
QUENCH!

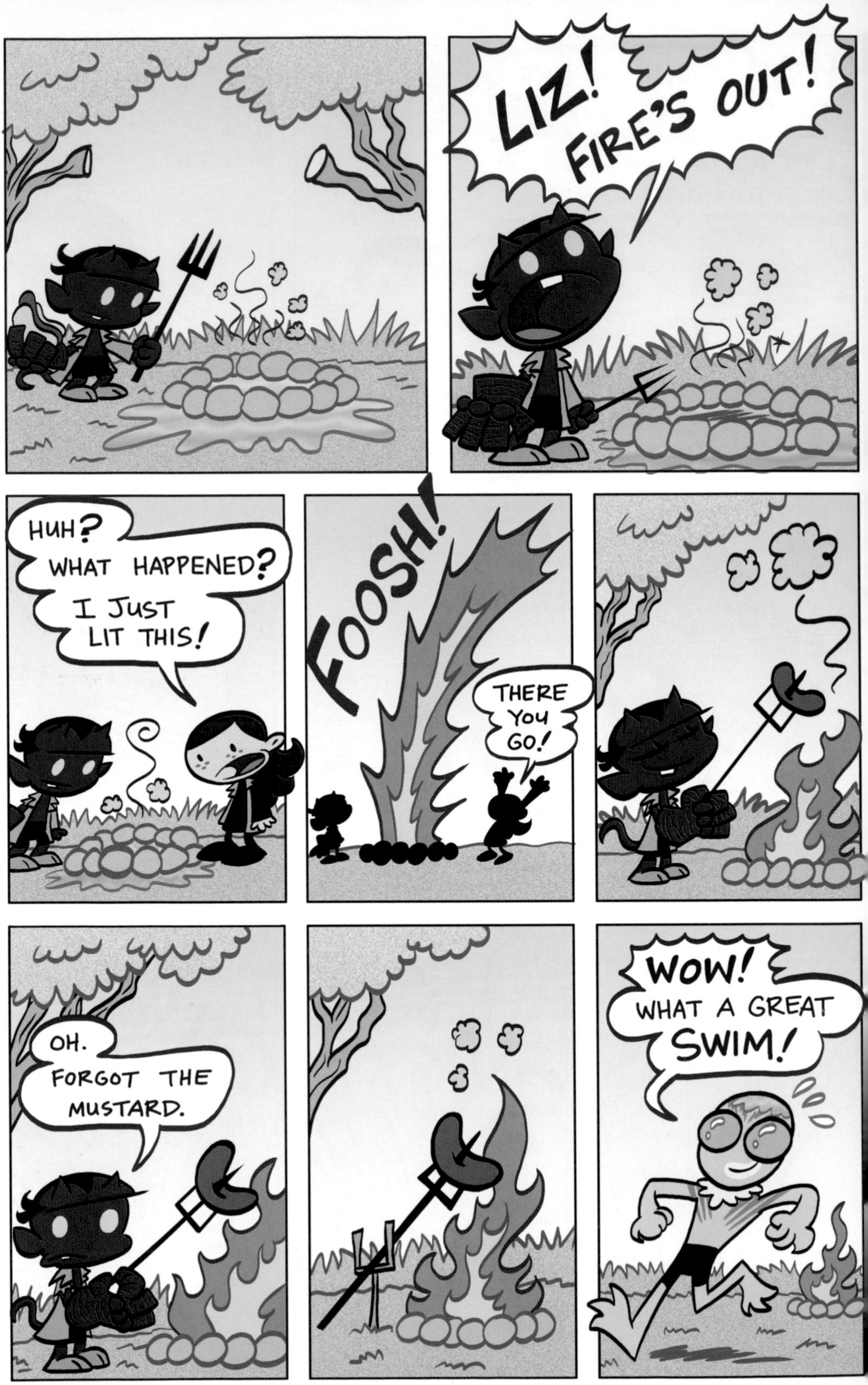
LIZ! FIRE'S OUT!
HUH? WHAT HAPPENED? I JUST LIT THIS!
FOOSH!
THERE YOU GO!
OH. FORGOT THE MUSTARD.
WOW! WHAT A GREAT SWIM!

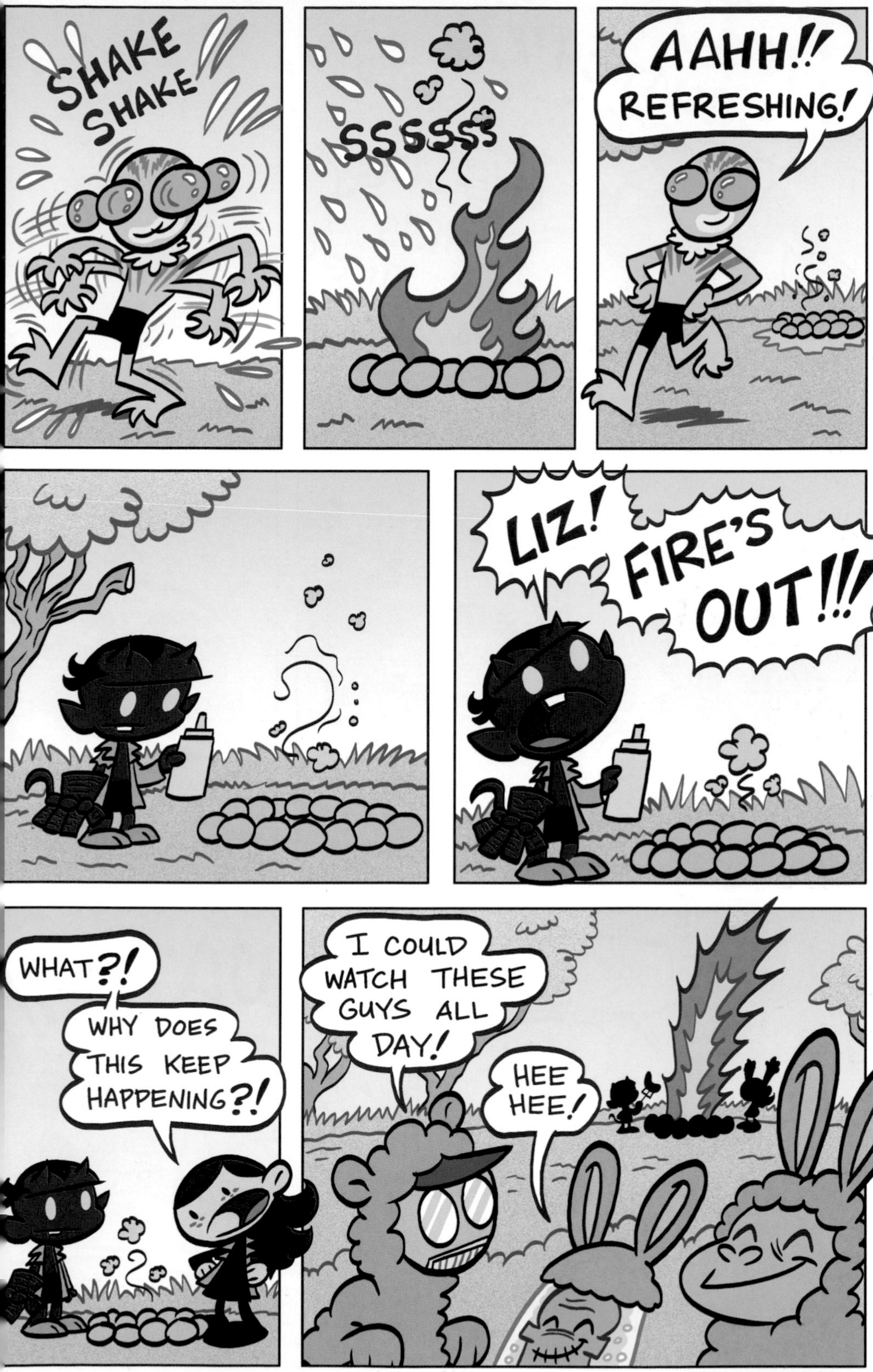
SHAKE SHAKE
SSSSSS
AAHH!! REFRESHING!
LIZ!
FIRE'S OUT!!!
WHAT?!
WHY DOES THIS KEEP HAPPENING?!
I COULD WATCH THESE GUYS ALL DAY!
HEE HEE!

—GETTING COMFY.

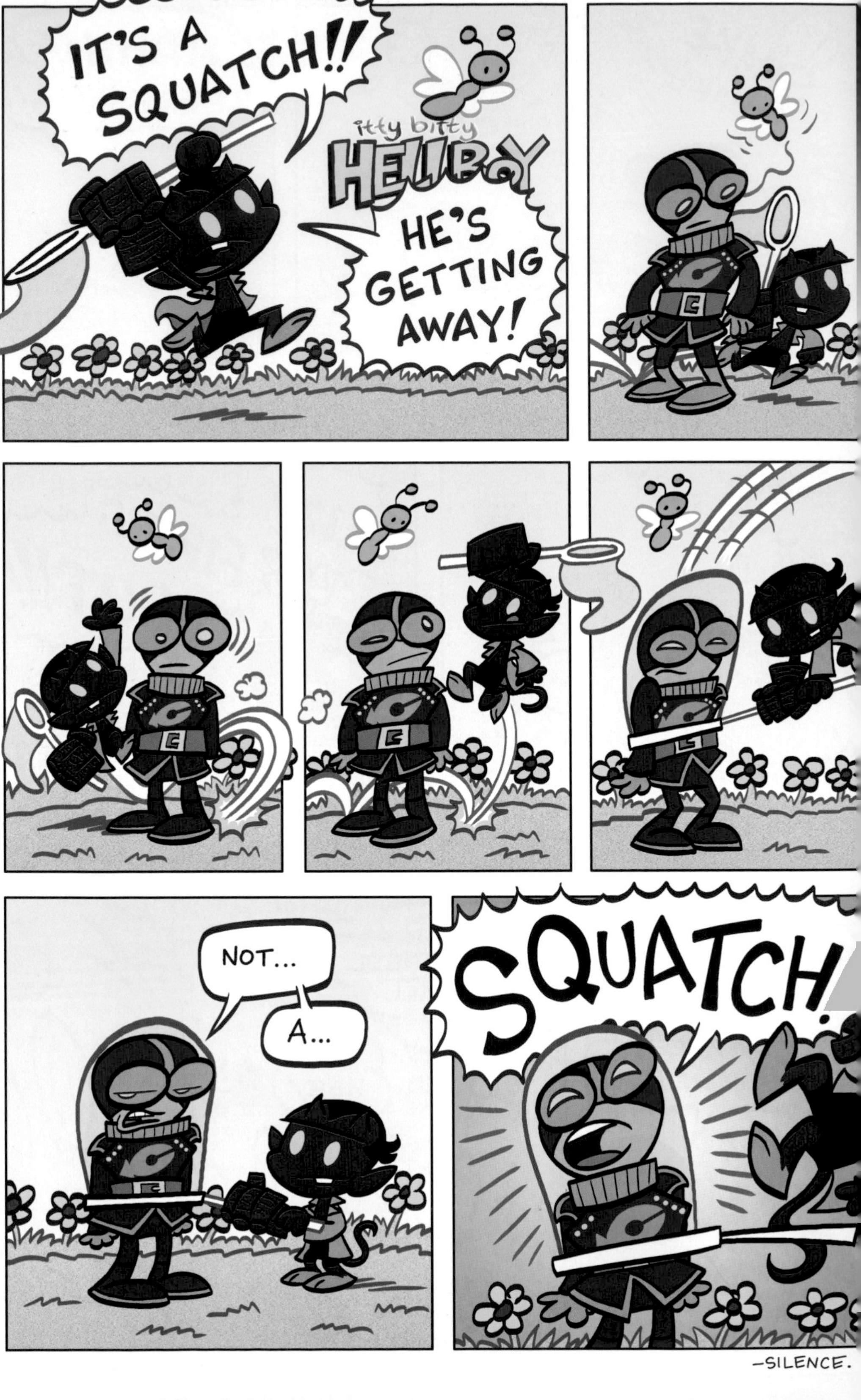
IT'S A SQUATCH!!
itty bitty HELLBOY
HE'S GETTING AWAY!
NOT...
A...
SQUATCH!

-SILENCE.

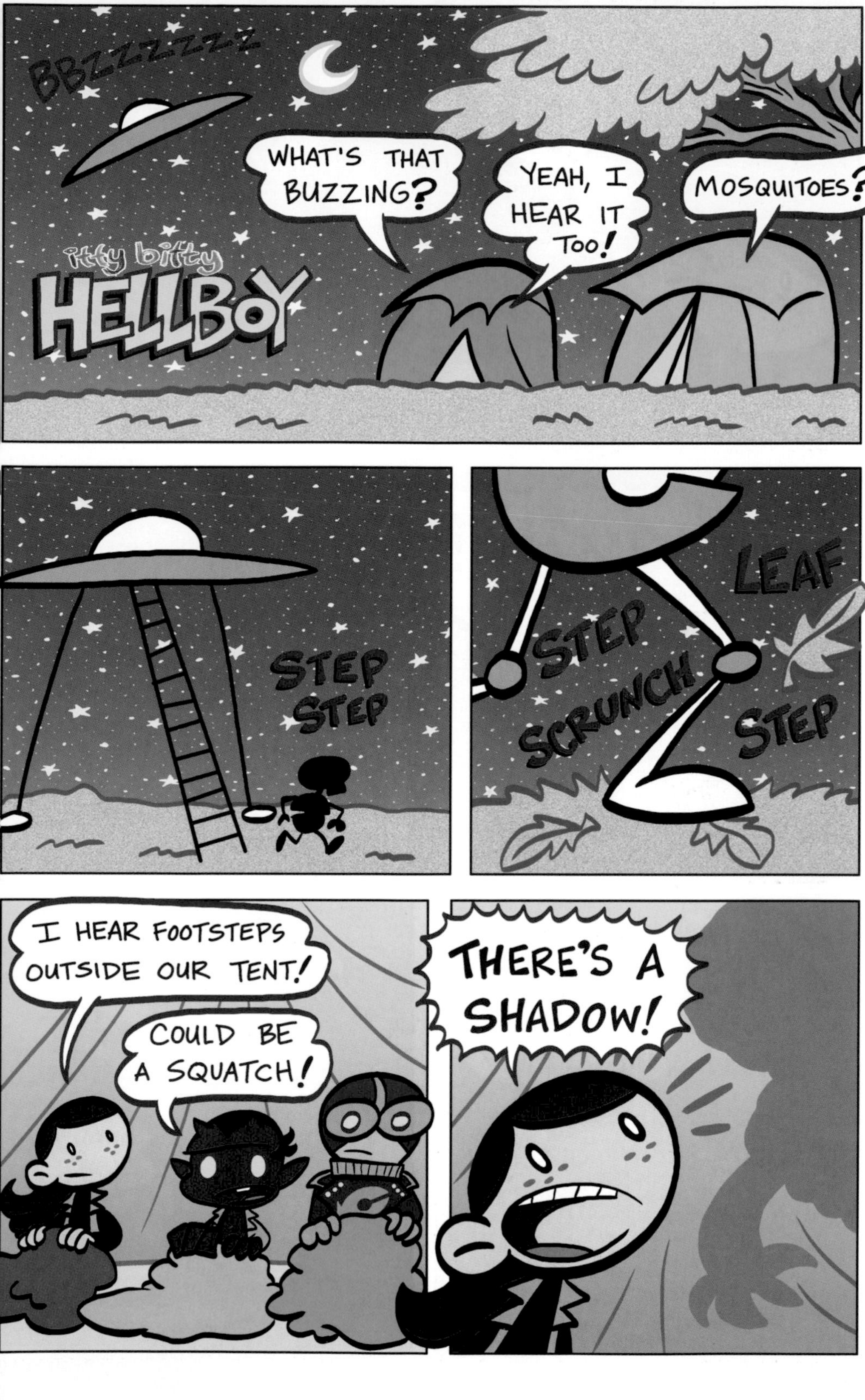
BBZZZZZZZ
itty bitty
HELLBOY
WHAT'S THAT BUZZING?
YEAH, I HEAR IT TOO!
MOSQUITOES?
STEP
STEP
LEAF
STEP
SCRUNCH
STEP
I HEAR FOOTSTEPS OUTSIDE OUR TENT!
COULD BE A SQUATCH!
THERE'S A SHADOW!

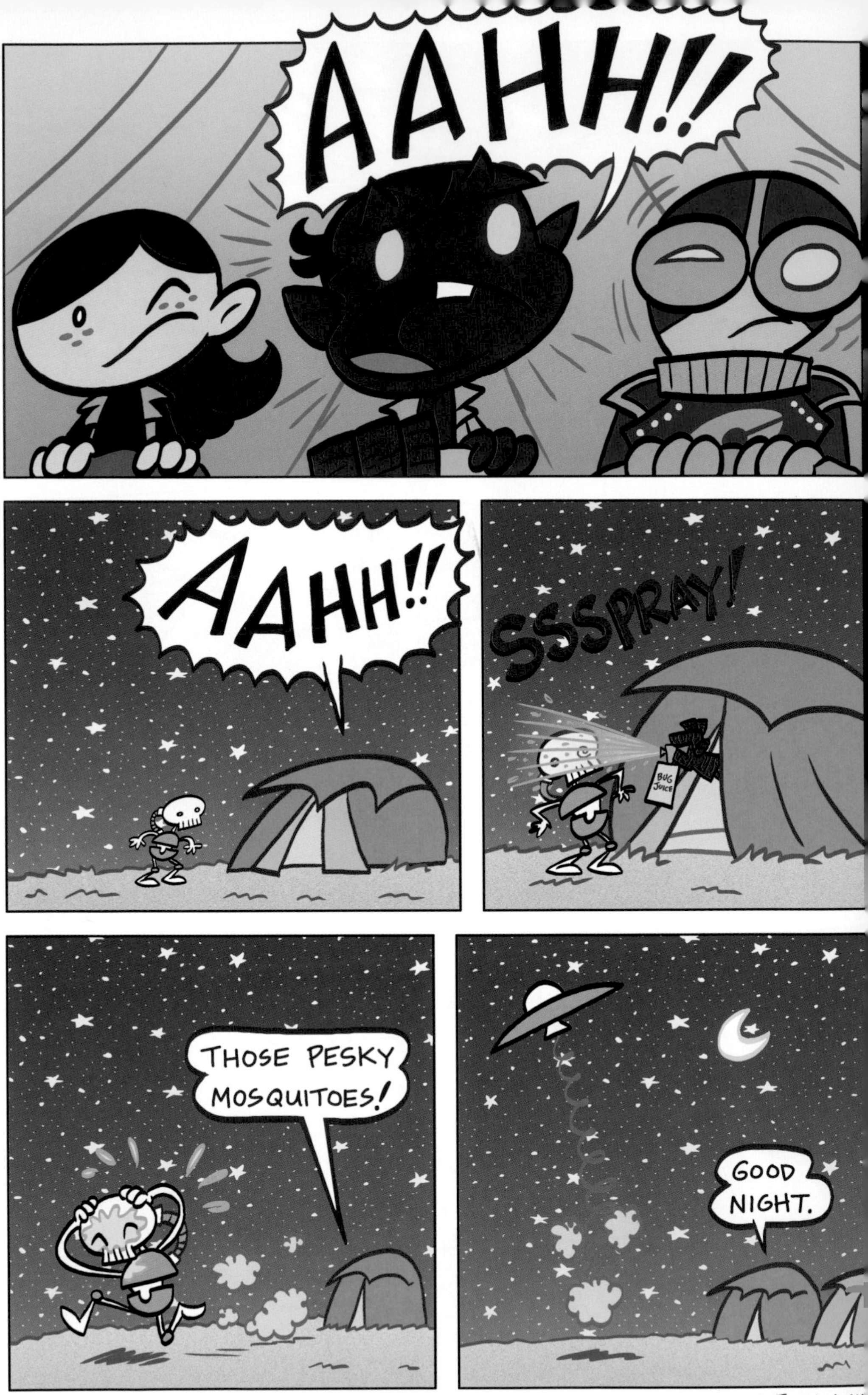
AAHH!!
AAHH!!
SSSPRAY!
BUG JUICE
THOSE PESKY MOSQUITOES!
GOOD NIGHT.

—U.F. OH YEAH

CHAPTER THREE

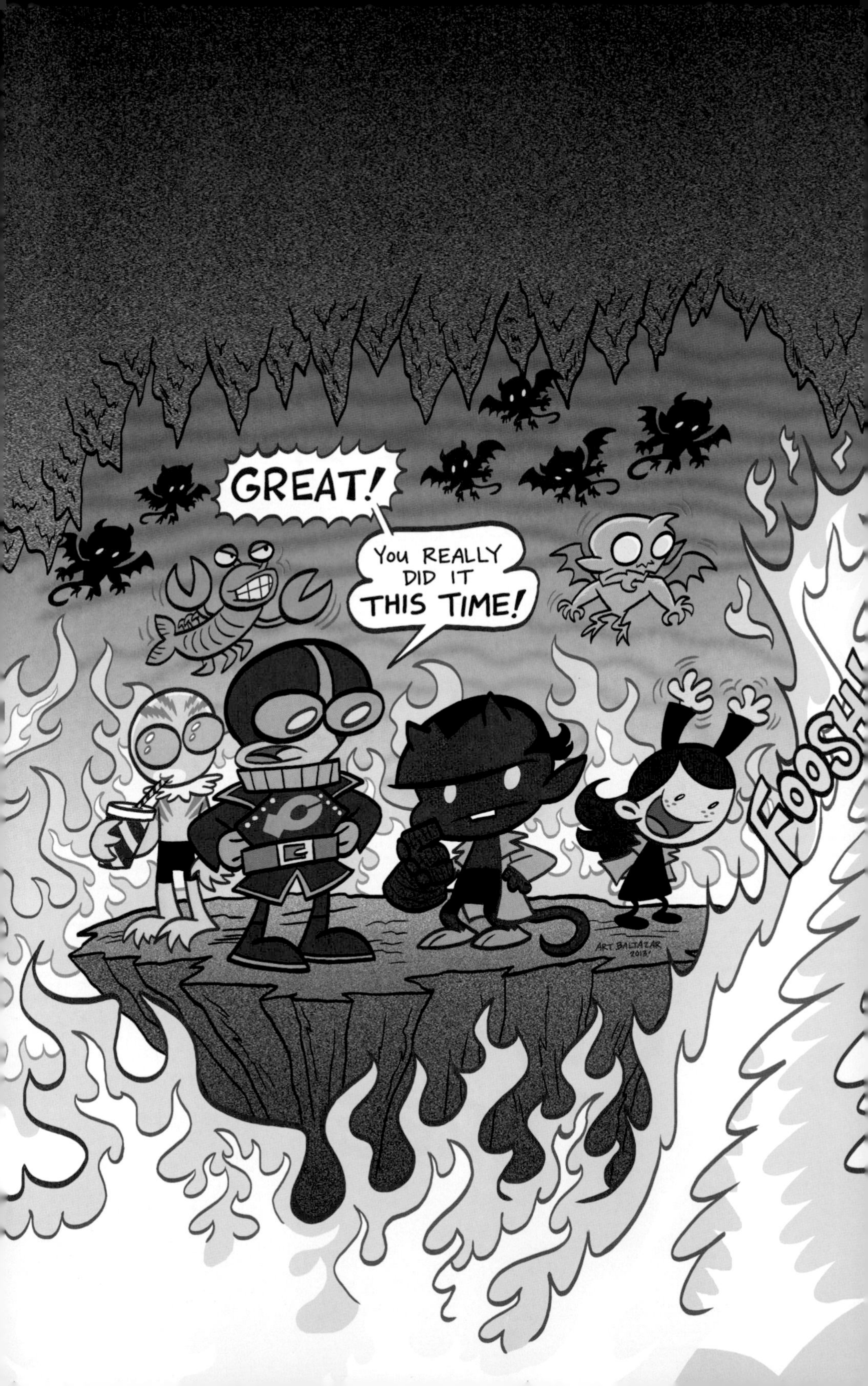
GREAT!
YOU REALLY DID IT THIS TIME!
FOOSH!
ART BALTAZAR 2013

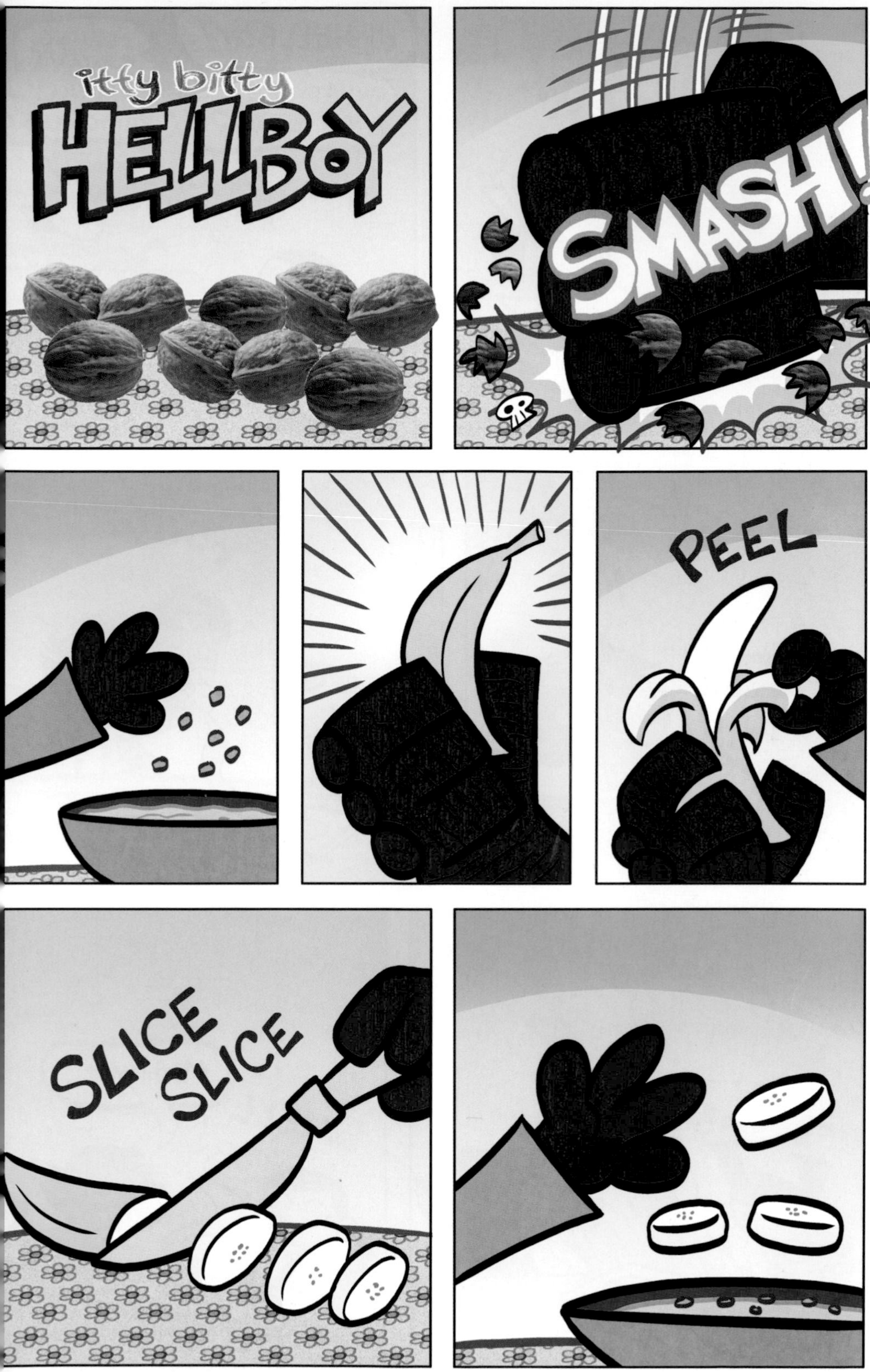
itty bitty
HELLBOY
SMASH!
PEEL
SLICE
SLICE

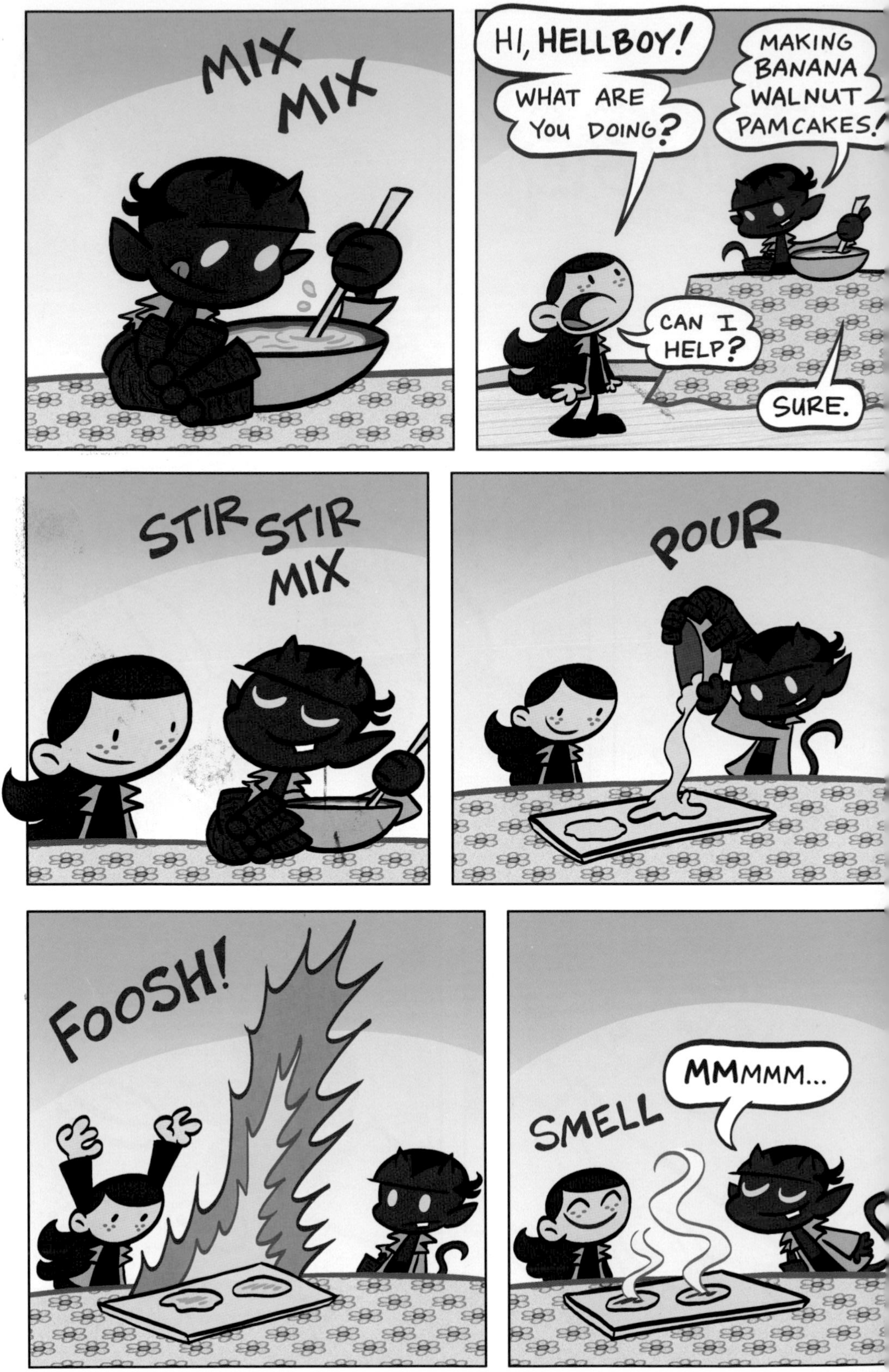
MIX
MIX
HI, HELLBOY!
WHAT ARE YOU DOING?
MAKING BANANA WALNUT PAMCAKES!
CAN I HELP?
SURE.
STIR STIR
MIX
POUR
FOOSH!
SMELL
MMMMM...

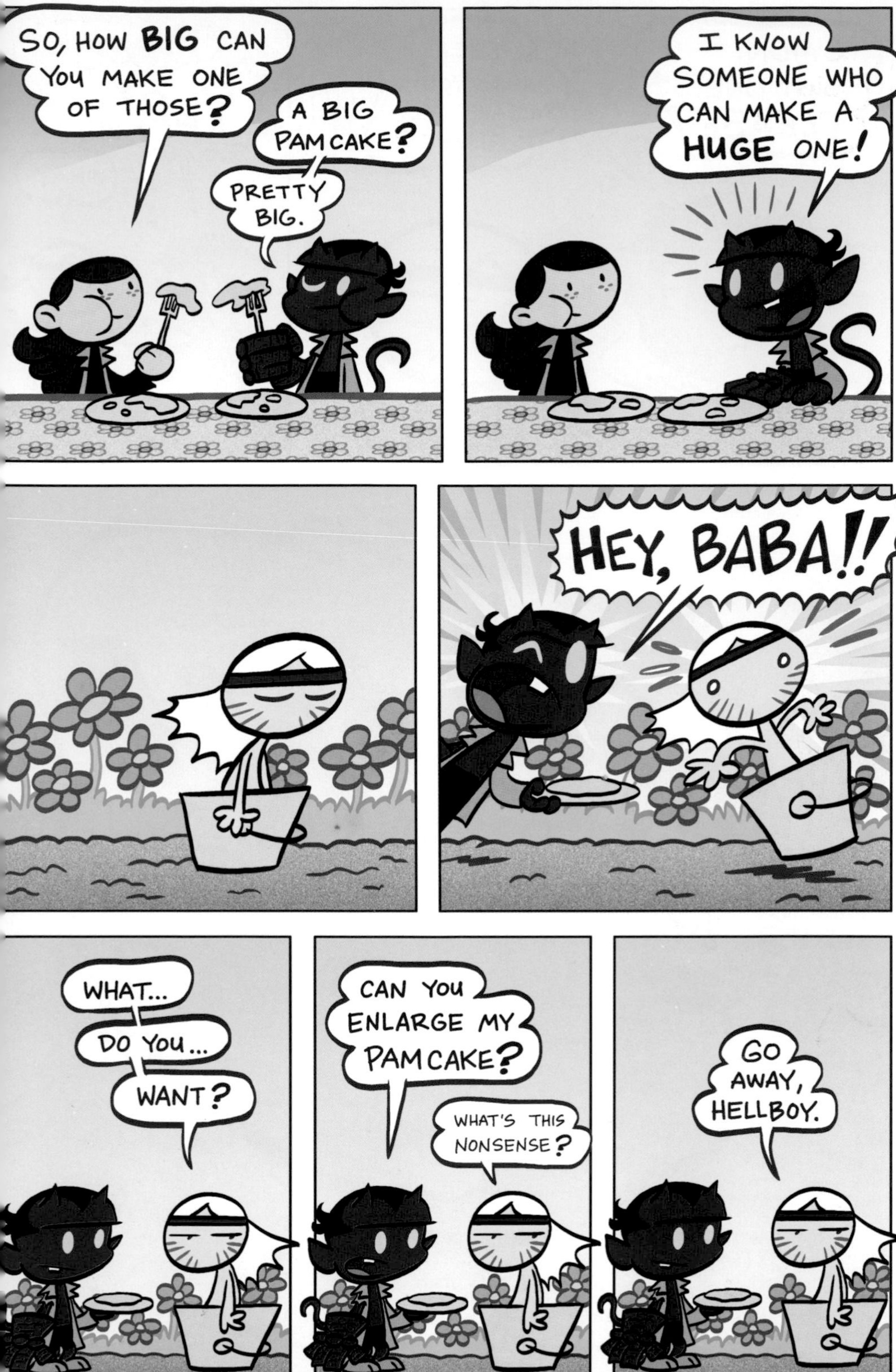
SO, HOW BIG CAN YOU MAKE ONE OF THOSE?
A BIG PAMCAKE?
PRETTY BIG.
I KNOW SOMEONE WHO CAN MAKE A HUGE ONE!
HEY, BABA!!
WHAT...
DO YOU...
WANT?
CAN YOU ENLARGE MY PAMCAKE?
WHAT'S THIS NONSENSE?
GO AWAY, HELLBOY.

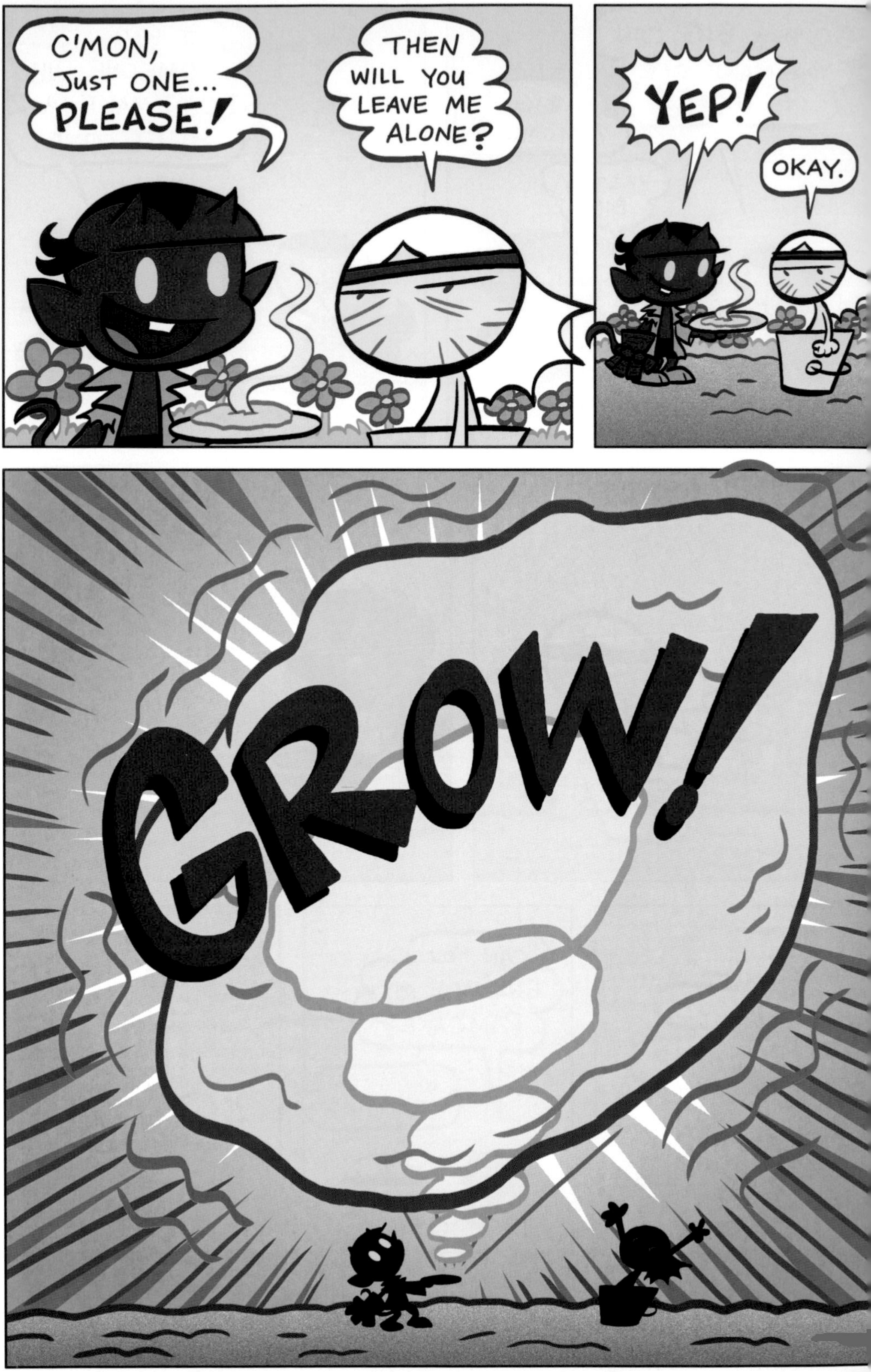
C'MON, JUST ONE... PLEASE!
THEN WILL YOU LEAVE ME ALONE?
YEP!
OKAY.
GROW!

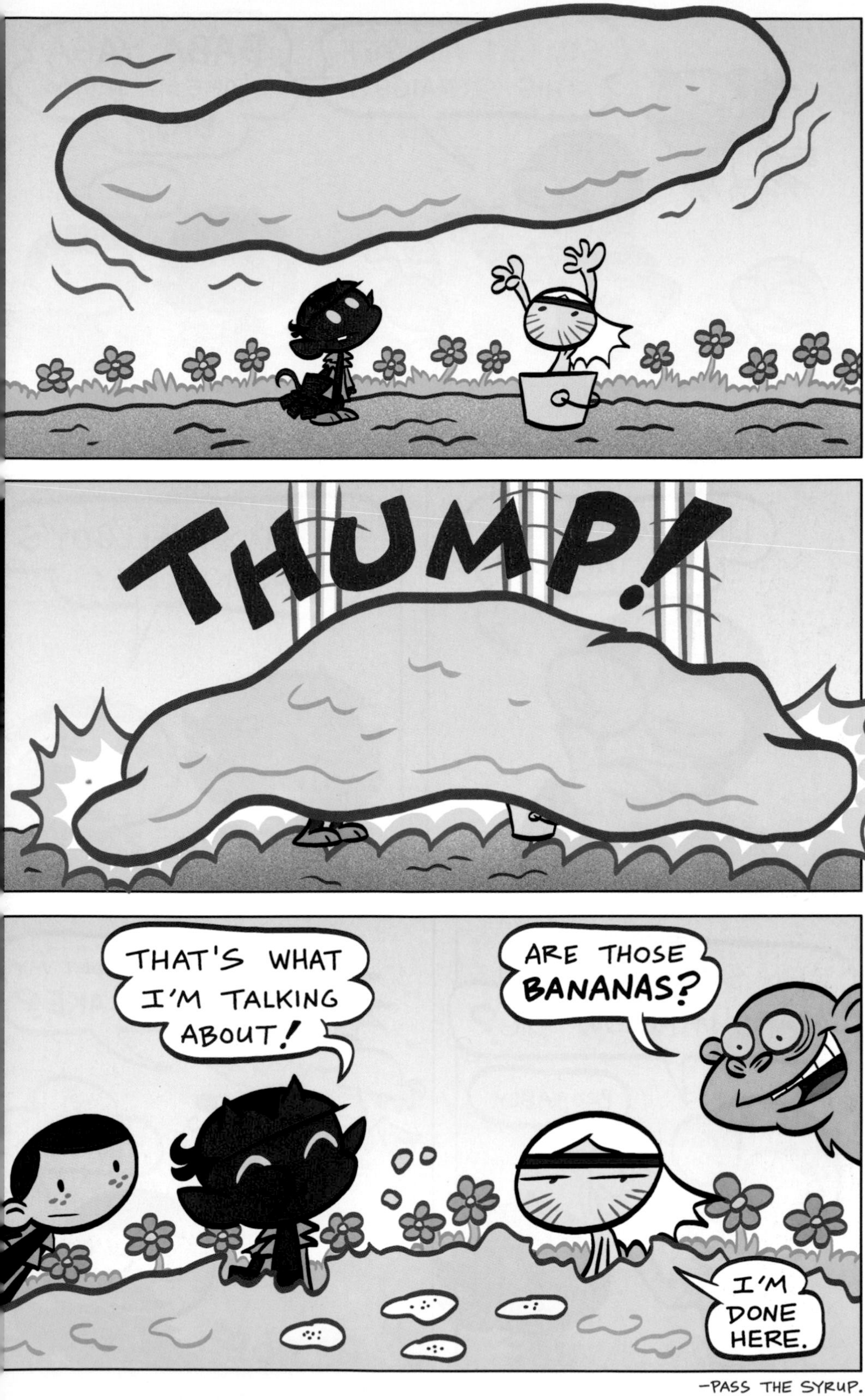
THUMP!
THAT'S WHAT I'M TALKING ABOUT!
ARE THOSE BANANAS?
I'M DONE HERE.

–PASS THE SYRUP.

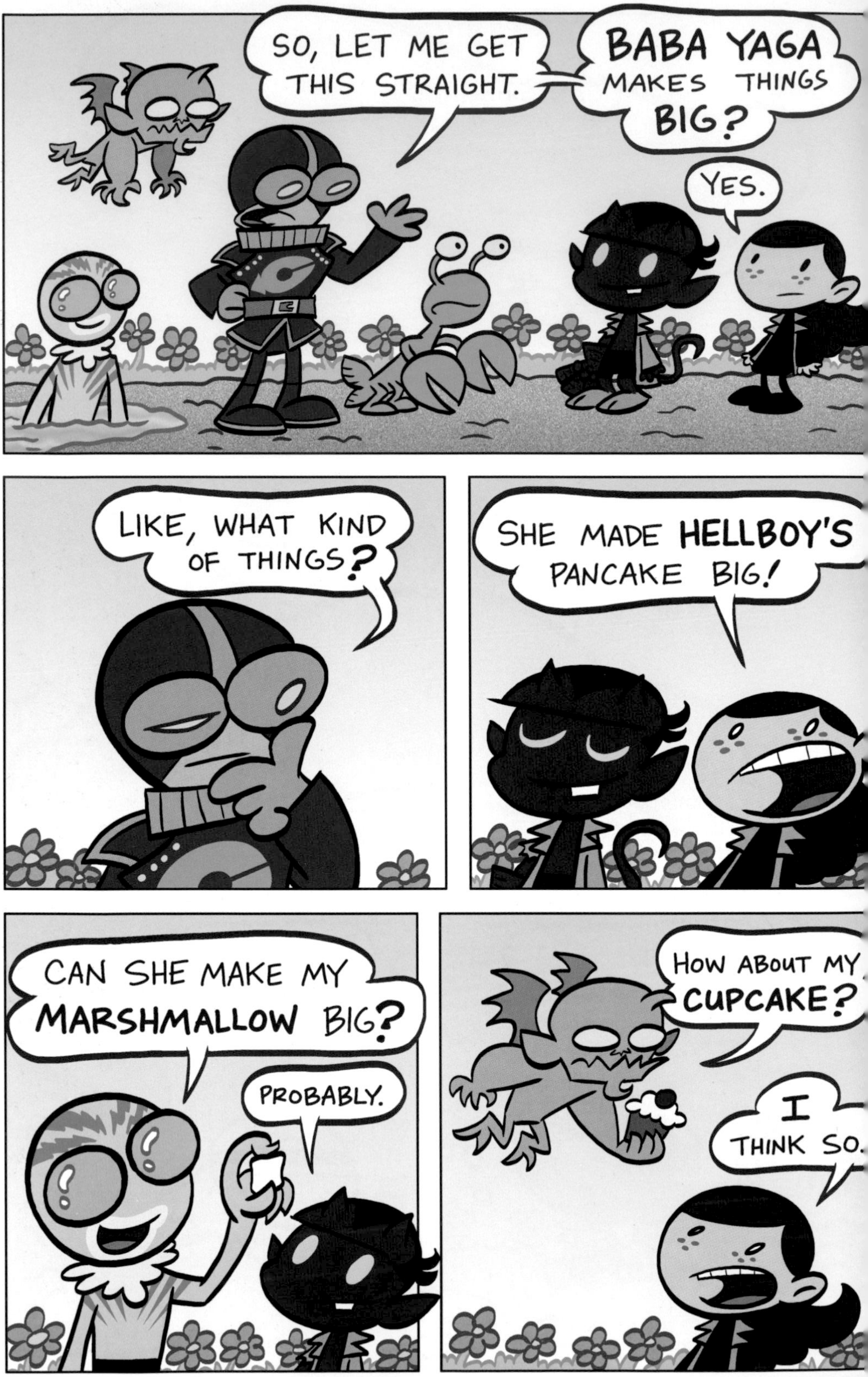
SO, LET ME GET THIS STRAIGHT.
BABA YAGA MAKES THINGS BIG?
YES.
LIKE, WHAT KIND OF THINGS?
SHE MADE HELLBOY'S PANCAKE BIG!
CAN SHE MAKE MY MARSHMALLOW BIG?
PROBABLY.
HOW ABOUT MY CUPCAKE?
I THINK SO.

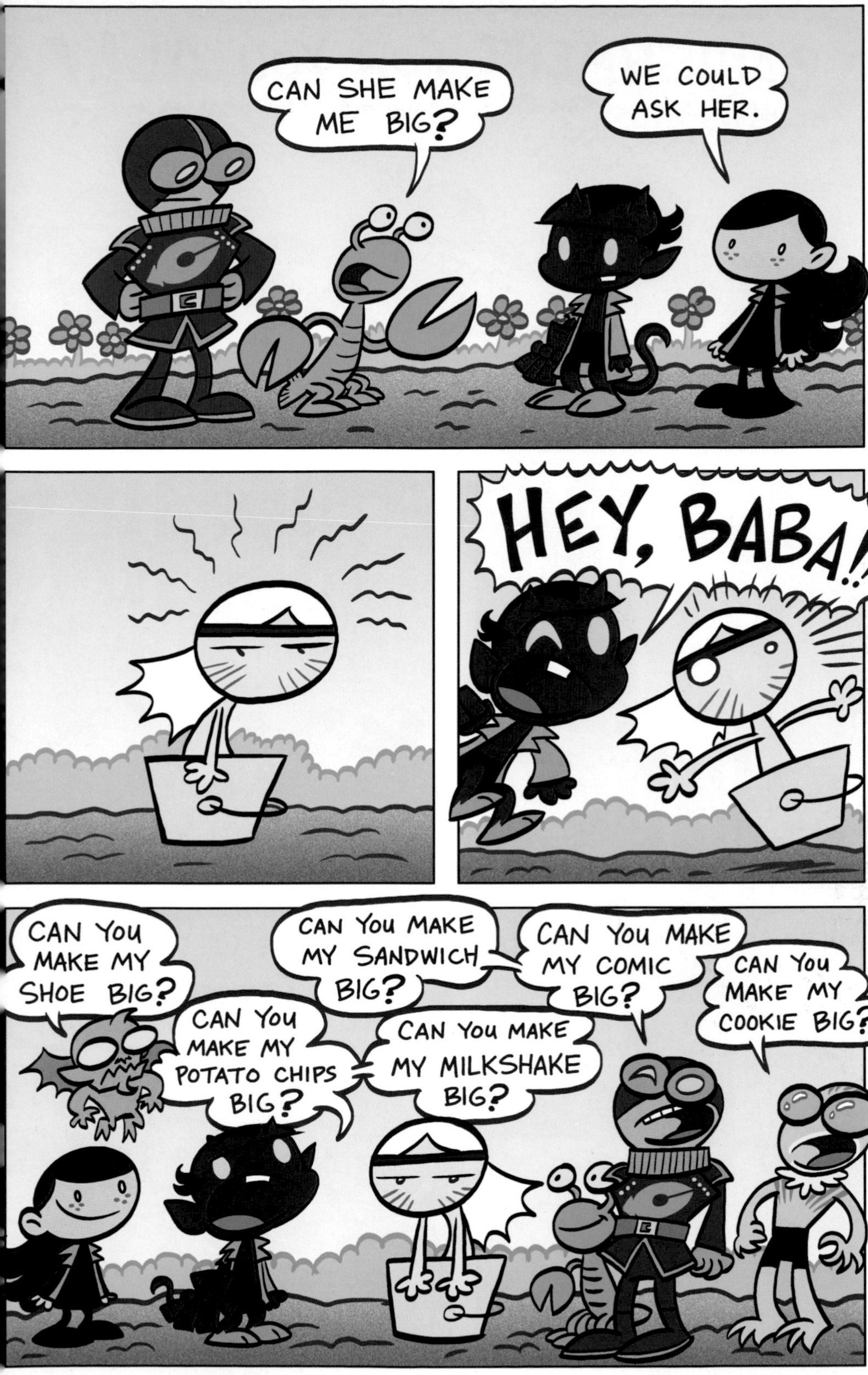
CAN SHE MAKE ME BIG?
WE COULD ASK HER.
HEY, BABA!!
CAN YOU MAKE MY SHOE BIG?
CAN YOU MAKE MY SANDWICH BIG?
CAN YOU MAKE MY COMIC BIG?
CAN YOU MAKE MY COOKIE BIG?
CAN YOU MAKE MY POTATO CHIPS BIG?
CAN YOU MAKE MY MILKSHAKE BIG?

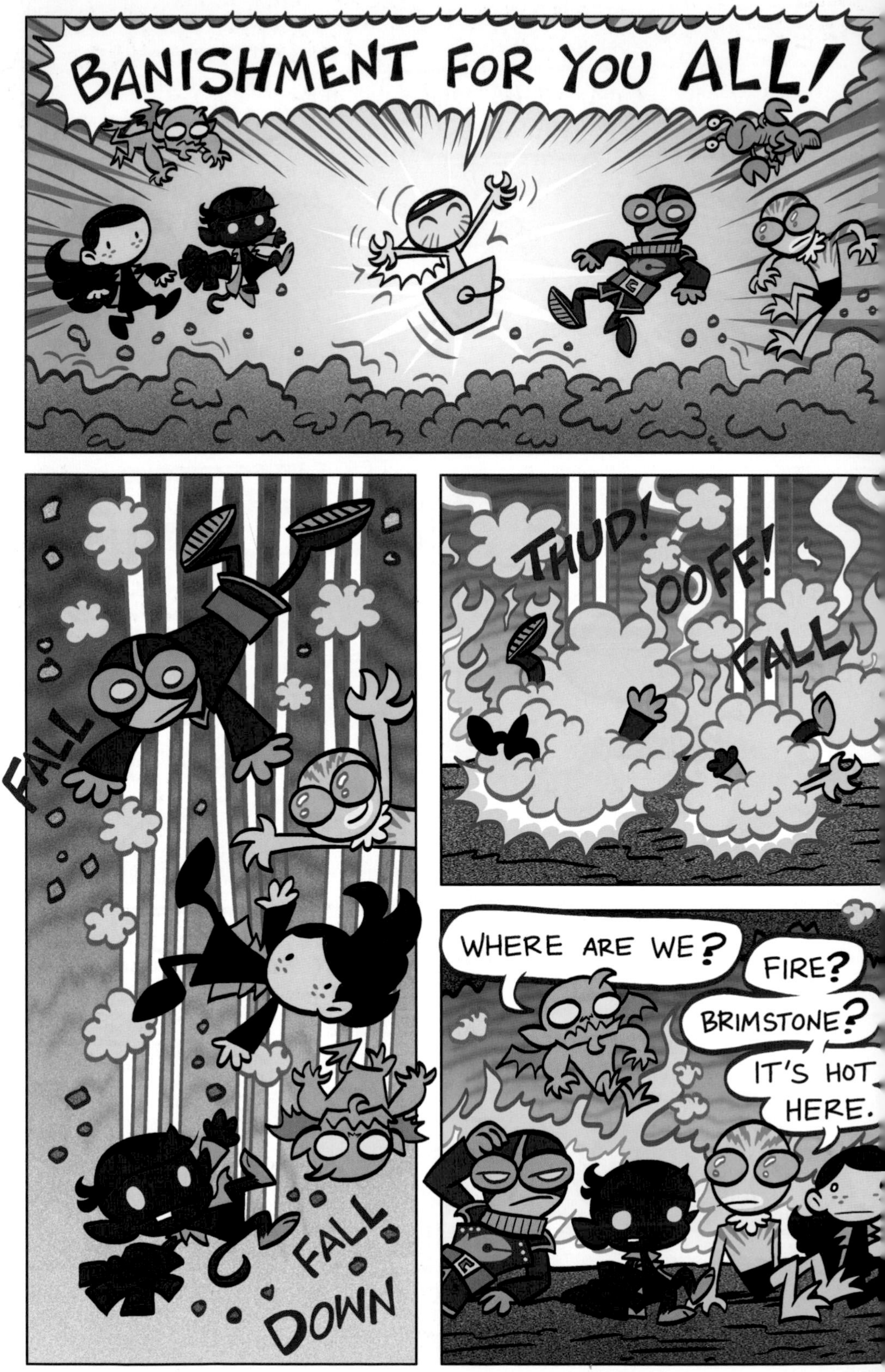

BANISHMENT FOR YOU ALL!
FALL
FALL
DOWN
THUD!
OOFF!
FALL
WHERE ARE WE?
FIRE?
BRIMSTONE?
IT'S HOT HERE.

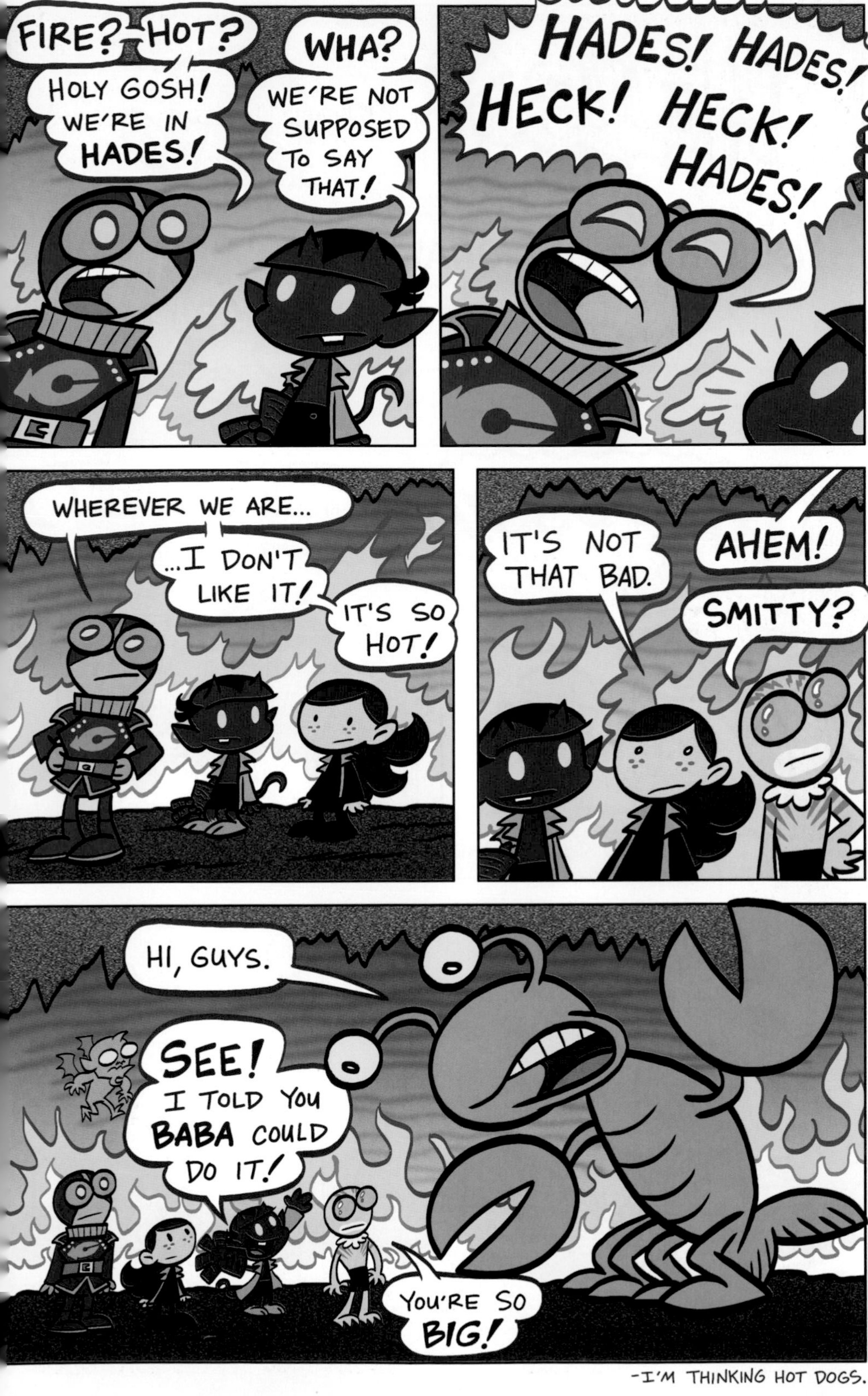
FIRE? HOT?
HOLY GOSH! WE'RE IN HADES!
WHA?
WE'RE NOT SUPPOSED TO SAY THAT!
HADES! HADES! HECK! HECK! HADES!
WHEREVER WE ARE...
...I DON'T LIKE IT!
IT'S SO HOT!
IT'S NOT THAT BAD.
AHEM!
SMITTY?
HI, GUYS.
SEE! I TOLD YOU BABA COULD DO IT!
YOU'RE SO BIG!

-I'M THINKING HOT DOGS.

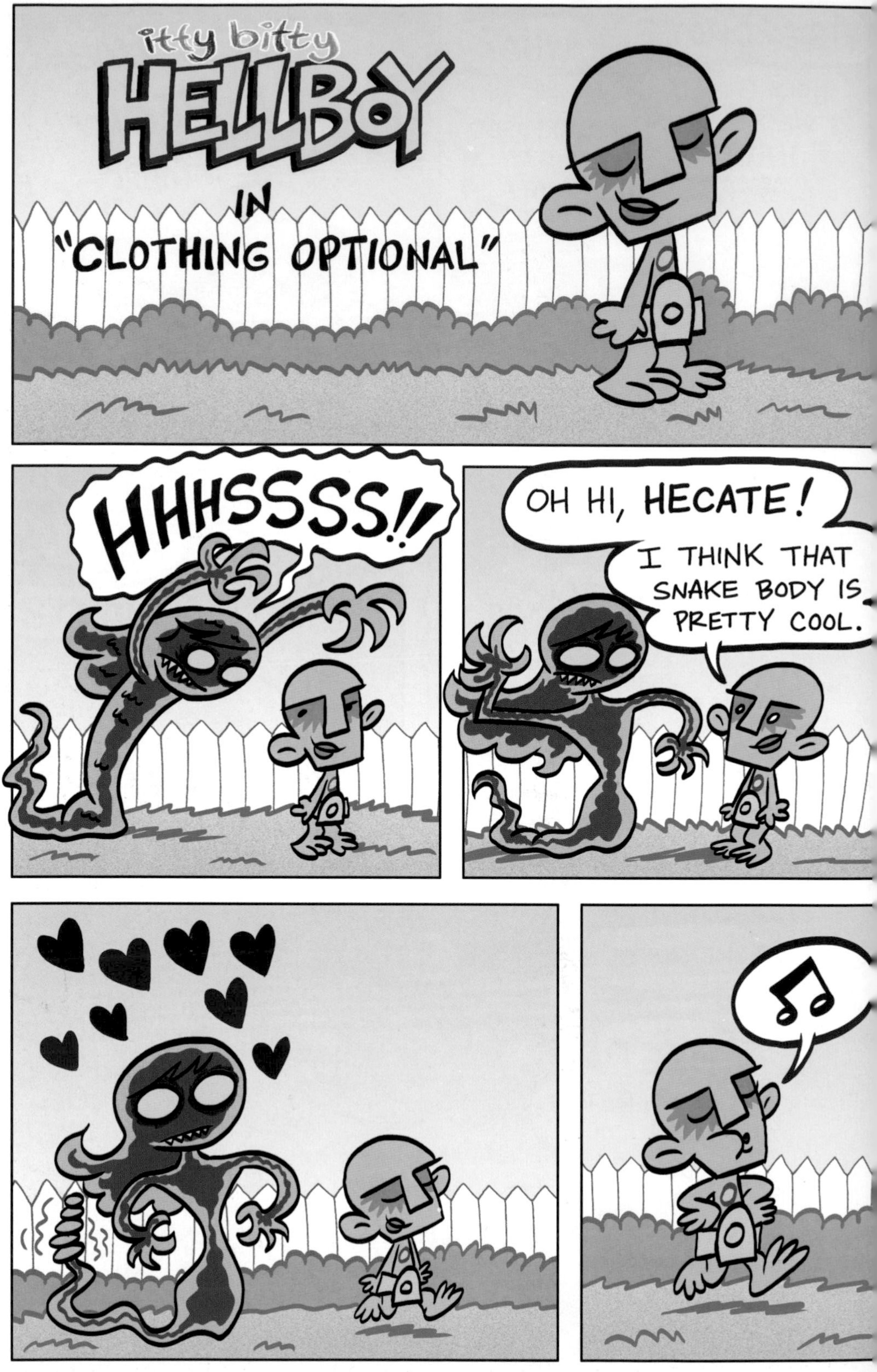
itty bitty
HELLBOY
IN
"CLOTHING OPTIONAL"
HHHSSSSS!!
OH HI, HECATE!
I THINK THAT SNAKE BODY IS PRETTY COOL.

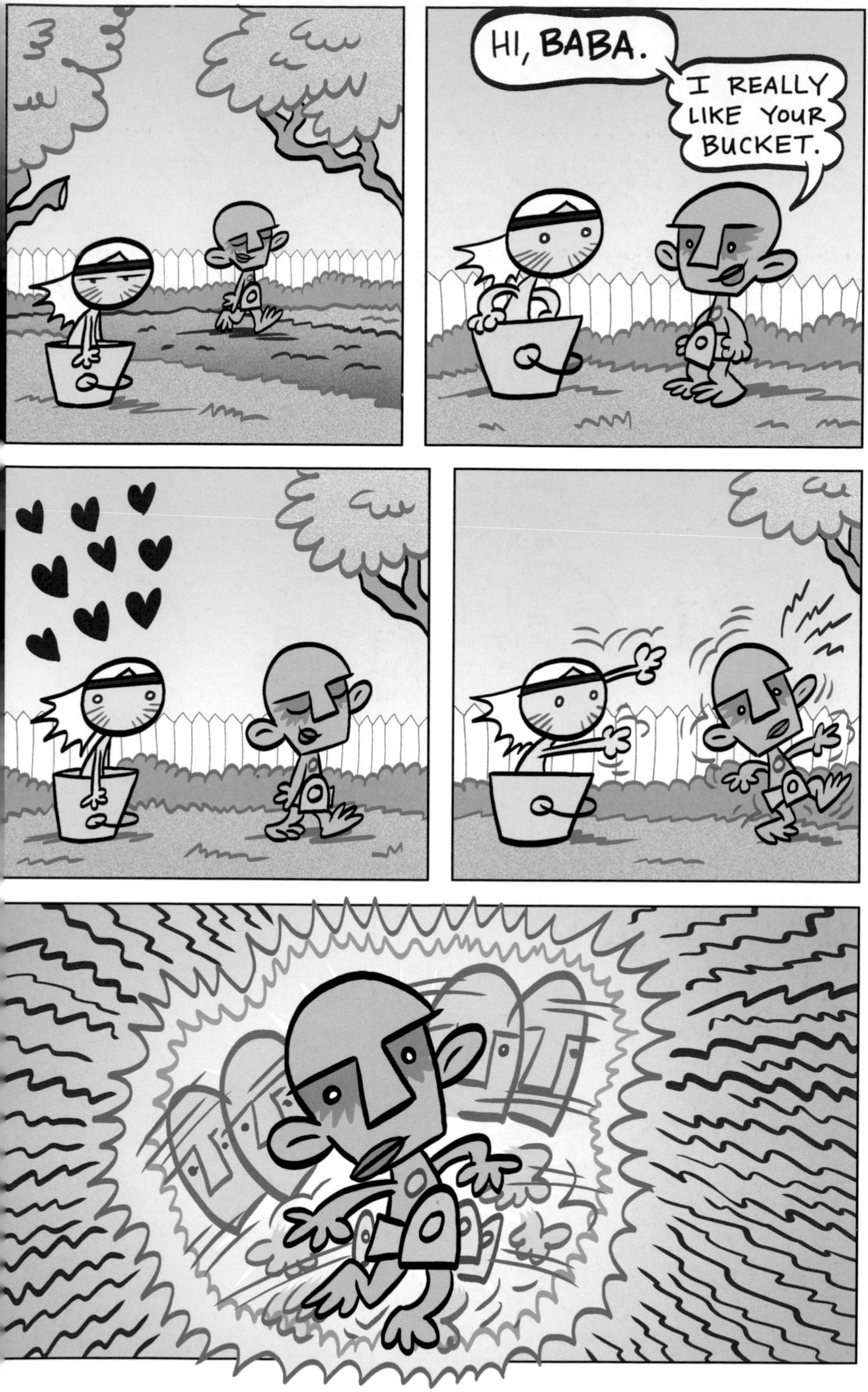
HI, BABA.
I REALLY LIKE YOUR BUCKET.

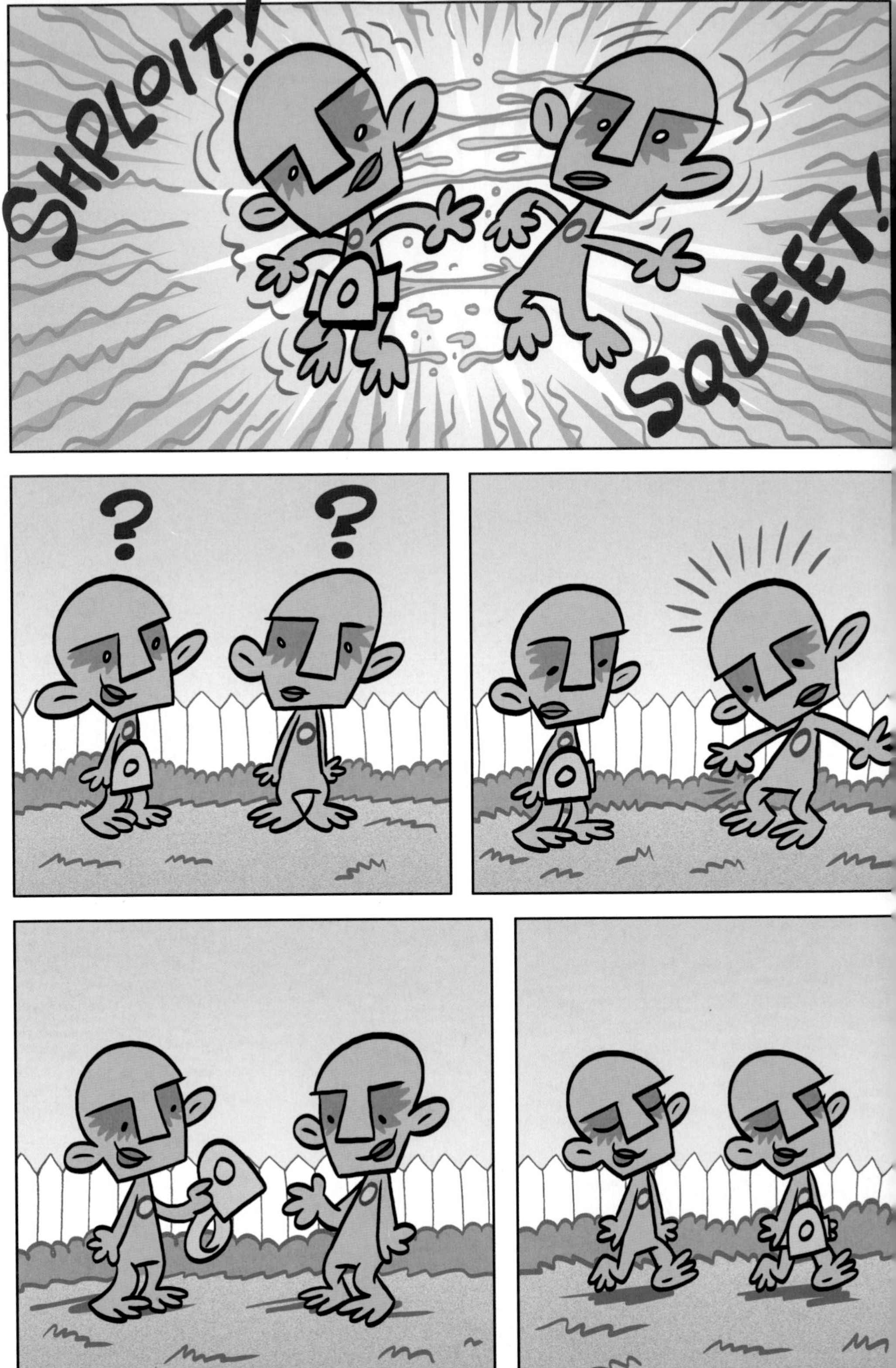
SHPLOIT!
SQUEET!
?
?

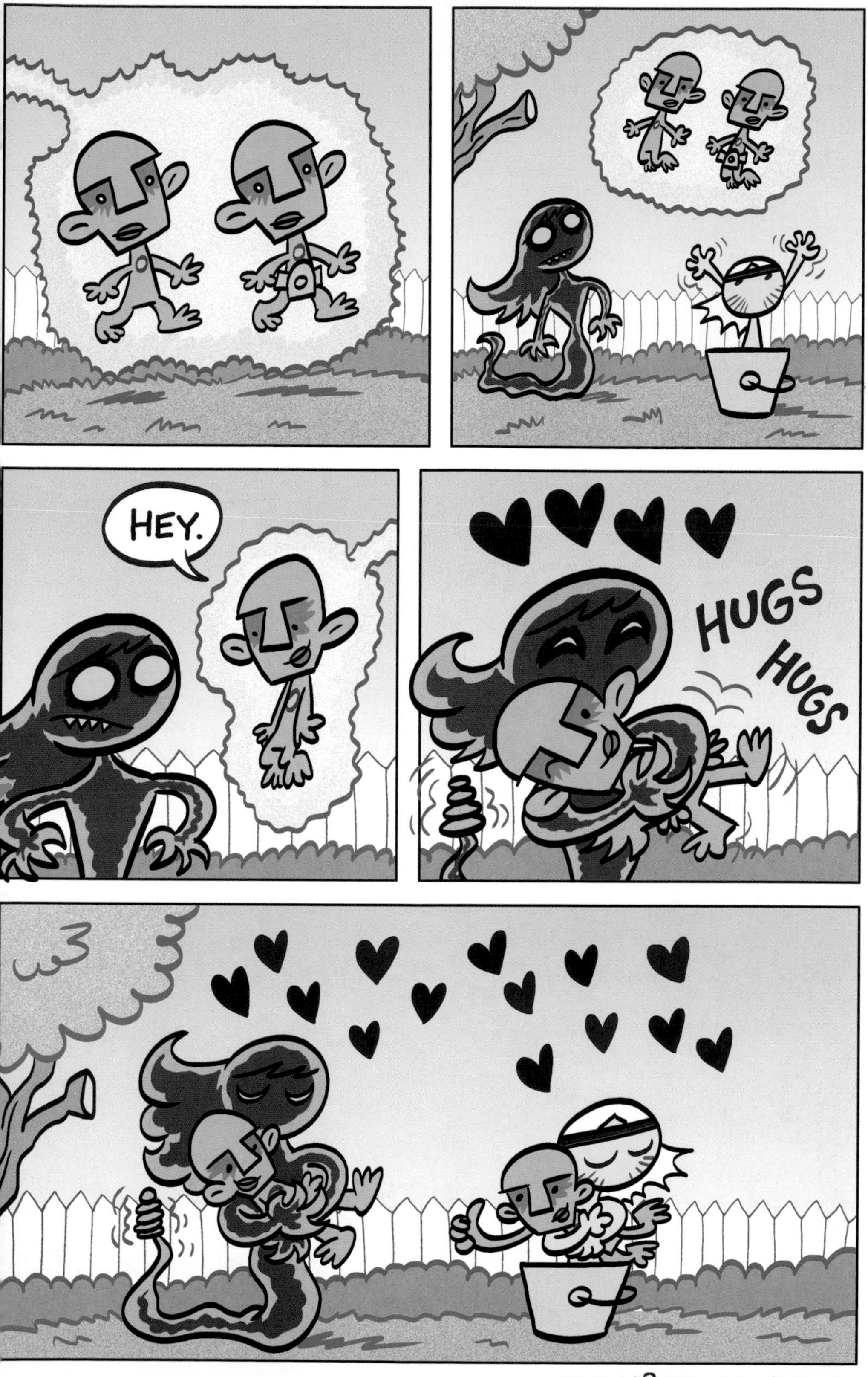
HEY.
HUGS
HUGS

—TRUE LOVIN'? RIGHT. I'M CONFUSED, TOO.

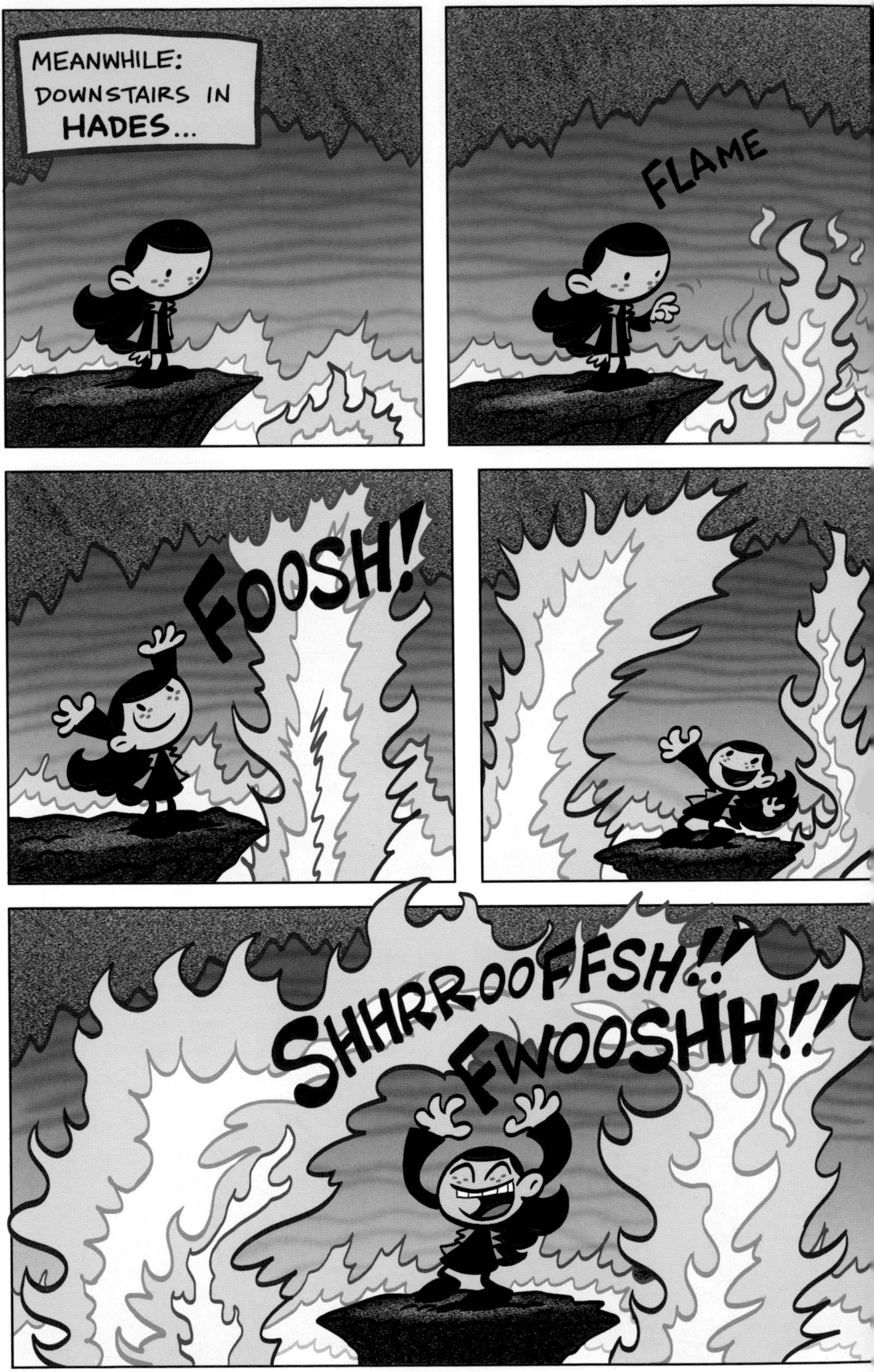
MEANWHILE: DOWNSTAIRS IN HADES...
FLAME
FOOSH!
SHHRROOFFSH!!
FWOOSHH!!

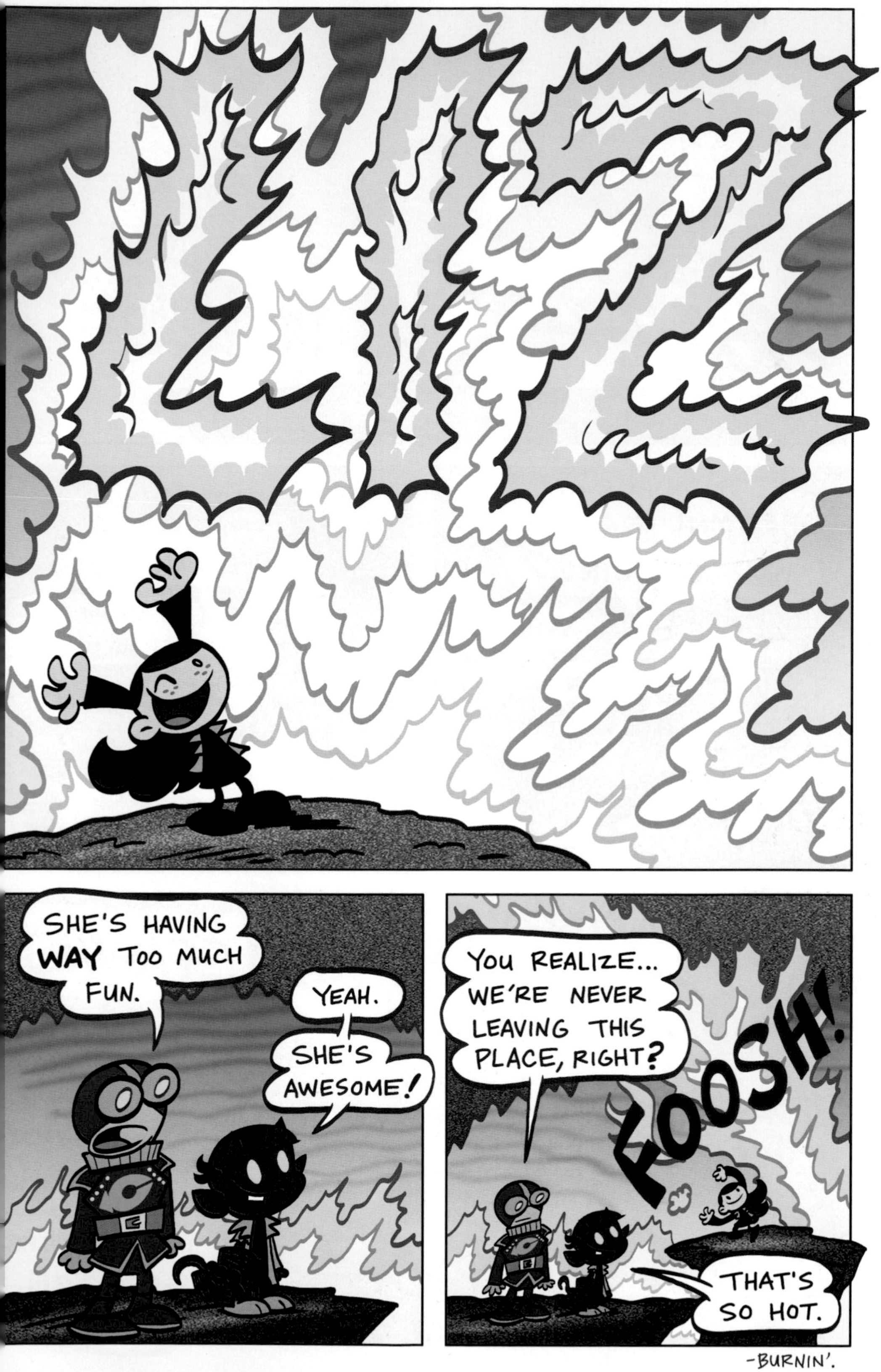
SHE'S HAVING **WAY** TOO MUCH FUN.
YEAH.
SHE'S AWESOME!
YOU REALIZE... WE'RE NEVER LEAVING THIS PLACE, RIGHT?
FOOSH!
THAT'S SO HOT.

-BURNIN'.

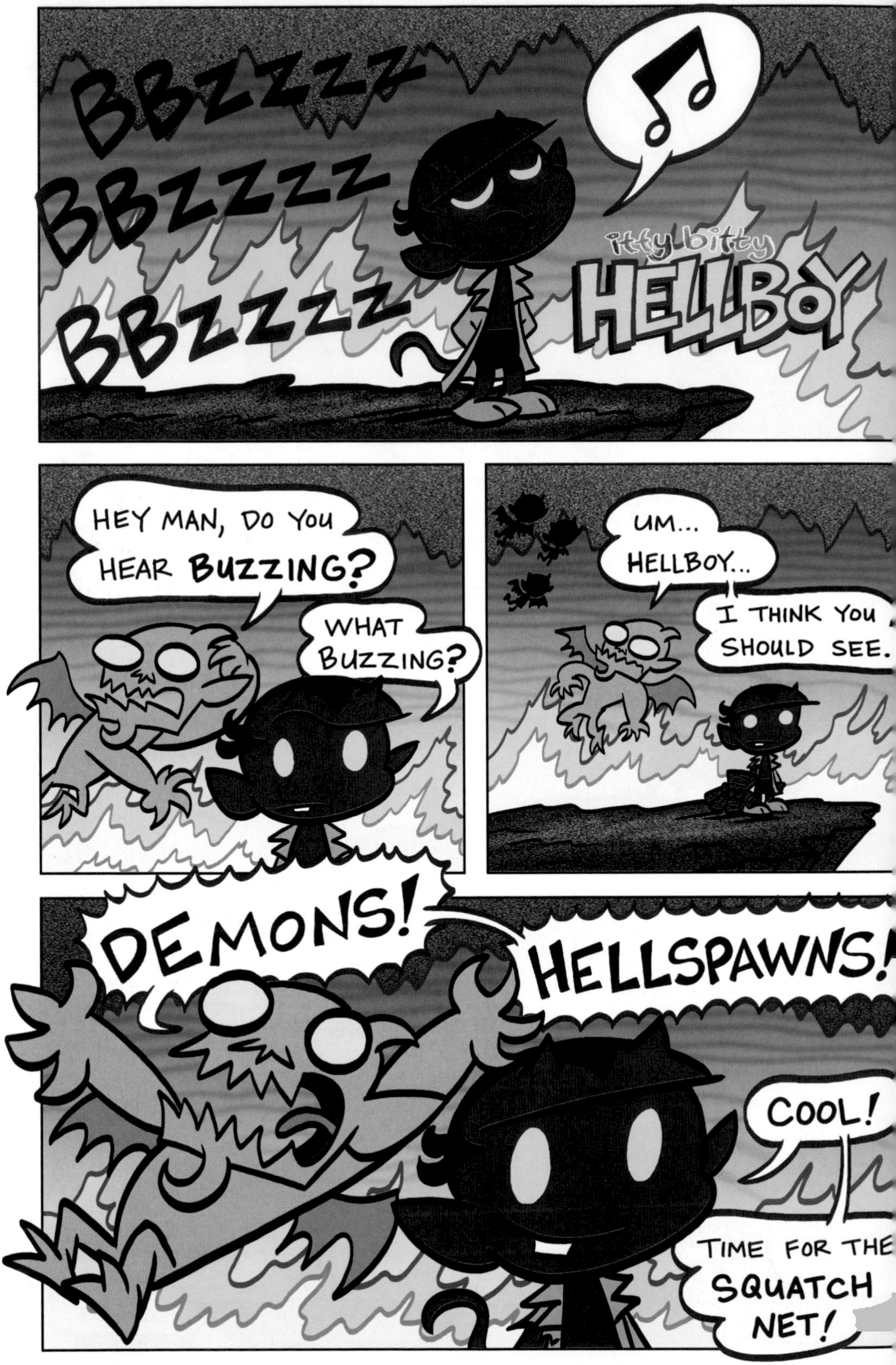
BBZZZZZ
BBZZZZZ
BBZZZZZ
itty bitty HELLBOY
HEY MAN, DO YOU HEAR BUZZING?
WHAT BUZZING?
UM... HELLBOY...
I THINK YOU SHOULD SEE.
DEMONS!
HELLSPAWNS!
COOL!
TIME FOR THE SQUATCH NET!

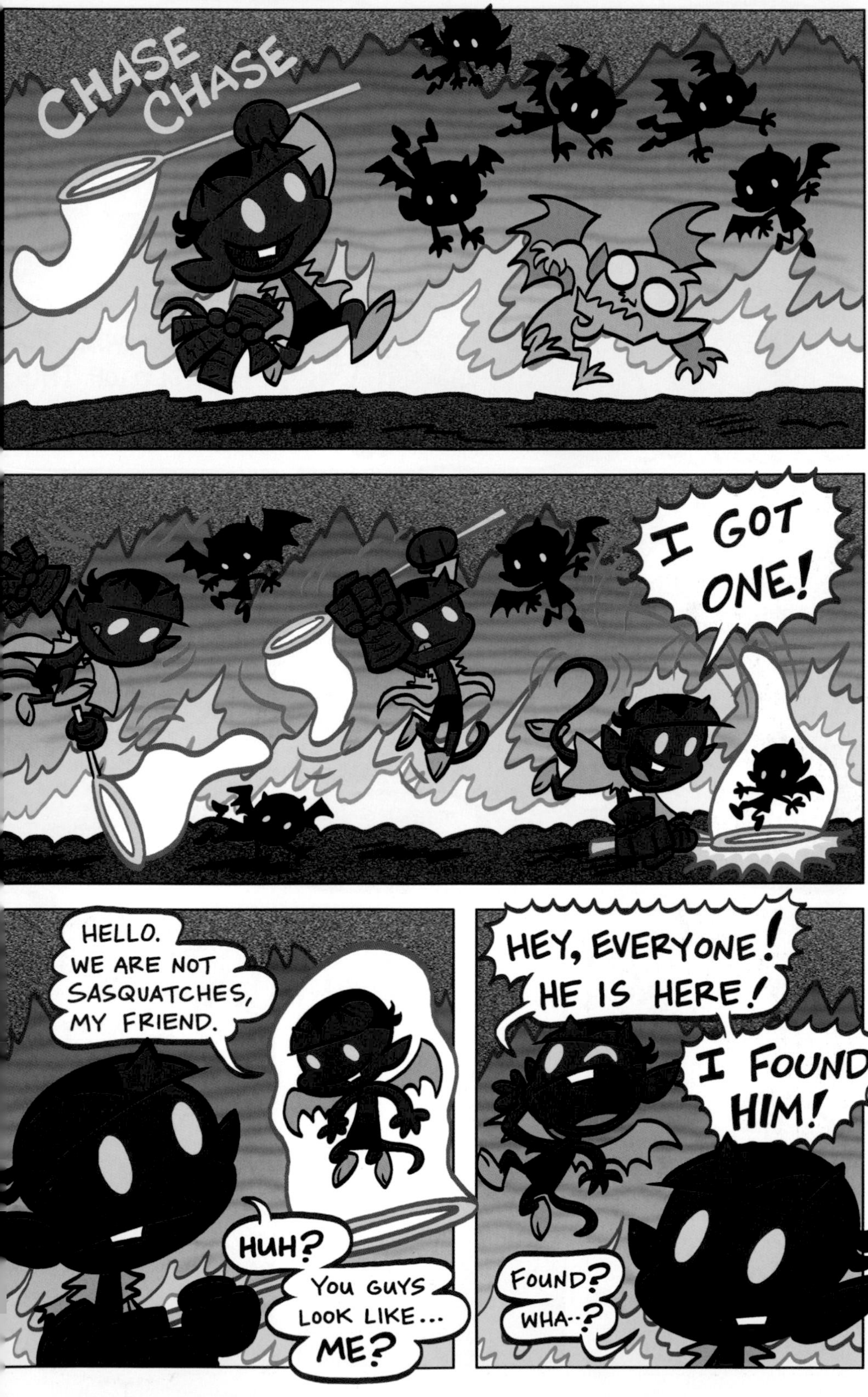
CHASE CHASE
I GOT ONE!
HELLO. WE ARE NOT SASQUATCHES, MY FRIEND.
HUH?
YOU GUYS LOOK LIKE... ME?
HEY, EVERYONE! HE IS HERE!
I FOUND HIM!
FOUND? WHA--?

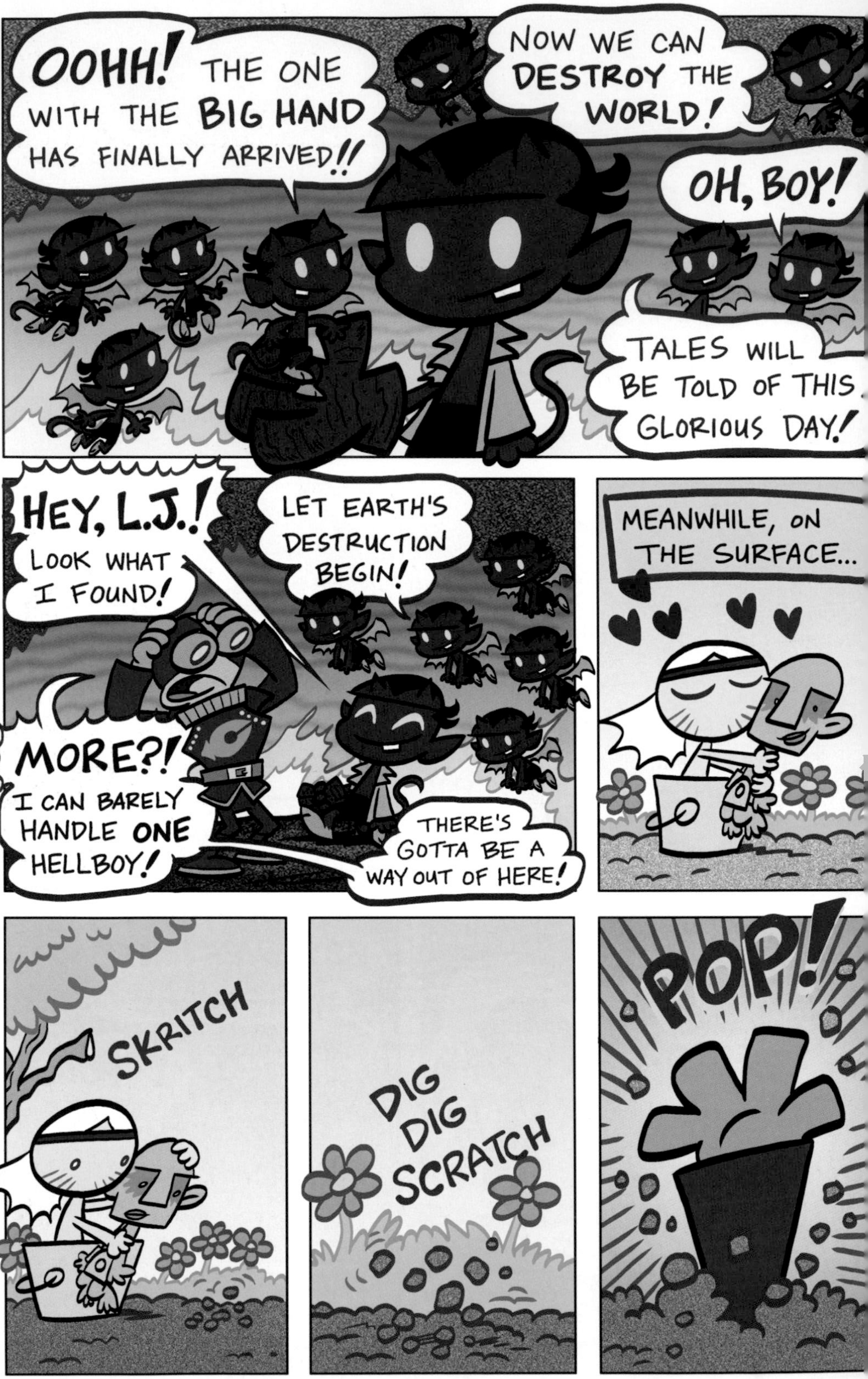
OOHH! THE ONE WITH THE BIG HAND HAS FINALLY ARRIVED!!
NOW WE CAN DESTROY THE WORLD!
OH, BOY!
TALES WILL BE TOLD OF THIS GLORIOUS DAY!
HEY, L.J.! LOOK WHAT I FOUND!
LET EARTH'S DESTRUCTION BEGIN!
MORE?! I CAN BARELY HANDLE ONE HELLBOY!
THERE'S GOTTA BE A WAY OUT OF HERE!
MEANWHILE, ON THE SURFACE...
SKRITCH
DIG DIG SCRATCH
POP!

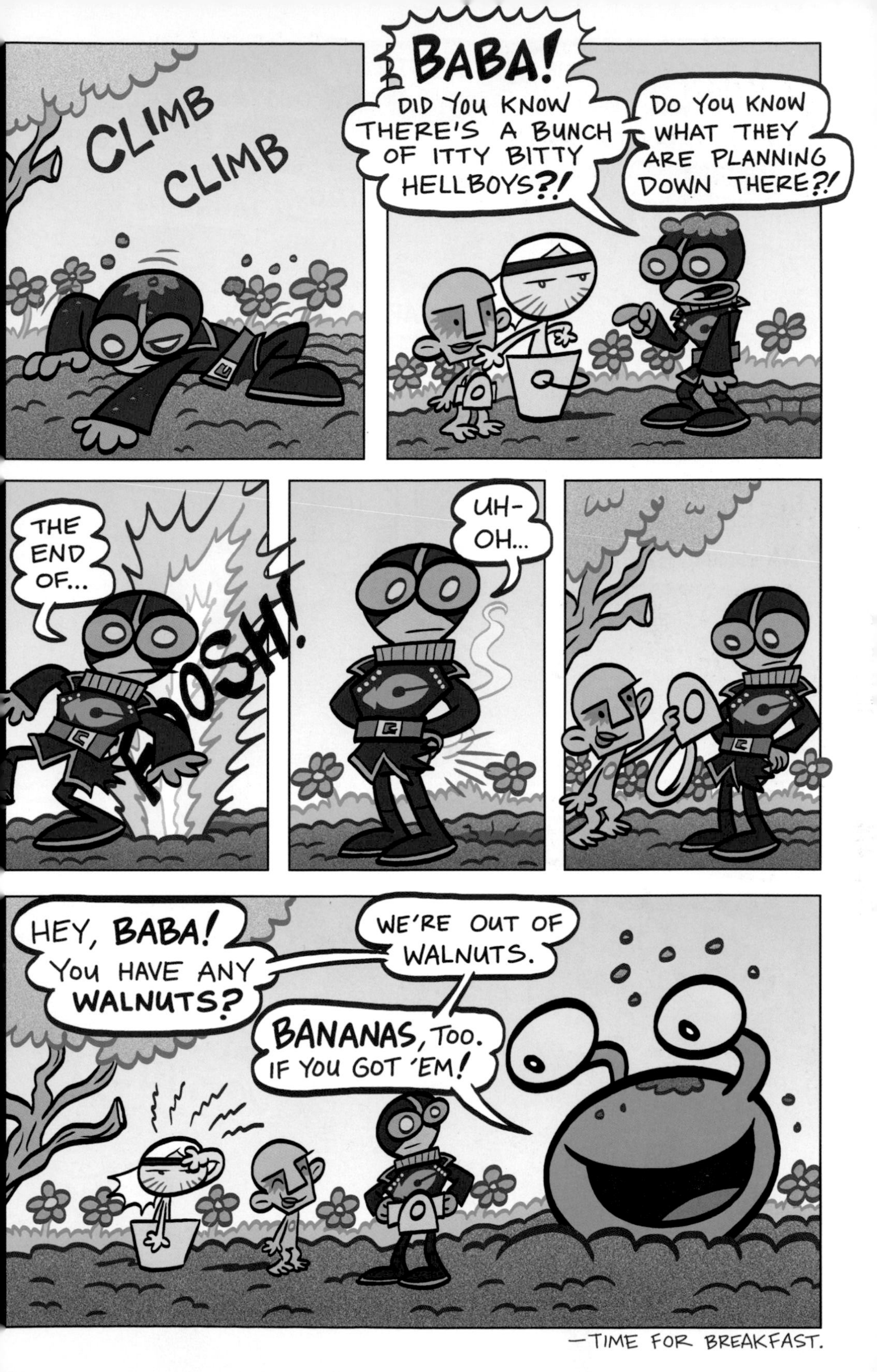
CLIMB
CLIMB
BABA!
DID YOU KNOW THERE'S A BUNCH OF ITTY BITTY HELLBOYS?!
DO YOU KNOW WHAT THEY ARE PLANNING DOWN THERE?!
THE END OF...
FOOSH!
UH-OH...
HEY, BABA! YOU HAVE ANY WALNUTS?
WE'RE OUT OF WALNUTS.
BANANAS, TOO. IF YOU GOT 'EM!

—TIME FOR BREAKFAST.

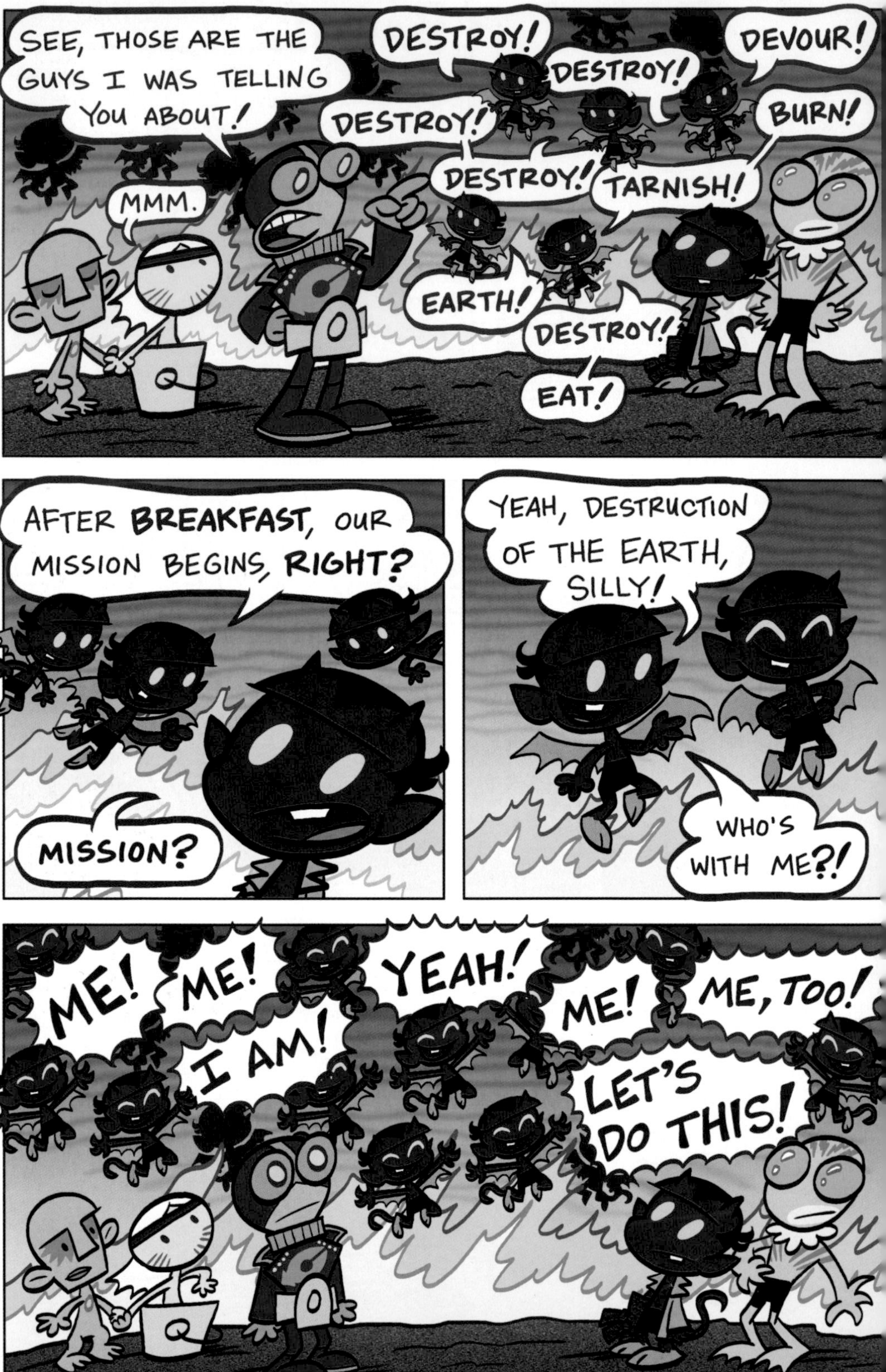
SEE, THOSE ARE THE GUYS I WAS TELLING YOU ABOUT!
DESTROY!
DESTROY!
DEVOUR!
DESTROY!
BURN!
DESTROY!
TARNISH!
MMM.
EARTH!
DESTROY!
EAT!
AFTER BREAKFAST, OUR MISSION BEGINS, RIGHT?
MISSION?
YEAH, DESTRUCTION OF THE EARTH, SILLY!
WHO'S WITH ME?!
ME!
ME!
YEAH!
ME!
ME, TOO!
I AM!
LET'S DO THIS!

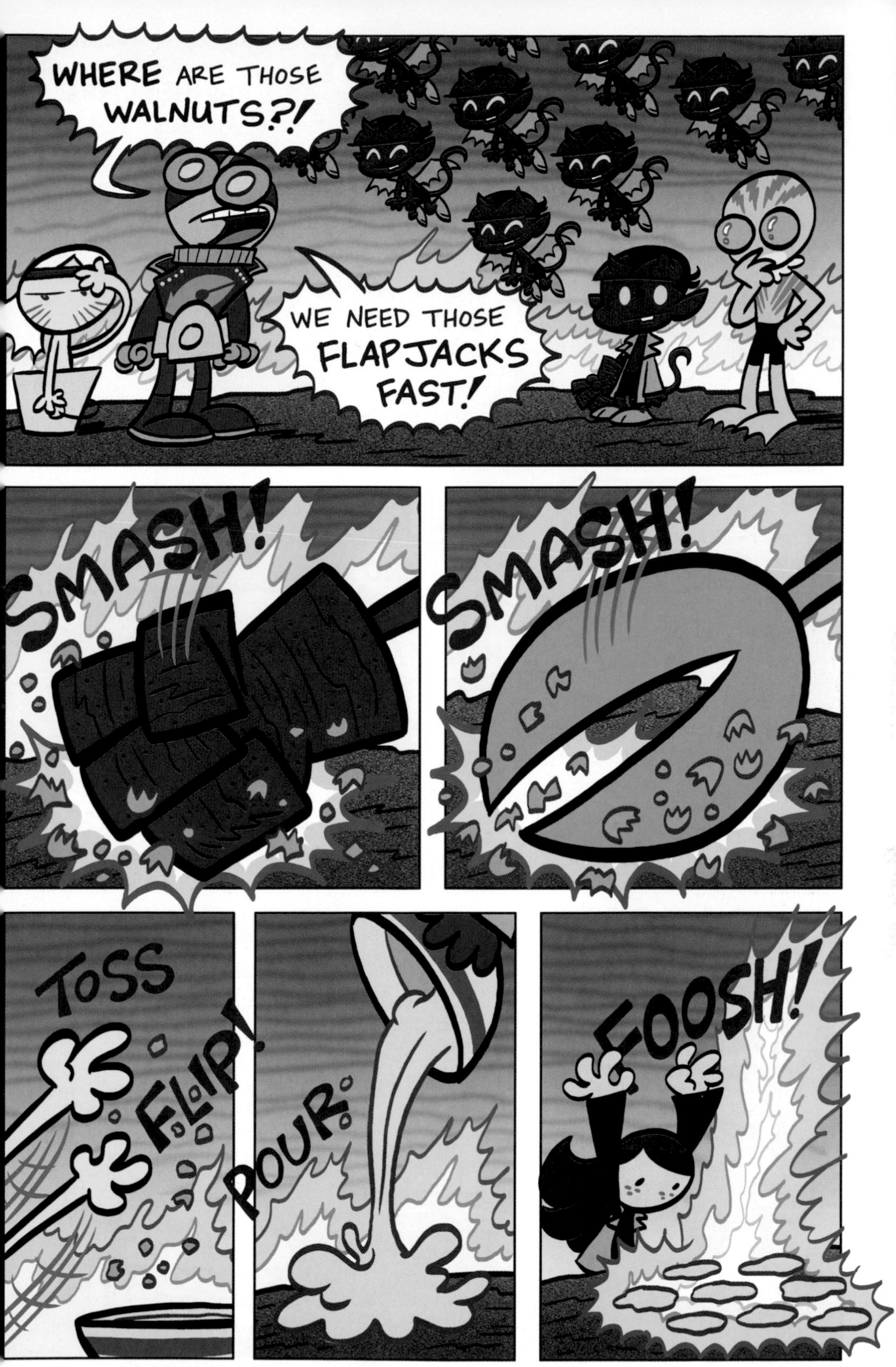
WHERE ARE THOSE WALNUTS?!
WE NEED THOSE FLAPJACKS FAST!
SMASH!
SMASH!
TOSS
FLIP!
POUR
FOOSH!

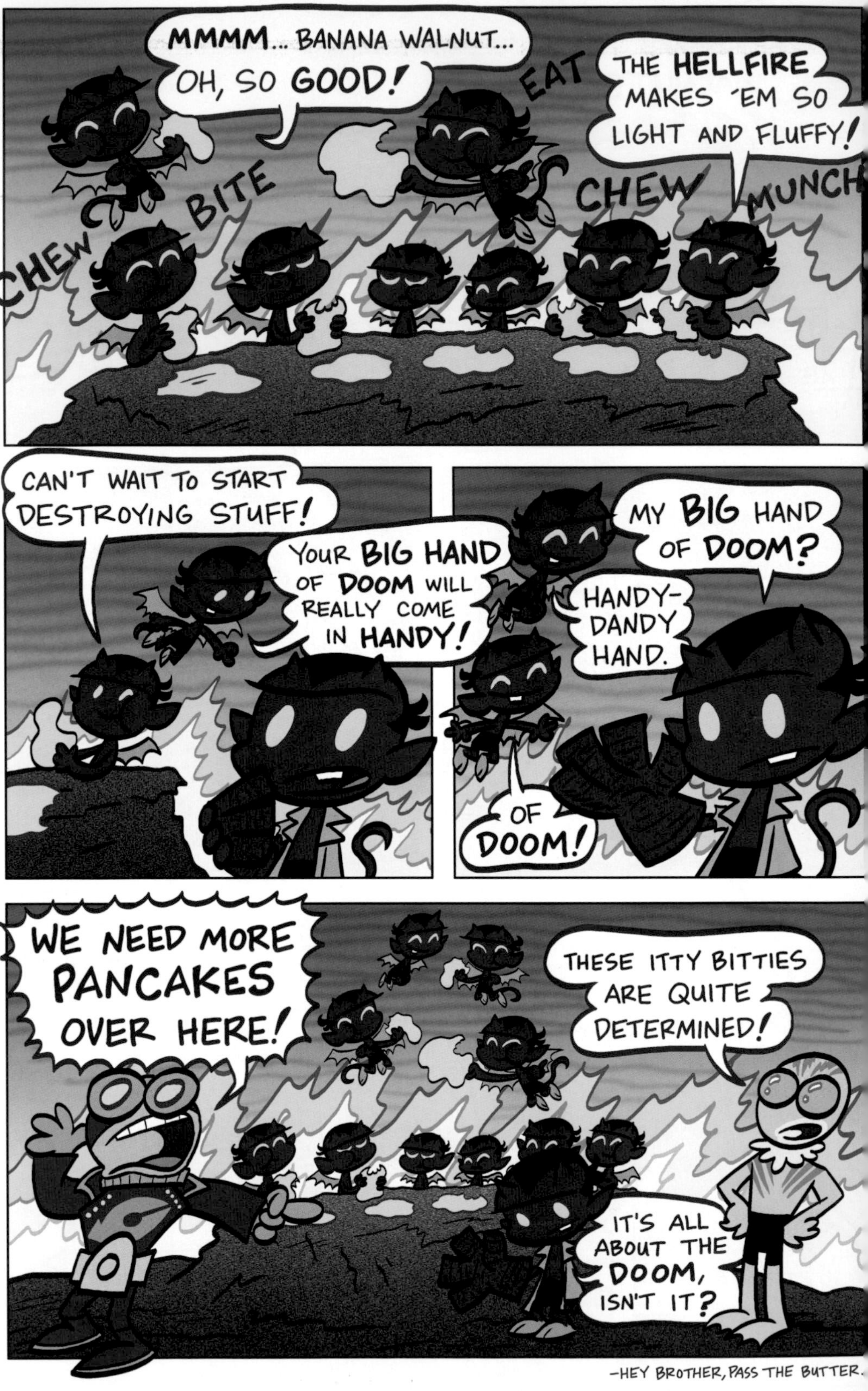
MMMM... BANANA WALNUT... OH, SO GOOD!
EAT
THE HELLFIRE MAKES 'EM SO LIGHT AND FLUFFY!
CHEW
BITE
CHEW
MUNCH
CAN'T WAIT TO START DESTROYING STUFF!
YOUR BIG HAND OF DOOM WILL REALLY COME IN HANDY!
MY BIG HAND OF DOOM?
HANDY-DANDY HAND.
OF DOOM!
WE NEED MORE PANCAKES OVER HERE!
THESE ITTY BITTIES ARE QUITE DETERMINED!
IT'S ALL ABOUT THE DOOM, ISN'T IT?

—HEY BROTHER, PASS THE BUTTER.

CHAPTER FOUR

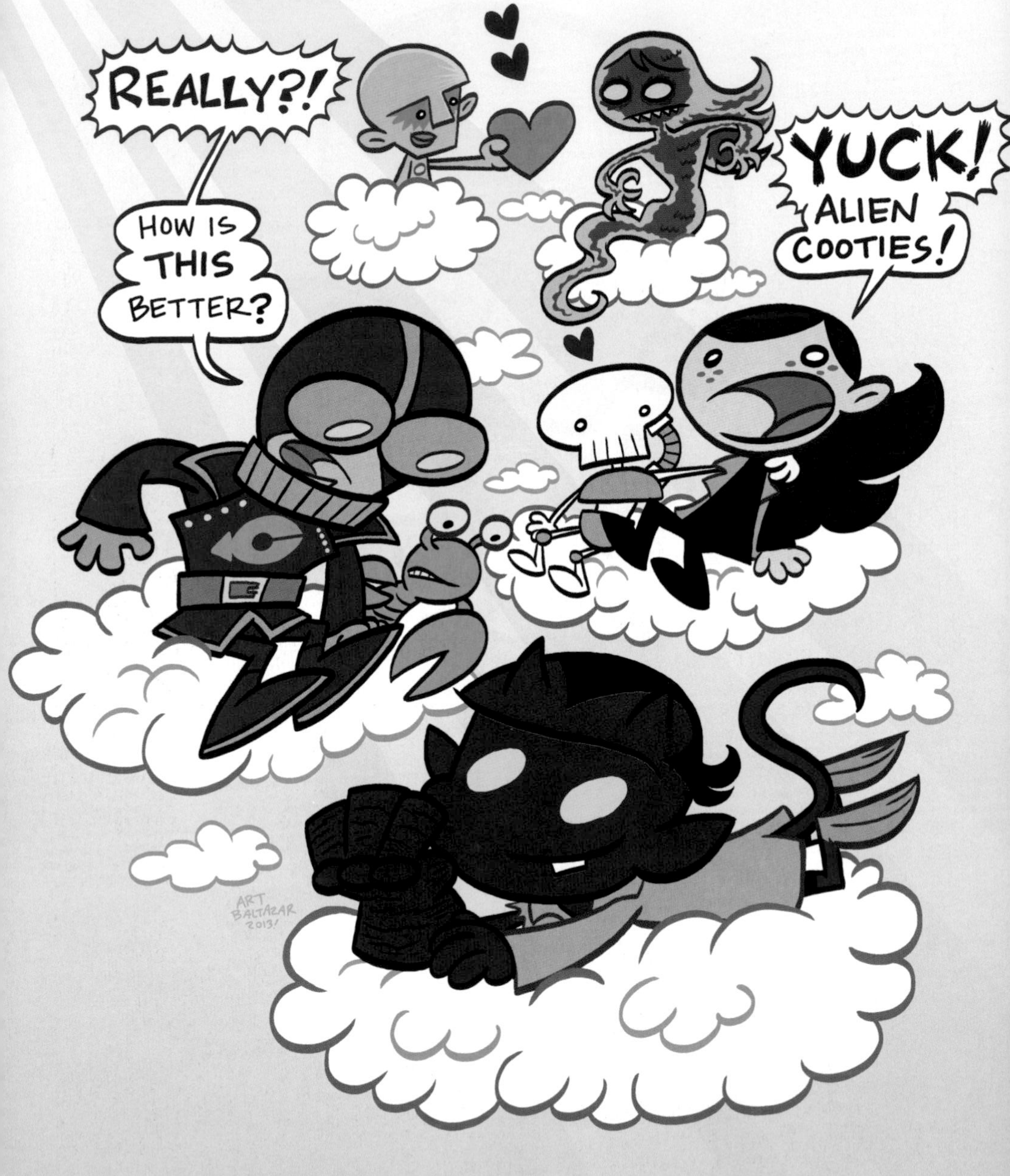

REALLY?!
HOW IS THIS BETTER?
YUCK! ALIEN COOTIES!
ART BALTAZAR 2013!

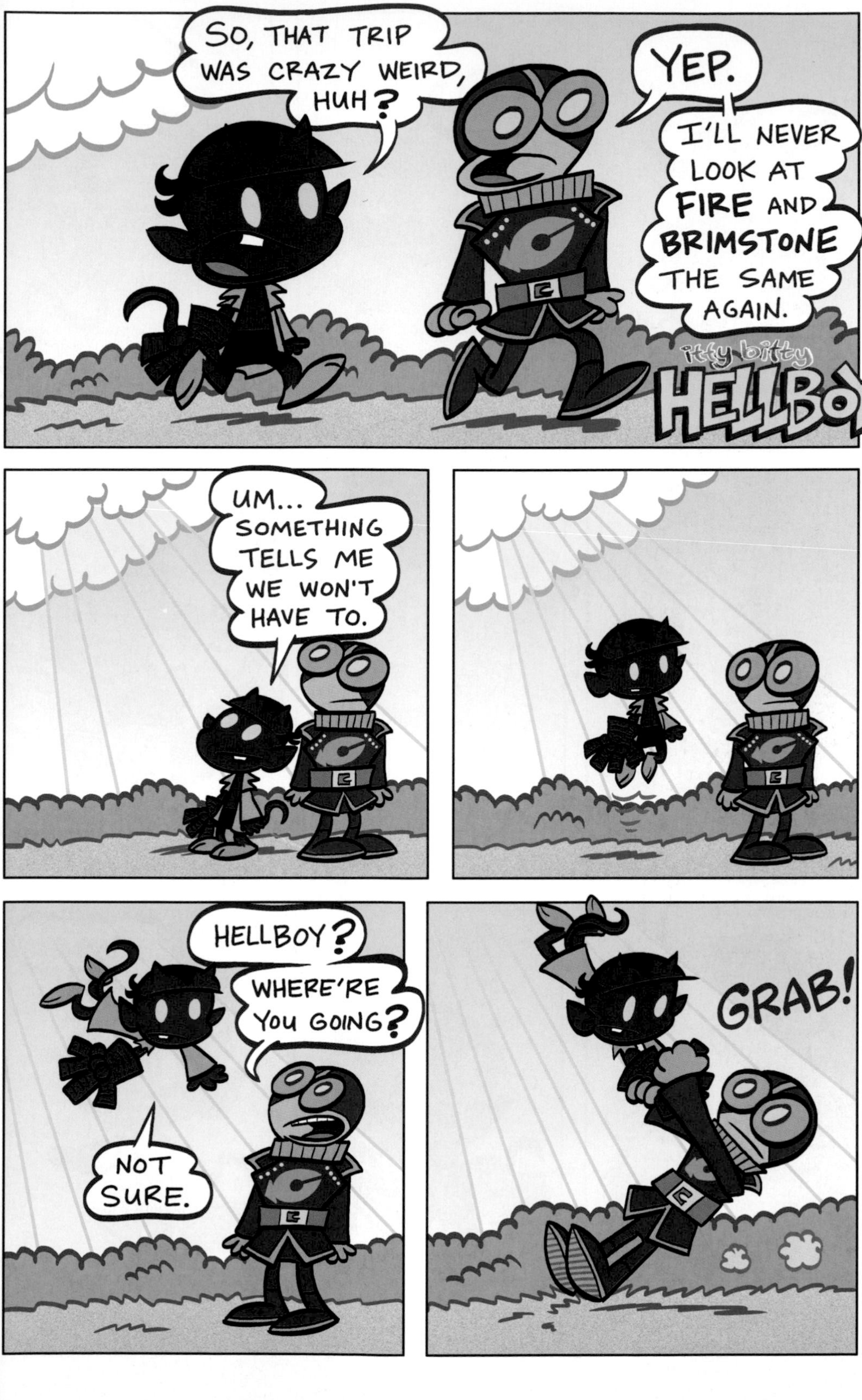
SO, THAT TRIP WAS CRAZY WEIRD, HUH?
YEP.
I'LL NEVER LOOK AT FIRE AND BRIMSTONE THE SAME AGAIN.
itty bitty HELLBOY
UM... SOMETHING TELLS ME WE WON'T HAVE TO.
HELLBOY?
WHERE'RE YOU GOING?
NOT SURE.
GRAB!

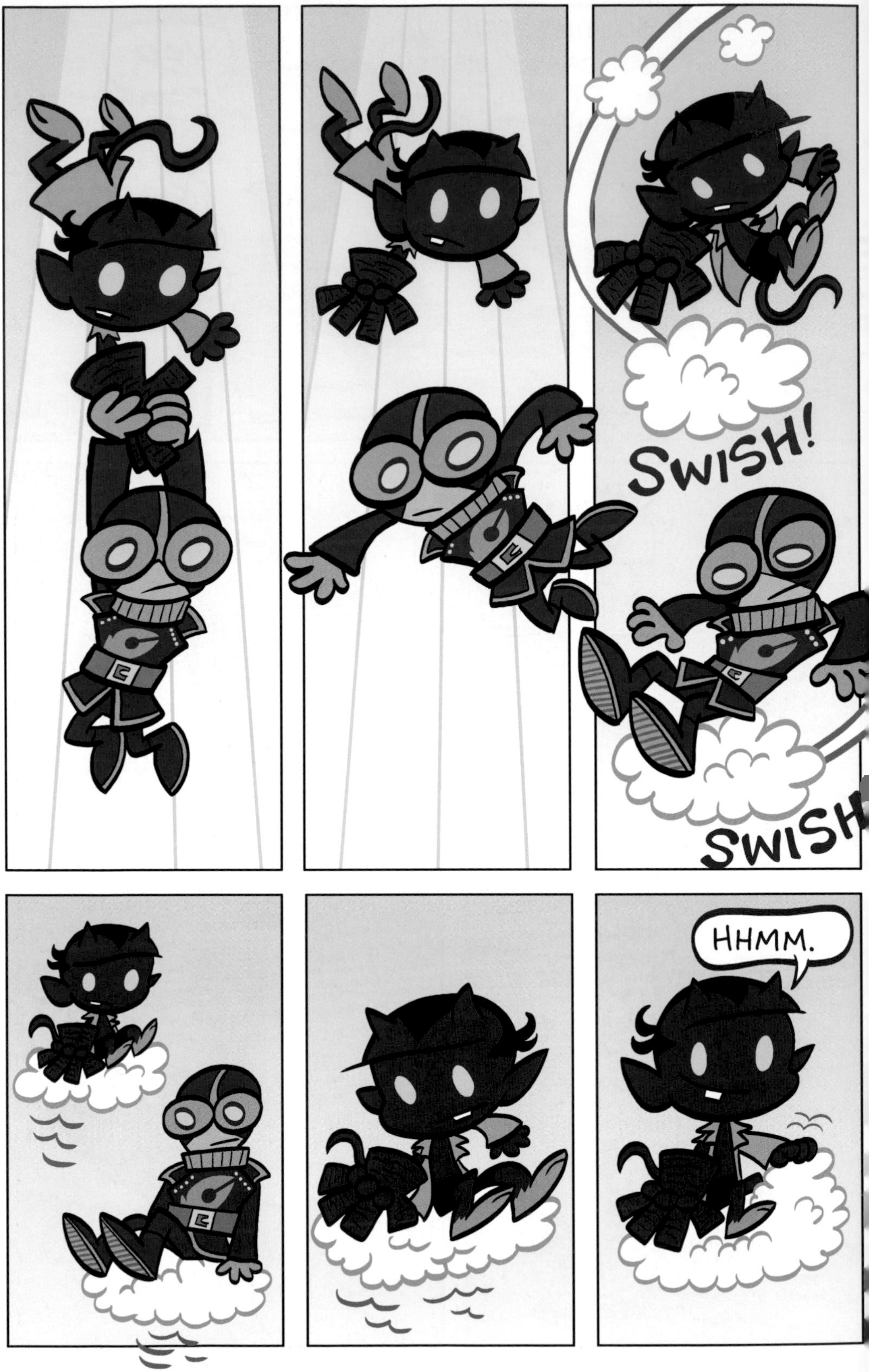
SWISH!
SWISH
HHMM.

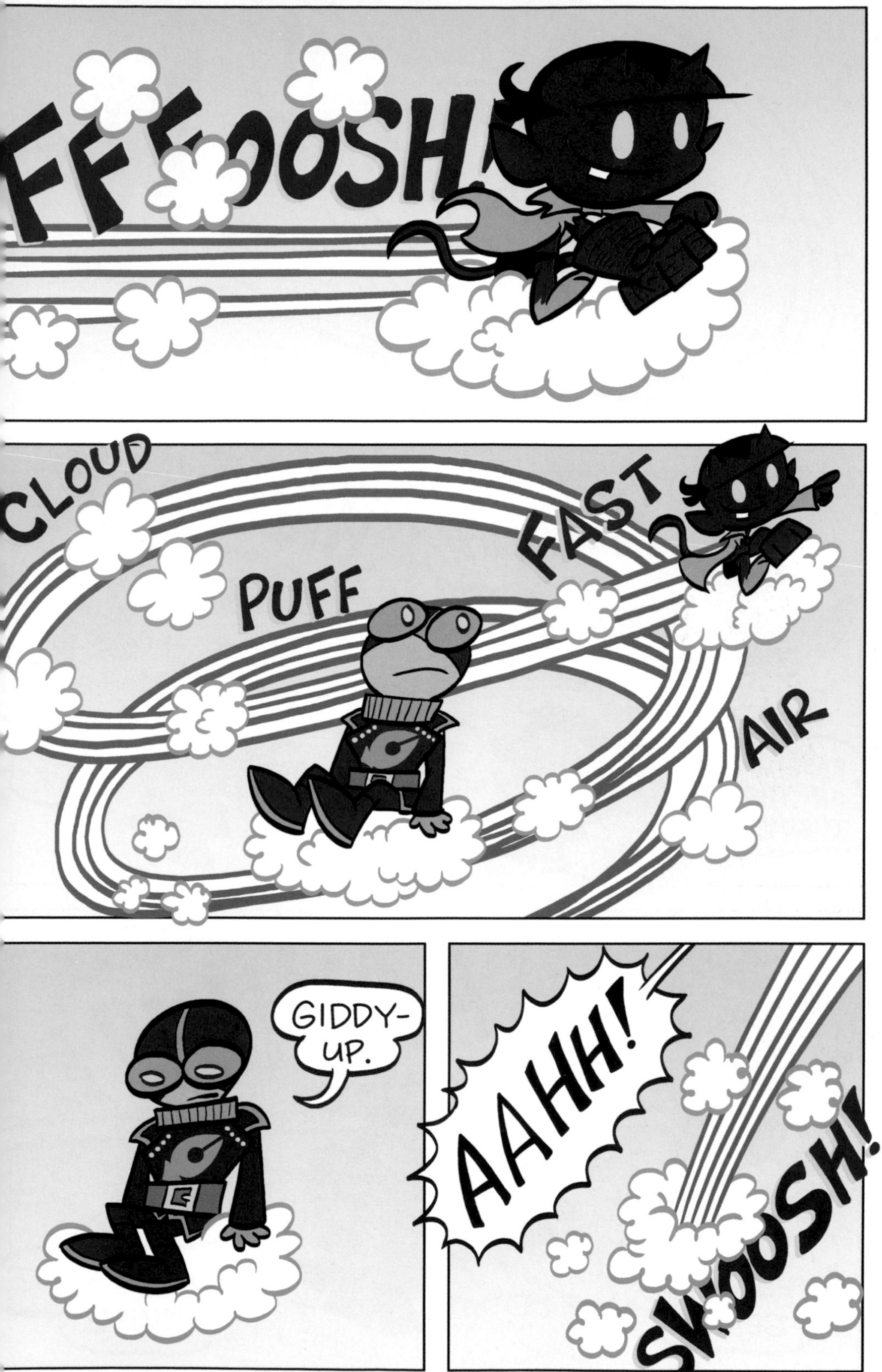
FFFOOSH!
CLOUD
PUFF
FAST
AIR
GIDDY-UP.
AAHH!
SWOOSH!

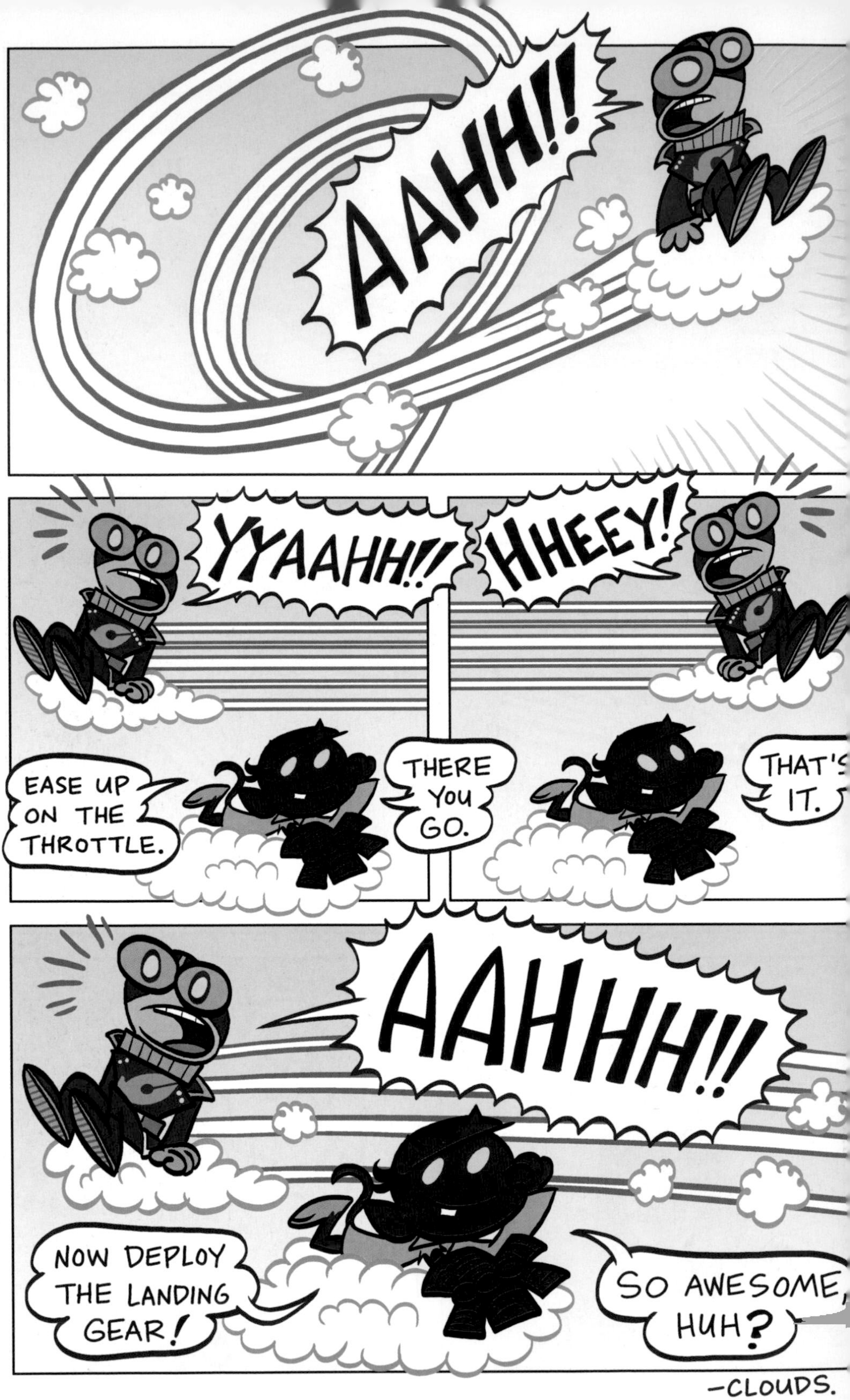
AAHH!!
YYAAHH!!
HHEEY!
EASE UP ON THE THROTTLE.
THERE YOU GO.
THAT'S IT.
AAHHH!!
NOW DEPLOY THE LANDING GEAR!
SO AWESOME, HUH?

—CLOUDS.

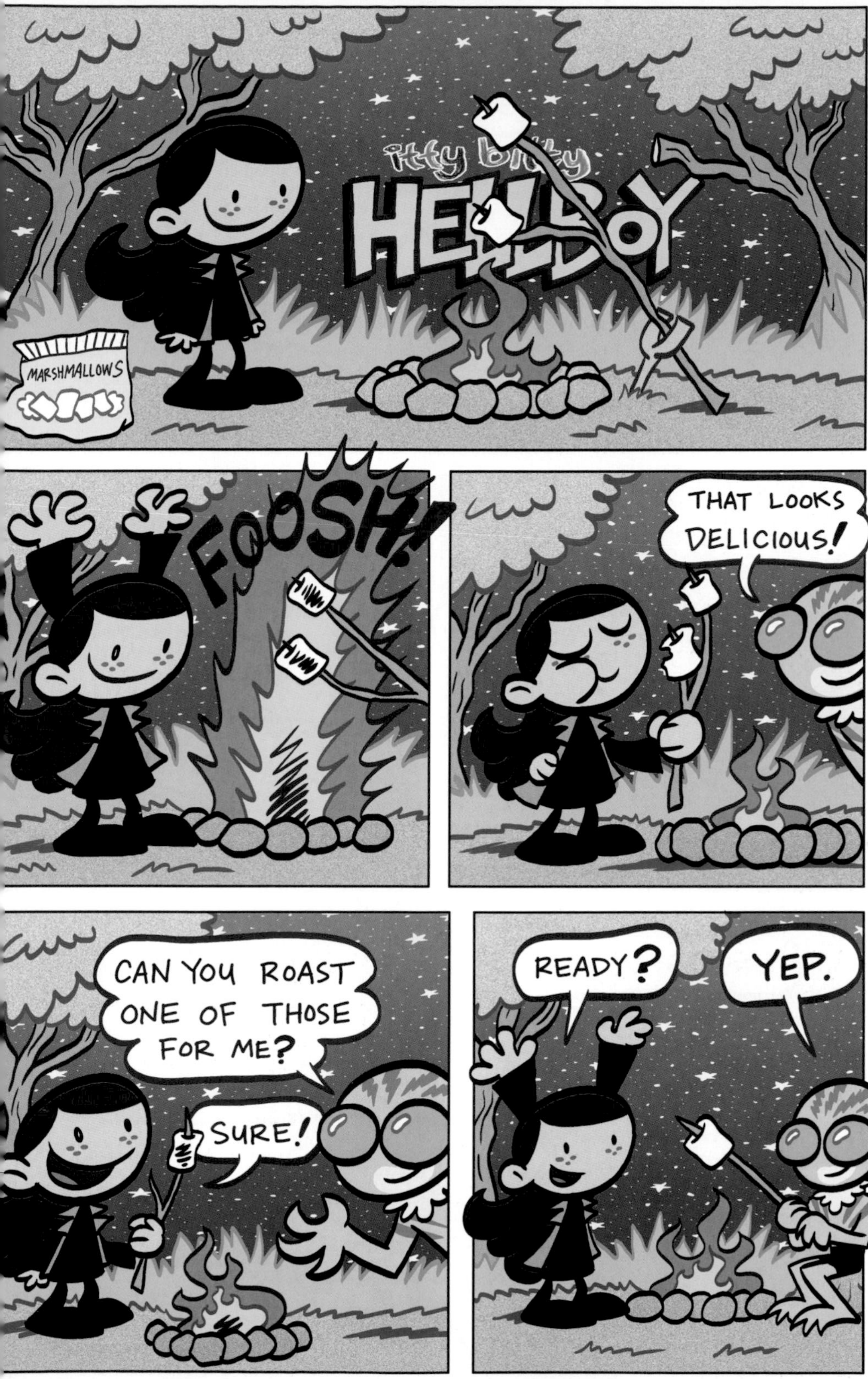
itty bitty
HELLBOY
MARSHMALLOWS
FOOSH!
THAT LOOKS DELICIOUS!
CAN YOU ROAST ONE OF THOSE FOR ME?
SURE!
READY?
YEP.

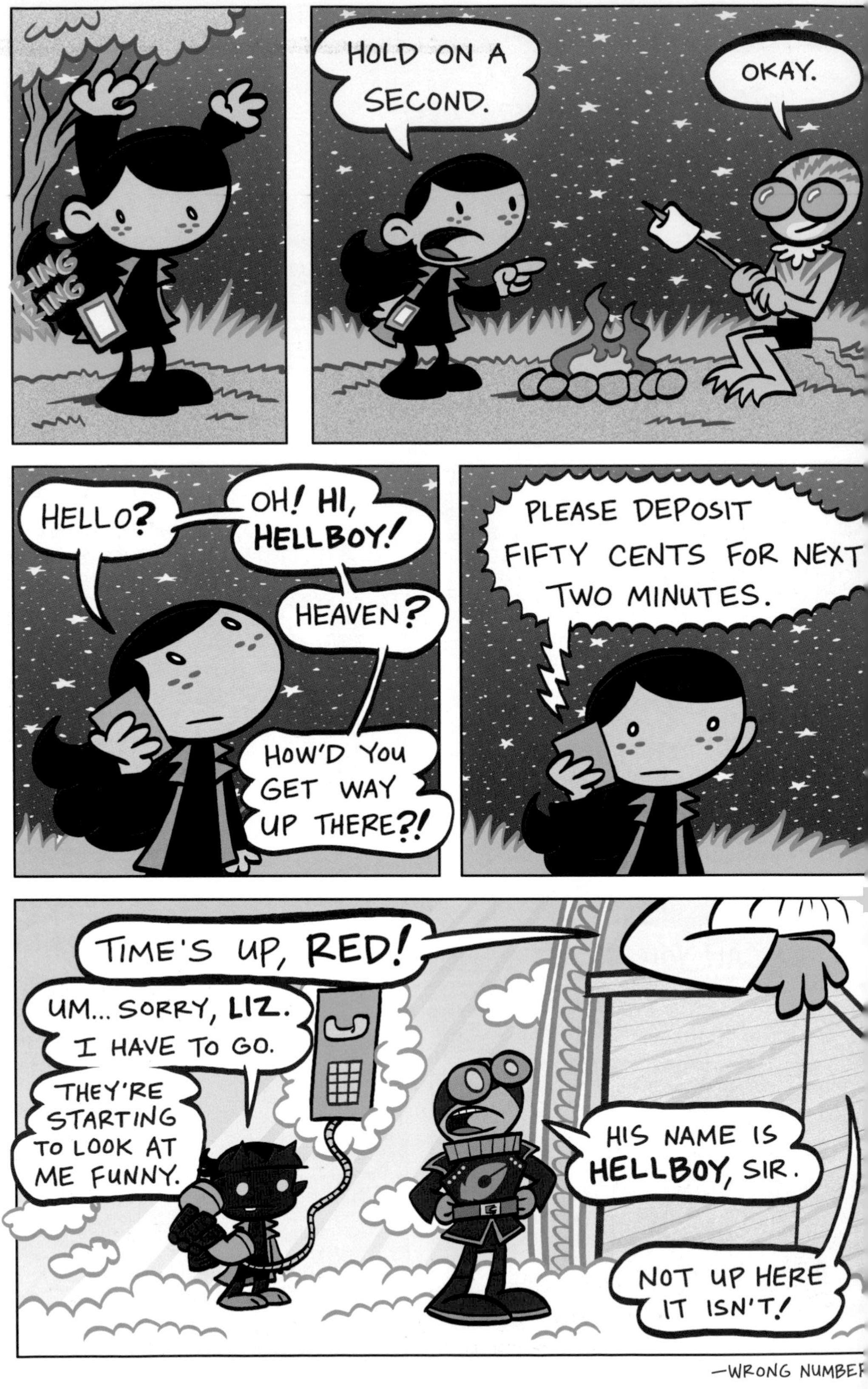
RING RING
HOLD ON A SECOND.
OKAY.
HELLO?
OH! HI, HELLBOY!
HEAVEN?
HOW'D YOU GET WAY UP THERE?!
PLEASE DEPOSIT FIFTY CENTS FOR NEXT TWO MINUTES.
TIME'S UP, RED!
UM... SORRY, LIZ. I HAVE TO GO.
THEY'RE STARTING TO LOOK AT ME FUNNY.
HIS NAME IS HELLBOY, SIR.
NOT UP HERE IT ISN'T!

—WRONG NUMBER

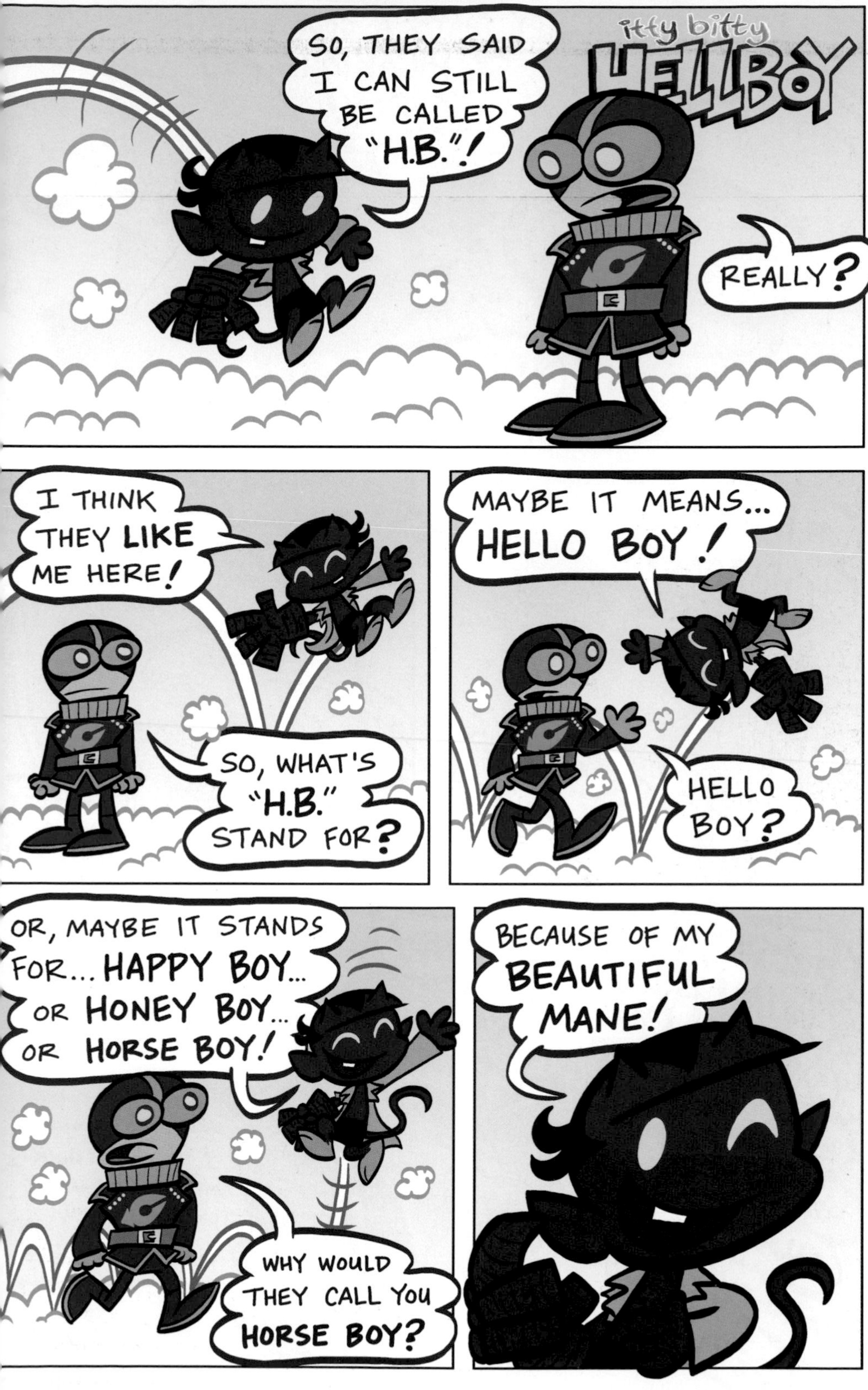
itty bitty HELLBOY
SO, THEY SAID I CAN STILL BE CALLED "H.B."!
REALLY?
I THINK THEY LIKE ME HERE!
SO, WHAT'S "H.B." STAND FOR?
MAYBE IT MEANS... HELLO BOY!
HELLO BOY?
OR, MAYBE IT STANDS FOR... HAPPY BOY... OR HONEY BOY... OR HORSE BOY!
WHY WOULD THEY CALL YOU HORSE BOY?
BECAUSE OF MY BEAUTIFUL MANE!

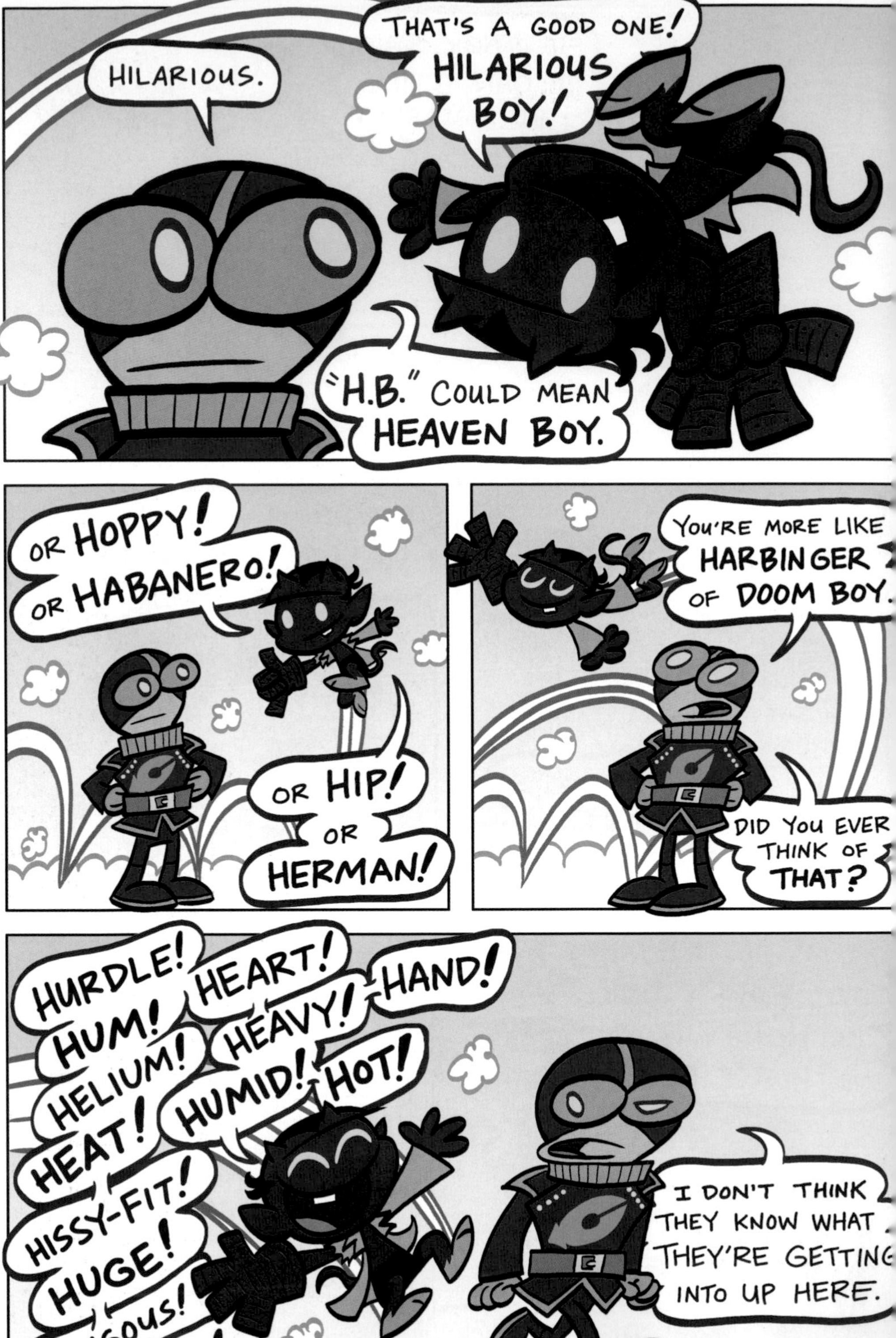
HILARIOUS.
THAT'S A GOOD ONE! HILARIOUS BOY!
"H.B." COULD MEAN HEAVEN BOY.
OR HOPPY! OR HABANERO!
OR HIP! OR HERMAN!
YOU'RE MORE LIKE HARBINGER OF DOOM BOY.
DID YOU EVER THINK OF THAT?
HURDLE! HUM! HELIUM! HEAT! HISSY-FIT! HUGE! HUMONGOUS! HEFTY!
HEART! HEAVY! HAND!
HUMID! HOT!
I DON'T THINK THEY KNOW WHAT THEY'RE GETTING INTO UP HERE.

-HUMANIT

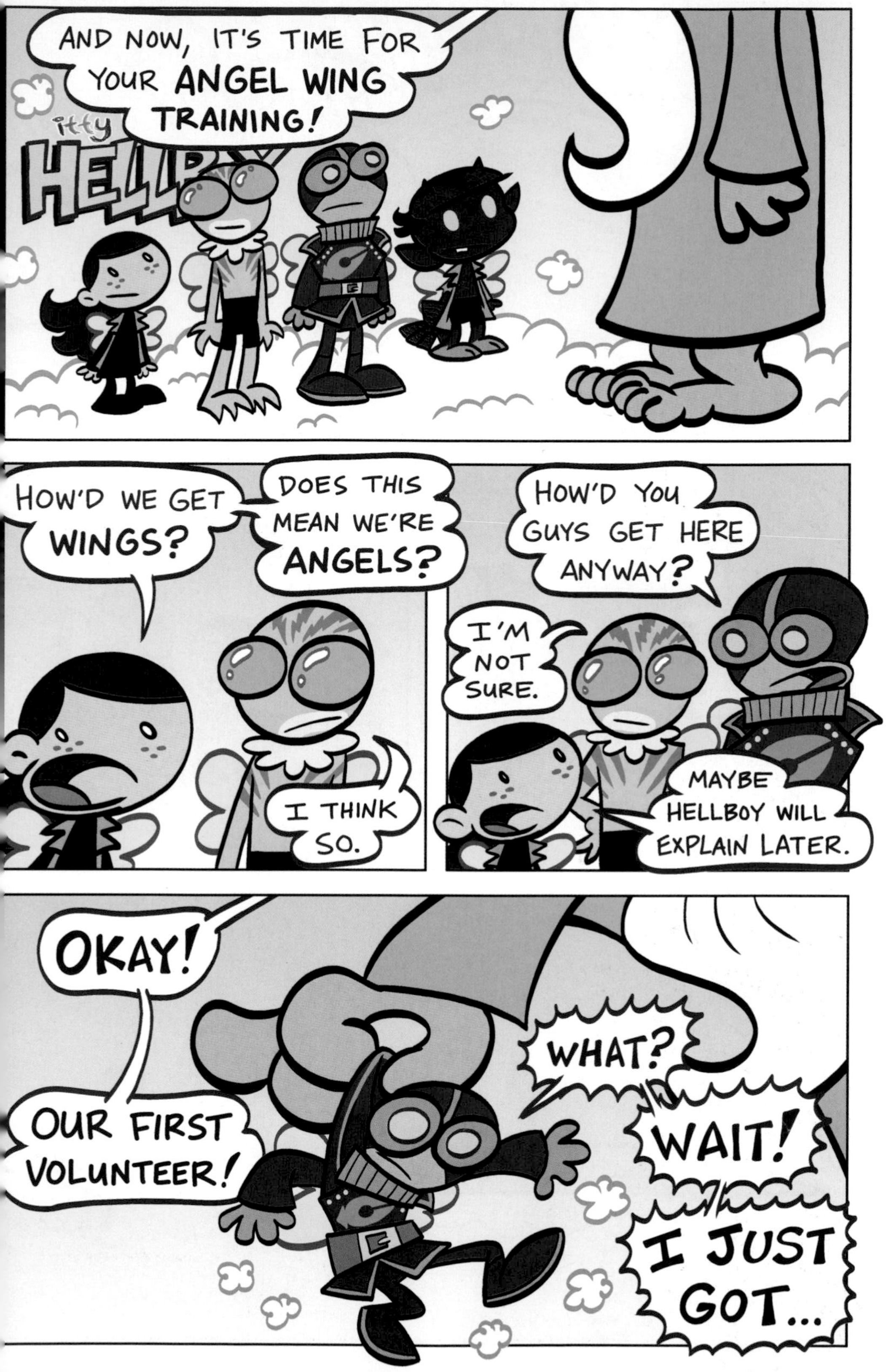
AND NOW, IT'S TIME FOR YOUR ANGEL WING TRAINING!
itty HELLBOY
HOW'D WE GET WINGS?
DOES THIS MEAN WE'RE ANGELS?
I THINK SO.
HOW'D YOU GUYS GET HERE ANYWAY?
I'M NOT SURE.
MAYBE HELLBOY WILL EXPLAIN LATER.
OKAY!
OUR FIRST VOLUNTEER!
WHAT?
WAIT!
I JUST GOT...

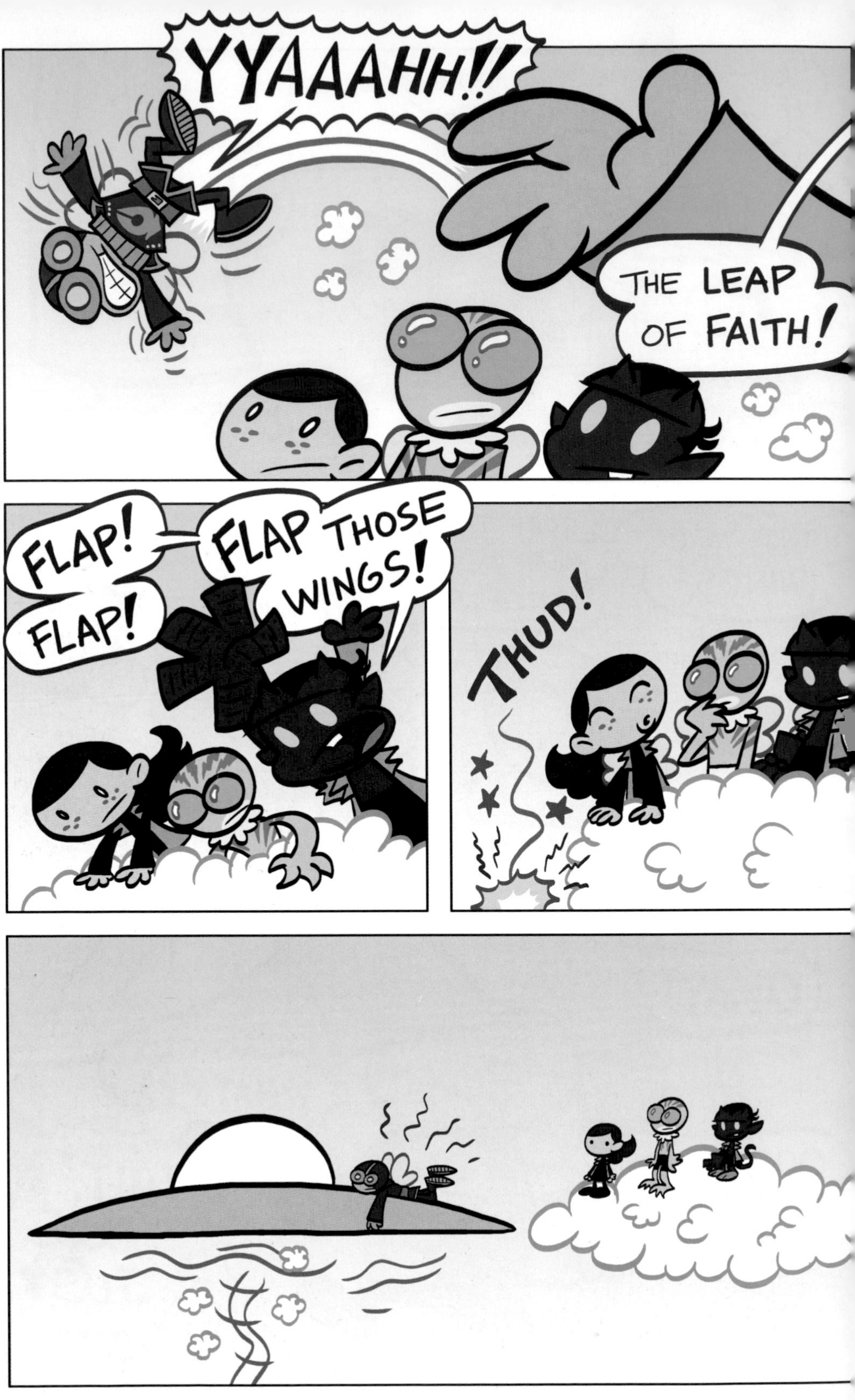
YYAAAHH!!
THE LEAP OF FAITH!
FLAP! FLAP!
FLAP THOSE WINGS!
THUD!

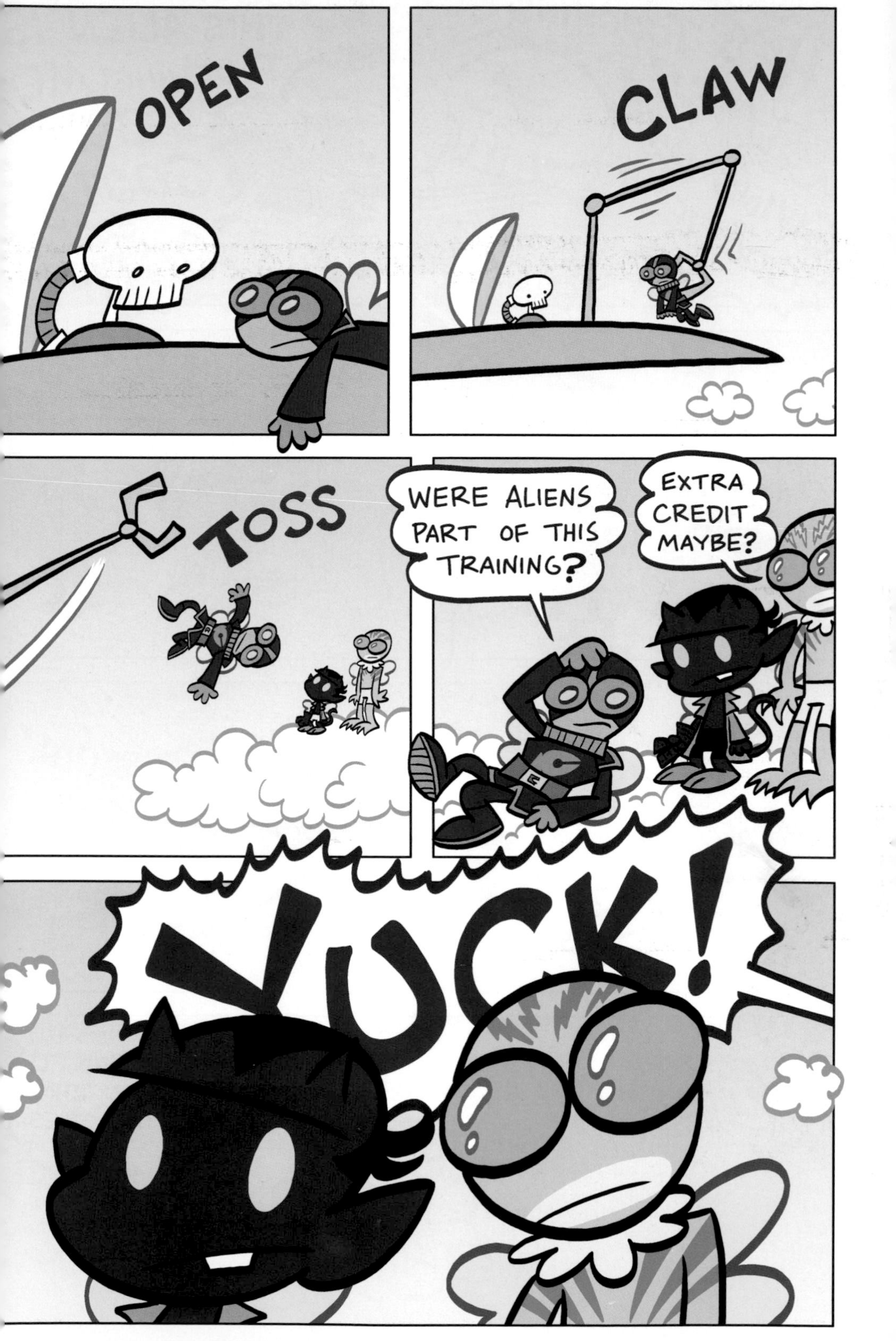
OPEN
CLAW
TOSS
WERE ALIENS PART OF THIS TRAINING?
EXTRA CREDIT MAYBE?
YUCK!

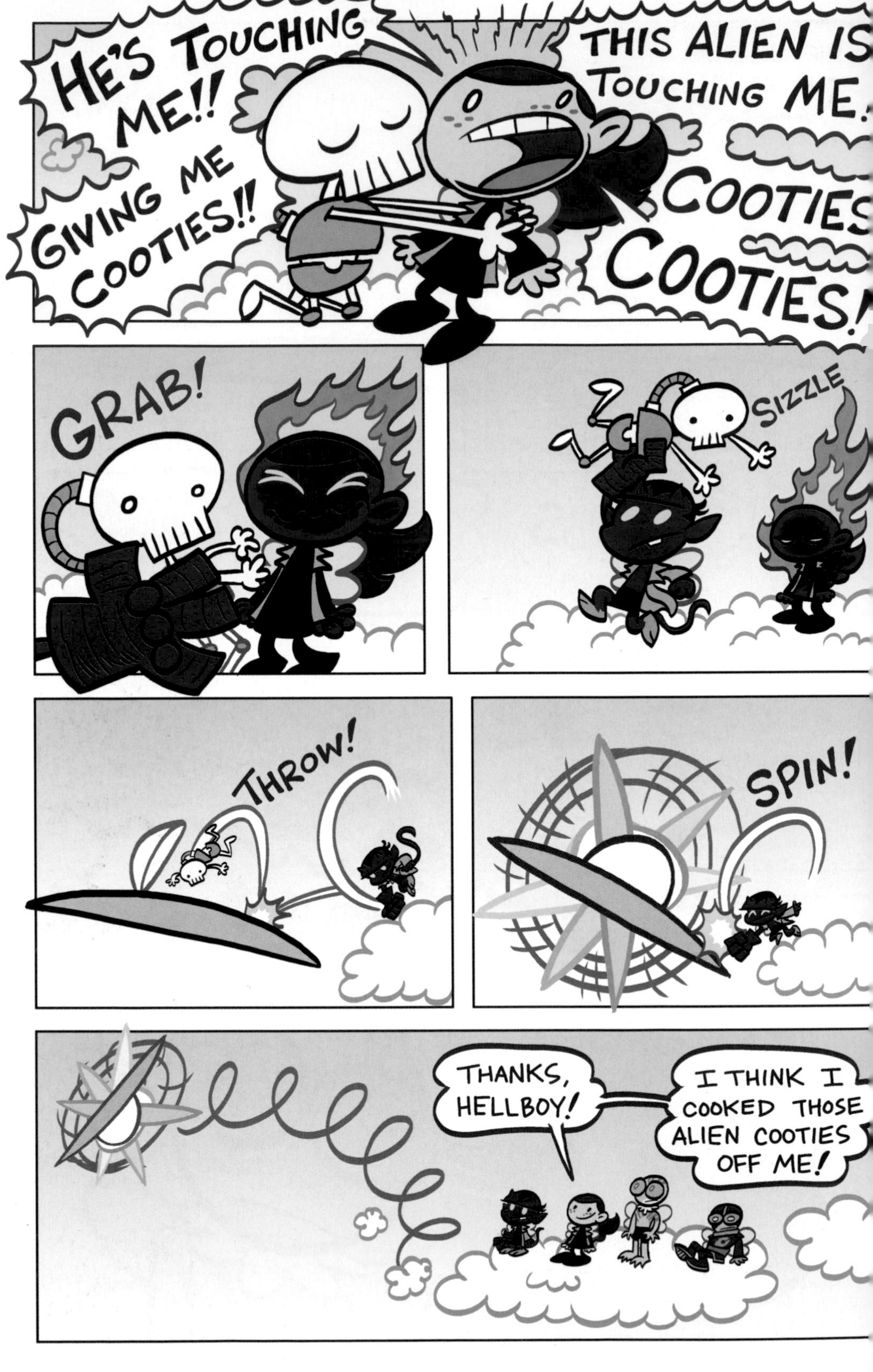
HE'S TOUCHING ME!!
GIVING ME COOTIES!!
THIS ALIEN IS TOUCHING ME.
COOTIES COOTIES!
GRAB!
SIZZLE
THROW!
SPIN!
THANKS, HELLBOY!
I THINK I COOKED THOSE ALIEN COOTIES OFF ME!

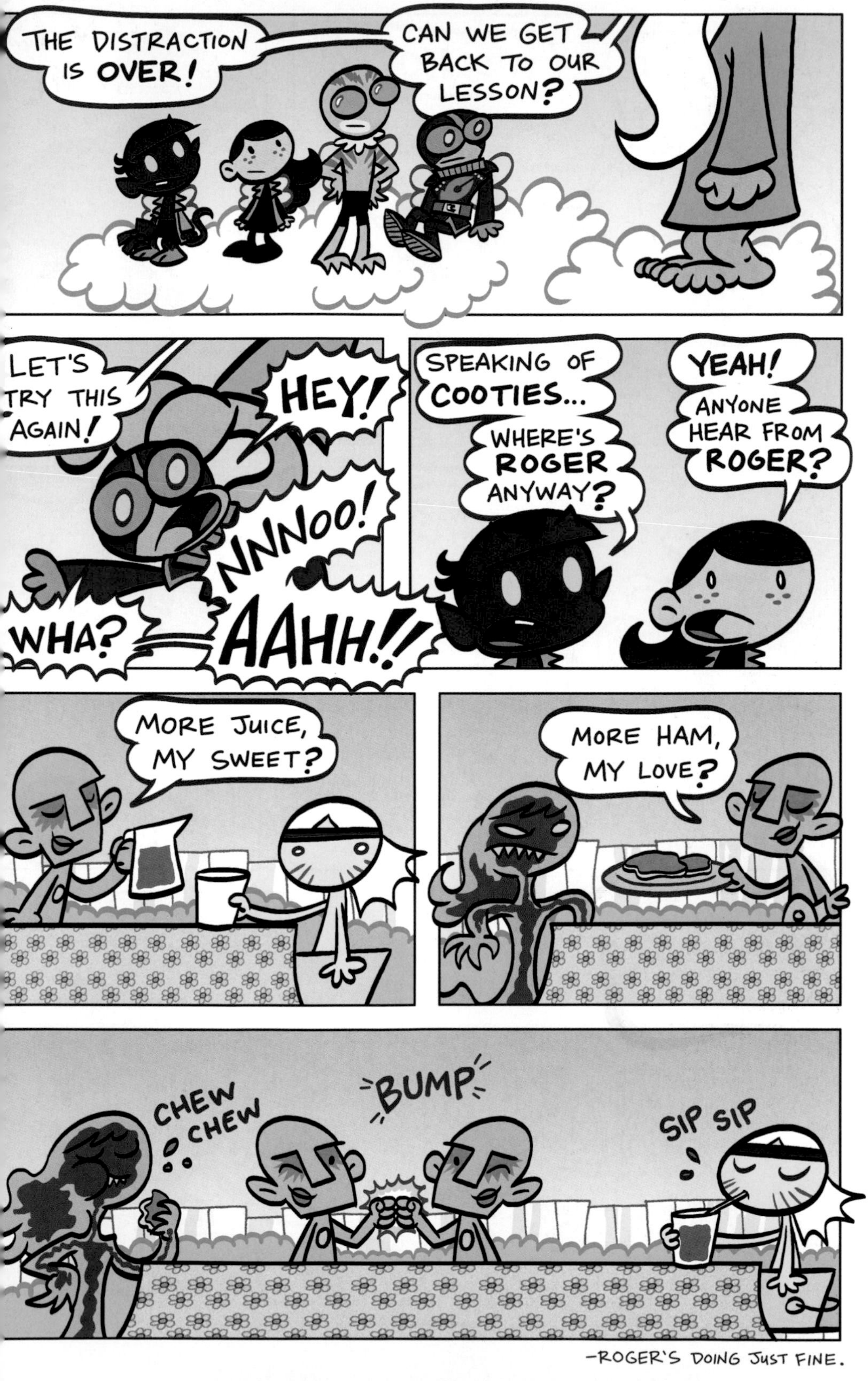
THE DISTRACTION IS OVER!
CAN WE GET BACK TO OUR LESSON?
LET'S TRY THIS AGAIN!
HEY!
NNNoo!
WHA?
AAHH!!
SPEAKING OF COOTIES...
WHERE'S ROGER ANYWAY?
YEAH!
ANYONE HEAR FROM ROGER?
MORE JUICE, MY SWEET?
MORE HAM, MY LOVE?
CHEW CHEW
BUMP
SIP SIP
-ROGER'S DOING JUST FINE.

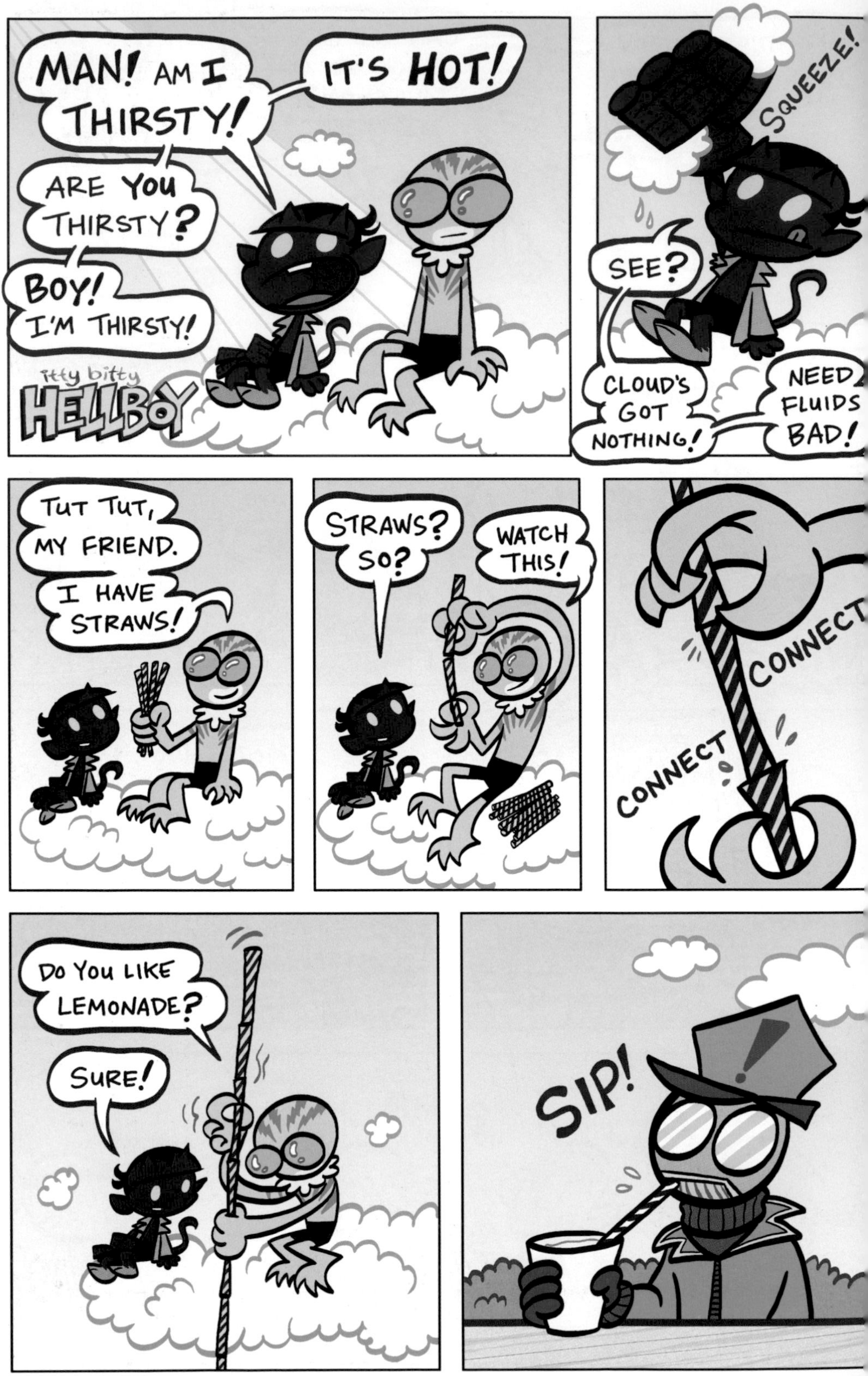
MAN! AM I THIRSTY!
IT'S HOT!
ARE YOU THIRSTY?
BOY! I'M THIRSTY!
itty bitty HELLBOY
SQUEEZE!
SEE?
CLOUD'S GOT NOTHING!
NEED FLUIDS BAD!
TUT TUT, MY FRIEND.
I HAVE STRAWS!
STRAWS? SO?
WATCH THIS!
CONNECT
CONNECT
DO YOU LIKE LEMONADE?
SURE!
SIP!

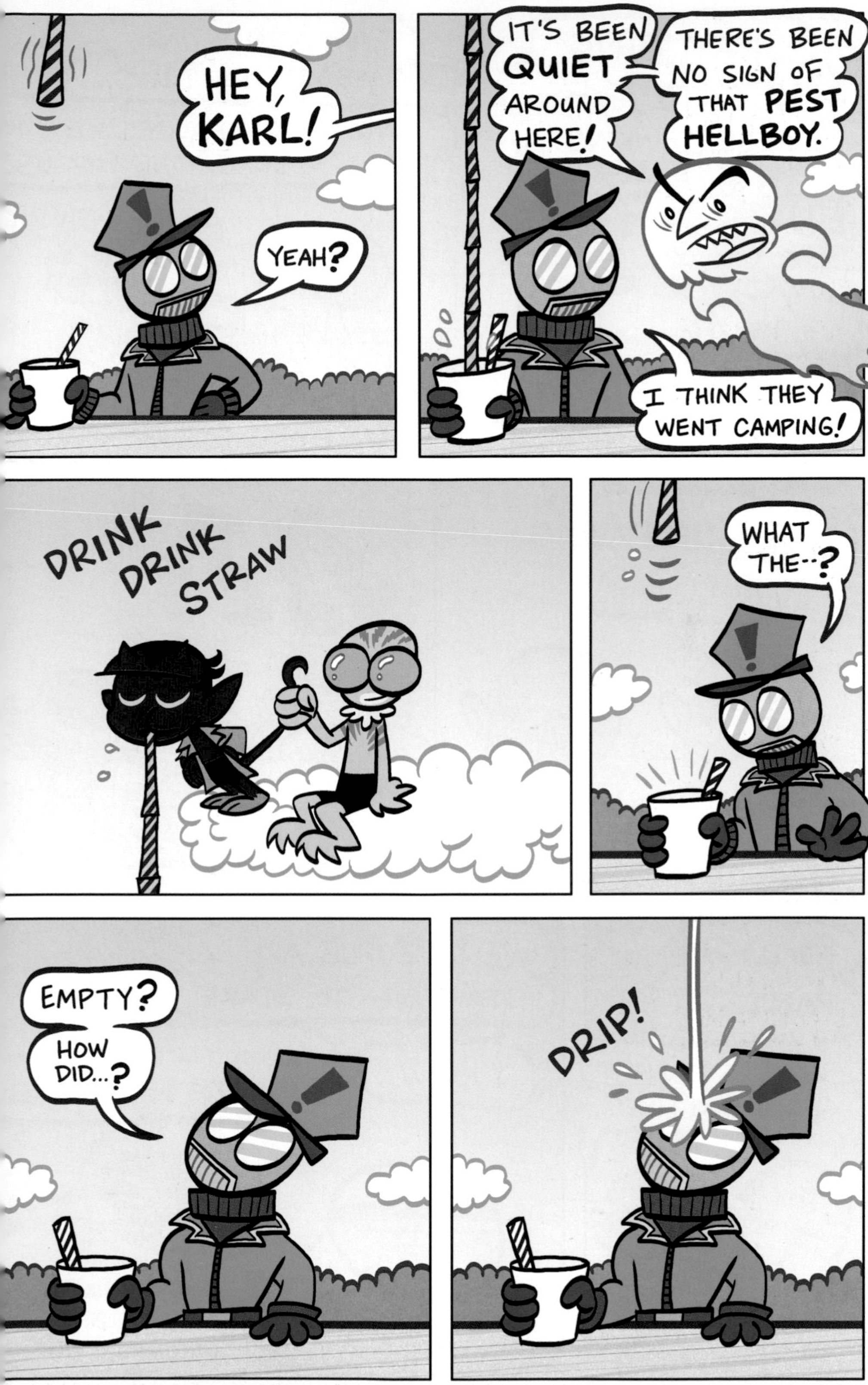
HEY, KARL!
YEAH?
IT'S BEEN QUIET AROUND HERE!
THERE'S BEEN NO SIGN OF THAT PEST HELLBOY.
I THINK THEY WENT CAMPING!
DRINK DRINK STRAW
WHAT THE--?
EMPTY?
HOW DID...?
DRIP!

—LOOKS LIKE RAIN.

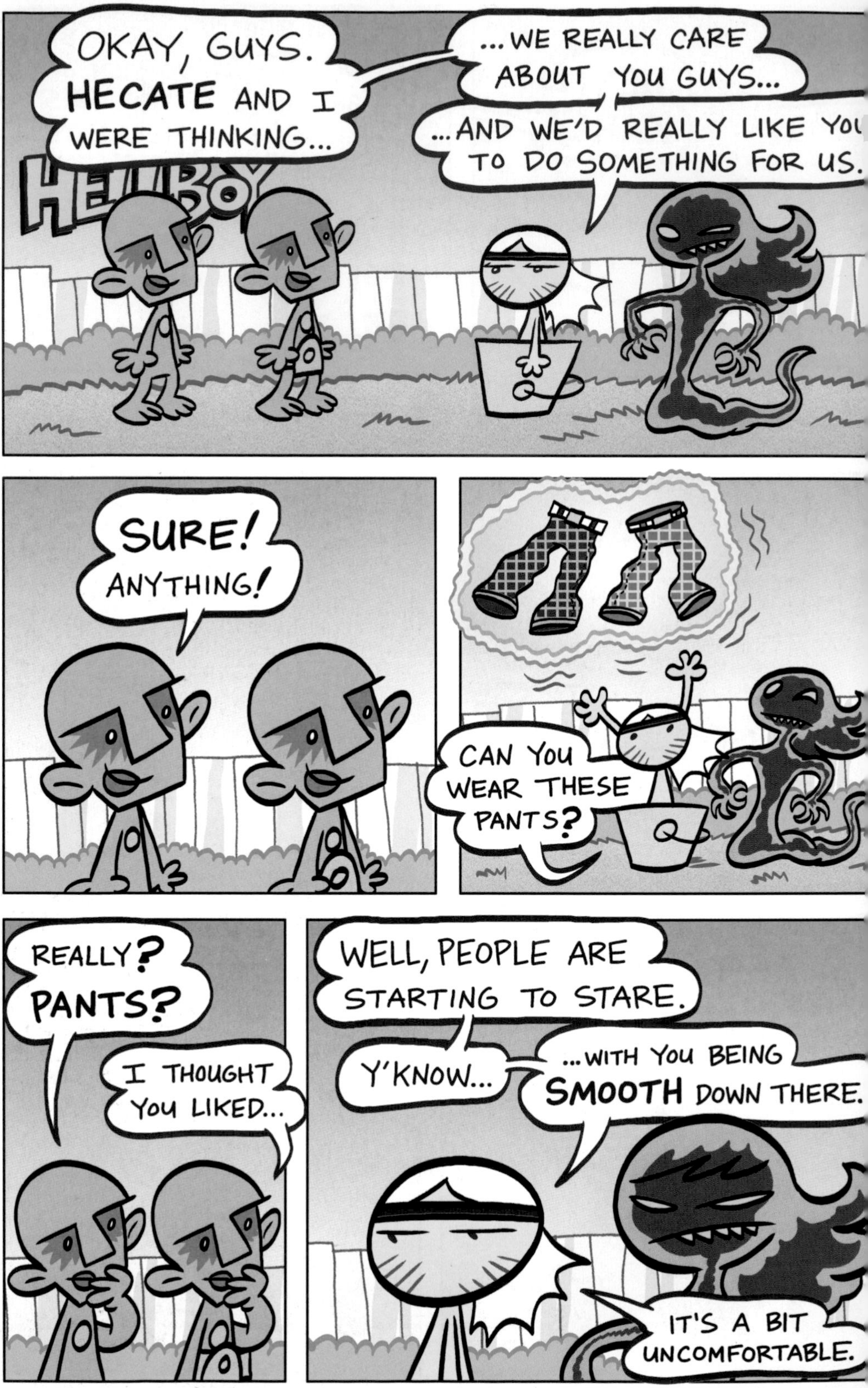
OKAY, GUYS. HECATE AND I WERE THINKING...
...WE REALLY CARE ABOUT YOU GUYS...
...AND WE'D REALLY LIKE YOU TO DO SOMETHING FOR US.
HELLBOY
SURE! ANYTHING!
CAN YOU WEAR THESE PANTS?
REALLY? PANTS?
I THOUGHT YOU LIKED...
WELL, PEOPLE ARE STARTING TO STARE.
Y'KNOW...
...WITH YOU BEING SMOOTH DOWN THERE.
IT'S A BIT UNCOMFORTABLE.

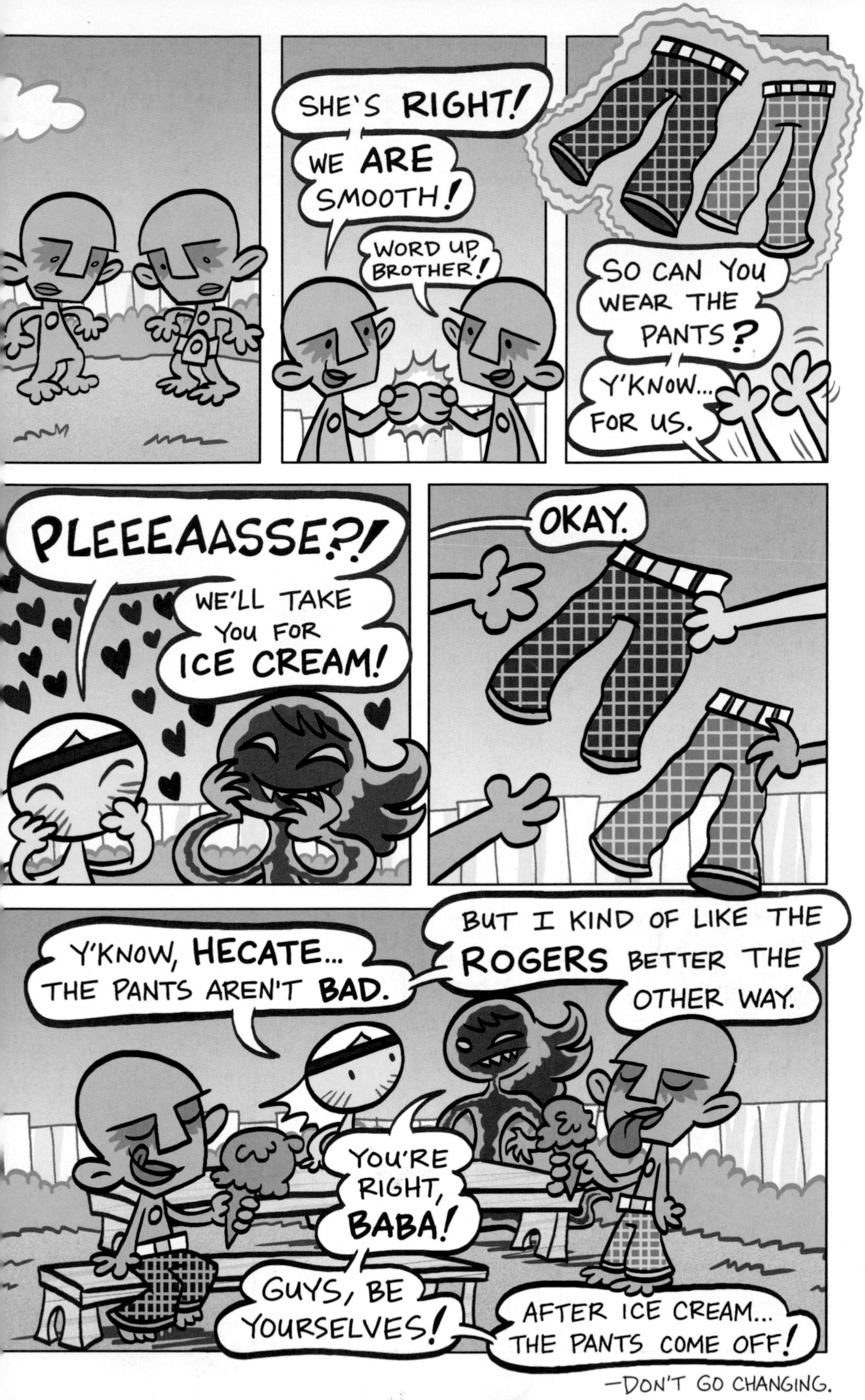
SHE'S RIGHT!
WE ARE SMOOTH!
WORD UP, BROTHER!
SO CAN YOU WEAR THE PANTS?
Y'KNOW... FOR US.
PLEEEAASSE?!
WE'LL TAKE YOU FOR ICE CREAM!
OKAY.
Y'KNOW, HECATE... THE PANTS AREN'T BAD.
BUT I KIND OF LIKE THE ROGERS BETTER THE OTHER WAY.
YOU'RE RIGHT, BABA!
GUYS, BE YOURSELVES!
AFTER ICE CREAM... THE PANTS COME OFF!

—DON'T GO CHANGING.

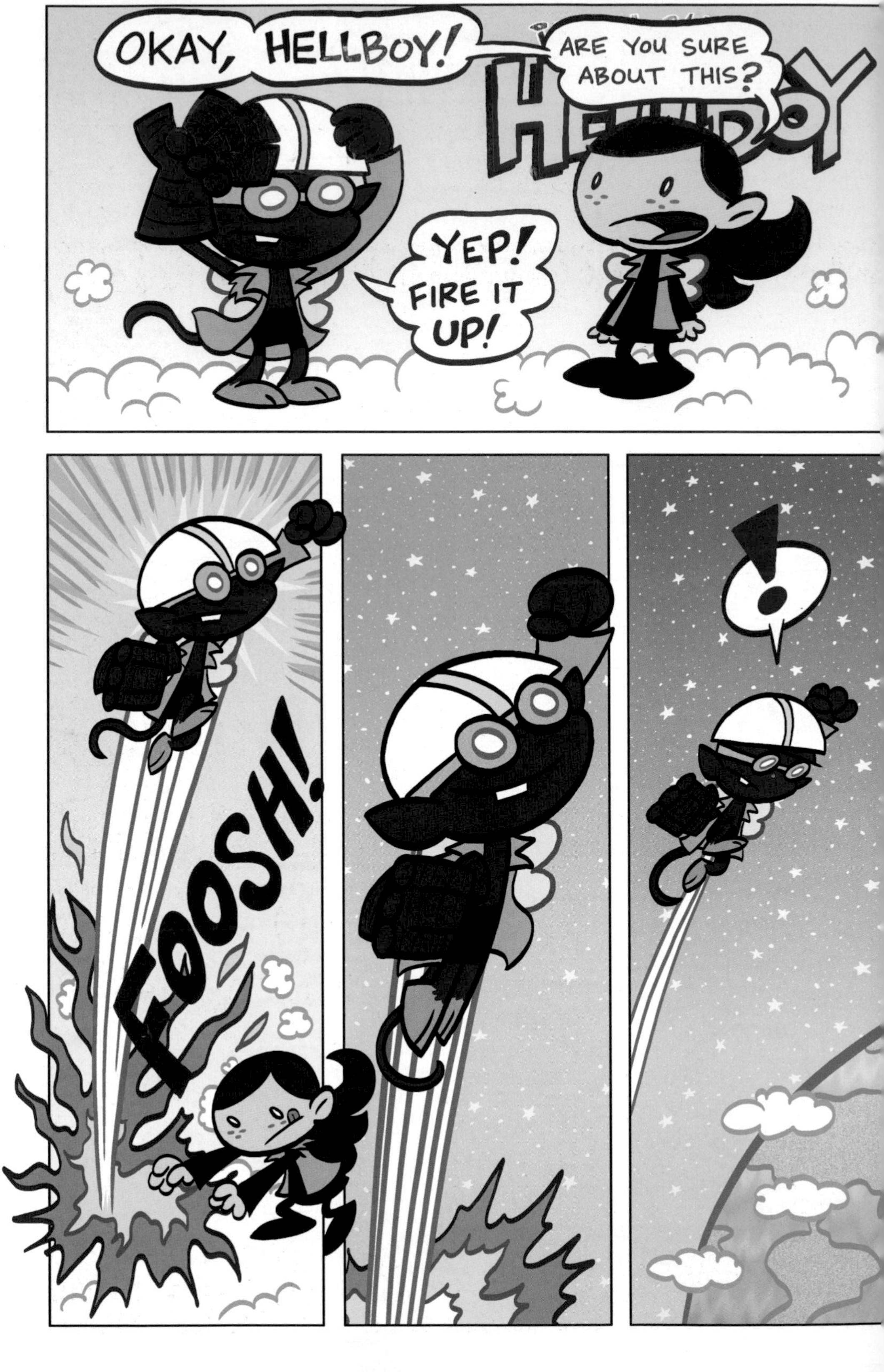
OKAY, HELLBOY!
ARE YOU SURE ABOUT THIS?
HELLBOY
YEP! FIRE IT UP!
FOOSH!
!

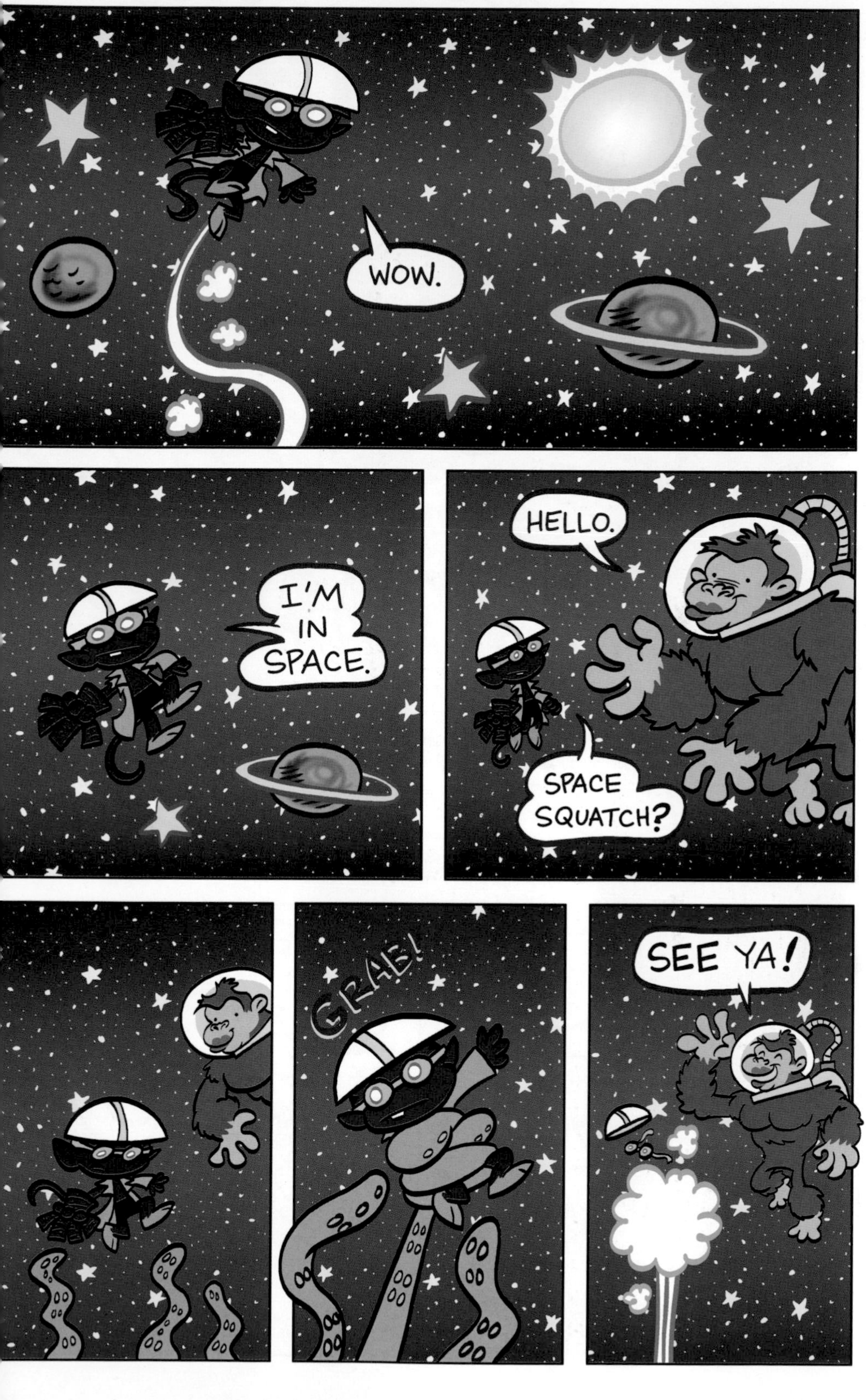
WOW.
I'M IN SPACE.
HELLO.
SPACE SQUATCH?
GRAB!
SEE YA!

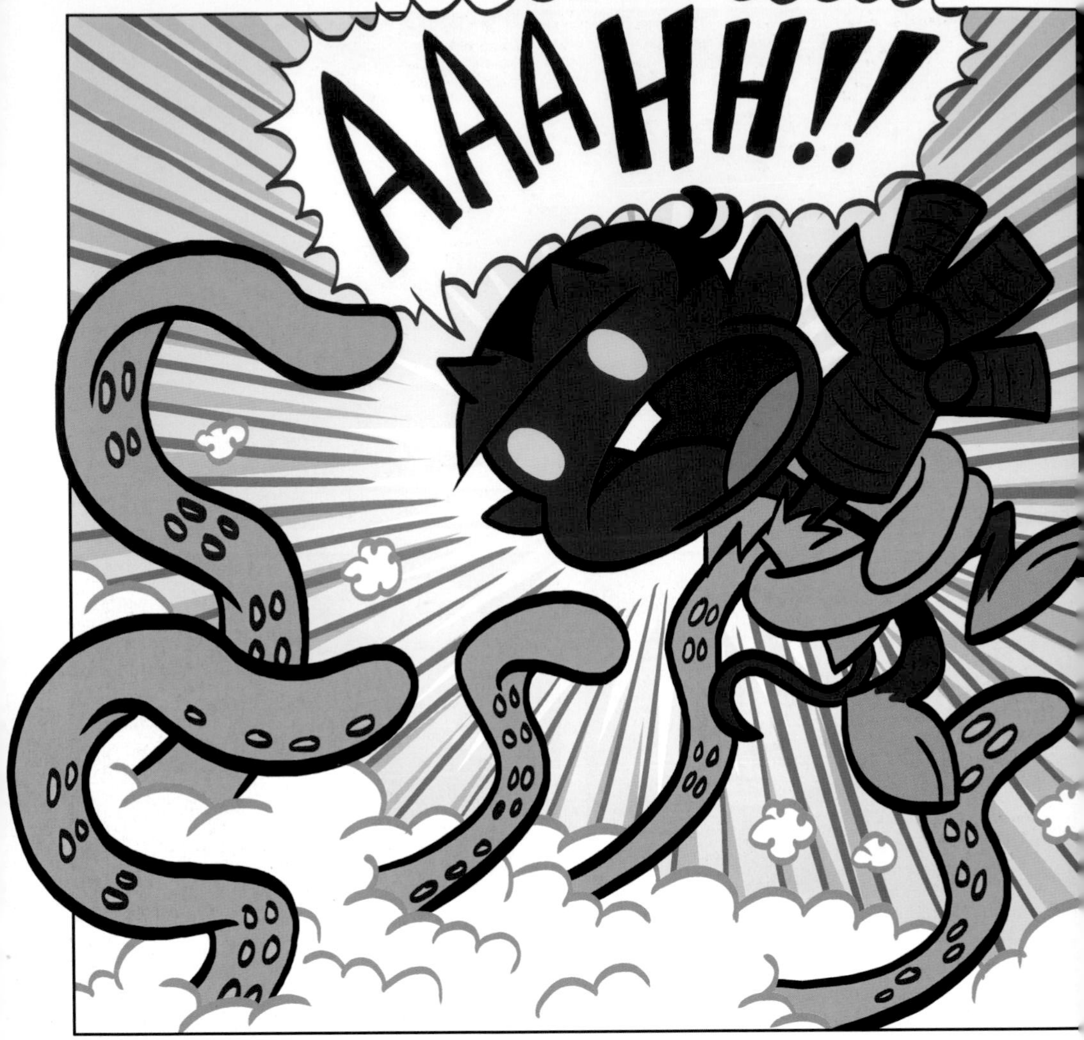
AAAHH!!
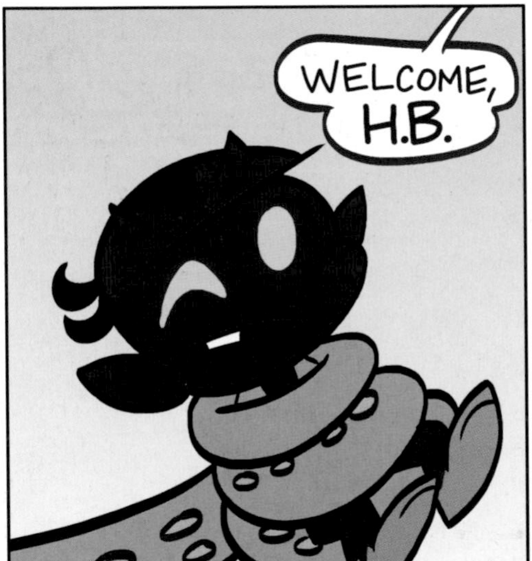
WELCOME, H.B.
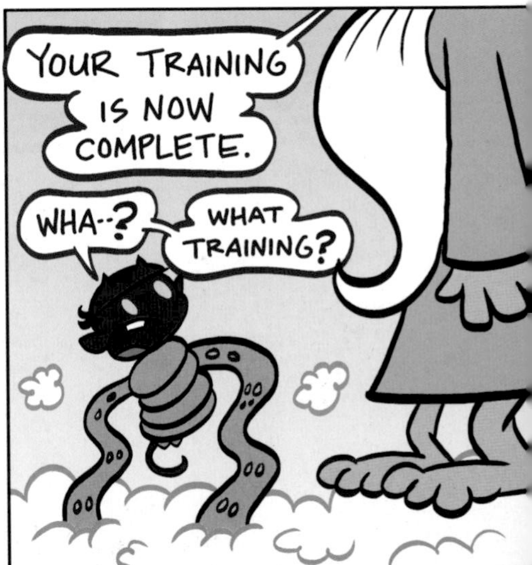
YOUR TRAINING IS NOW COMPLETE.
WHA--?
WHAT TRAINING?

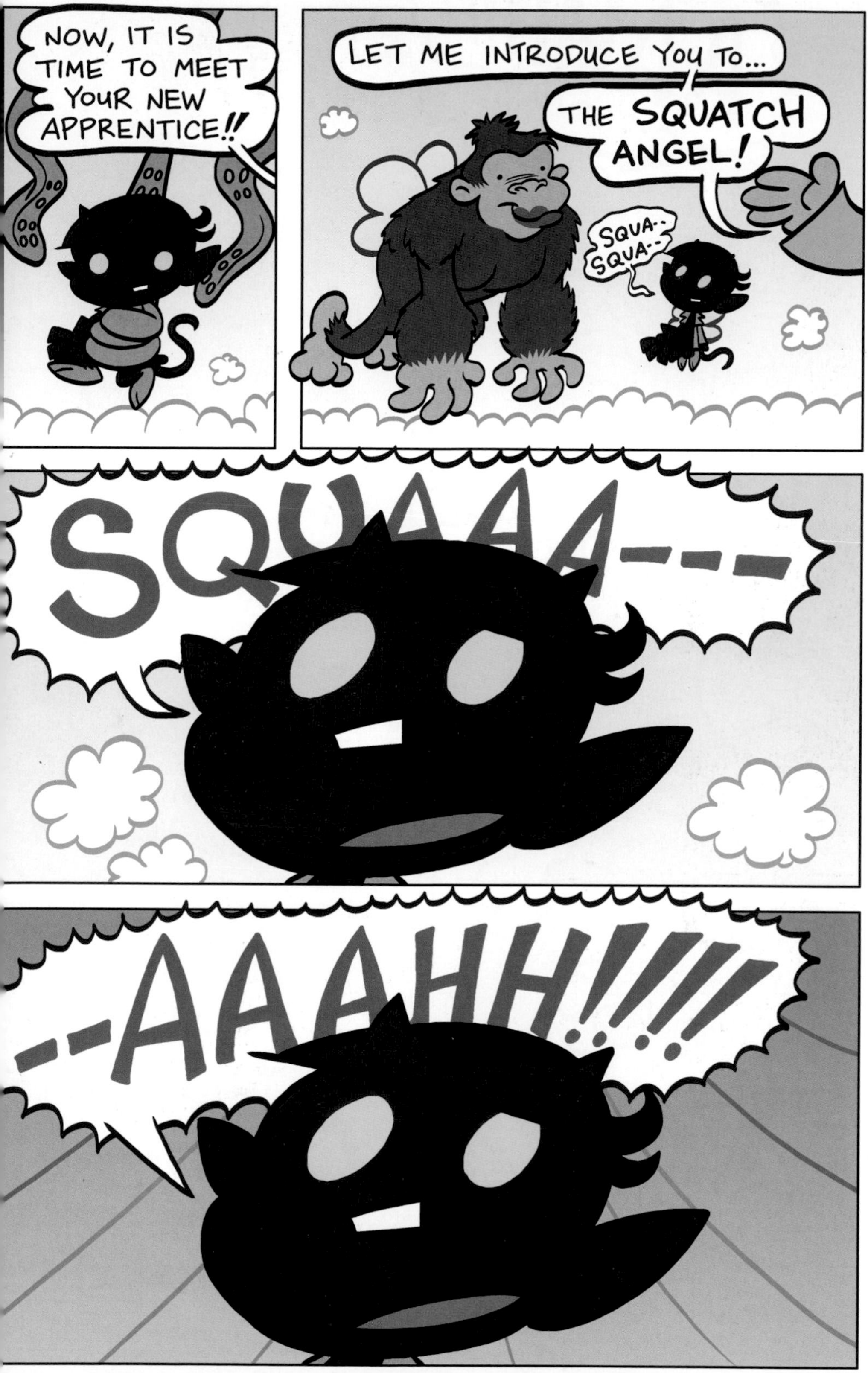
NOW, IT IS TIME TO MEET YOUR NEW APPRENTICE!!
LET ME INTRODUCE YOU TO...
THE SQUATCH ANGEL!
SQUA-- SQUA--
SQUAAA---
--AAAHH!!!!

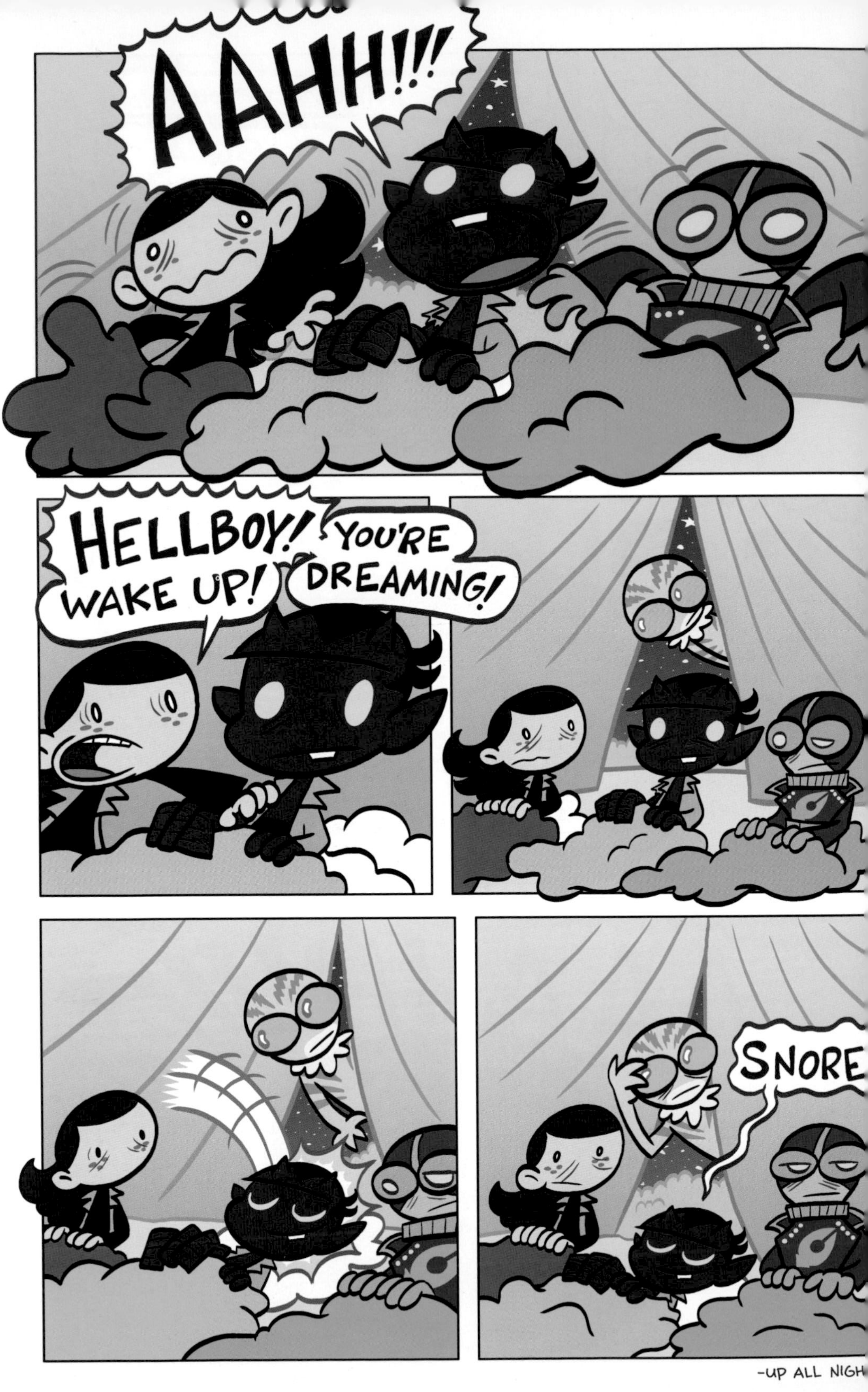
AAHH!!!
HELLBOY! WAKE UP!
YOU'RE DREAMING!
SNORE

-UP ALL NIGH

CHAPTER FIVE

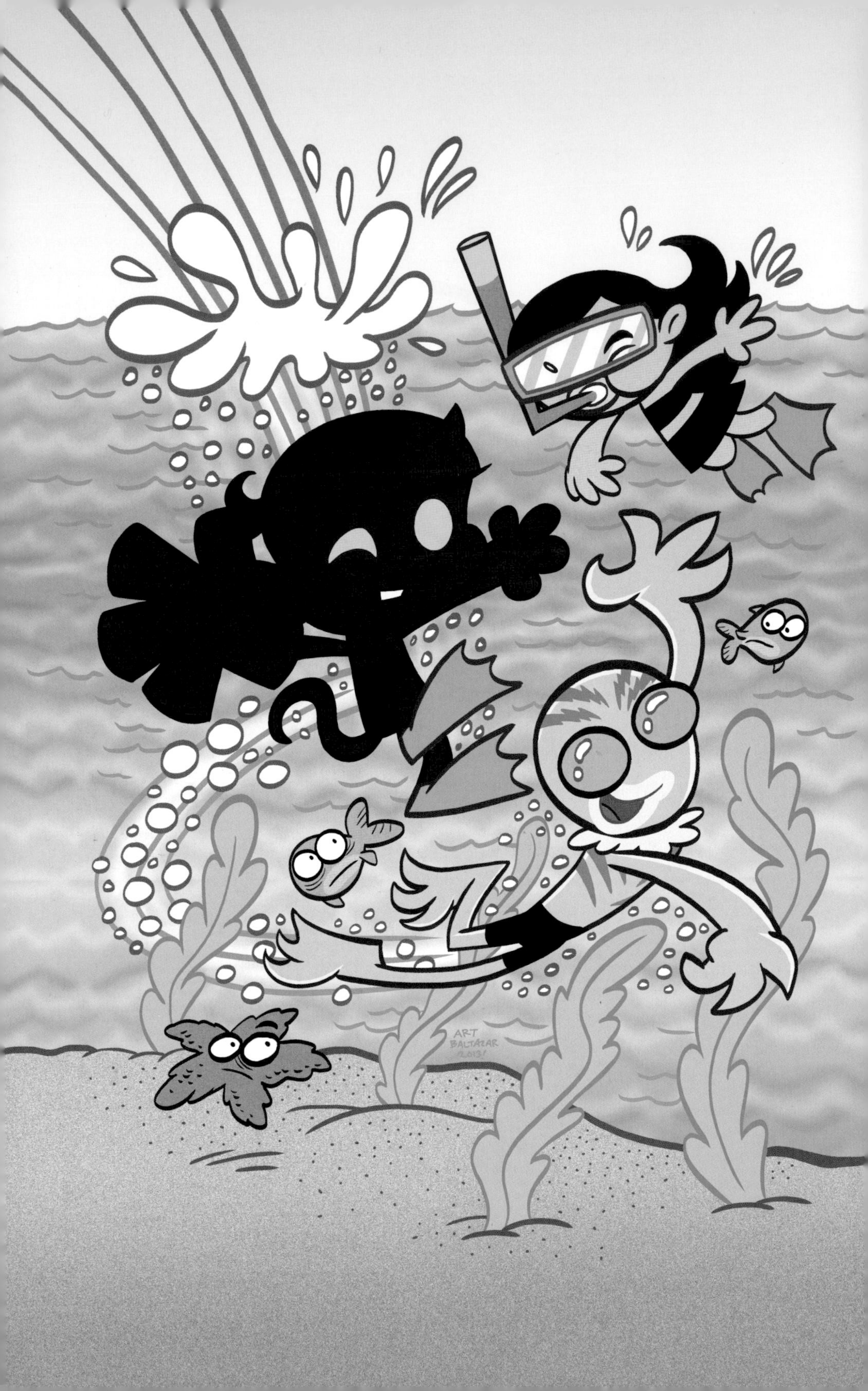
ART
BALTAZAR

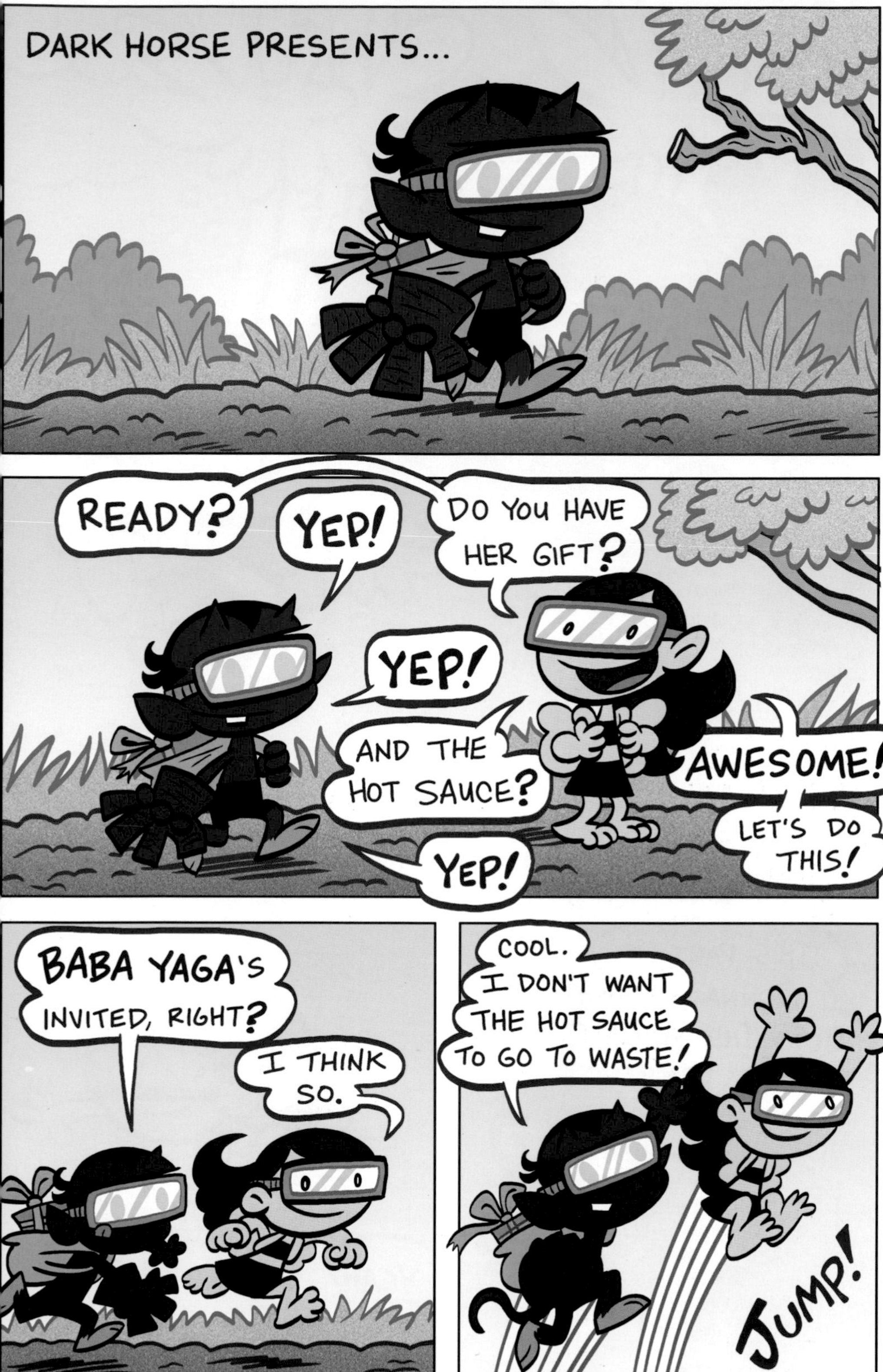
DARK HORSE PRESENTS...
READY?
YEP!
DO YOU HAVE HER GIFT?
YEP!
AND THE HOT SAUCE?
YEP!
AWESOME!
LET'S DO THIS!
BABA YAGA'S INVITED, RIGHT?
I THINK SO.
COOL. I DON'T WANT THE HOT SAUCE TO GO TO WASTE!
JUMP!

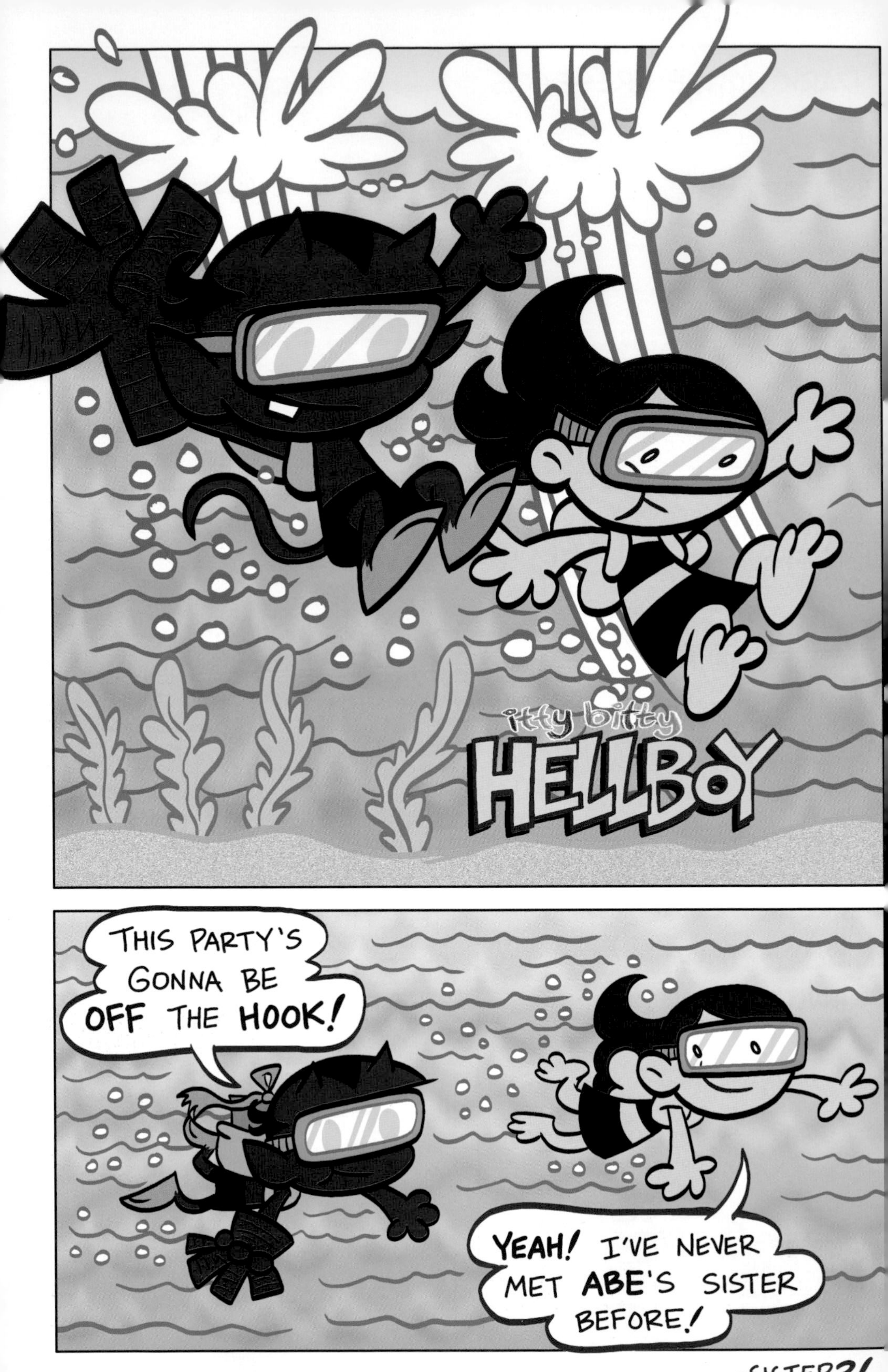
itty bitty
HELLBOY
THIS PARTY'S GONNA BE OFF THE HOOK!
YEAH! I'VE NEVER MET ABE'S SISTER BEFORE!

-SISTER?!

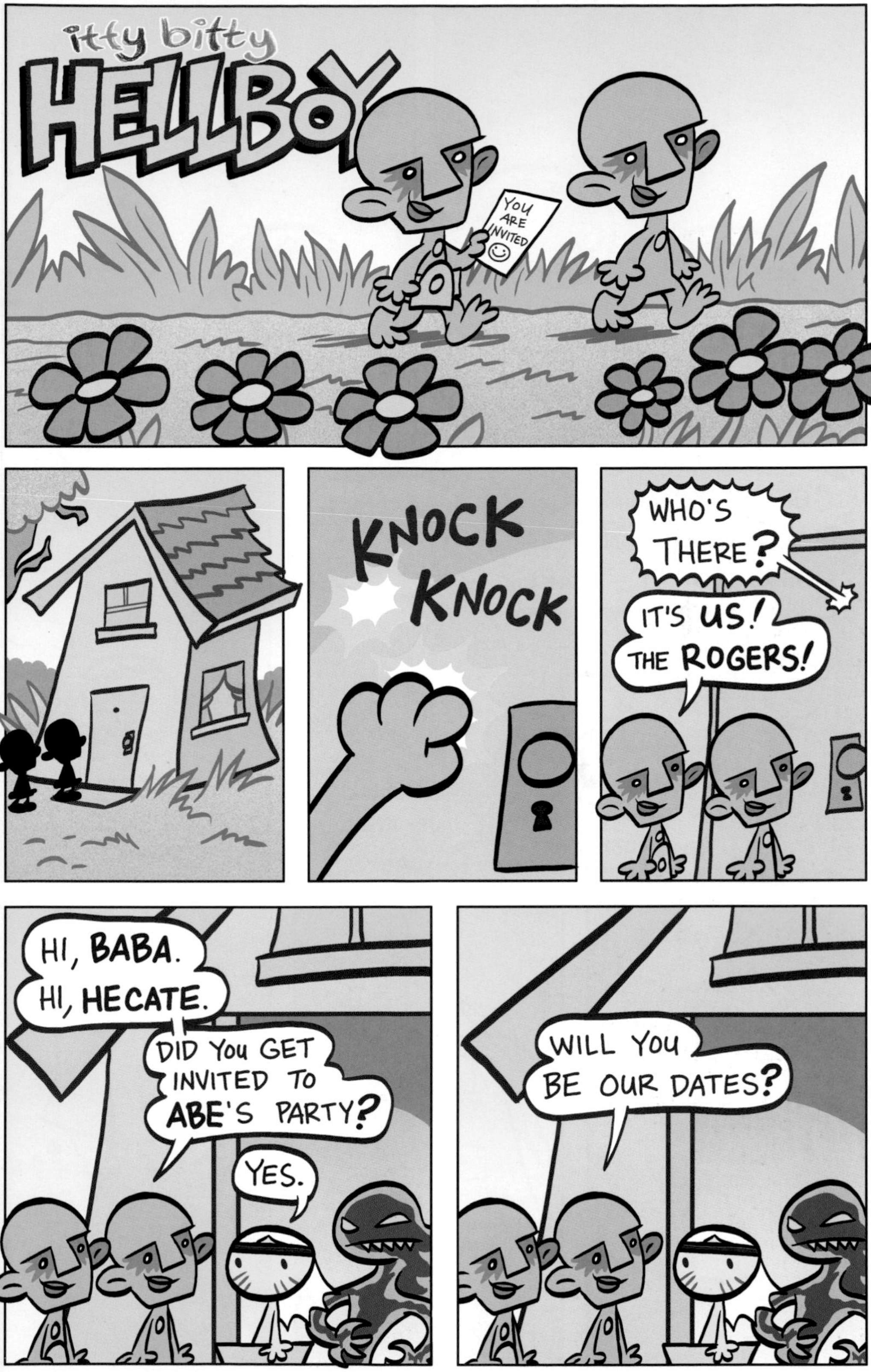
itty bitty
HELLBOY
YOU ARE INVITED
KNOCK
KNOCK
WHO'S THERE?
IT'S US! THE ROGERS!
HI, BABA.
HI, HECATE.
DID YOU GET INVITED TO ABE'S PARTY?
YES.
WILL YOU BE OUR DATES?

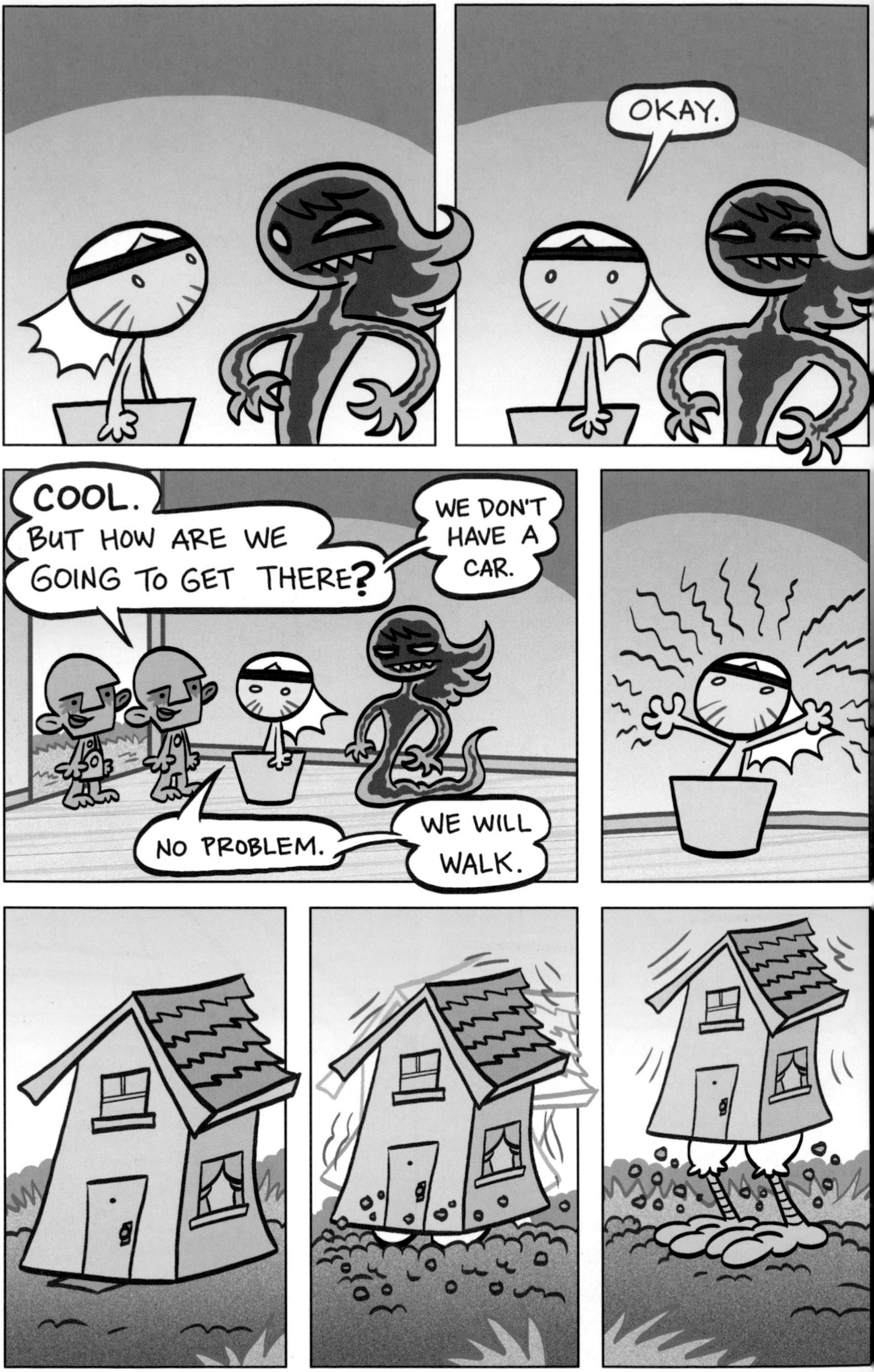
OKAY.
COOL. BUT HOW ARE WE GOING TO GET THERE?
WE DON'T HAVE A CAR.
NO PROBLEM.
WE WILL WALK.

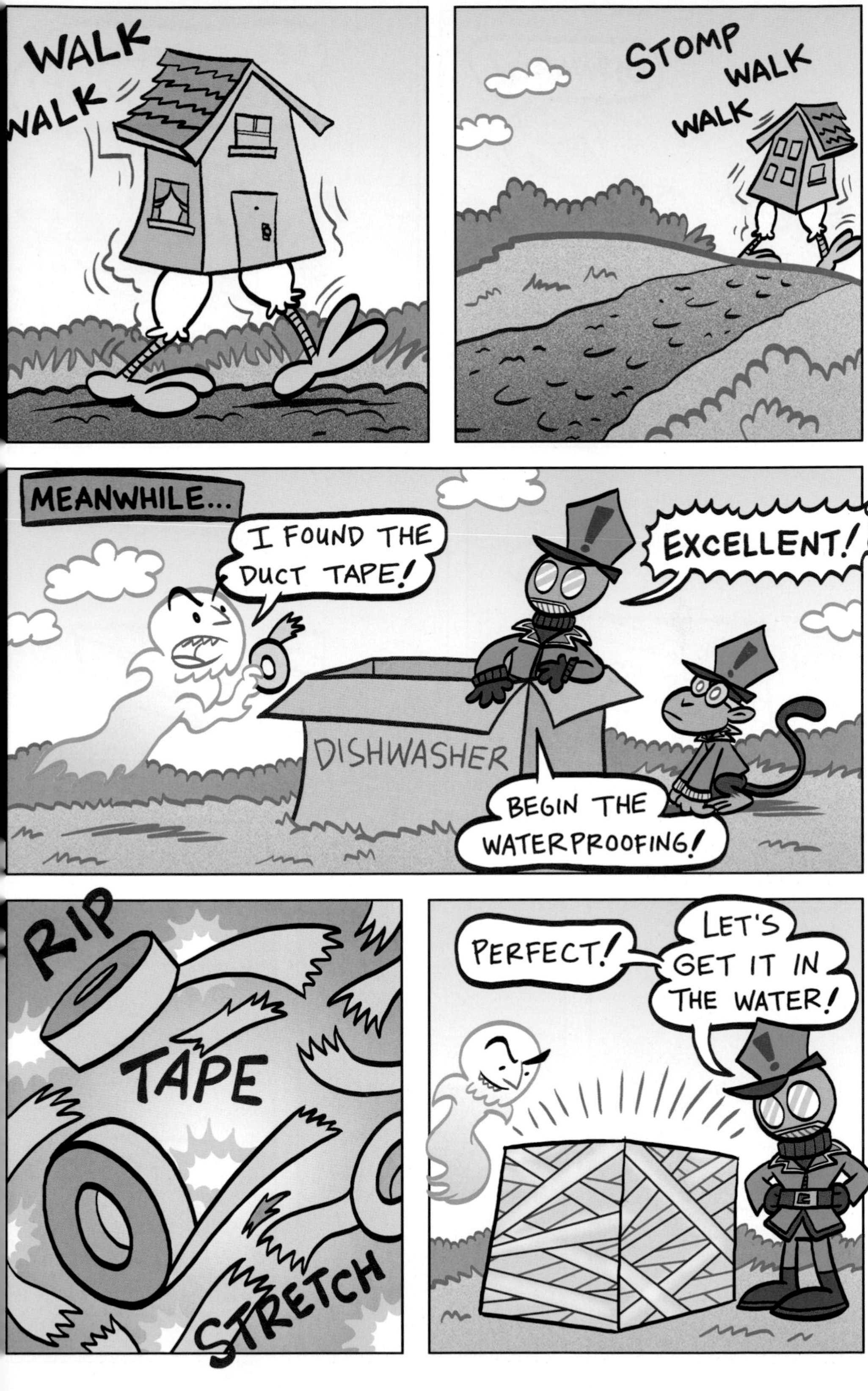
WALK
WALK
STOMP
WALK
WALK
MEANWHILE...
I FOUND THE DUCT TAPE!
EXCELLENT!
DISHWASHER
BEGIN THE WATERPROOFING!
RIP
TAPE
STRETCH
PERFECT!
LET'S GET IT IN THE WATER!

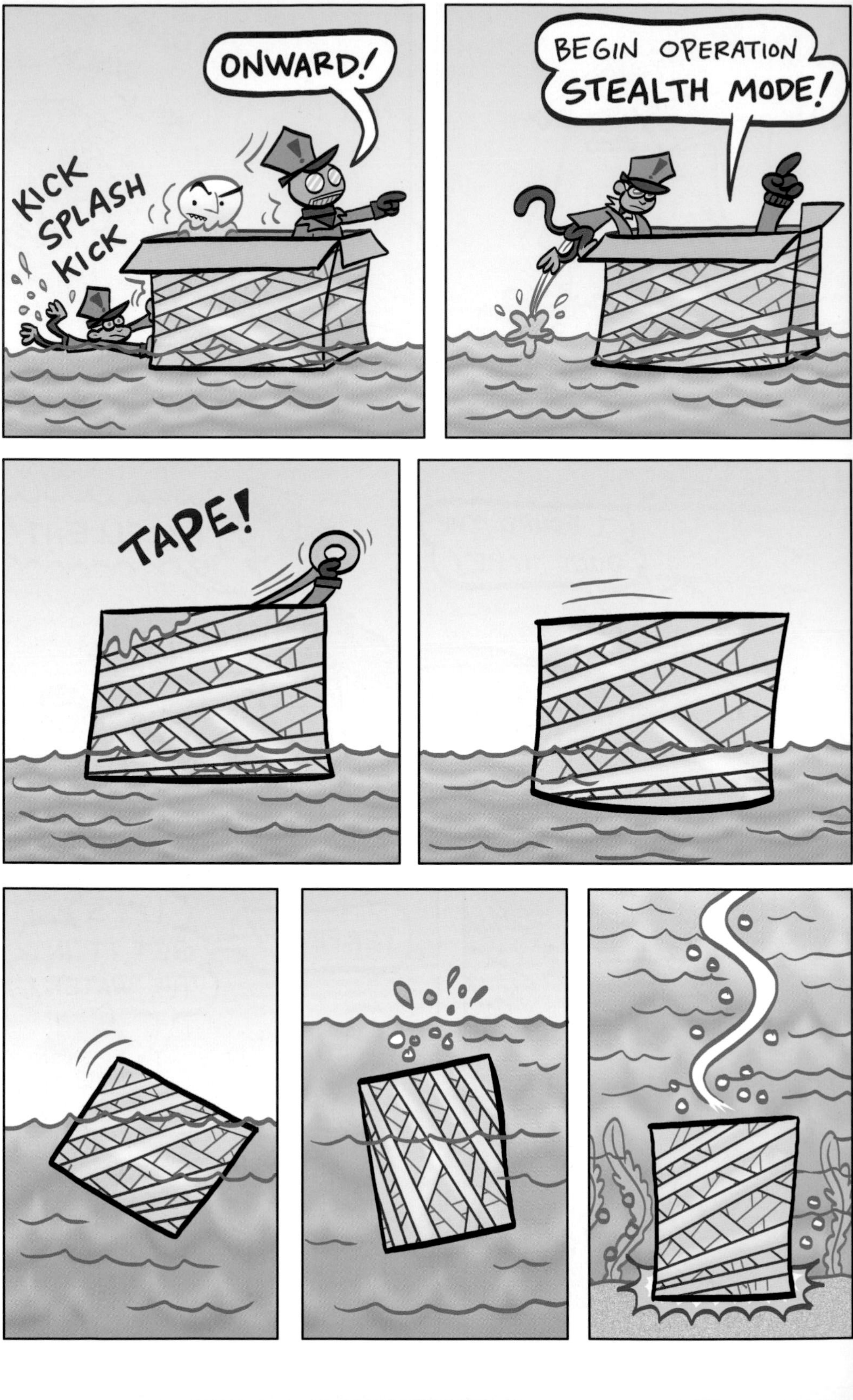
ONWARD!
KICK
SPLASH
KICK
BEGIN OPERATION STEALTH MODE!
TAPE!

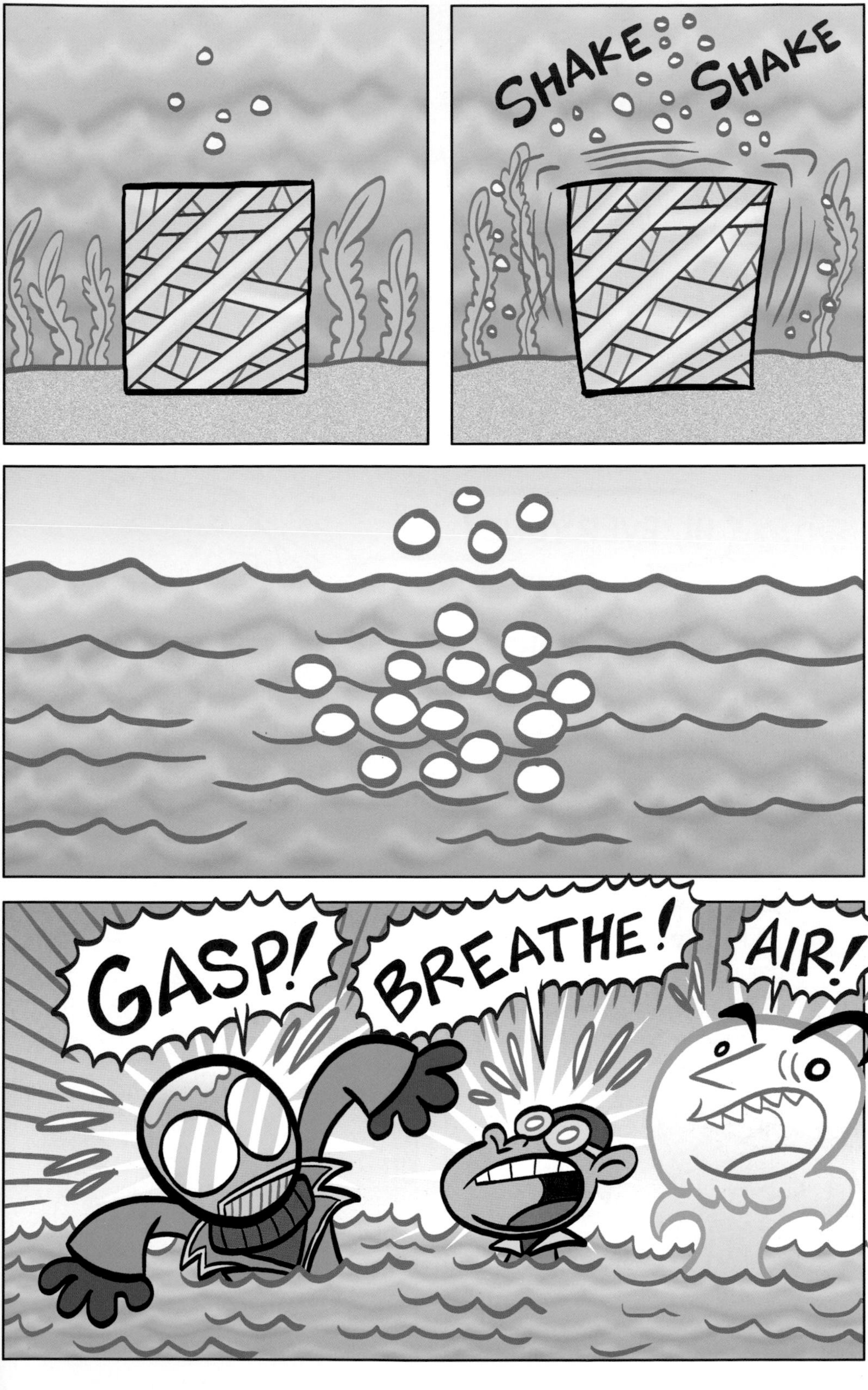
SHAKE
SHAKE
GASP!
BREATHE!
AIR!

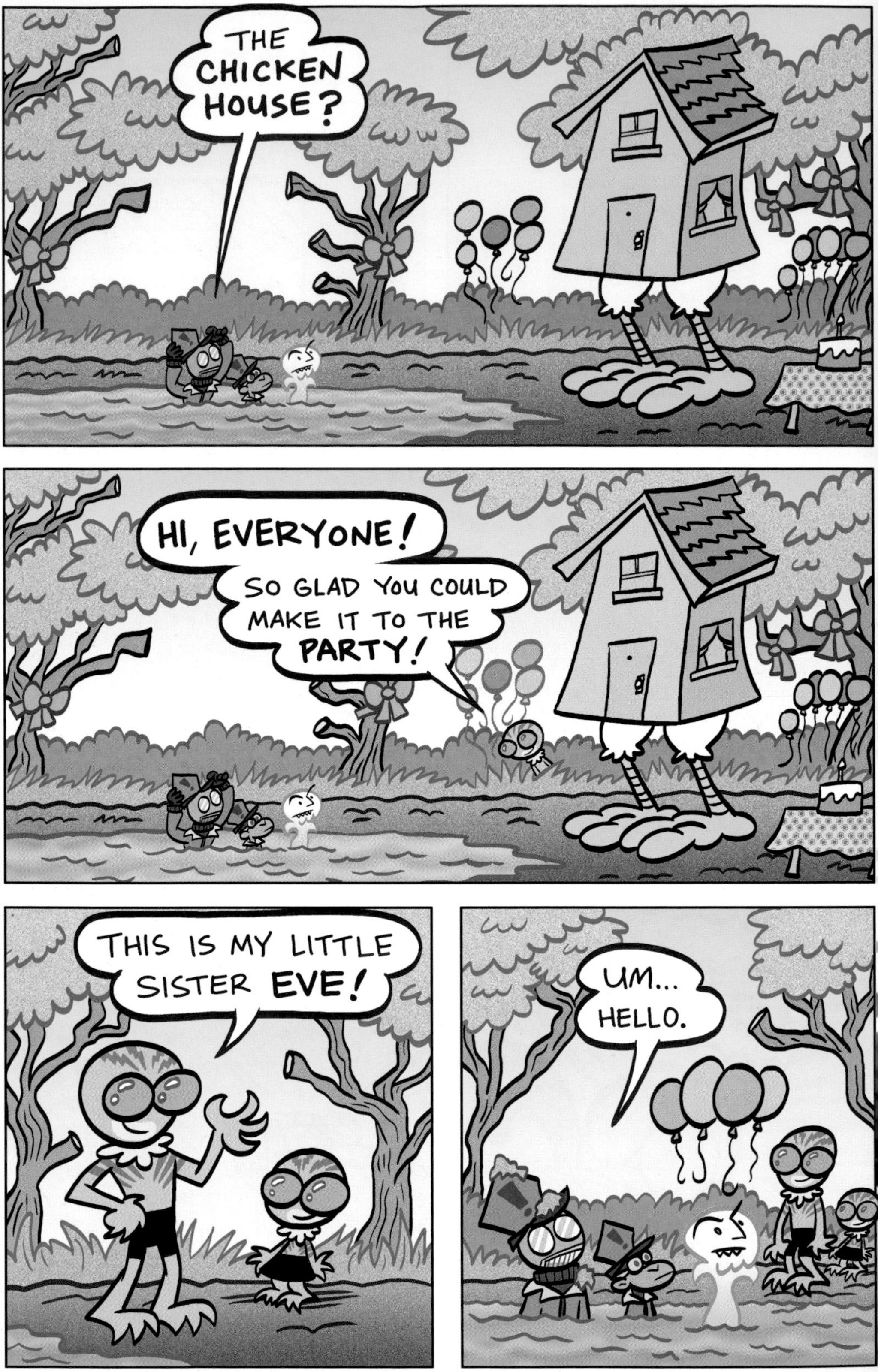
THE CHICKEN HOUSE?
HI, EVERYONE!
SO GLAD YOU COULD MAKE IT TO THE PARTY!
THIS IS MY LITTLE SISTER EVE!
UM... HELLO.

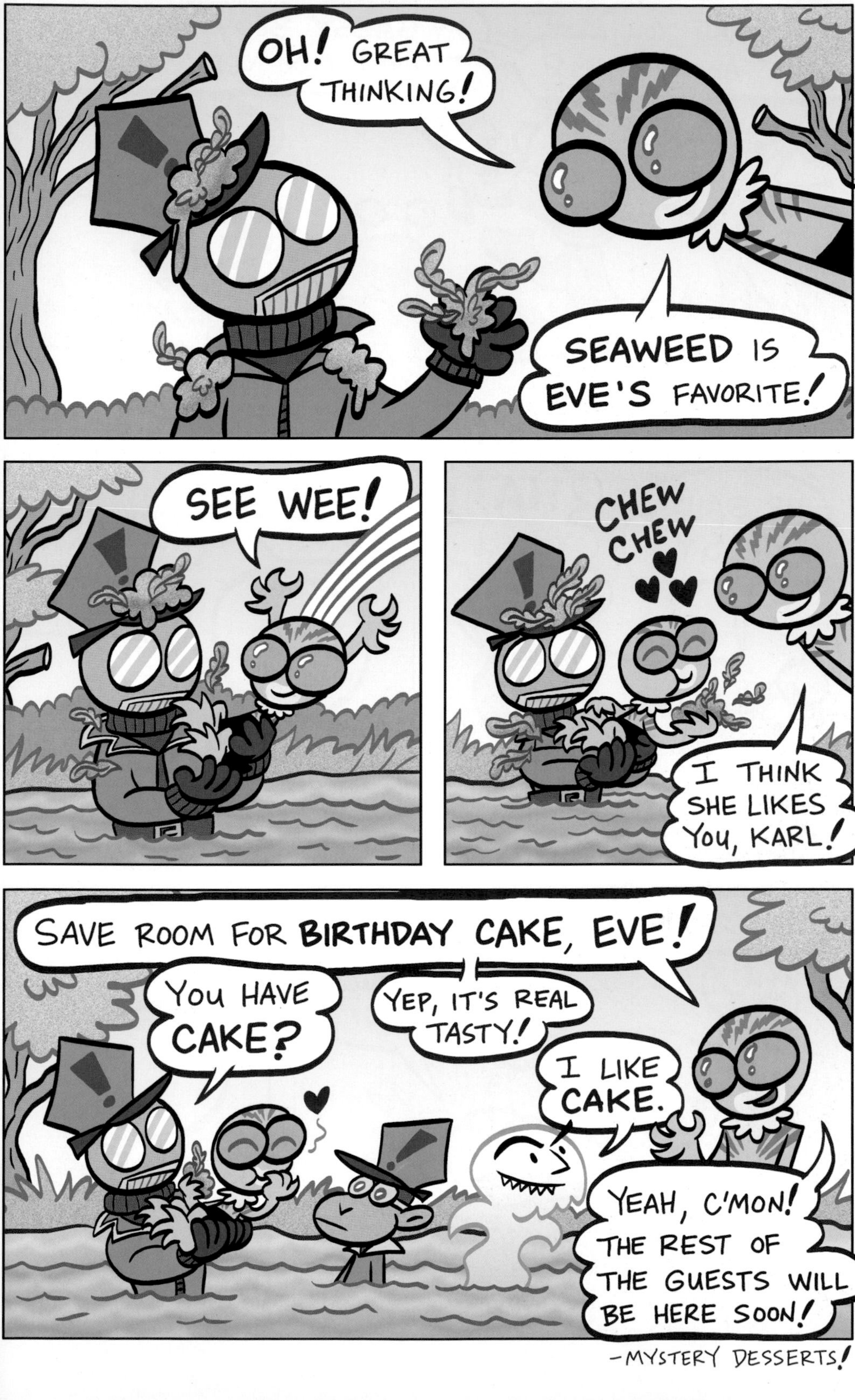
OH! GREAT THINKING!
SEAWEED IS EVE'S FAVORITE!
SEE WEE!
CHEW CHEW
I THINK SHE LIKES YOU, KARL!
SAVE ROOM FOR BIRTHDAY CAKE, EVE!
YOU HAVE CAKE?
YEP, IT'S REAL TASTY!
I LIKE CAKE.
YEAH, C'MON! THE REST OF THE GUESTS WILL BE HERE SOON!
-MYSTERY DESSERTS!

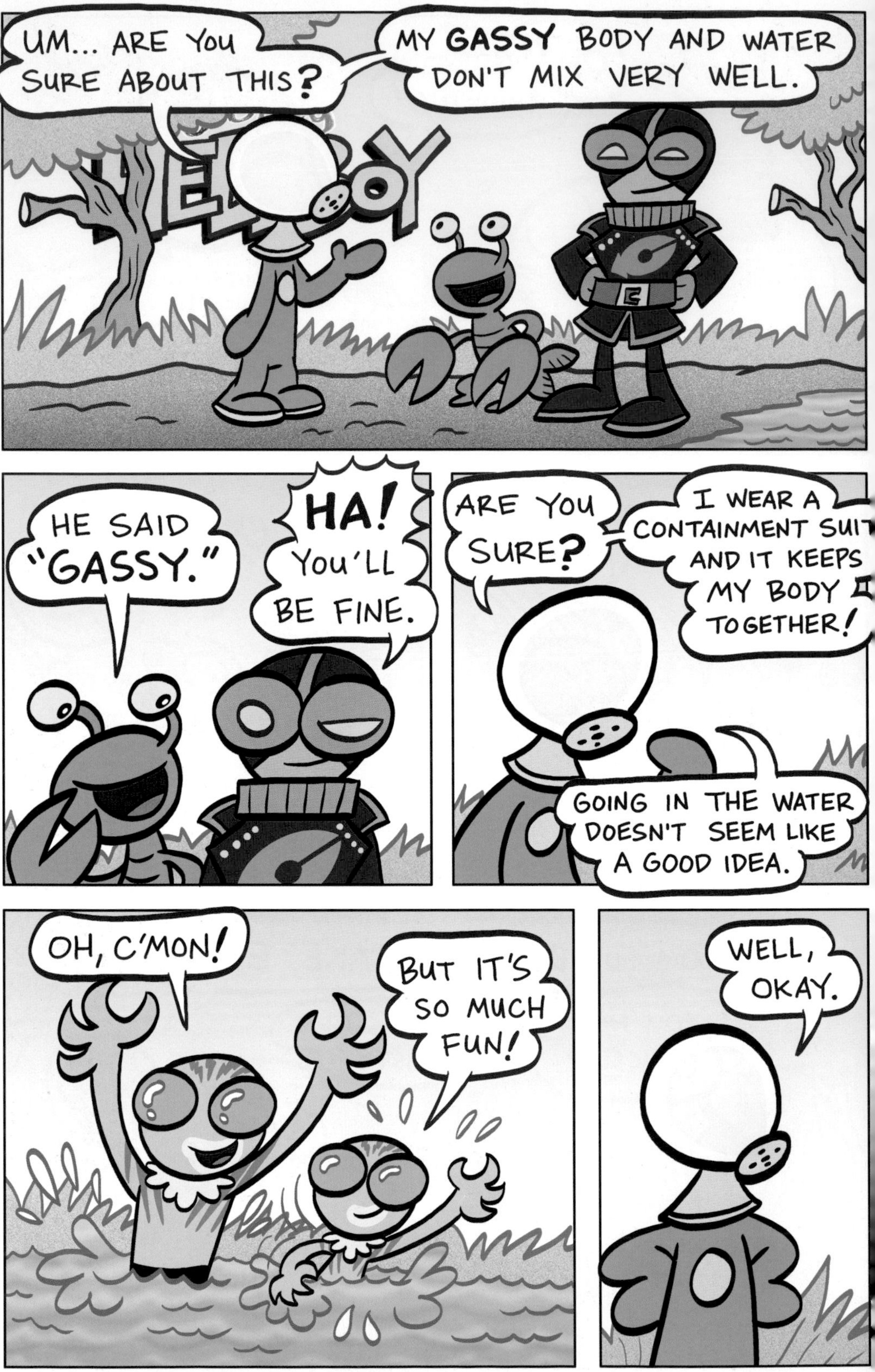
UM... ARE YOU SURE ABOUT THIS?
MY GASSY BODY AND WATER DON'T MIX VERY WELL.
HE SAID "GASSY."
HA! YOU'LL BE FINE.
ARE YOU SURE?
I WEAR A CONTAINMENT SUIT AND IT KEEPS MY BODY TOGETHER!
GOING IN THE WATER DOESN'T SEEM LIKE A GOOD IDEA.
OH, C'MON!
BUT IT'S SO MUCH FUN!
WELL, OKAY.

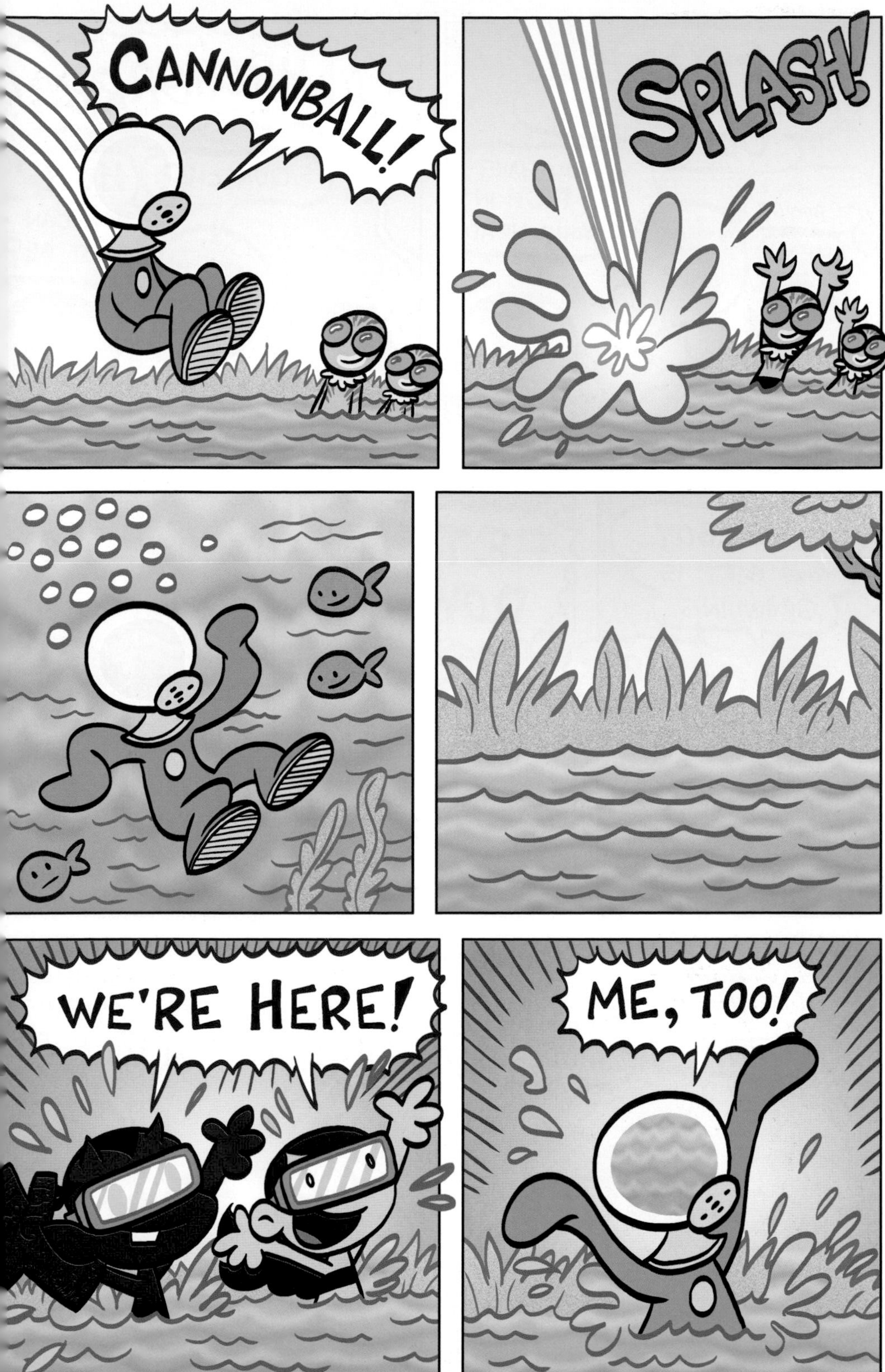
CANNONBALL!
SPLASH!
WE'RE HERE!
ME, TOO!

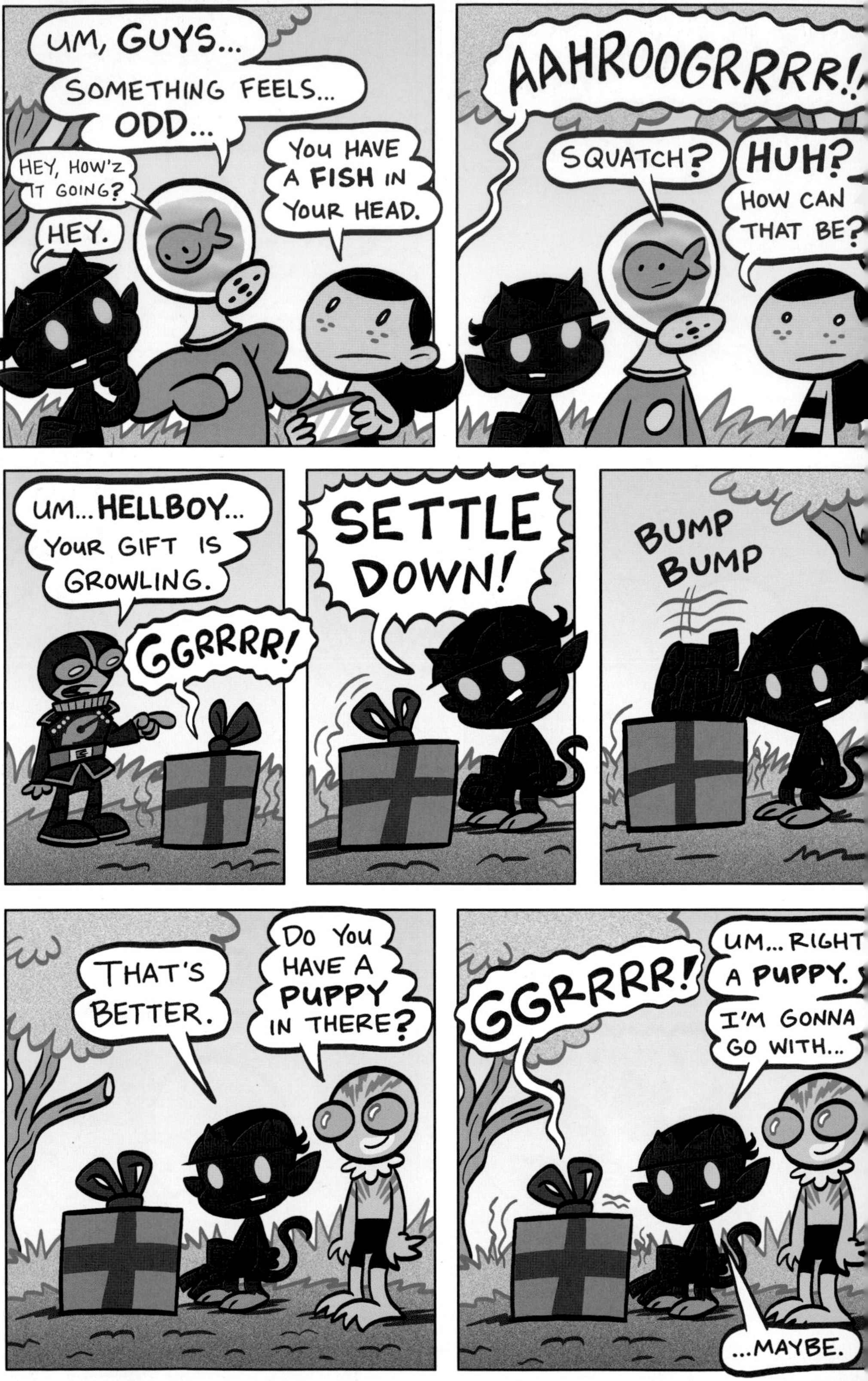
UM, GUYS...
SOMETHING FEELS... ODD...
HEY, HOW'Z IT GOING?
HEY.
YOU HAVE A FISH IN YOUR HEAD.
AAHROOGRRRR!
SQUATCH?
HUH? HOW CAN THAT BE?
UM... HELLBOY... YOUR GIFT IS GROWLING.
GGRRRR!
SETTLE DOWN!
BUMP BUMP
THAT'S BETTER.
DO YOU HAVE A PUPPY IN THERE?
GGRRRR!
UM... RIGHT A PUPPY.
I'M GONNA GO WITH...
...MAYBE.

—NOT A SQUATCH

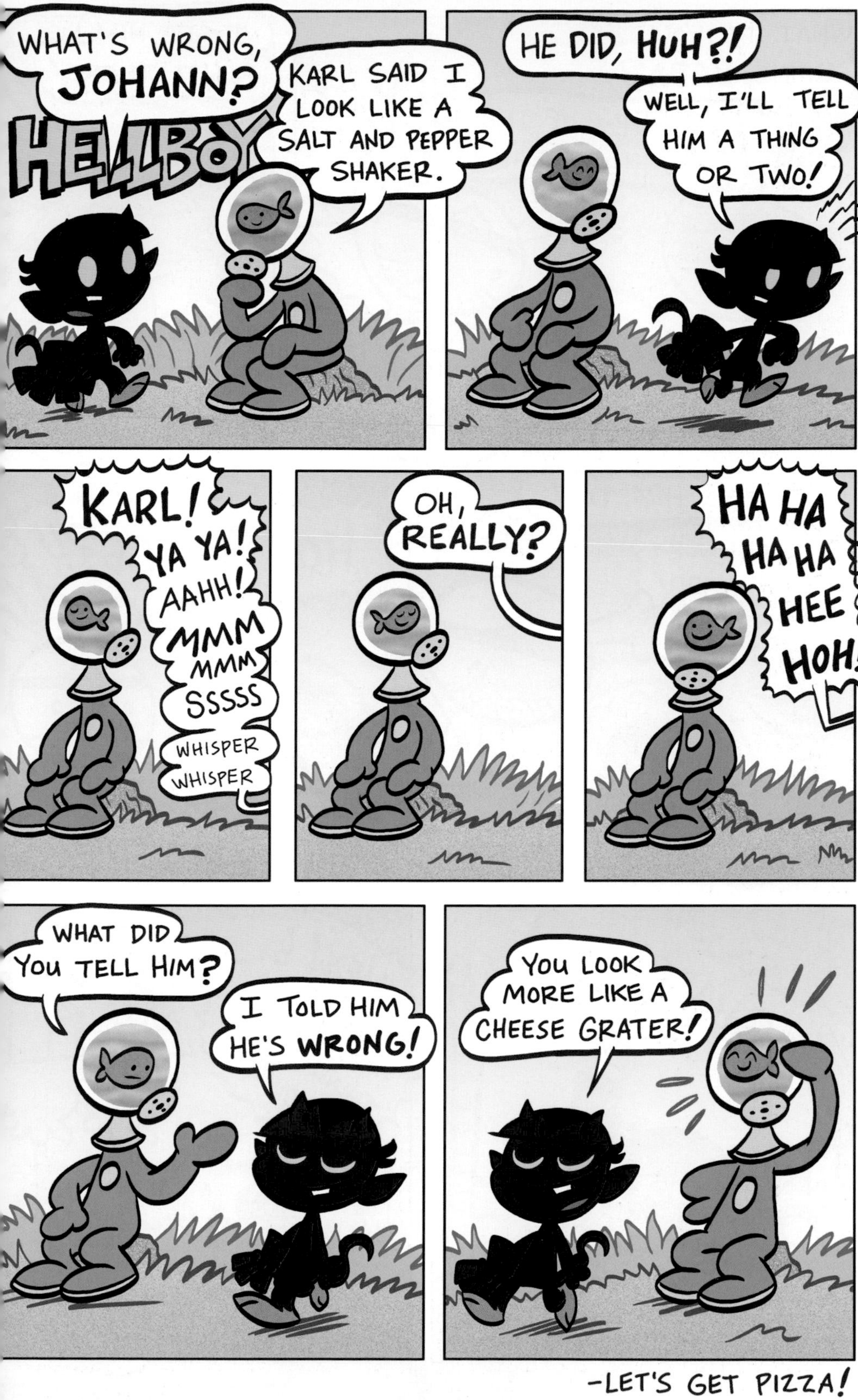
WHAT'S WRONG, JOHANN?
HELLBOY
KARL SAID I LOOK LIKE A SALT AND PEPPER SHAKER.
HE DID, HUH?!
WELL, I'LL TELL HIM A THING OR TWO!
KARL!
YA YA! AAHH! MMM MMM SSSSS
WHISPER WHISPER
OH, REALLY?
HA HA HA HA HEE HOH!
WHAT DID YOU TELL HIM?
I TOLD HIM HE'S WRONG!
YOU LOOK MORE LIKE A CHEESE GRATER!

-LET'S GET PIZZA!

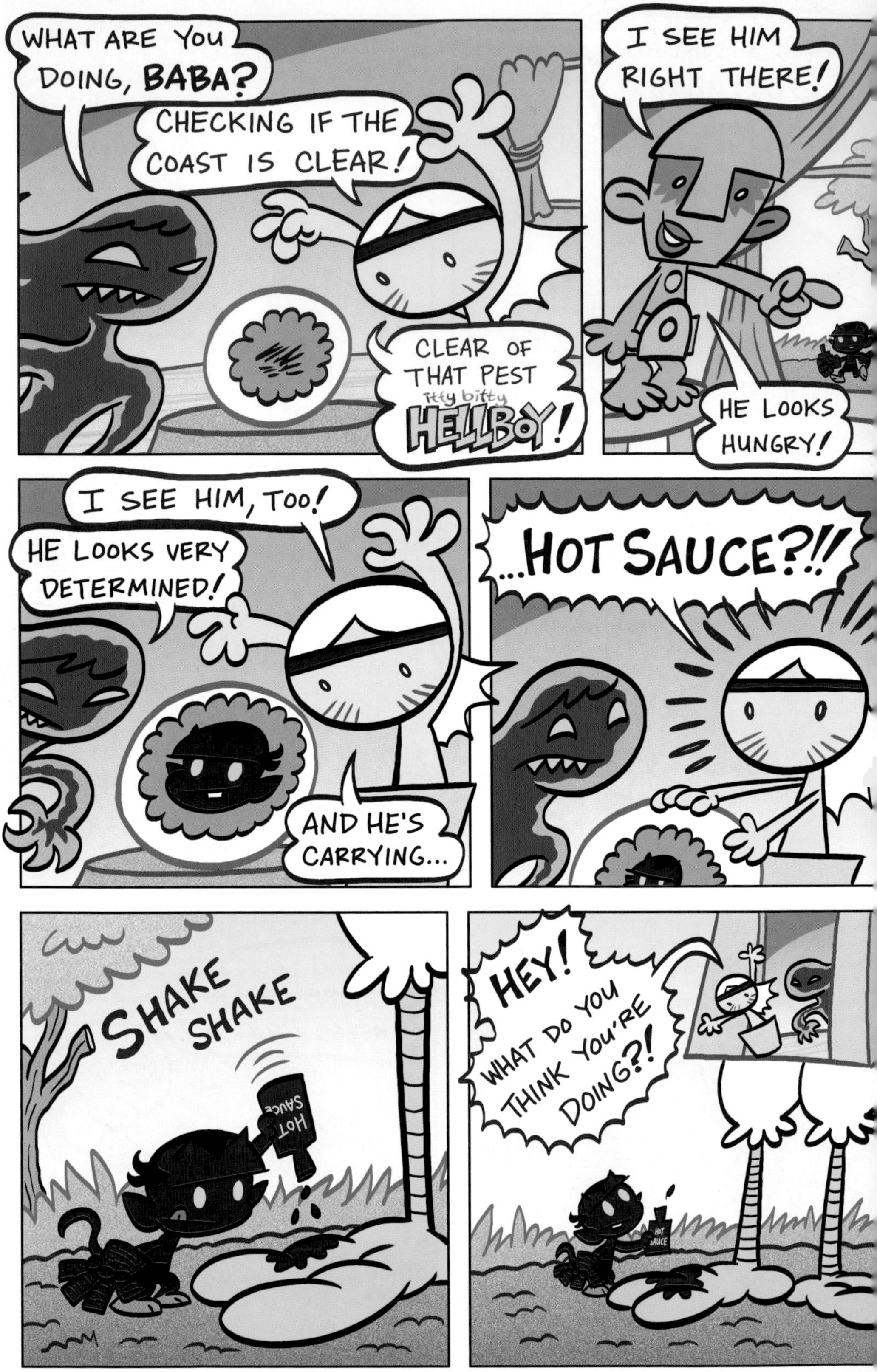
WHAT ARE YOU DOING, BABA?
CHECKING IF THE COAST IS CLEAR!
CLEAR OF THAT PEST itty bitty HELLBOY!
I SEE HIM RIGHT THERE!
HE LOOKS HUNGRY!
I SEE HIM, TOO!
HE LOOKS VERY DETERMINED!
AND HE'S CARRYING...
...HOT SAUCE?!!
SHAKE
SHAKE
HOT SAUCE
HEY!
WHAT DO YOU THINK YOU'RE DOING?!
HOT SAUCE

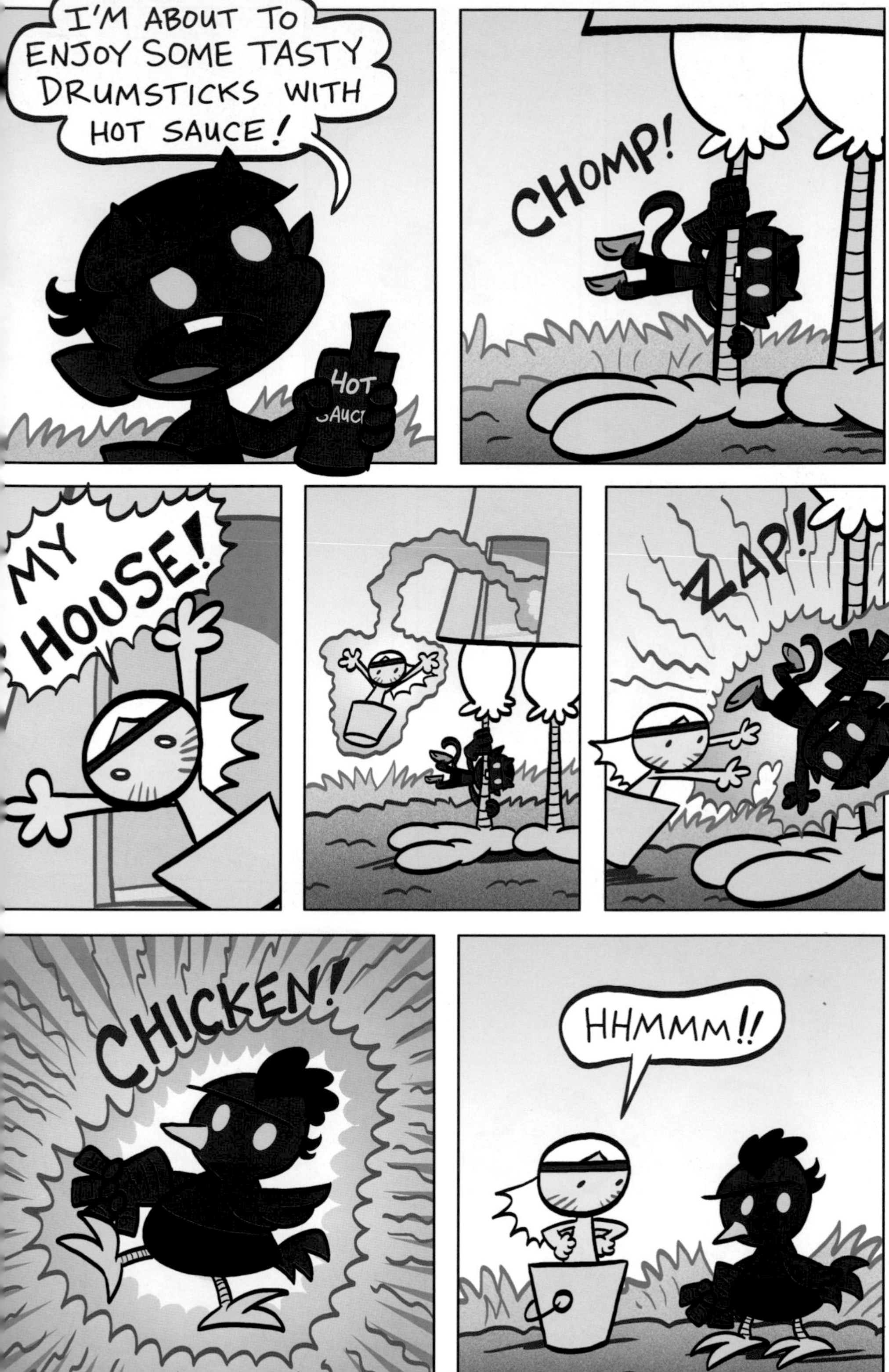
I'M ABOUT TO ENJOY SOME TASTY DRUMSTICKS WITH HOT SAUCE!
HOT SAUCE
CHOMP!
?
MY HOUSE!
ZAP!
CHICKEN!
HHMMM!!

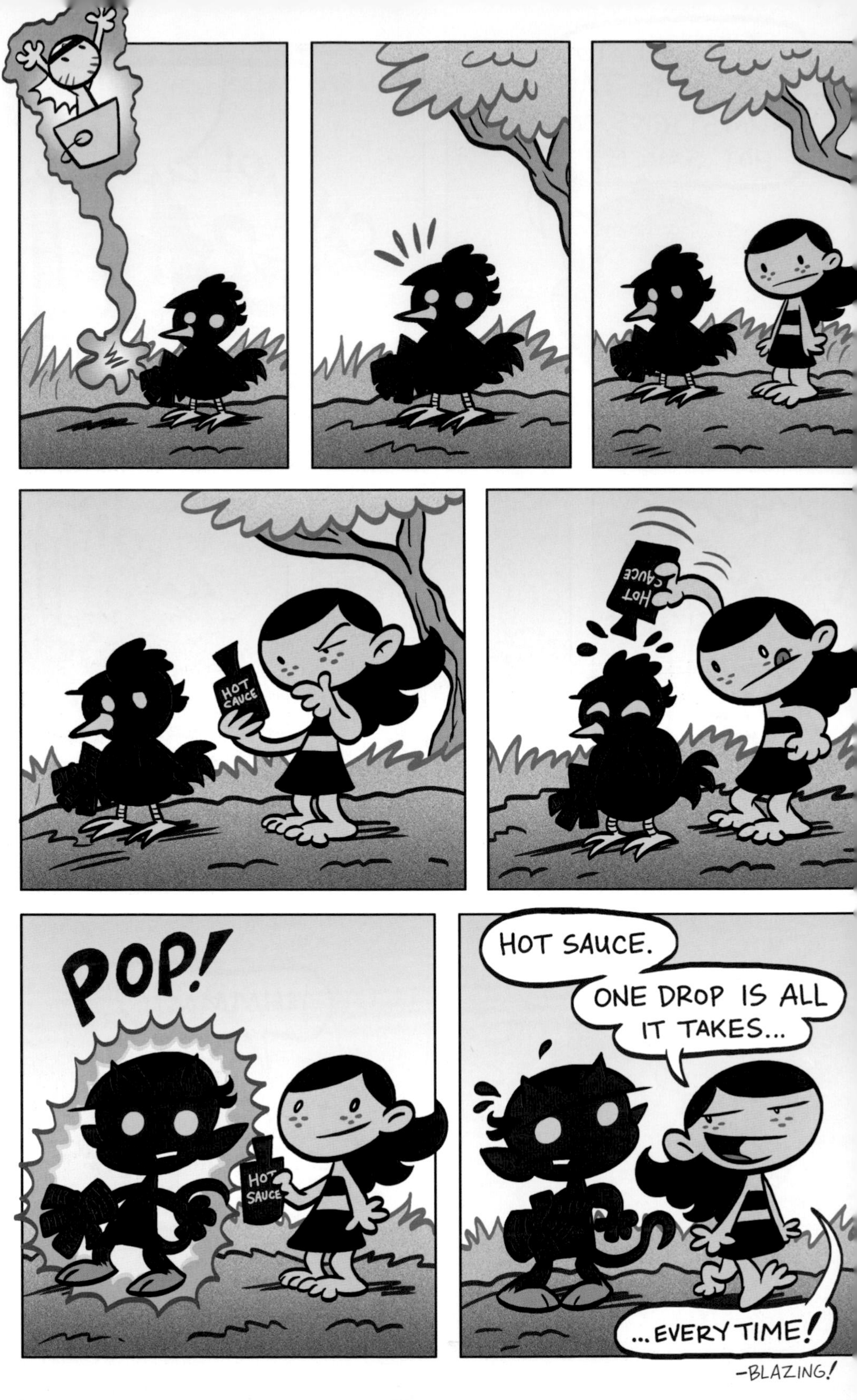

HOT SAUCE
HOT SAUCE
POP!
HOT SAUCE
HOT SAUCE.
ONE DROP IS ALL IT TAKES...
...EVERY TIME!

-BLAZING!

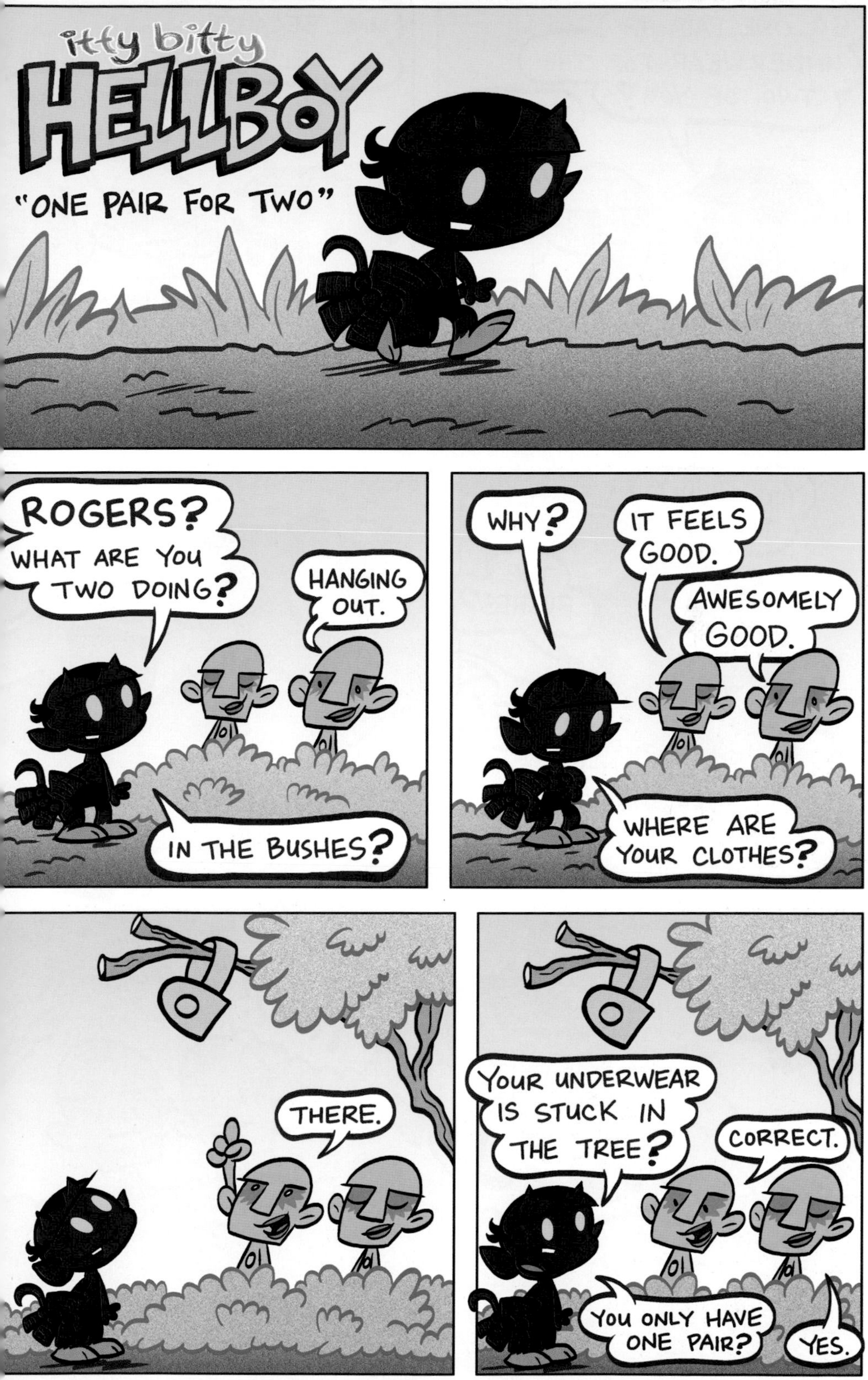
itty bitty
HELLBOY
"ONE PAIR FOR TWO"
ROGERS? WHAT ARE YOU TWO DOING?
HANGING OUT.
IN THE BUSHES?
WHY?
IT FEELS GOOD.
AWESOMELY GOOD.
WHERE ARE YOUR CLOTHES?
THERE.
YOUR UNDERWEAR IS STUCK IN THE TREE?
CORRECT.
YOU ONLY HAVE ONE PAIR?
YES.

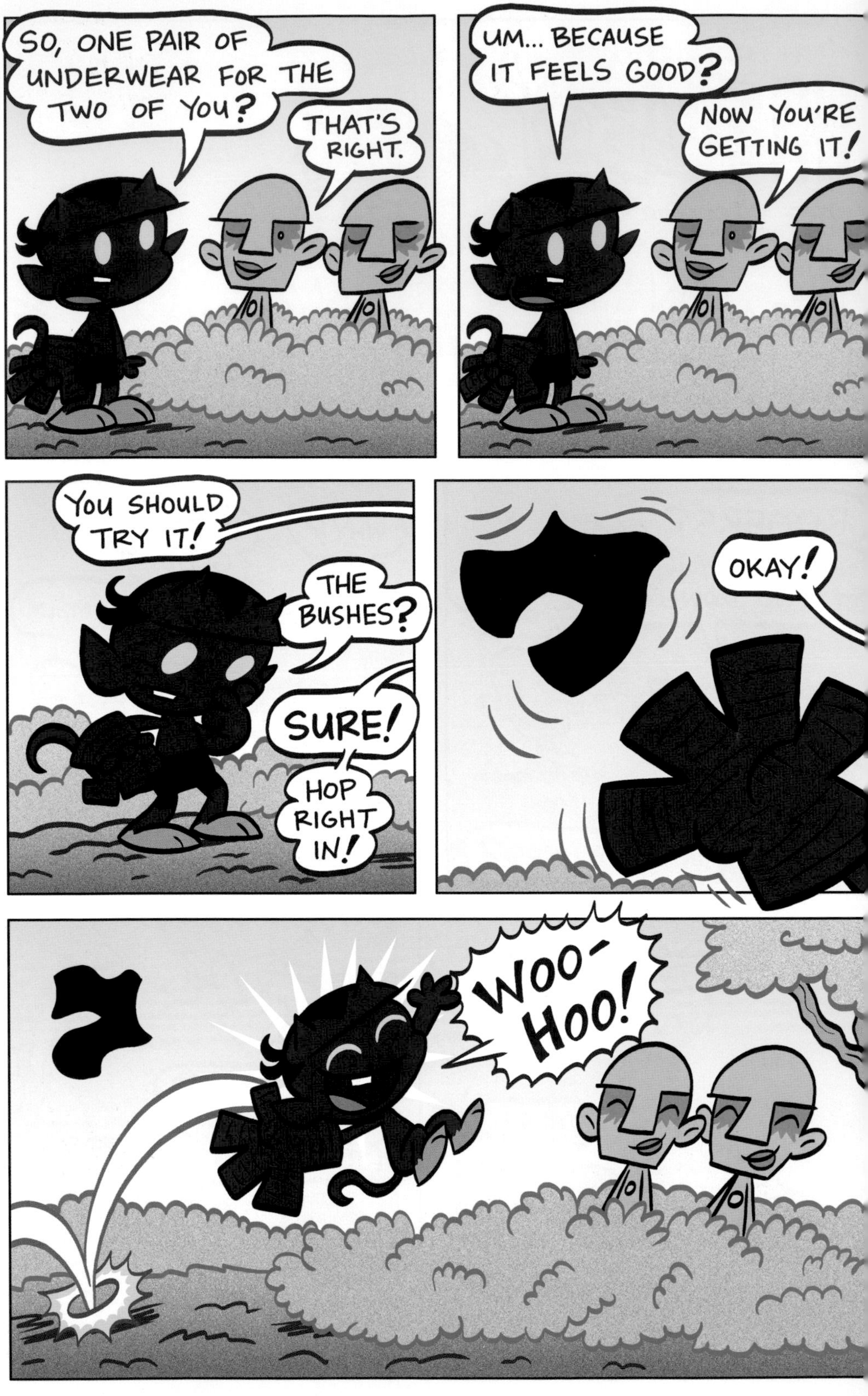
SO, ONE PAIR OF UNDERWEAR FOR THE TWO OF YOU?
THAT'S RIGHT.
UM... BECAUSE IT FEELS GOOD?
NOW YOU'RE GETTING IT!
YOU SHOULD TRY IT!
THE BUSHES?
SURE!
HOP RIGHT IN!
OKAY!
WOO-HOO!

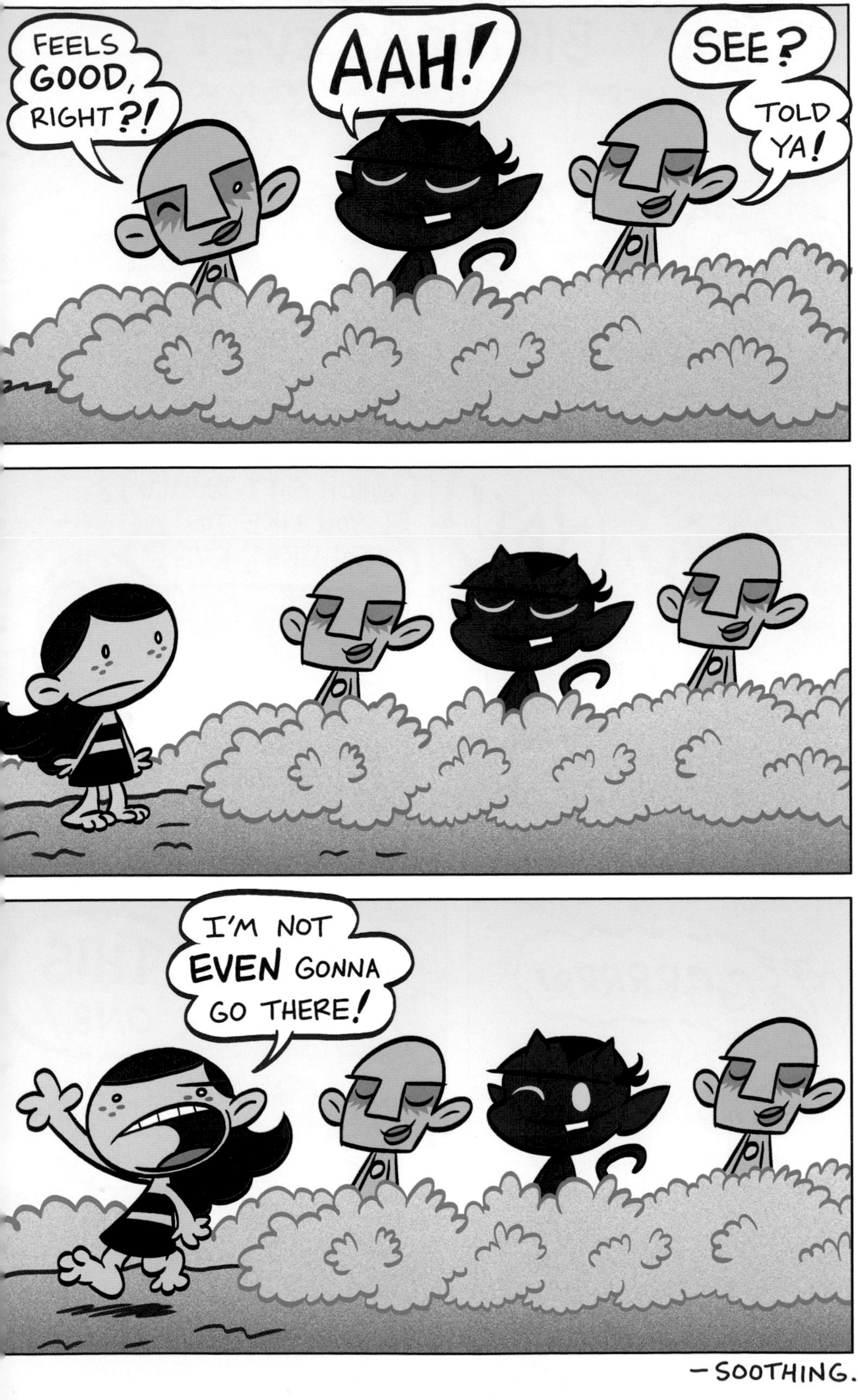
FEELS GOOD, RIGHT?!
AAH!
SEE?
TOLD YA!
I'M NOT EVEN GONNA GO THERE!

— SOOTHING.

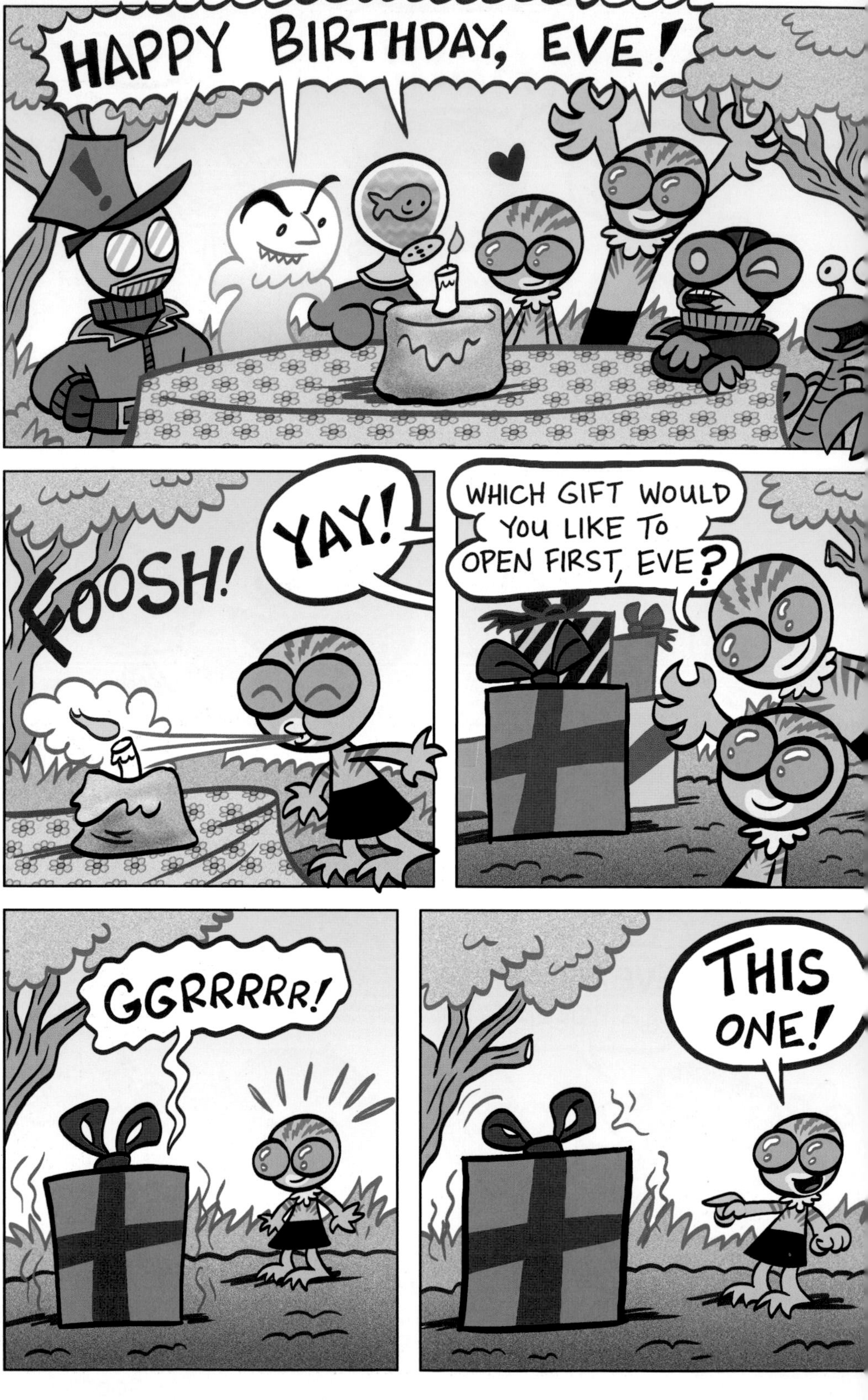
HAPPY BIRTHDAY, EVE!
FOOSH!
YAY!
WHICH GIFT WOULD YOU LIKE TO OPEN FIRST, EVE?
GGRRRRRR!
THIS ONE!

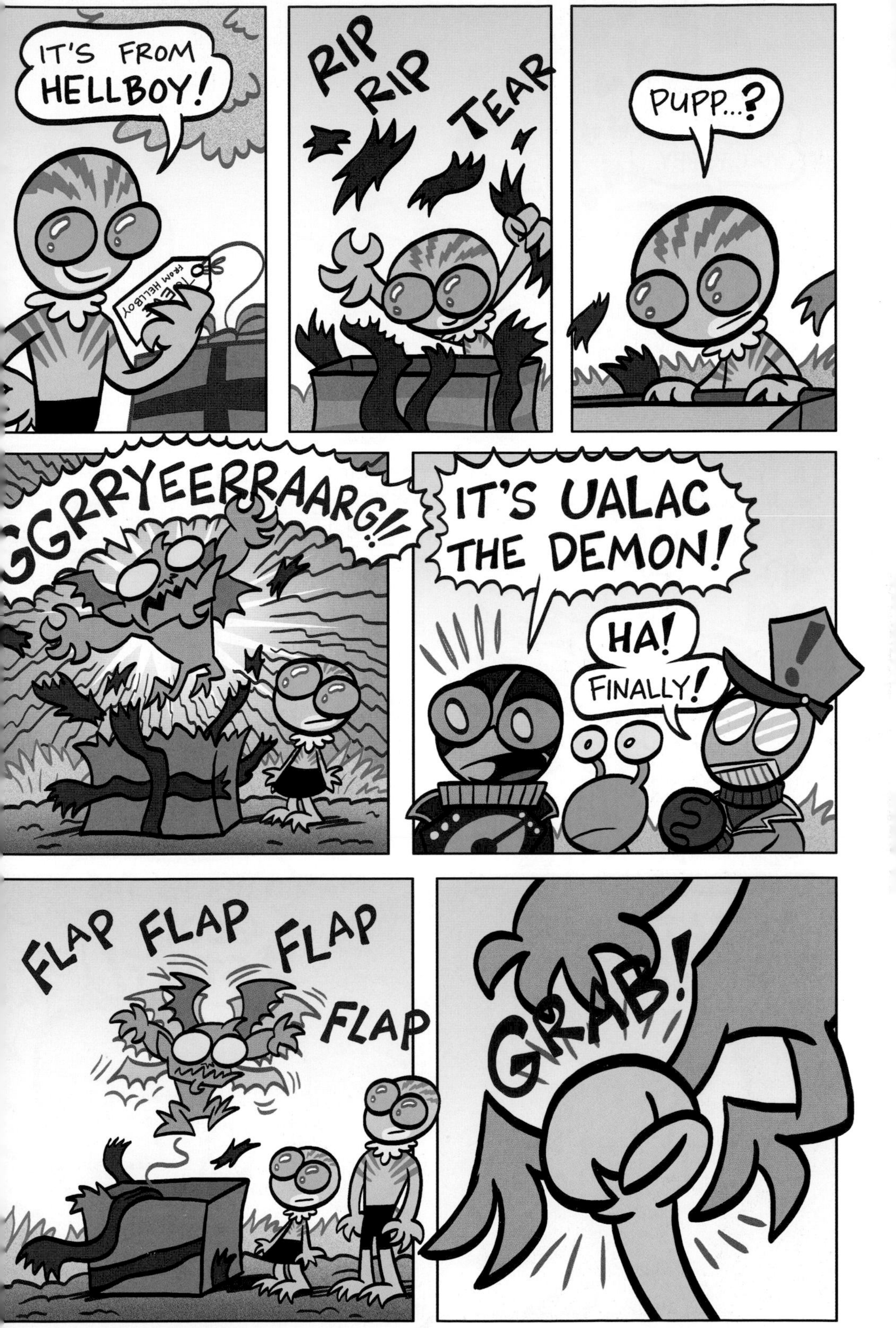
IT'S FROM HELLBOY!
TO: [illegible]
FROM HELLBOY
RIP
RIP
TEAR
PUPP...?
GGRRYEERRAARG!!
IT'S UALAC THE DEMON!
HA!
FINALLY!
FLAP FLAP FLAP
FLAP
GRAB!

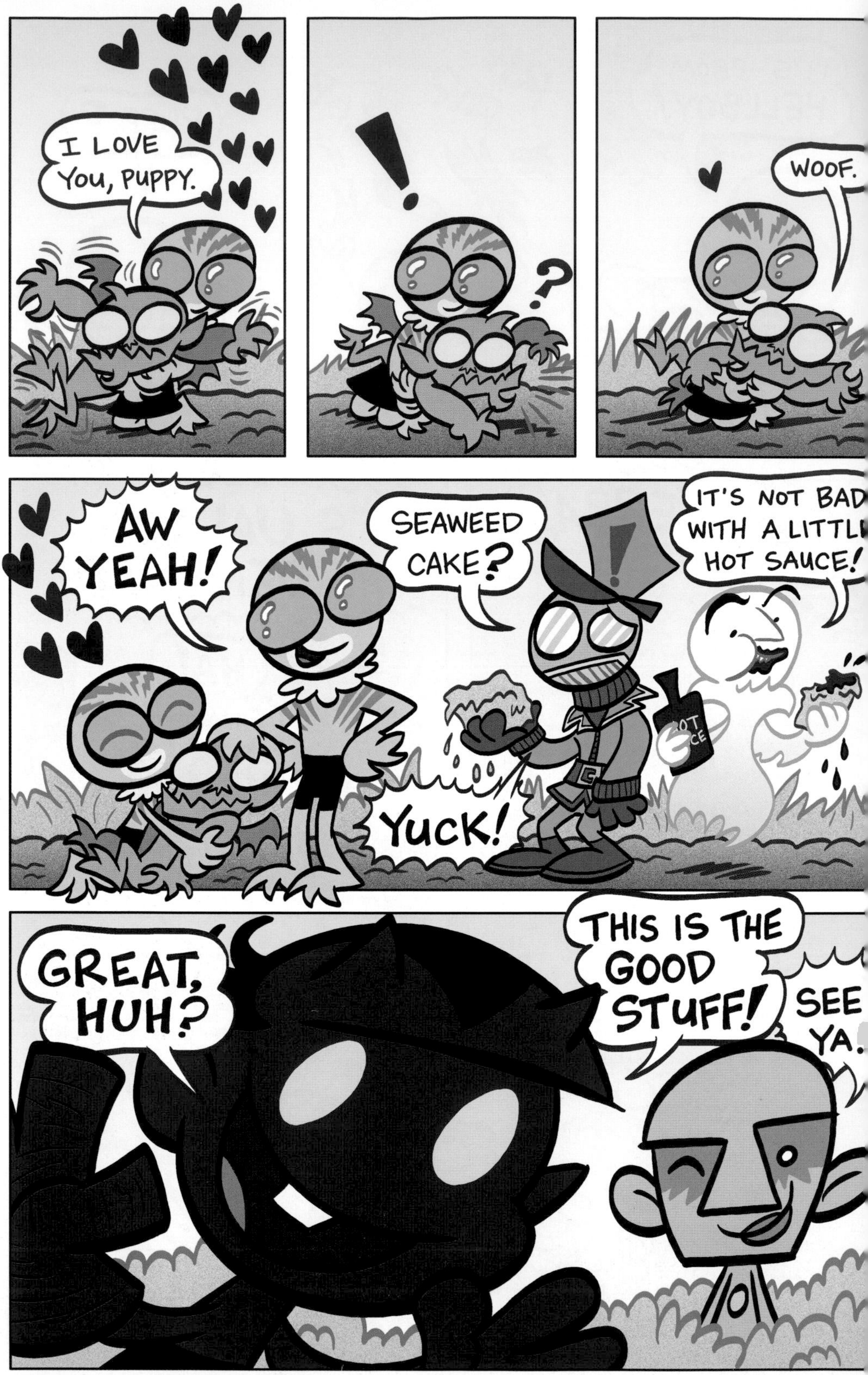
I LOVE YOU, PUPPY.
!
?
WOOF.
AW YEAH!
SEAWEED CAKE?
!
IT'S NOT BAD WITH A LITTLE HOT SAUCE!
YUCK!
GREAT, HUH?
THIS IS THE GOOD STUFF!
SEE YA.

-ITTY BITTY END!

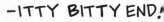

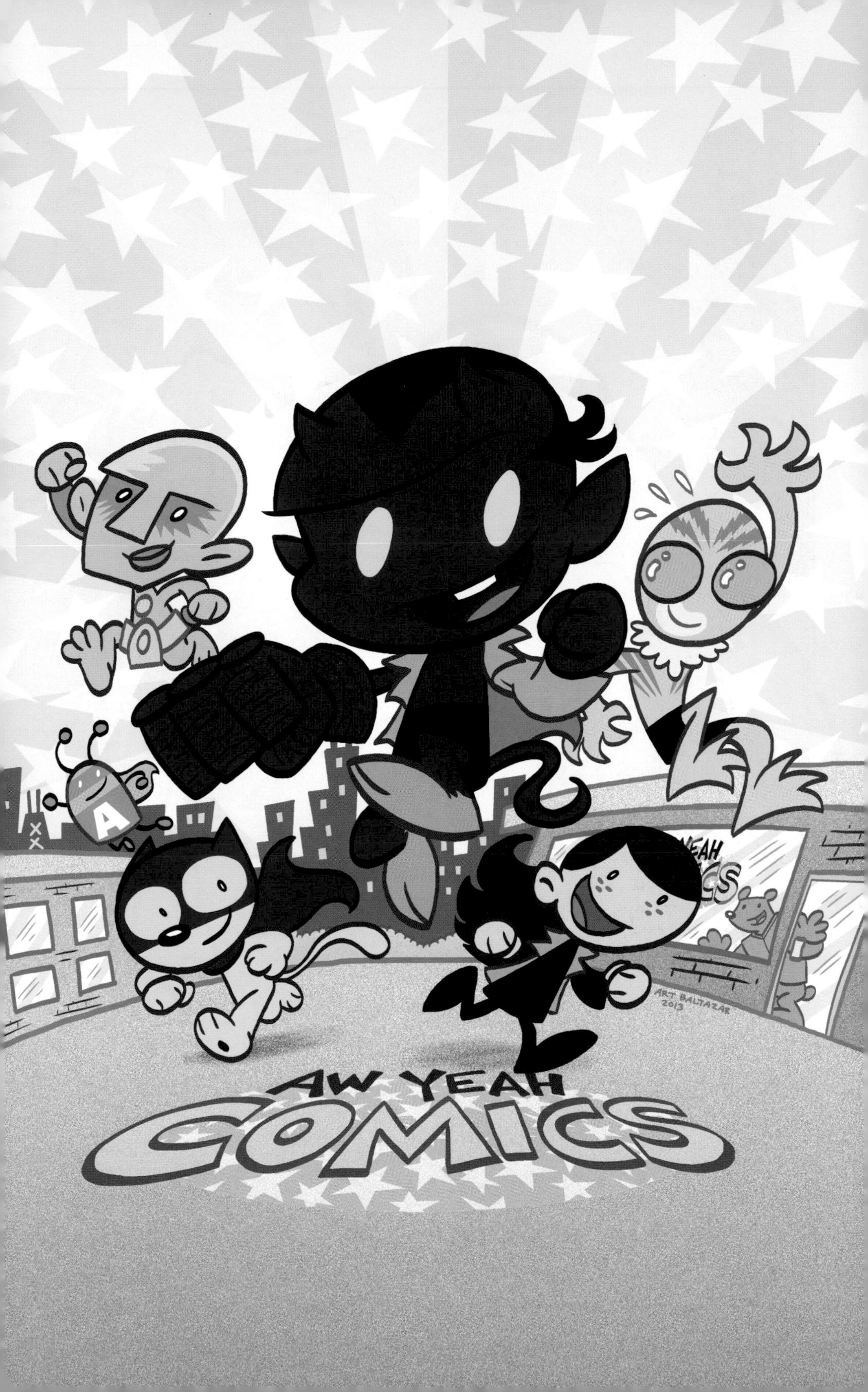
AW YEAH
COMICS
ART BALTAZAR
2013

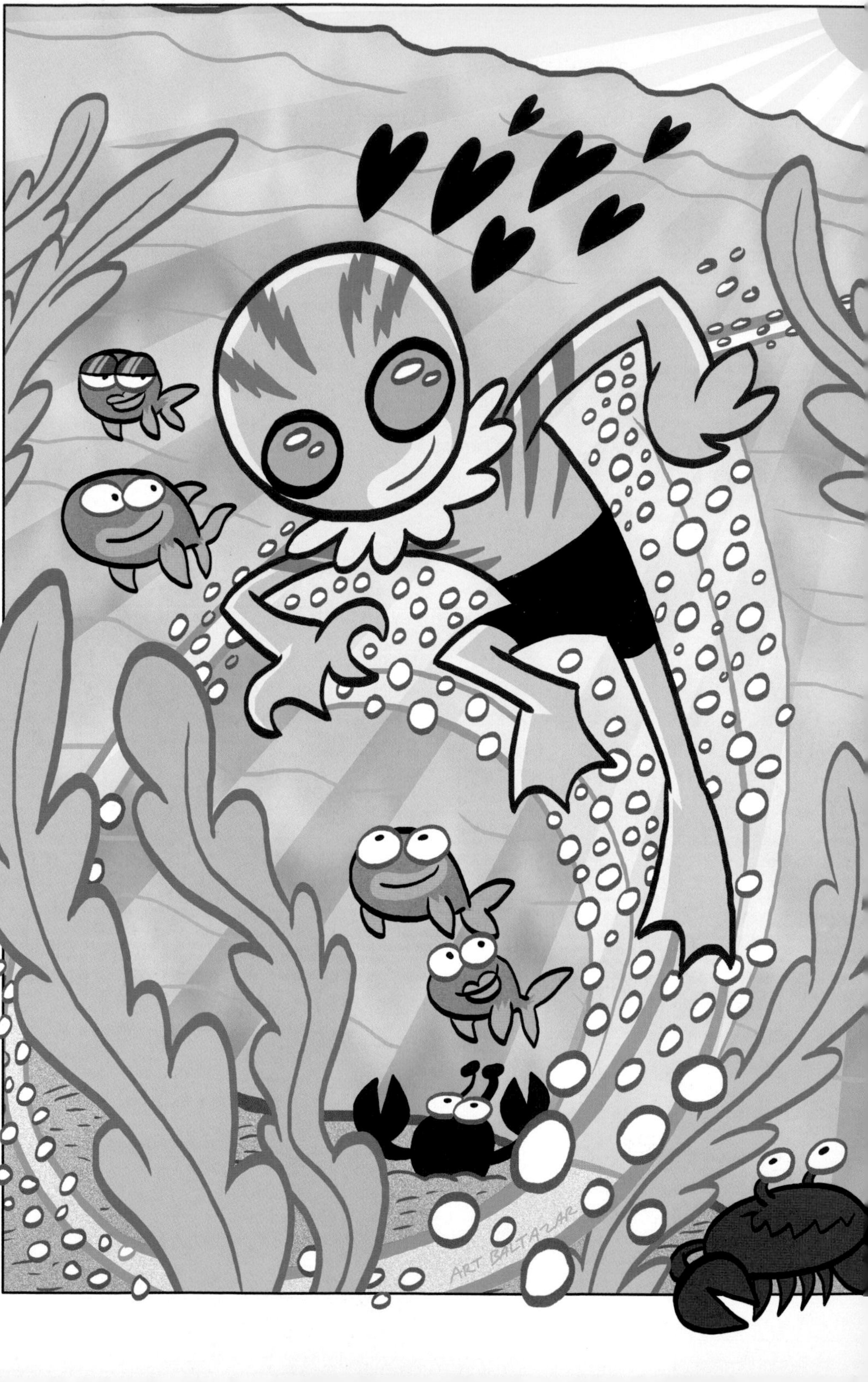
ART BALTAZAR

MIKE MIGNOLA'S HELLBOY

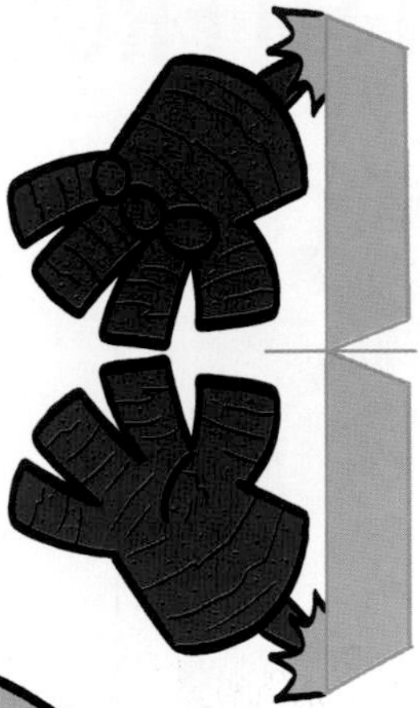

STEP 1: Print this page on cardstock or regular paper. Use scissors or a craft knife to cut out Itty Bitty Hellboy's body and each of his arms. Do not cut along blue lines in the body or arms—these lines are where you will fold the paper.

STEP 2: Take Itty Bitty Hellboy's body and make all of the folds along the blue lines for the body and the tabs. Make each fold away from you except for Itty Bitty Hellboy's legs. For Itty Bitty Hellboy's legs, fold the top blue line toward you and the bottom blue line away from you. This will help him sit on the edge of a table or shelf.

STEP 3: Glue the tabs to the inside of Itty Bitty Hellboy's body. The glued tabs will create a box (his jacket).

STEP 4: Fold each of Itty Bitty Hellboy's arms in half along the blue line and glue the two sides together. Glue each arm to Itty Bitty Hellboy's sides.

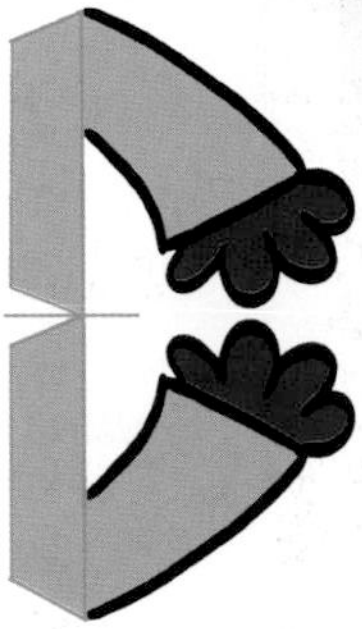

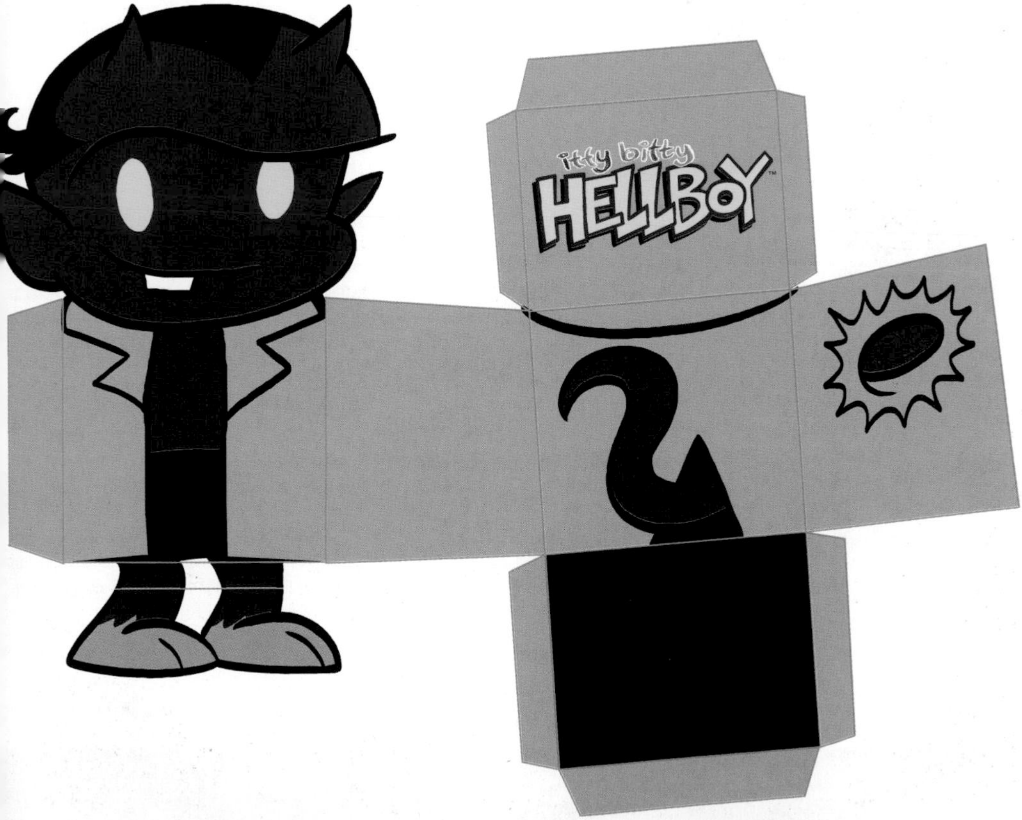
itty bitty
HELLBOY™

ALSO FROM DARK HORSE

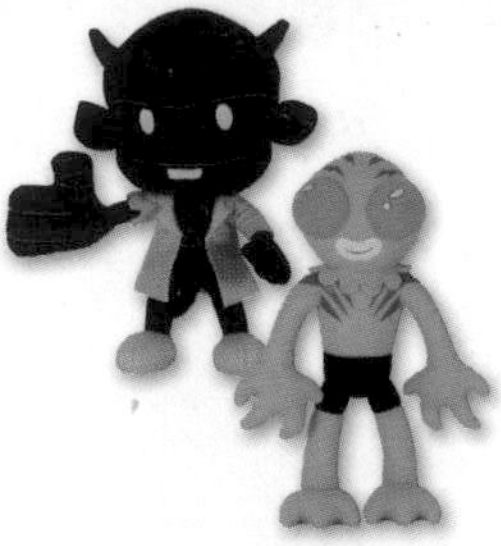

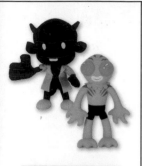

ITTY BITTY HELLBOY PLUSH: HELLBOY, ABE SAPIEN

Based on the hit cartoon treatment of Mike Mignola's characters are these itty bitty spot-on collector plush dolls. Aw Yeah, Hellboy!

HELLBOY: 7 61568 25139 5 | 7.25" tall | $14.99
ABE SAPIEN: 7 61568 25140 1 | 8.5" tall | $14.99

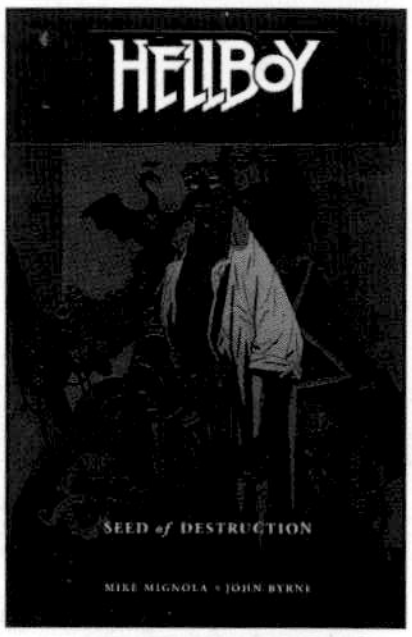
HELLBOY
SEED of DESTRUCTION
MIKE MIGNOLA • JOHN BYRNE

HELLBOY VOLUME 1: SEED OF DESTRUCTION TPB

Mike Mignola and John Byrne

Hellboy is one of the most celebrated comics series in recent years. The ultimate artist's artist and a great storyteller whose work is by turns haunting, hilarious, and spellbinding, Mike Mignola has won numerous awards in the comics industry and beyond. When strangeness threatens to engulf the world, a strange man will come to save it. Sent to investigate a mystery with supernatural overtones, Hellboy discovers the secrets of his own origins, and his link to the Nazi occultists who promised Hitler a final solution in the form of a demonic avatar.

978-1-59307-094-6 | $17.99

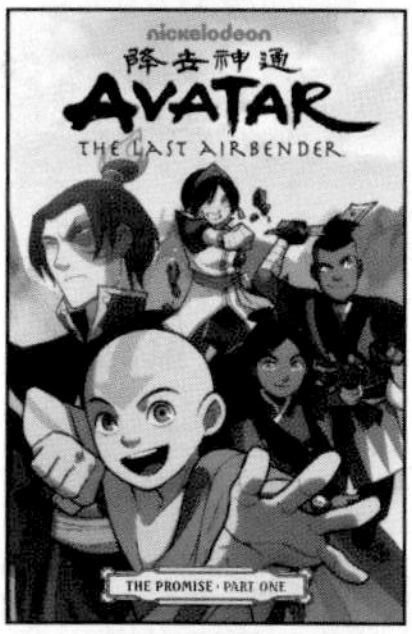
nickelodeon
AVATAR
THE LAST AIRBENDER
THE PROMISE · PART ONE

AVATAR: THE LAST AIRBENDER—THE PROMISE PART 1 TPB

Gene Luen Yang, Michael Dante DiMartino, Bryan Konietzko, and Gurihiru

The wait is over! Ever since the conclusion of *Avatar: The Last Airbender*, its millions of fans have been hungry for more—and it's finally here! This series of digests rejoins Aang and friends for exciting new adventures, beginning with a face-off against the Fire Nation that threatens to throw the world into another war, testing all of Aang's powers and ingenuity!

978-1-59582-811-8 | $10.99

BRODY'S GHOST BOOK 1 TPB

Mark Crilley

Brody hoped it was just a hallucination. But no, the teenaged ghostly girl who'd come face to face with him in the middle of a busy city street was all too real. And now she was back, telling him she needed his help in hunting down a dangerous killer, and that he must undergo training from the spirit of a centuries-old samurai to unlock his hidden supernatural powers. Thirteen-time Eisner nominee Mark Crilley joins Dark Horse to launch his most original and action-packed saga to date in *Brody's Ghost*, the first in a six-volume limited series.

978-1-59582-521-6 | $6.99

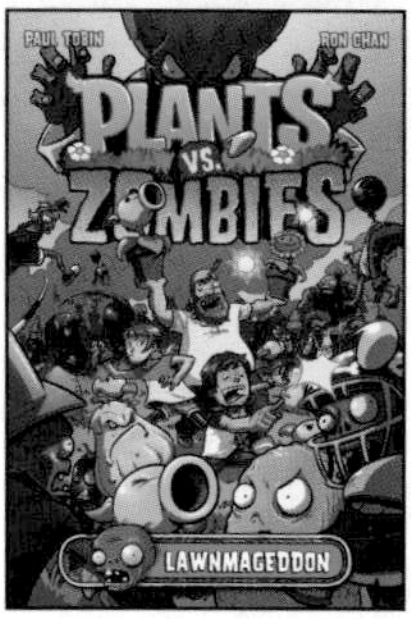
PAUL TOBIN
RON CHAN
PLANTS VS. ZOMBIES
LAWNMAGEDDON

PLANTS VS. ZOMBIES: LAWNMAGEDDON HC

Paul Tobin and Ron Chan

The confusing-yet-brilliant inventor known only as Crazy Dave helps his niece, Patrice, and young adventurer Nate Timely fend off a "fun-dead" neighborhood invasion in *Plants vs. Zombies: Lawnmageddon*! Winner of over thirty Game of the Year awards, *Plants vs. Zombies* is now determined to shuffle onto all-ages bookshelves to tickle funny bones and thrill . . . brains.

978-1-61655-192-6 | $9.99